I Vow to Thee

Book 1 – Revolution

William E. H. Walker

For Zoe, always.

Oxfordshire

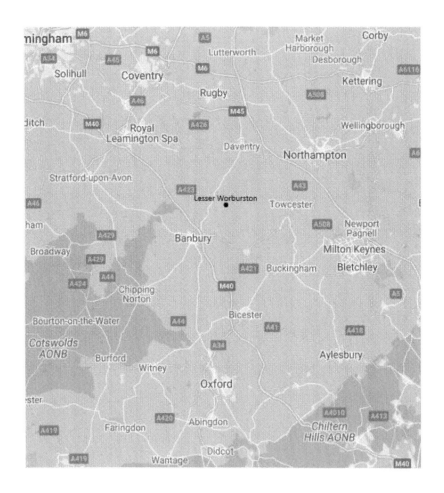

Lesser Worburston

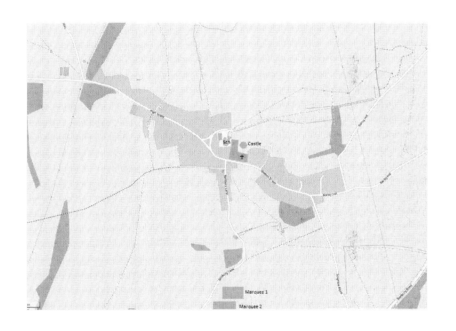

Westminster

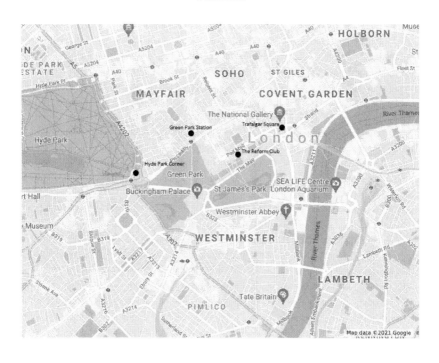

Prologue

The spring air cooled in the fading light of May's sun. The first stars were just visible as cirrus clouds flitted before the rising sickle moon. From the meadow behind them an owl hooted, while the gate on its rusty hinges whined in the breeze like a wounded mouse. It had rained heavily that morning leaving the ground under him sticky and slick, as though he writhed in tar.

He cradled his head in his hands and the tears rolled from his blackened eyes to stain his cheeks to mix with the dark blood and cloying sludge that engulfed his body. Through his swollen and battered lips, he gasped for air and choked out the words they had told him to say, 'I am filth. I am disease. I am nothing.'

'Again.' One of his tormentors delivered a hard kick to his ribcage, sending molten agony through his body. As the fire spread within, he cried out, 'I am filth! Disease! I am nothing!'

'Again!' The back of his legs exploded, and his body twisted in pain. Every cell burned, broken bones screamed, frayed nerves sent bolts of agony through his crumpled frame as he drifted on the edge of consciousness. As darkness closed in on him his soul clawed for life. It scoured his body in search of hope and found the well he kept deep within him. The one place they could never touch. His never-ending constant. He drank deeply and a flood of relief washed through him like a tsunami of love.

He raised his bleeding face from the filth he stared blindly into the void that had swallowed his world and screamed, 'I am not filth! I am not disease! I am someone!' The words ended in a wild howl as all his terror and anguish expelled into the night.

A punch to the throat cut the scream short. He choked, spluttering yet more blood over his body to mix with the filth.

'Who's there?' An eerie cry from close by. *An angel?* he thought.

His eyes were closing, he was losing consciousness, he was dying. And that was okay.

'I say, you there. Who are you?' The voice, high and wavering, was coming from a place beyond his comprehension. It was followed by the sound of running, retreating. He was alone.

He lay where they had finally let him fall, his right arm and left leg shattered. Ribs more broken sticks than a cage. Blood pulsing from a golf club-inflicted wound on his scalp. His death mask was all bloodied eyes, crumpled nose and broken jaw. He lay soaked in their urine, fingers twitching as though playing a ghostly piano.

'My God, are you all right?'

My God indeed.

He felt life ebb from him into the ground he had tended so lovingly all these years. Was this how it was meant to end? Was this his reward for devotion?

The light was fading. The voice was talking quickly but he couldn't comprehend the words. It didn't matter. He let go and the peace of the everlasting night enveloped him. Was this death? *Please let this be death.*

Then sweet, sweet release consumed him.

Day 1

'When hatred judges, the verdict is just guilty.'
—Toba Beta

03:46

The Man crouched in the long grass, his military-issue trousers repelling the dew. Pulling open the doors of the electronic components of the cellular base station, he attached explosive glass vials to each bundle of wiring and circuit board.

Thirty seconds.

He glanced around him, eyes searching the darkness for signs that he was discovered, but the night was still. So still, his steady breathing sounded deafening in his ears. Above him countless stars swam in the immeasurable blackness. So many stars, so much creation. It warmed his heart. Even with the reduction of street lighting in recent years, the city's foul sky remained a ruin by comparison. Adjusting the balaclava, the Man itched his nose before fixing cold eyes on the soft glow of his watch.

Fifteen seconds.

He pulled the trigger from his pocket, connected it to the explosives and held it out over the mass of wires and cables.

Five seconds.

He was so still, so silent, so calm. His training had made him sure. It had made him ready.

Three, two, one…

He pulled the trigger and watched the small pops blow apart the vials and electrical components. The acid stripping away metal and plastic as it ate its way through the system.

He rose, stepping back as the small explosions spread, causing sparks and smoke as they went off. The Man took the phone from his pocket and checked its screen: full signal. As the caustic substance continued to eat its way down the wires and through the circuit boards, the Man kept his eyes focused on the slowly rotating readout on his phone. No signal. And no quick fix for that mess. Replacing the phone, the Man took a torch from his jacket and pointed it downhill where the road lay hidden in the gloom. Three quick flashes, three in return.

Returning to his bag, he lifted the silenced FNX 45 Tactical and placed it in its holster before lifting the bag onto his back and setting off down the hill, his eyes watching the ground as he picked his way over the rough terrain toward the old broken gate in the thick hedge.

I Vow to Thee – William E. H. Walker

He nodded to the man in the police uniform and stepped up to the open boot of the waiting car, placing the bag next to the others before getting in the passenger's side. The three other occupants were silent as he gently closed the door. Everyone remained mute as they pulled off down the narrow country lane. They only had a minute to drive and there was no need to speak, each having carried out their task successfully.

He had cut the phone signal while his colleagues in the back had stood watch. His driver had visited the quaint cottage on the edge of the village where the old lady lived with her cats and chickens.

Not a word, that was the rule. Not a word until the job was done. Tonight, they were changing the world. That had been His message before they left that morning.

'Tonight, we will create a new Britain. What happens tonight will resonate in history. What happens tonight will reverberate for decades. What happens tonight will scare them more than they ever thought possible.'

The Man watched the hedgerow pass as the words ran through his head. '*...tonight won't be compared to Nine Eleven, it will succeed Nine Eleven as the ultimate wake-up call. You're trained well. You are experts at what you do. You are ready. And you will change the world.'*

They pulled up in the middle of a narrow street and silently climbed out. The driver and front passenger crossed the road to the left, while the Man and his fellow passenger moved to the right. Surveying the scene, the Man could see other cars spread evenly down the road. One car for every six houses, 96 houses in all. He remembered the layout of the village from their training. A large T-shape with a council estate bolted onto one end. A small village green complete with manor house, memorial trees and a track that led to the primary school. Opposite was the church behind which sat the remains of an Iron Age castle. It was a typical Oxfordshire village. A mix of stone and brick houses ranging from the absurdly large to the tiny post-war emergency dwellings like those currently to his left. This could be anywhere, but it had to be here.

He checked his watch: three minutes to get ready. His partner tapped his back and pointed to the small card held under the shielded XED light. They knew these instructions by heart, but it was part of the plan. Review and confirm, always check twice.

1. No. 2 Railway Cottages 3-2A-1C-0D-Mortice – 1st-2AR-1CL

2. No. 1 Railway Cottages 4-2A-2C-0D-Electronic – 1st-2AR-2CL

3. The Old Police Cottage 1-1A-0C-1D-RE-Cylinder – 1st-1AL

4. Bluebird House 4-1A-3C-0D-MP & Latch – 1st-1AL, 1CLR, 2CMR

5. No. 2 Farm View 2-2A-0C-1D-Mortice – 1st 2AL-LLO

6. No. 1 Farm View 3-2A-1C-0D-MP-1st 2AL-1CL – *RSL*

I Vow to Thee – William E. H. Walker

The Man tapped his partner twice on the shoulder and they ran quietly toward the small redbrick semi with a copper number two on the door. The other occupants of the car crossed the street where the driver jumped expertly over a gate and disappeared from view.

Two minutes, six seconds to go.

His partner tapped him once on the back before twisting away and vanishing around the back of the house. The Man waited as he recalled, '...*you were chosen not because of your training. Many of you had none before joining us. You were chosen not because of who you are, for you are from all different walks of life, different backgrounds and circumstances. You were chosen because of who you could be. Because you are special. And that is who you are today. The Chosen few. Today, you fulfil your destiny.'*

Forty-five seconds.

He took the Prolox D27 automatic lock pick from his pocket. Glancing about him, he could see one of his partners crouching in a doorway. The lonely streetlight picking his visage out from the darkness.

The street was so still it might have been painted. The village serene as its occupants slept on. The arrival of the visitors had gone unseen. A slight breeze rustled the leaves of a stately oak tree, bats flitted deftly between the houses and the old iron gate on the path next to the church creaked softly on its hinge. The war memorial stood resolute before a Tudor cottage with roses in the garden. Postcard England incarnate.

Here, everyone still said hello to each other as they passed in the street, popped round for tea before the village fete and checked up on their elderly neighbours.

Even in today's world, where politics was played out at knifepoint and wars fought for the benefit of corporations, their doors would be left unlocked for visitors. Kids could still ride their bikes on the road and talk to strangers without fear. This was not one of those villages near a motorway taken over by commuters who spent less time there than they did in London. This was a community, a family, a message.

You're going to change the world.

A fox shrieked in the darkness. The Man breathed in deeply and held it. Three, two, one, go.

He pushed the pick into the lock and it clicked open in a second. No waiting, he had practiced this many times on the replicas. Open the door just far enough for him to slip inside. He thought, *Hallway, stairs directly ahead, no furniture, coats often hung on the banister.*

He moved quickly and silently to the stairs, avoiding the raincoat slung over the banister, his gun out before him moving with his eyes.

2A right, he thought and turned there first. Bedroom door slightly ajar, the floor creaking softly as he moved across the landing and into the room.

I Vow to Thee – William E. H. Walker

Isabelle Jacklyn had moved to Lesser Worburston five years previously with her new husband Tim. At just 24 she had been fortunate to receive a gift from her parents for a deposit. Along with Tim's steady income from managing a warehouse in Banbury, they had been able to buy the little train workers terrace so Isabelle could pursue her dream of becoming an ostler in the village stables.

Symone was born 13 months later. A beautiful child – everyone said so – she was quiet and fey with auburn hair and quizzical eyes. She had recently started at the local primary school, allowing Isabelle more time with the horses and to dream of owning her own stable and of taking her daughter riding one day. She had the picture clear in her head. They would trot across the fields every weekend before coming home, wet and grinning, to find Tim had cooked a huge roast dinner with steaming mugs of tea. A simple life. No stress, no worries, just a happy, joyful life.

Isabelle had it all planned out. Symone would go to the private school at Stowe, which they had been saving for ever since she was born. She would win awards, write poems and star in school plays. She would make many friends and be the most popular girl in her class, always getting the highest grades with humility and pride. They would all move to one of the larger houses in the centre of the village with their new little boy, currently six weeks old within her. There they would have one more child, hopefully another girl, and grow old together in their peaceful little world. Isabelle smiled in her sleep, dreams of her wonderful life playing through her mind.

The bullet went through her left eye, taking out the back of her head and spraying skull, blood and brains over her pillow. Tim's eyes instantly opened but the .45 ACP bullet hit him in the middle of his forehead. He was dead before he knew what was happening.

The Man moved quickly back out of the room and across the landing, his heart rate raised as he took the first victims of the night. The child's door was open and he slipped inside. The silenced muzzle was an inch from the side of her face when he pulled the trigger, all but removing the top half of Symone's skull before he left the room and went down the stairs.

Back in the hall, he turned left into the living room and through to the kitchen. Two light taps on the back door, one in return, and the shadow outside moved away and over the fence.

He silently moved through the house and out the front door, closing it gently behind him, listening for the click of the pins as it locked. Across the street, his colleague was entering a second house. Staying low, the Man ran quietly to the next door. *Two adults, two children*, he thought.

The electric lock took longer to overcome than the older mortise or cylinder style, but the pick had it open in under 10 seconds. The Man moved quickly up the stairs. Noisier than the last house, they creaked and moaned under his boots. Movement from the bedroom to the right, but he did not check. *Just keep moving*, he told himself.

Liam Fennel, a tubby little man in his mid-thirties, worked for the Co-Op funeral service and smelt constantly of cigarettes and a knock-off aftershave called Celvin Kline. He, like almost all of those who worked in such a job, possessed a jovial manner when not working with the recently bereaved, quick to laugh and comfortable with himself. He had sat up in bed when he heard movement on the stairs and was checking the time when the shadow demon entered his room.

A single vowel had escaped his lips before the bullet tore into his forehead. His wife, Elizabeth, who was often described as acting more like the Queen than the Queen herself, didn't even lift her head before she too died.

The Man turned and crossed the landing. Bedroom one, the petite girl of eight lay with her mouth open and a stuffed dog in her arms. The bullet passed through her mouth and into her brain.

Last room, door firmly shut, tough to open, resistance on the floor, a light on inside. He put his shoulder to it and heard a murmur from within.

'Dad?' a drowsy voice asked.

A teenager, the Man knew he was 15 and called Harris. TV left on as he slept, he was sitting up in bed half-asleep. He saw the Man push the door past his pile of clothes and into his room. Harris saw the covered face, the black clothing and the gun in his hand. He opened his mouth to cry out as his head snapped back and his body tipped out of bed onto the pile of clothing on the floor.

Back out of the house and onto the street. Five minutes gone.

He found he was sweating despite the moist spring chill in the air. It was harder than training, the images of the children would stay with him.

This time it was his turn to wait. It had been decided the rear entrance was the best point of entry for this home. He stopped outside the front door and waited, his eyes scanning the street. Over the road he saw the tell-tale flash of two shots fired in an upstairs window, pair seven were bang on schedule.

Standing ready beside a Land Rover a few doors down from his current position, the street watcher was ready to catch runners. No police uniform needed for him, just those positioned on the roads out of the village lest someone try to disturb their mission. Further down the street a dark shape slinked out from the darkness of a doorway and into the next house.

Waiting there, crouching in the darkness, his ears picked out the tiny sounds of his partner moving toward the window. He looked through the small pane of glass in the door in time to see his partner kill the dog and tap twice against the fanlight. He tapped once in reply and crept onto the cottage next door.

He counted as he moved. It would take his partner 16 seconds to exit the house and get to the back door of the cottage; it would take him 12 to reach the front.

He climbed over the small stone garden wall as he knew the gate creaked terribly and he crept up to the front door. He had just placed the pick in the lock when a crash split the night. A front door had been

I Vow to Thee – William E. H. Walker

thrown open and a woman stood on the threshold. She was dressed in T-shirt and knickers, her hair wild, face hidden by shadow from the bright hallway light behind her. She had not taken two steps on to the pavement before a bullet took her in the side of the head and she folded to the ground, bathed in the light from her door. Within seconds a figure appeared beside her, another from the door, switching the light off as they passed. They picked her up and carried her now still body quietly back inside, closing the door behind them.

The Man had been side-tracked; he was behind schedule. He cursed himself and placed the pick back in the lock.

Fred and Teresa had grown up in the village. They had known each other since they were four years old and had been a couple for as long as anyone could remember. 'It must be true love' had been said to them more times than either could count.

Teresa worked in a local solicitor's office in town, while Fred taught at the village school. Francis and the twins had all attended and their father had taught them. It was something the other pupils constantly reminded them of.

Francis, a shy, quiet boy, had struggled with the teasing, but since he had joined the academy in Banbury he had come out of his shell and was clearly happy. He was now learning to play the guitar and doing well in class.

The twins were a handful and always up to something. So much so that no one ever called them by their names. They were just known as 'The Twins' or, on the rare occasions they were to be found separately, 'Which of The Twins are you?'

Fred had really struggled to teach them, something Teresa failed to fully understand. When they had left his class, their next teacher had made a point of calling her in to talk about their use of moulding glue in the classroom door and on the teacher's chair.

'They'll grow out of it,' she'd assured Fred. 'They're just energetic.'

He had sighed and agreed, although he was not convinced, and left for his karate class that evening feeling a bit of a failure. He'd been taking classes for about eight years now and was getting good at it. No competitions past local level, but he had won a few of those and Teresa was always there to support him. She said she liked how toned it made him. He had to admit that he did as well.

He was dreaming of karate as he died. Teresa could never remember her dreams.

Francis died with his eyes open, as the press of the gun's silencer on his forehead had woken him. His last thought was 'mum.' The Twins were awake when the Man entered their room. He shot the first in the head as she stared at him agog. The second was trying to climb over her bed and took two in the back. As she slumped over, he moved forward and put another in the back of her head to be sure.

I Vow to Thee – William E. H. Walker

The Man left the room and slipped back downstairs. A double tap of knuckles on the kitchen window, a single in return.

Two more to go. Seven minutes 24 seconds gone.

When the Man opened the door, he fished a small bone from his breast pocket and dropped it in front of the small Bichon Frisé who had come trotting over to see what the fuss was about. As he entered, he kept the muzzle of his pistol pointing at its head as the dog greedily gnawed at the bone.

Isaiah and Nancy had lived in number 2 Farm View for 47 years. They had planned to die there. The Bichon Frisé's life ended with a quiet bullet to the head as it ate.

Last one. Nine minutes eight seconds.

Suddenly there was a bright flash – the rear security light had been activated. The Man dropped against the wall, his nerves suddenly alive, his body taut and his gun raised. He kept himself perfectly still and slowed his breathing. Not a sound was heard. Ahead of him a snake-like shape dissolved from the darkness into a man who slivered from a house and moved across the road to a car. He had to move now. He stood quickly and crept to the front door, swapping the pistol's magazine as he went.

Gerald, Sue and their new-born son were all asleep in the bedroom. The Man killed Gerald first, then Sue and then their infant son. As the six-month-old died he experienced a pang of regret, but he knew it was necessary. There was no other way. People die in war; it was for the cause. The baby would never see the world they were creating, but he had been sacrificed to bring it about. His name would be remembered.

Two taps on the back window and he was away and moving quietly back down the road to the car. The Man climbed into the back and quietly closed the door behind him as his partner got in on the other side. They waited. Seconds later, the other passenger emerged from a house and crossed the road. Glancing to his right, he saw her as she climbed over a small wall from the rear of the houses opposite before jogging across the road to join them. Settling herself into the driver's seat they pulled silently away, the slight whine of the motor the only sound. The convoy grew as they drove through the village as the other teams returned to their vehicles and followed them.

Turning onto the High Street, they saw one other person had been woken during the raid and was now being carried, motionless, back into their house. As they reached the edge of the village, the Man's partner leaned forward and handed a list to the passenger in front. He rolled the window down as they approached the dark figure stood by the sign.

I Vow to Thee – William E. H. Walker

Welcome to Lesser Worburston

Please drive carefully

He handed the person the pages and said, 'Done.' His voice was flat, emotionless.

'Take the left,' came the reply.

They drove off into the night, the car that followed them pausing at the figure to be given their instructions. When they reached the crossroads a mile out of the village, they turned left and accelerated gently off down the winding country lane. Their crimes left for others to discover as they slipped away slowly and sedately as though nothing had happened.

The last car to approach the sign pulled up and stopped. The driver got out and faced the motionless figure.

'All done?'

'All done. Seven unaccounted for, only one unexpected; four runners stopped.'

'All doors closed?' asked the new arrival.

'All except one,' replied their subordinate.

'Any interference?'

'None.'

'Go.'

The subordinate who'd been directing the cars from the village got into the Land Rover and drove away. The other watched them leave before pulling off his balaclava and enjoying the feeling of the cool night prickling against his skin.

They had done it: 397 people in just over 18 minutes. No one would ever forget this. They had struck their first blow. Stage two would be put into motion soon but stage one appeared to be an unequivocal success. A brand-new Jaguar XF-E pulled up quietly beside him and he got in. Time for some sleep. After all, it was nearly 4.00 am and the milkman would be coming soon.

I Vow to Thee – William E. H. Walker

06:23

Kinsella

The report of a body found in an isolated Oxfordshire village was passed along the chain and Detective Inspector Maria Kinsella of Thames Valley Police was assigned to the investigation. Before she had left Kidlington HQ, she'd called in the Scene of Crime Investigations Team and some extra support from the local force.

As her police-issue BMW i6 sped up the M40, she reflected on the call. 'Elderly lady found shot in her bed this morning when her milkman noticed her door left open and received no reply to his calls. The 999 call was placed by Peter Shull in the neighbouring village as no reception at the scene. No further details known at present.'

She ran her hand through her shoulder-length flame-red hair before glancing at herself in the rear-view mirror. *You look knackered,* she said to herself.

She hammered down the outside lane, blue lights flashing and siren blaring, yet it still took nearly a minute for the Mercedes to move out the way. 'Idiot.' She scowled at the driver as she passed, not that he looked across or apologised. They never did.

Kinsella had been a DI for two and a half years. At 38 she was considered one of the top detectives in her jurisdiction. She'd only been a DS for two years before her promotion, partly due to the death of her old boss, DI Wingate, who was taken by a sudden stroke before his time.

Moving with her husband to Summertown in North Oxford, she'd been ready to leave the force and focus on raising a family. But six years on her children remained naught but wisps of hope in her nightmare marriage to her hedge fund manager husband. Kinsella shook herself in her seat. That was the past; her future was just beginning.

She took a deep breath, held it for four seconds and released. Then another. She felt her body begin to relax. She had once been told stress was a hormone or enzyme or something that the body found impossible to hold on to when you focus on your breathing. She wasn't sure it was true, but it worked nonetheless.

She blinked, her eyelids heavy as though weighted. She twisted her head, hoping that somehow this would help shake off the deep desire to sleep, but still the fog lay over her, inviting her to drift off. She put the car in self-drive mode, released the steering wheel, rubbed her eyes and stretched out as best she could in the cramped car. A long groan escaped her lips. She would sleep well tonight. She would go home, shower... no... a bath! Why not? She had the water stored. She would bathe, have a small dinner, stretch out diagonally in her king-size bed and sleep for a week.

She was struck by the realisation that it was her bed now, not theirs. How long had that been the case? Her husband stayed in London most of the time and although she was now used to the arrangement, it had taken a lot for her to stop hating him. There had been more than one night of tears and too many bottles of wine. More than one morning waking on the kitchen floor, her head throbbing and gut churning. All those tears just so he could bed "*her*". It wasn't fair.

They barely talked these days. She hadn't even bothered to tell him when she'd spent those weeks away on the Church retreats. Why should she? Over two years she'd spent eight weeks in Scotland and he'd not even called, let alone noticed her absence. She could probably have stayed at the camp for months, and had wanted to in fact, and he'd probably not even come home. She wished she had stayed. It was so calm up there. So far from the torture of everyday life. So much to focus on that was bigger than her. She rubbed her eyes again and flicked the car back into manual-driver mode. There was no point dwelling on it. The camps had ended six months ago and wouldn't return. Now there was just the late-night TV, the takeout and the 3.00 am bedtime. Last night had been different, though. Last night she had not slept a wink.

She reached for the coffee cup beside her and took a sip; still too hot. She grumbled quietly to herself, *Need coffee. Need caffeine.* The car headlights flashed again at the obstinate Ford Focus in her path. *Idiots*, she thought, again, as the car swerved into the middle lane and out of her path.

Like clockwork, her thoughts turned back to her husband. She had known about his affair for the past three years. Silvia Hutton, the luscious Director of HMC Bank with the legs and breasts of an Amazonian Goddess and the easy charm of a talk show host. And don't forget to mention a former model and Oxbridge graduate.

"Lips like a suction cup" had been the overheard comment from her husband's colleagues. She'd met her at some Christmas bash the year before and had been almost amused by how awkward they had been together. She remembered asking if she and her husband had to work closely together? And if Silvia

I Vow to Thee – William E. H. Walker

worked under him? Kinsella remembered the perverse joy she felt as his cheeks turned scarlet when Silvia had answered yes. Kinsella couldn't resist adding, 'Well, make sure he doesn't ride you too hard to get what he wants from you!' Silvia had laughed, but her eyes had skittered like a young bird and she'd made excuses to scurry off.

She was married at the time too, of course. Some European banker. Gerard? Donald? Could be Hugo even? He spent as much time in Manchester and Berlin as Kinsella's husband did in London. Kinsella knew Silvia had left him about a year ago, the divorce finalised just last month. Would her husband ever ask her for the same? Or was he happy with his second life? Leaving her to play the part of dutiful wife whenever he needed. No, the part of the dutiful Mrs-waiting-patiently-indoors while he ravaged his way around Europe with the beautiful warrior princess looking like something out of Wagner's Ride of the Valkyries.

Kinsella wasn't fine with it, of course, but it wasn't going to change anytime soon, and divorce was, for her at least, out of the question. She'd learned to live with the truth, just as she had learned to live with the realisation that she had wedded a man she no longer loved. Had she ever? Or had infatuation with the tall, athletic, charming banker clouded her judgement? She was no longer certain. Either way there was nothing she could do about it now, although she prayed she wouldn't have long to wait for it to all be over.

No more. Don't let him occupy your mind, you don't need him to feel whole, you're stronger than him. She focused her mind on the road before her. She was done with him. For now at least.

Turning off the motorway, Kinsella sped down the increasingly narrow roads toward the inevitable revelations. It was another 20 minutes before she arrived in Lesser Worburston. The house was on the very edge of the village. No more than 30 yards from a large sign that bid visitors welcome.

Two constables were busying themselves with cordoning off an area around the house. Another two were hammering on the front door of a large white stone house two doors up from her, while a final two stood watching her park, clearly eager to give her news. To her right, a youth vaped great clouds of righteous pineapple while leaning against his car with phone in hand; to her left an ambulance crew tended to a terrified fat man in a white coat. The milkman, she guessed. He looked as though half the life had been squeezed out of him.

Getting out, she arched her back trying to wake tired muscles before walking over to the two officers waiting for her. *Be present*, she told herself. *Don't let your tiredness show.* 'DI Kinsella.' She flashed her badge, 'What do we have here?'

'PC Abboud, Ma'am, that's PC Davis.' His accent was pure Birmingham.

'What's your first name, Abboud?'

'Omar, Ma'am.' He stood so rigidly to attention Kinsella wondered if he'd strain something.

'Omar it is then.' She gave him a half-smile, trying to keep things friendly. 'What happened?'

Omar's reply was as though he were reading the recipe for beans on toast. 'Myris Grantham, Ma'am, 65-years-old, found in her bed. She's been shot.'

'The singer?' she said, sounding surprised and looking past Abboud to his colleague.

'Yes, Ma'am. She was found by the milkman.' Omar's arm shot out as though on a piston. 'He's the one with a blanket over him over there, Ma'am – Donald Chiefly. He arrived this morning to drop off her usual bottle and found the door wide open. Said he tried calling out to her but got no reply, so he ventured inside and found her upstairs. He's been sick in there and he's not doing too well, Ma'am.

Not my concern, Kinsella thought.

Abboud continued. 'The call was placed by the young man hovering over there.' He pointed at the man vaping youth. 'Peter Shull, 21, driving through the village on his way to work and discovered the milkman sitting in the middle of the road. No reception here so he drove over to Greater Worburston.'

'Okay. Was this a robbery?' she asked, watching the bird's flitter between the rows of small trees. Their song drifting over to her on the breeze.

Davis replied, eager to be involved. 'Doesn't look that way, Ma'am, nothing looks disturbed. She's upstairs. It's…' He paled slightly, an involuntary shake of the head. 'It's not nice up there.'

'First shooting?' She could see how shaken he was. Poor kid. He didn't look more than 25.

Davis shook his head. 'Second, Ma'am. But this one's different, she's just a little old lady. The last one was when I was stationed in Leeds. Young bloke, you know… it's different.'

'She's not that old constable, remember your ageism training.' She shot him a look, and he nodded his understanding.

Kinsella considered the house. The stonework looked weathered in the morning light. The pointing needed doing. Signs of damp in the corners where the roof met the wall. The thin front garden, all overgrown bushes and leggy plants. A giant foxglove stood tall and proud in the centre of some stinging nettles, its princess pink flowers moving gently in the breeze. *Looks like someone hadn't time or inclination to tend it properly for quite a while*, she thought.

She was nodding as she took it all in. 'Okay. Well, no one else goes in till SOCO have had a look. They're on their way. Any witnesses?'

'Don't know, Ma'am. Neighbours aren't talking to us,' Abboud replied.

She swivelled her head slowly to look at the two constables. 'What do you mean, the neighbours aren't talking to you?'

Davis looked awkward. 'We've knocked on doors Ma'am, but no one has answered yet.'

Kinsella made a show of looking incredulous. 'Right, well, you two take those four,' she pointed at the four constables now huddled in a group pretending not to be listening, '…and keep trying. Bang on doors, wake them up. Someone must have seen or heard something.' Kinsella checked her watch. 'Someone should be awake by now. Anyone with kids for starters.'

'Yes, Ma'am,' they said in unison, both eager to be helpful, and they trotted off to collect their colleagues.

As she plucked a dead rose from an overgrown bush, she called after them, 'Check the back doors as well.'

Kinsella watched Abboud and Davis walk purposefully over to the grand house next door. A double-fronted Georgian affair with bay windows and ivy creeping over the door frame. Future possibilities floated through her mind. *Could I buy one on my own? Retire to a place like that maybe? I could using his life insurance. Also, I'll get a fair bit for the house…*

PC Abboud was hammering a door knocker as though trying to gain access to hell. The sharp, metallic crack echoing off houses and up the desolate street. No response.

The houses on the right were all large, stately buildings. The type with a drawing room or parlours. Larders, dining rooms and grand pianos. One was of grey stone with an impressive red slate roof. Next to it was a redbrick manor with impressive rose-filled front gardens surrounded by a small wrought iron fence. *No solar panels on the roof for you*, she thought, *Can't ruin the look of your beautiful homes to save the planet.* Her house might be large, but they hadn't been able to avoid the mandatory addition of solar. Somehow this village seemed to have been missed off a list when the Mandatory Solar Power Directive 2025 was put out. Was it because a Civil Servant lived here? *Surely not.*

The houses on the left were smaller and a mishmash of styles. Although all a reasonable size, they varied between the 1960s 'let's-stick-plastic-under-the-window-for-some-God-awful-reason' bungalows to the 1990s middle-income three beds designed to look unique but with exact replicas in a thousand towns and villages across the country. These all had solar panels and the obligatory sonic composter attached to the side. All had cars on the driveway. All had their curtains closed. A cat sat cleaning its paw on a garden wall paying no heed to the commotion caused by the officers banging on doors. Its long pink tongue flicked between its outstretched paws. No dirt on him.

'Omar, check the windows. See if you can see in anywhere,' she called.

Abboud moved around from the red manor's front door and looked through the first bay window, cupping his hands to his face. Across the road his colleagues were banging on doors and calling out, hoping to attract the attention of the occupants.

Would I be bored in a village? Living life at two miles an hour? Baking cakes for the school fete and going to coffee mornings? She shook her head. Dreams, that's what they were. You don't make Superintendent in a village. Kinsella was driven out of her ponderings by the arrival of the Scene of Crime Officers, their van bumping up against the verge as they parked. A heavyset woman in her mid-forties exited the driver's side.

'Sally, good to see you.' Kinsella smiled and shook the SOCO lead's hand.

Sally smiled back in return. 'DI Kinsella, bit early isn't it? You look tired, love.'

Kinsella cursed inwardly. She needed to do better at hiding it. 'Yeah, I am a bit I suppose. Did they fill you in?' Her voice was slightly beyond breezy, but Sally didn't seem to notice.

'Yeah, gunshot victim.' She shook her head. 'How old?'

'Sixty-five.' Kinsella informed her.

'Sixty-five?' Her surprise was evident in her tone. 'Not likely to be gang-related then I take it?'

Kinsella laughed politely. 'No signs of robbery apparently, but I was waiting for you before I went in. We don't get many murders out here so I want to make sure we're doing everything we can. Didn't want to leave footprints across your scene.'

Sally nodded her thanks, her eyes moving over the outside of the building. 'Who's been in so far?'

Kinsella pointed at the paramedics. 'The milkman sat there on the back of the ambulance, the two EMT and the two officers first on the scene. Oh, and probably the young lad filming us on his phone over there.' She felt her anger rise and thrust her finger out to where the youth leaned against the bonnet of his car. 'Oi!' she yelled at him, 'If one second of that film gets online, I'll have you!' He nearly dropped the phone in surprise before quickly putting it in his pocket, looking for all the world like a schoolboy told off by a teacher. Kinsella turned back to Sally, who was smirking at her. Kinsella smirked back. 'Kids! Anyway, no one else as far as I know. She's upstairs by all accounts.'

Sally Magnaught looked across at her partner 'Get dressed Simon, we're going to take a look.' She looked back to Kinsella. 'You coming?'

'If you'll take me?' she smiled. Kinsella looked to where Abboud was shining his torch through a window, while Davis hammered at the door. 'Omar, still no answer?' she called.

His body tensing as though electricity passed through it. 'No, Ma'am. Nor over the street or next door. Going to have a look in the garden, see what we can see.'

'Okay, mind how you go. Don't want to have to tell the super you've ruined your trousers now, do we?'

Davis cracked a smile while Abboud remained serious. 'No, Ma'am.'

'Keep it light,' she said to Sally. 'Village lady getting murdered in her bed is going to have everyone a little spooked. It's not what you'd call your usual village crime, is it?'

Donning the white, papery protective suit of the Scene of Crime Officer, Kinsella followed Sally to the door of the cottage. Sally paused and studied it. 'It's not been forced,' she said. 'No splintered wood or anything.' She shone a small torch on the door lock. 'No scratch marks round the cylinder. Nothing unusual at any rate. First bet of the day: automatic lock pick. Photograph this please, Simon. The lock especially, then mark it up for removal and follow me.' Simon nodded and pointed the camera at the door lock while Sally moved forward into the hall. 'Nothing broken here, nothing turned over.' She examined a delicate white occasional table near the door, running her finger over the wood and lifting a picture frame. 'Dust would suggest nothing's been moved.'

'The milkman who found her, apparently he's left a pile of vomit at the top of the stairs,' Kinsella called to her as she stepped inside.

'Uh-huh,' Sally replied absently, her torch moving slowly and methodically over the floor and walls. Simon stepped past Kinsella to walk beside Sally, scanning the other side of the narrow hallway.

Kinsella followed, taking in the space. The hall, with flaking yellow paint and dusty pictures, had three doors leading off it. To her left what appeared to be a living room preserved from the 1990s. A stained wood dresser took up most of one side of the room. Old black and white photos of relations long-dead sat beside more recent pictures of an attractive woman in her twenties on stage wearing little clothing. Mottled pink wallpaper peeling at the corners and damp stains showing through the gaps gave the room a musty doll's house feel. A once-yellow sofa long past its prime gradually fell apart in the middle of the room. Faded pink roses, blurred by sun and years, spread over its surface between the stuffing poking through moth-eaten holes.

An orangey brown wingback chair, complete with cigarette burns and water stains, sat in the corner, a new DAB radio beside it. *Funny how something so familiar can seem so out of place*, she thought. Digital tech in an analogue room.

She turned to the room on the right, glancing down the hall and past the stairs to the door that lead to the kitchen. The dining room held a scuffed circular table big enough for eight. Four padded chairs, gradually releasing their stuffing onto the burned and threadbare carpet. A bureau, which must have once been expensive but now was pretty much worthless, and glass cabinet filled with crystal decanters containing various shades of brown liquid were all else the room had to offer. She noted that all the crystalware was chipped and stained.

A large portrait hung on the far wall surrounded by the flaking lime green paint. Kinsella moved toward it, taking it in. A striking man and the same beautiful woman as in the living room, now on a festival stage and picked out in two spotlights. The raised arms of a crowd intruded along the bottom of the photo while the couple themselves held each other close, an eternal look of longing passing between them. Myris Grantham in all her pop star glory. This would have been before the rumoured drugs, the abuse, the failed marriages. This was her in her prime.

'DI Kinsella,' Sally's massive voice boomed from upstairs.

'Coming.' She turned from the picture and walked back into the hall to ascend the stairs. She avoided the gift left by the milkman and stepped into the bedroom beside Sally. Simon already had his camera to his eye and was photographing the scene in minute detail.

Kinsella took her first look at Myris Grantham and sucked her breath in through her teeth. It was as though someone had painted a bright red fan around her while she slept. A near-perfect semi-circle encompassed her as though she were trying to grow wings.

'This wasn't murder,' Sally said solemnly. 'This was an execution.' Kinsella exhaled as Sally walked slowly around the bed to point at the blood and skull fragments sprayed over the pillows. 'By the looks of it, they lifted her and placed the gun against her forehead – see the splatter angle?' Her thick finger pointed at the extent of the gore. 'If she'd been killed lying in bed it wouldn't be under her, it wouldn't have fanned out like that. I'm guessing they came in here, one lifted her off the bed and the other shot her at point-blank range. There's an indentation around the entry wound that suggests a silencer. Whoever did this had planned it. They wanted to make a scene, but not be heard.'

'They?' Kinsella was interested to hear the theory.

Sally nodded, staring at the naked corpse. 'Yep, I'm guessing.' She sniffed, 'One to lift her and hold her, the other to shoot her. Though someone could do it alone, I suppose. She doesn't look too heavy.' She sniffed again. 'Angle of the blood splatter suggests the shooter were standing on the right-hand side of the bed.'

'Type of weapon?'

Sally shook her head. 'Too early to tell.' She moved over to a small hole in the wall and peered in. 'Bullet is in there, but we'll have to run ballistics on it. Any idea why she was killed?'

I Vow to Thee – William E. H. Walker

'None yet. She was a singer in the eighties and nineties, famous and infamous by all accounts. Downstairs doesn't seem to have been ransacked, or up here. Doesn't seem like she had much worth taking anyway. Royalties would've dried up years ago.' Kinsella ran her finger over the corpse's ear. 'Was she abused in any way?'

Sally bent down closer to the body. 'Doesn't look like it at first glance, but I'll have to examine her when we've photographed everything. I'll let you know.'

'Thanks.' Kinsella walked out of the room and across the brown-carpeted landing. She opened the door to the room opposite and switched on the light. A spare bedroom. Double queen-size neatly made with too many scatter cushions. What was the point in those? All you did was put them on the floor before you got into bed. A couple of generic-looking pictures and a chest of drawers that, like the rest of the house, was gradually decaying to dust. *And now she will too*, Kinsella thought. Regretting the frivolity as soon as she thought it.

'DI Kinsella! DI Kinsella!' Davis's voice, loud, alarmed.

'Yeah?' She moved to the top of the stairs and looked down at him.

'No one is answering anywhere on the street.' Davis looked thoroughly confused and concerned. Abboud stood rigid beside him, still and silent.

Kinsella screwed up her face. *Here we go*, she thought. 'What? Anywhere? You've been to every house?'

'Yes, Ma'am. Been in the gardens too. Can't see anyone about. It's like they've all gone out,' Davis said.

'Right, well…' She drummed her fingers on the banister. 'I'll have to have a look then.'

Outside she stripped off the protective clothing and walked with Davis and Abboud to the big Georgian house next door. 'You've been in the garden, right?' she asked.

Abboud nodded once. 'Yes, Ma'am. No one visible anywhere.' He had yet to show any true emotion. Was he capable of doing so?

The four other officers came over to join them. 'No one answering anywhere, Ma'am. It's like they're all hiding from us.'

Kinsella slammed her fist into the door three times. 'Police, open up!' she called.

No answer.

She took a couple of steps back and looked up at the windows. Not a curtain twitched. She moved on to the next house and planted her face against the pane, her hands cupping her face against the glare. It

I Vow to Thee – William E. H. Walker

only took her a second to see it. 'Omar,' she said, quietly. He moved to her. 'What do you see on the floor behind the door there?' She moved aside to allow him to look in.

He mimicked her pose and scanned the room. 'Looks like a dog, Ma'am,' he said.

'Yes, it does.' She scratched her eyebrow. 'So why isn't it moving or barking?'

Abboud straightened up and looked at her for direction. 'Don't know, Ma'am.'

Kinsella whistled. The dog didn't move. Abboud banged on the glass. The dog didn't move.

'I think it's dead Ma'am', he said. The other officers were crowding in to look.

'Do any of you have a ram in your car?'

'I do. PC Patrick, Ma'am,' said the officer, jogging off to retrieve it.

'Your plan, Ma'am?' Abboud asked. Kinsella noted that his iris were almost black. So much so the definition was lost between them and the pupil. It made her feel momentarily cold.

Kinsella addressed the group, noting how energised they all seemed. 'We have a murder victim in the house down there, a dead dog in this house and no one is answering their doors or moving about. My plan is to open this door and find out what killed the dog.'

'Should we wait for a warrant?' asked one of the constables.

'You can, but I'm going in here to see what killed that dog.' Kinsella was looking up at the top floor windows. 'No sign of life, and what appears to be a dead dog led me to believe a crime has been or is currently being committed on these premises. Any objections?' They shook their heads. 'You, what's your name?'

'PC Bradley, Ma'am.'

'Get on the radio Bradley. Inform HQ of the situation. I don't want this coming back to bite me.'

'No signal, Ma'am. We've not been able to raise anyone.'

'Have you tried all over the village?'

'We've walked up and down it, Ma'am.' He looked sheepish. *He's just a kid too*, Kinsella thought.

'Right, well, we'll breach here and you'll have to drive somewhere with reception, where'd the kid get it? Greater Worburston? Once you get a signal radio this in from there.'

PC Patrick returned carrying the short cylindrical police-issue ram as Bradley sprinted off to his car. Kinsella stood aside as Patrick stepped forward and slammed the door lock with it. The white paint chipped and the door shook, but it held. Panting, a look of confused annoyance on his face, Patrick hit it again and the door flew inward a few inches before bouncing back.

I Vow to Thee – William E. H. Walker

Kinsella pointed to Abboud. 'You first,' she said. 'Try not to touch anything.' Abboud nodded and stepped toward the door. He had to force the body of the dog to gain access, leaving a smear of blood in its wake. Kinsella, PC Davis and a now sweating PC Patrick entered behind him.

They were in the living room of a two-up, two-down terrace, nicely presented with modern furniture and features. Davis bent down to the dog, lifting its head. 'Jesus!' He exclaimed, jumping back. 'It's been shot in the head!'

There was silence for a moment. All four stood staring at the dark hole where the dog's eye had once been.

PC Patrick turned to Kinsella. 'I don't get it,' he said quietly.

Kinsella roused herself. 'Davis, go check upstairs, will you?' Davis nodded while looking confused, and walked away upstairs. 'Abboud, can you check the kitchen for me?'

'Yes, Ma'am.' He snapped his heels and marched through to the kitchen. Kinsella turned to look at the room. Nothing in there must have been older than a year. Clean lines and sharp corners, minimal furniture. It looked like an Ikea house. Like someone had lifted one of the display homes straight out of the shop and plonked it here. Not bad, but too much for her.

'Fuck me!' Davis's voice wobbled from upstairs. 'Jesus, Ma'am! Jesus! We've got another two up here.'

Kinsella braced herself. 'What do you mean, another two what?' she called up the stairs.

'Fuck me!' He was panicking now. She could hear it in his voice. 'I can't...'

'Davis, what is it?' The sound of retching was followed by PC Davis falling backwards at the top of the stairs. He cleared his throat, 'There's a man and woman here, in bed. They've... they've been shot. Same as before.'

Abboud had come back quickly from the kitchen at the sound of PC Davis's raised voice. Now he stared at her, making Kinsella's skin crawl beneath his dark, emotionless eyes. She moved first, with PC Patrick following close behind her. At the top of the stairs was a thin landing and small PVC-framed window. Davis leaned heavily against the wall, his face ashen and his breathing heavy.

She placed a hand on Davis' shoulder. His face pale and sweaty, eyes searching her face for an answer she couldn't give him. 'Keep it together,' she coaxed him. 'Stay strong.'

Stepping past him into the bedroom, she readied herself for what she must see. The man and woman were lying next to each other, hands resting together. She had been shot once. A small red hole in between her eyes, her head on the pillow, the once white fabric now a deep crimson. He had two wounds, one in his neck and the other in his cheek. There was blood on the sheet, on the pillows, duvet and floor.

Kinsella studied the details of the scene. 'He'd been awake. Someone fired too quickly and hit him with a nonfatal shot in the cheek so had to shoot again. He'd have bled out,' she said. 'She'd died in her sleep. She was killed first, and he'd woken to the noise, disturbing the attacker and managing to get up from the bed.' A picture of the living room flashed in her mind and she knew the hardest part was still to come. 'Patrick.' She spoke quietly, a slight tremor to her voice.

'Ma'am.' He stood in the doorway behind her, unconsciously shaking his head.

'Downstairs, by the door, there were kid's shoes…'

'Ma'am?' Uncomprehending. He was going into shock; he'd not seen this before.

'A child.' Her voice hardening. 'A child, Patrick. Where is the child?'

He shook his head again, bewildered. 'Don't know, Ma'am.' She could see the distress etched into his face. Would it ever leave him?

Her eyes moved to the closed door of the room opposite. The paint was eggshell, but the door was so covered in stickers and drawings it could've been anything. She stepped quickly to it and grasped the knob. The small chalkboard attached to the door read "Jennifer" in cursive script. Davis had recovered enough to join her and was currently glancing nervously over her shoulder at the door. She could smell the breakfast mushroom and eggs on him.

She took a deep breath and pushed the door wide open. Jennifer looked to be asleep in her bed. Her tiny body curled around a large sparkly stuffed unicorn, head buried in the pillows and long hair hiding her face.

Davis let his breath out loudly. 'Thank God! She's okay.'

Kinsella took two steps forward and pulled gently at the toy with trembling fingers. Jennifer's arm fell limply away. Kinsella pulled again, wrenching it free of the girl. A noise like a dying cat escaped Davis' lips. She no longer had a face. It had been replaced by brain matter, splintered bone and a well of blood.

Patrick turned away, his hand over his mouth, Davis collapsed and Abboud ran up to join them. He crouched in front of Davis. 'Phil, Phil, you okay?' he asked. The clearly genuine concern was still hidden behind the monotone voice.

Davis just pointed. Abboud turned and saw the girl. Kinsella still stood in the open doorway, the stuffed unicorn dangling in her hand. Jennifer's blood dripping from it onto the landing carpet. 'Break open the other houses, Omar.' She hadn't turned to face him, but there were tears in her eyes. 'Patrick?' She turned to the young PC who stood looking unwell on the landing and said, 'Drive to Greater Worburston after Bradley. Call everyone. And I mean everyone. Get them all here.'

08:23

Singh

By the time the Chief Constable Alex Singh arrived, the first houses on Queen Street and the High Street had been breached and their owners found dead in their beds. The officers who were still able to continued down the street breaking in doors.

There were now 26 police units in the village and a total of 57 officers undertaking the grim task from all the local forces and many from further afield. The ambulance service had sent 12 vehicles from the local area, though their employment was with the police officers rather than wounded civilians. The fire service were helping the police gain access to the houses, the swing of their axes splintering the strangely stilled atmosphere. Sally and Simon were still the only SOCO unit on the ground and were now in their fifth house examining bodies and recording their findings for future investigation.

Almost half of those present were sitting in doorways, leaning on cars or just staring into space after what they had seen. A major incident had been declared and the counter-terrorism unit were on their way.

Singh hadn't wanted to believe the reports. This sort of thing didn't happen in the depths of the English countryside. The worst crimes did of course happen. Just last year a man had murdered his wife, cut her up and fed her to their pigs. But not terrorism. And certainly not a whole village of people, as they now suspected. Pulling up on the village green, he saw a scene reminiscent of his tour of duty in Afghanistan. Broken men and women stumbling around him. The hollow expressions of the newly haunted.

Here an officer crying, there a man wiping fresh vomit from his mouth. Some even openly smoking in uniform, seemingly unaware of their surroundings or his arrival. One lad, a young chap of about 22, stumbled around slowly, his mouth moving without sound and his pale face quivering slightly. PTSD in the making.

I Vow to Thee – William E. H. Walker

Singh got out of the car and called the first person he saw. 'You there!' The PC was sitting on a bench staring into nothing. 'Who's in charge here?'

His voice roused her, and she looked over at him. Tears stained her cheeks, her eyes hollow and lifeless. 'DCI Wentworth, Sir.' Her shaking arm lifted to point at a man in a long coat, blue jeans and black trainers standing with a small group by a mock Tudor house called "The Olde Shop."

At the sound of his name, DCI Wentworth glanced up and saw the CC looking at him. Singh had known Wentworth for some years now and liked him. He was 43-years-old, average height at around five foot nine or so, close-cropped dark hair and the sort of hazel eyes that flashed in the sunlight. His skin the colour of varnished oak, but today it carried a tinge of grey. They had attended many drinks parties and worked on a good number of cases together. Singh would have thought him a friend if it weren't for the difference in rank. Wentworth always seemed a little uneasy with him. Not mistrustful or keen to impress, just a little too eager to please. *He looks 10 years older*, Singh thought as he strode toward him. They met in the middle of the road. 'Phillip.' Singh's voice was curt but not impolite as they shook hands.

'Sir.' There was an edge to his voice, like he was holding something back.

'What happened Phillip? I'm getting confused reports.' Behind him, the crack of a door being forced open distracted the men for a second. Two firefighters had broken into a little house set back down a long drive. They disappeared inside.

'I don't know where to start, Sir. This morning DI Kinsella attended what we believed to be the murder of former singer Myris Grantham found shot in her bed sometime last night. While attempting to rouse the neighbours Kinsella noticed a dog had been killed in a neighbouring house. Believing a crime might be ongoing she had one of the constables break down the door and they entered, whereupon they found the second victims…' He swallowed. 'Two adults and a child.' Singh could tell he was doing everything he could to hold it together.

'A kid?' Singh couldn't believe his ears.

'Indeed, Sir. All three shot in their beds as well. Now we're opening all the houses up and…' He paused; Singh readied himself to hear this. 'They're all dead, Sir. All shot. Everyone. Men, women, children. Even…' Wentworth's voice was hoarse, '…even a baby.'

Singh met his gaze. His DCI looked like he might cry. 'Any survivors?' *There must be survivors*, he pleaded silently.

Wentworth wiped his cheek. 'None found so far, Sir. No. Whoever did this seems to have taken every one of them in their sleep.'

Singh struggled to digest the words. Everyone taken in their sleep. How do you break into a whole village of houses and not wake anyone? The silence dragged out and his face struggled to achieve a suitable expression.

'Sir?'

The word roused him 'What are,' Singh's mouth was dry, and he coughed slightly to cover it. 'What are we doing now?'

'Checking all the houses Sir, those still able. Half our team have just sort of... stopped.'

'I can see that.' His voice was harsher than he intended. The truth was Singh couldn't blame them. Who knows what they'd discovered in the houses?

'Can't blame them, Sir.' Wentworth echoed his thoughts. 'There are kids in their beds murdered while they were asleep.' His voice wobbled slightly and he wiped his eyes again.

'Easy Phillip,' Singh said, softening his tone. He placed a firm hand on Wentworth's shoulder.

'Sorry, Sir. We're up to 67 so far and we're only about a fifth of the way through the village. We've not seen anyone alive yet sir. So...'

'You're assuming it's the whole place?' He couldn't keep the fear from his voice. *God no, this isn't possible*, he thought. Wentworth nodded and Singh's stomach lurched. Images of long-ago villages played out in his mind. Bodies piled on bodies and set on fire. He blinked them away. 'Okay,' he said and turned in a slow circle, taking in the strange mix of almost frantic activity and zombie-like grief the likes of which one only experienced on a battlefield. He had to snap into command mode. *Control yourself, control the situation.* 'Harry, come here will you?' His assistant came over to him and Singh leaned in and said, 'I've some calls for you to make.'

'We've got no reception here, Sir,' Wentworth interjected. 'Something's wrong with the phones, not one is working. No internet or landlines. Looks like whoever did this disabled it all somehow. I've got officers going to the cell tower and I've asked for a mobile unit to be brought in.'

'Good man. How have you been communicating?' Singh asked.

'We've had to send runners out of the village. Reception picks up in Greater Worburston just over the hill there.' He pointed north.

'Right, thank you Phillip.' Singh turned back to Harry. 'Drive over to Greater Worburston. Call the counter-terrorism unit first and tell them what we're looking at here. At least 67 dead but inform them it could be more. Then call the Ministry of Defence – we need to cordon off the whole area. Tell them I want soldiers, at least 100. They're to patrol the area around the village and help us here. Then call the

Commissioner, she'll want to speak to the Home Office. Find out how long the mobile comms unit will be, then see if you can get me an up-to-date map of the village – one that shows all the houses. Lastly, I want a list of all residents. How many we're expecting to... locate. Okay?' His commands had been reflex. There were processes to follow, and that helped him regain control of his emotions.

Harry nodded. 'What shall I say has happened, Sir?'

Singh paused, trying to find the words. 'Tell them a major incident is confirmed, most likely linked to terrorism and it appears that all the residents have been killed.'

Harry paused as if checking he'd heard correctly. He noted Singh's expression and nodded. 'Yes, Sir'

'Good, get going.' Harry jogged off to his car. 'Phillip, have you posted police on the roads into the village?'

'Yes, there are three in and out. I've sent officers to cordon them off.'

'Anyone tried to come through?'

Wentworth shrugged. 'No idea, Sir – sorry. We've no communication with them.'

Singh cursed quietly. Stupid question. 'Who's your second?'

'DI Kinsella, but she's in a bit of a state.' He nodded in the direction of a worn stone on the village green. It had once been a horse mount, now it sat so weather-beaten at its centre it resembled an uncomfortable stone chair. 'SI Harrow and CSI Farmer are apparently on their way, Sir.'

'Thanks. Look, I'll be back with instructions for you shortly. Can you round up the Fire Services Commander so we can have a chat?' Wentworth nodded and Singh looked over to Kinsella. Her body bowed over, head in her hands as though she were a wilting flower. He recalled her from previous meetings. She'd been at a retirement party in the local pub, all smiles and confidence and a sparkling wit. That was just three weeks ago and now he hardly recognised her. He seemed to remember the Commissioner had taken a liking to her as well. She'd said Kinsella looked like a woman on a mission. He composed himself as he approached. 'Kinsella.' She looked up; her expression haggard as though denied sleep for a week. 'How're you doing?'

'Fine, thanks.' Her voice was brittle like thin ice.

'Too much, isn't it?' He was struggling to know what to say.

She blinked as though only now recognising him. 'Sir, I'm sorry. I'll be okay. It was just the kid.' She started to rise.

'It's okay.' He rested his hand on her shoulder and she sagged back down. 'Stay here for a while, we can talk when you're ready.'

She wobbled on her feet. 'Thank you, Sir. I'll be okay.' She looked anything but.

'I know, I know.' He gently pushed her back down on the stone. 'I have some organising to do but I'll be back to check on you.' Singh patted her shoulder and Kinsella nodded weakly. He left her there and walked back over to DCI Wentworth who was in deep discussion with a couple of firefighters and a PC. The conversation stopped as he approached.

Wentworth spoke first. 'Sir. This is Station Officer Mendez.' The smooth-skinned Latino looked grave as he shook Singh's hand. 'Sub Officer McClaw, his second.' Another handshake, another prematurely aged face. 'And PC Omar Abboud. He was first on scene.'

Singh was surprised as he turned to face the young PC. He'd expected to find the first on in a similar state to Kinsella. Instead, the man stood to attention before him looking alert and assured. His mouth cut a blade-straight line through his face, and those eyes, so dark and full of menace, made Singh want to shiver. His voice betrayed none of his feelings as he addressed the PC, 'Abboud, I can't imagine what you've been through today. How are you doing?'

Abboud answered promptly, his voice emulating his stance: rigid and direct. 'Fine, Sir. Thank you.'

Singh regarded him closely. He was standing so straight his muscles twitched while those unfathomable eyes focused on a spot not quite Singh's eyes. *Unmoving and unmoved*, Singh thought. He couldn't express exactly why he felt uneasy. There was just something about the man he couldn't put his finger on. He intuitively knew he wanted him away from here. 'I want you to do me a favour, Abboud. We have police officers securing each road into the village. We need to know their situation and they're to expect the army, counterterrorism, and no doubt before long, the press. They're to hold the reporters and TV crews there and keep all roads clear. Understand?'

'Absolutely, Sir.' Abboud stared at him implacably.

Singh's mouth twitched but he nodded his thanks. 'Good man. Tell them that additional officers will be joining them soon. Where's your car?' Singh tried to look him in the eye. Black as night. Cold as stone.

'Down at the entrance to the village, Sir. Where we found the first—'

'Use mine,' Wentworth interrupted, 'It's just behind you there.' He took his phone from his pocket, tapped the screen and Abboud's pocket pinged. 'You've access now.' Abboud nodded and marched toward the BMW.

I Vow to Thee – William E. H. Walker

'Phillip.' Singh spoke quietly as Abboud walked away. 'Dispatch another man to the same location with the same message in five minutes.' Why did he mistrust him? He turned back to the firefighters. 'Now, Mendez, McClaw, what do you have for me?'

Mendez answered. His voice had a smooth, musical lilt to it. 'So far we've forced entry to 38 houses for your officers. No threats detected. All occupants are dead, as are their pets.'

'Their pets?' Singh asked.

'Best guess is they were killed so they didn't alert their owners,' McClaw said, his voice deep and gravely with a strong Aberdeen accent.

'Do we know if it's the whole village yet?' Singh asked.

'We can't say for definite, no.' Mendez replied. 'But we've yet to find a soul alive.'

Singh's mind was working swiftly. 'Priorities then. Let's open every house and see if anyone comes out. How many with you, Mendez?'

'We have 16, but with the available tools we can open four houses at a time. It's slow going.'

'How many houses do we think there are?' Singh asked.

Wentworth spoke up. 'I sent an officer round to count. He said there was about 95, give or take.'

'Right.' Singh was working through his options. 'How many officers do we have Phillip?'

'In total 57, Sir. But of them I'd say we've lost 15 or so. Only one SOCO unit so far though, Sally and her assistant. I sent a PC out to Greater Worburston a while ago to call in others. We're expecting more from Hertfordshire, Warwickshire, Gloucestershire, Northamptonshire, some from London and more besides.'

'Good job.' Singh's eyes landed on a grey-haired sergeant weeping openly on the doorstep to a white bungalow. There would be time to help her later. 'We can't investigate every scene, so we're going to do what we can and open every house to confirm our fears. Mendez, Wentworth, I want you to divide your teams into six. Phillip, keep 10 officers with you and leave four here with me. Smash or kick the doors in if you must, but gain access. I want to know if this really is as bad as it looks.'

Mendez looked ready to object, but Singh raised a hand. 'Given what we've seen so far I think it's highly doubtful there will be any gas leaks, boobytraps or other dangers, but we do need to keep some checks in place, which is why I want one of your crew in first into each house.' Mendez nodded in agreement.

'You really think someone could do all this?' McClaw asked in a whisper.

Not a time to dwell. 'Sadly, yes,' Singh answered. 'So, to your teams gentlemen. We'll have CTU arriving soon so let's give them something to investigate.' They nodded and moved off quickly, summoning their officers to them as they went.

Singh remained staring at the war memorial. Although it was May, a wreath of poppies still lay on the lichen-stained stone, battered and faded like forgotten glory. Just above it were the names F. G. Kilmer and R. G. Kilmer. *Brothers, maybe? Father and son?* Singh realised he wasn't breathing and sucked in a long, deep breath. He had to keep it together. An entire village murdered. Surely not. Suddenly he was back in Afghanistan leading the men over the rugged sun-blasted terrain. Peterson disappearing in a cloud of bloody smoke. His pulse raced and he closed his eyes to fight his rising fear. Fists clenched, nails digging into his palms.

'Sir?' The voice came from behind him.

He opened his eyes and spun around. Kinsella stood close by. Her green eyes red-rimmed from crying. 'Kinsella,' he said, trying to smile. 'How are you doing?'

'Okay Sir, thank you.' She shifted on her feet. 'Sir, I need to be useful, Sir.' Singh noted the repetition. He scrutinized her face. She looked like she'd been awake for days. 'I'm inclined to send you home to rest.' He struggled to recall her first name, '…Maria.' It finally came to him.

She visibly bristled. 'With respect, Sir. There's no way I'm resting now. And until CTU arrives I'm one of only a few detectives we have here.'

She was right, of course, but she looked like she was ready to collapse. Singh caught the eye of one of the paramedics and waved them over. 'I'm sorry Maria, I need you to rest now. You don't have to go home, CTU will want to speak with you when they arrive. For now, I'm going to ask you to go see the paramedics.'

'I'm not injured though.' Her voice was cold.

'Not physically maybe, but you've been through the mill this morning and I need you to get some rest.' He saw her fists tighten.

'I'm not tired.' She wasn't backing down. She looked ready to fight.

'Maria.' He tried to soften his voice. 'You've done brilliantly. Your initiative is to be praised, but you've done enough for now. You need to rest for a while so you'll be valuable when needed.' The two paramedics joined them.

'I don't need a rest, Sir. I just found a murdered woman, a murdered couple and a murdered child. What I need to know is why?' Each word was spat out.

Singh smiled at her. 'I get that. Maria, look at me.' She looked into his eyes. 'You're one of the best we have, and we need you at your best.' He pointed to the medics. 'These two will take you to relax for a while. Once you've rested I want you back at my side. But not before, understand?'

Kinsella looked left and right at the two green-clad men. 'Sir,' she said reluctantly before allowing herself to be gently escorted away.

Singh stood alone on the quickly emptying village green. The general hubbub abated as officers spread out down the street to complete their gruesome tasks. Singh heard a familiar noise from overhead as rotors slashed the air. He turned toward the noise, which was growing quickly louder and, lifting his hand to shield his eyes, watched the helicopter fly over a house to his left. It was a Chinook, and from the growing cacophony he could tell more were following. He breathed deeply. 'That's better.'

Singh called his four PCs to him and gave them their tasks. One was to go to the army commander and ask him to join Singh on the green. One was to liaise with Wentworth on the current situation. One was to open the school to be used as a command base and medical centre and the last was to act as his assistant until Harry came back.

Three more Chinooks joined the first landing somewhere behind the school. Another SOCO unit arrived a moment later followed by a sleek black BMW i8S. The CTU team, he guessed. *Thank God for that*, he thought, and walked over to meet them.

08:46

The Man sat silently and closed his eyes, listening to bird song return now the helicopters had landed. He didn't smile, but he wasn't angry. He felt nothing really. The radio was on. Evan Davis' voice seeping into his half-sleep. There were no reports on the Today Program. No news yet at any rate, but he didn't expect there to be. They'd only be about a quarter of the way through checking the houses by now. He noted the time and adjusted himself in his seat, closing his eyes once more. He could afford a quick nap before he had to get going. It had been a successful night, after all.

I Vow to Thee – William E. H. Walker

08:47

Freemark

Julia Freemark clamped her phone to her ear, a rapidly cooling cup of coffee in front of her. Her oval face, with high cheekbones and unmarked skin, was still as she listened to the voice. Her ocean-blue eyes were focused on the dinosaur her daughter had drawn at school that was now pinned to the fridge. 'No communication at all?' she asked for the second time.

'None.' Frank, her editor's voice, blunt as ever. 'Seems that every copper in the county and beyond is descending on the place, but no one's sure what the fuck is going on. Latest I heard was from a mate at Thames Valley HQ. He said there was some murder up there, but it's gotta be more than that.' Frank's voice was animated with the potential for a big scoop.

'Anyone famous live there?' She put the cup down and walked over to her pad and typed in "Lesser Worburston – Murder" but nothing came up.

'Not that we know, my man wasn't in the loop. Works in the mailroom. He walked in on the end of a briefing. DCIs come out and told everyone to get over there on the double and prepare for a long day. Then every copper in the place ups and leaves at the same time with the berries and cherries flashing, sirens going off, the whole works. I've asked him to see what he can find out.'

Freemark nibbled at the inside of her lip. 'I know the place. I grew up around there. I'm about 30 minutes away so I'll head over there and see if I can find out what's going on.'

'Thanks, Jules. Let me know what you find out. Can you get something over to me by two?'

'No problem. I'll ping something in. Bye.'

'Bye,' Frank put the phone down.

Freemark picked up her cup of coffee and took a sip, then screwed up her face. Damn: cold. 'Stephen?' she called, putting the cup in the sink.

Her husband popped his head into the kitchen. His dark hair was still a wet mess from the shower. 'Don't ask, she's already got her coat on and we're leaving now. You got a long one today?'

She smiled at him. He was brilliant. 'You're a legend, you know that right?'

'Of course!' he grinned. 'You going to be late?'

'Not sure. Probably not. Something's happened in Lesser Worburston. No doubt a fuss over nothing.' She cupped his face and kissed him, her fingers stroking his freshly shaved cheek, then reached for her bag and keys before slipping her phone into her inside pocket.

'Mummy!' Her daughter Maddie came running into the kitchen. Freemark went to her, bent down and wrapped her up in her arms, breathing in her scent. 'We're rehearsing the summer play today mummy!'

'I know, my love. Who are you playing?'

'I'm a sunbean!' she grinned. Her mispronunciation made Freemark chuckle.

'A sunbeam, Wow! And what a lovely, bright, beautiful sunbeam you'll be.' She kissed her cheek and stood up. 'Though I'm not sure what a sunbeam is meant to do on stage...' She spoke quietly so only Stephen could hear. He smiled at her as she left the room. 'Bye love, I'll be back as soon as I can. Bye Maddie, have fun at school.'

Closing the front door behind her, she squinted against the morning light. It wasn't cold, but the hour still held a slight chill. No frost any more at least, just the dew on the grass and car windows. Her Fiesta was across the street, and she crossed to it quickly, got in and started the motors. Just as she was pulling out her phone rang. It was Frank again. She said, 'Fiesta, answer.' A ping and Frank's face appeared on the console. 'More info for me Frank?'

'Are you on the road yet?' His voice sounded a little more tense than usual.

'Yep, just left. ETA 9.30 am.'

'I'm not sure what to make of what I'm hearing from my boy at Thames Valley. According to him it might be some sort of terrorist attack.'

'Terrorists?' Her instinct was to recoil but then the absurdity of the notion hit her and she laughed. 'Are you having me on?'

Frank's head swung from side to side on the screen. 'I'll be honest with you, I asked him the same thing but he swears blind it's true.'

Her smile stayed. 'I think he's taking the piss Frank. I'm going to get there and find a chicken's escaped and is terrorising the village.'

I Vow to Thee – William E. H. Walker

Franks' reply was serious, ignoring her joke. 'Jules, I don't think he was. He sent me photos of the station. It's empty Jules. Not a soul about, no cars in the yard.'

Her smile faded. 'Terrorists attacking a little village in the arse-end of nowhere? What am I walking into Frank? Is this bombing or a shooting or… what?'

He sighed. 'Not sure but take care and call me regularly with any updates.'

'Yeah, no worries. Find out more for me though please Frank. If you can.'

'Yeah of course. Bye.' He hung up. Freemark drove quickly, lost in thought. Terrorism? There must be a mistake. It must be his mate in the HQ having a laugh with him and she was the butt of the joke. She switched on the DAB and tuned it to Radio 4. Evan Davis was questioning someone on the current situation in South Sudan.

'…and yet you consistently block legislation to increase military personnel in the country. How do you marry that up with your desire to see Islamic Jihad defeated?'

A woman's voice. 'I don't think more soldiers is the answer. What we need is to join forces with our allies and work out a strategy to remove them from the towns they still occupy. Yet all we've seen from this government is a total lack of leadership in dealing with Islamic Jihad. Since we pulled out of Syria two years ago, we've seen nothing but procrastination and obfuscation. We've left it up to the Americans and Russians to fix the issues with little involvement from ourselves. Now we know where their leadership is in Qatar and the size of their organisation, yet we are doing nothing while they continue to grow their power base in South Sudan.'

'Thank you, we're going to have to leave it there. That was Chana Kapoor, Shadow Defence Secretary. And to remind you, we were expecting to be joined by Simon Barns, Minister of State for the Armed Services, but he has just cancelled without comment.'

Martha Kearney's voice. 'Now, what does your shopping say about you? According to a new study by the University of East Anglia, it's a lot more than you think…'

She switched the radio off. *Minister cancels radio interview?* She thought. *Coincidence? Doubtful.* She sped up. She needed to know what was happening.

09:18

Miller

'With all due respect, you're not telling me anything at all.' Natasha Miller's voice filled the ornate Cabinet Room. 'How was this accomplished? Who did it? And why? I need answers, and you're not giving me any.'

Michael, the Prime Minister's private secretary, scratched at the paper as he recorded the minutes. Stewart, the Cabinet Secretary sat to her left, rereading the notes provided by MI5 and MI6 just minutes earlier.

'More importantly, how were you not aware this was going to happen?' remarked the man sitting to her right.

The room, although large enough to comfortably accommodate 40 people, felt stuffy and confined for the 10 people who currently occupied it. Prime Minister Natasha Miller sat back in her chair, her grey eyes fixed on the Head of MI5 sitting opposite her. Defence Secretary Marko Flint and Home Secretary Douglas Howard, currently sporting an expression of extreme smugness, sat mutely. Howard's portly belly was squashed against the table in front of him, his tailored suit doing little to compliment his bulk. Having asked what he believed to be the most pertinent question, he leaned back, the chair creaking beneath him as he steepled his podgy fingers under his chin. *Pompous bastard*, she thought.

Michael Blackley, the Head of MI5, looked across at him as though mirroring Miller's own thoughts. 'As I said, there was no chatter. No rumours, no discussion, no coded transmissions. Whoever did this, they're not any of the usual suspects.' He was a tall, sturdy looking man. Ex-military with the unmistakable poise of a soldier. He returned her gaze with neither obsequiousness nor contempt. 'As far as I know this wasn't orchestrated in the UK. None of our operatives knew anything. GCHQ has pulled a blank. They've not heard a peep of this. I'm going on record to say it must have been planned abroad and the perpetrators shipped in.'

I Vow to Thee – William E. H. Walker

'I doubt that,' observed the thin, wiry man sitting to his right. 'Looking at the little we know so far, given the size of the village we're going to have at least 370 deaths with the last confirmed count being 87, which wouldn't be possible to carry out in the manner it was without extensive training. It would take around 50 people coming into the UK over the past few weeks and months to carry this out, probably by various means from planes to ships to the tunnel. Not a mean feat in itself but...' He paused to adjust his glasses. 'We're talking about trained fighters here, probably from Syria, Afghanistan, Iraq or even South Sudan. The belief in the cause required to carry out something like this? Yes, of course some people are highly motivated. But getting those sorts of people into the country without anyone noticing, no alarms ringing?' He shook his head slowly and deliberately. 'It's not going to happen; we'd have identified the movement all across Europe and we'd have known. The CIA has nothing, nor do the DGSI, FSI, Mossad, Interpol, the Chinese Ministry of State Security, you name it – no one saw this coming. Or they've not told us if they did.'

'Someone must know!' The PM struck the table, her face set in a grimace she hoped made her appear formidable. The men opposite her didn't flinch. 'Are you saying you couldn't have missed it?'

Jeremy Hudson, Head of MI6, adjusted his tie and took a moment to compose himself. 'I don't think it's likely, no. None of those on our watchlists have acted out of character in the past few weeks or months, no online chatter, covert activity, nothing. None of our allies know anything.' Another adjustment of his tie. 'No, I think it's more likely they're home-grown.'

You're trying to ensure MI5 takes the heat for this, Miller thought.

Jeremy continued. 'Regardless, we've got everyone available out asking questions, we are doing all we can.'

The PM sighed heavily, her body sagging as though punctured. She ran her hands through her greying hair. She had politicians in charge of her secret services when she needed soldiers. *More fool me*, she thought. 'We're not getting anywhere. I'm going to have to make an announcement soon before this gets out organically and we're accused of incompetence, failure to act or whatever. I need something to tell the press.'

As soon as the reports began to mount up and the full scale of the previous night became clear, Miller had Michael call a press conference for 11.00 am. 'We're getting out in front of this,' she'd said. 'I'm not waiting till the whole world finds out before we tell them. I'll let them know myself.' Now she was regretting that decision. If there were to be any speculation or a climb down, better to let the local commissioner do it.

The door opened and a stout man marched crisply into the room. 'General, what's the situation?' Miller asked him without preamble.

His face was that of an Oxford scholar. Narrow hawk-like eyes, a large, bulbous nose and wide mouth. He carried with him an overarching air of competence and experience. The sort of man who looks like he'd smell of books but could break your neck with one hand and carry on reading without losing his place. He cleared his throat. 'Prime Minister; gentlemen.' He sat down without waiting for an invitation and placed his hands on the desk. 'I can report that as of 09:10 this morning, we have 120 personnel on the ground, joining with the emergency service personnel already in situ. We've closed all access to Lesser Worburston in Oxfordshire and imposed a no-fly zone below 25,000 feet at a radius of 10 miles. This has included grounding all flights out of Oxford Airport and Silverstone Racetrack. We've set patrols around the area to ensure no curious onlookers get close. We've set up a command unit in the school and we are currently drafting in SOCO units from every force in the country. There are 97 houses in total.' His voice had remained at the same timbre throughout his report. 'We are currently in the process of erecting marquees in fields near the village to give focal points to those who will invariably descend once the press conference is over.' Miller thought she detected a note of annoyance in that last sentence. The General continued. 'CTU have requested for tents to be erected over as much of the village as possible but that's proving unfeasible. Instead, we'll look at fingertip searches of the ground and isolate anything that might prove useful with the investigation.'

'Why?' asked the Defence Secretary, looking confused.

Miller rubbed her eyes in frustration. *Idiot*, she thought.

The General turned to face him, his expression placid. 'The perpetrators would have moved from house to house. With the weather changeable at this time of year, they want to ensure the ground remains dry and preserve any evidence of movement. With the current focus being to discover if it really is the whole village, they're worried there may be little consideration being taken to preserve the scene. They argue this would give us a better chance of catching those responsible, though they admit the likelihood is slim.'

Defence Secretary Marko Flint sat to the right of the Home Secretary and scratched his massive, flabby chest and sniffed. *Why are all my Ministers so fat?* Miller asked herself as she caught sight of the sweat stains under Marko's arms.

The General hadn't seemed to notice or was better than she at hiding his thoughts. 'From what I've been told, it is as feared: every occupant of the village has been killed. Men, women, children.'

'Good God,' said Michael from behind him. The Prime Minister eyed the man before turning back to the General. 'Are you sure there aren't any survivors?'

He shook his head solemnly. 'Doesn't look like it, Prime Minister, I'm afraid not.' The room was deathly quiet as the occupants digested the news.

Miller was the first to rouse herself. 'Any evidence of why this was done?'

The General shook his head again. 'Nothing yet, no. They were clever, though.'

'How so?' Flint interjected.

'They cut the phone lines, used acid on the cell tower and cut the internet connection. Most of the victims were executed with a single shot to the head or heart.'

'Which suggests they were professionals,' said the Head of MI6 helpfully.

'Indeed,' the General answered. 'Or had at least been training for this for some time. We have evidence that some people were woken up. The way they fell, for example, suggests they were sitting when they died. There are a couple who received multiple wounds and weren't lying naturally. The theory is they were out of bed when they died and then placed in their beds afterward.'

'How very macabre.' Michael Blackley played with this cufflink as he listened.

Miller wanted to slap him. 'But no idea who did this? None at all?' Her mouth was dry, she needed a drink. Was 9.00 am too early for a drink? Even on a day like today?

The General was shaking his head. 'No, not at this time.'

Her fingers drummed on the table. 'Well, what can you tell me?'

'We believe they drove into the village and parked up along the road. There are several tread marks on the verges that appear to have been made last night. All victims were killed with a 0.45 round – also known as the Lord's calibre among the more rabid aficionados over the pond – which makes tracing their origins difficult.'

'Too many options to pick from to be much help there.'' Jeremy Hudson said, dismissively.

'Exactly, but we're looking at up to 50 people all with the same calibre weapon, a shipment like that?' Blackley countered.

The MI6 chief considered it. 'Yes, worth looking into of course.' He reached for his phone and typed in a message. 'And now it is.'

'Will it all be the same gun?' Miller asked.

'There are more than a few handguns and rifles that use a .45, but I would put money on them all being the same. Find one you like and stick with it,' the General said. Miller was feeling frustrated. 'Fine, MI6 is looking into the shipment. What's Counter Terror up to?'

'Commissioner Slender is due to see you in half an hour, Prime Minister,' replied Stewart smoothly.

Miller nodded as she thought. She liked Slender. She was a stern, iron-hard woman but there was something about her Miller liked. She'd always been deferent to Miller. Respecting her position and authority. Maybe that was it? But she undoubtedly should be here for this meeting. 'Why isn't she here now?'

'She wasn't invited Prime Minister. This is an intelligence briefing.' His tone hadn't changed, yet all could hear the condescension in his voice.

Miller felt herself anger and she made an effort to pull herself back to the present. 'Anything else, General?'

He slowly shook his head. 'I'm afraid that's all we have at present, Prime Minister.'

'Fuck.' This time it was Miller's turn to swear. 'Thank you, General. Geoff, your opinion?'

Her Home Secretary looked uncomfortable but thoughtful. 'Go slowly. Let's make sure we do this investigation right. The public will expect answers, they'll want grisly footage and facts, and they'll want revenge. But if we force this to satisfy that need, we'll be likely to get it wrong. And then…' He spread his arms and bobbed his many chins in a gesture meant to symbolise calamity.

'Agreed, but we also can't afford to be seen to be doing nothing.' Miller turned to her Defence Secretary. 'Marko?'

He was looking sicklier than ever these days. It was an open secret his diabetes was causing him issues. She could swear he'd put on a stone in weight in the past few months. Marko-bloody-Flint, she'd only kept him around because he used to be someone; now look at him. More blubber than a Japanese whale market. She'd have to move him on in the next reshuffle.

'I think we need to give the public confidence in our administration. I think we can safely say this was the work of Islamic extremists—'

'Forgive me, Mr. Secretary,' the Head of MI5 intervened. 'How can we have confidence in that?'

Flint bristled. 'Well, who else could it be? They do this sort of thing all the time in Syria, Sudan, et cetera.'

'Yes, Sir,' said the MI6 Chief, 'but there they have carte blanche to do as they please. As I said, there is no way that many heavily-armed fighters could get into the country unnoticed.'

I Vow to Thee – William E. H. Walker

'Small boats from Calais?' Marko asked petulantly, his cheeks billowing out like a frigate's sails as he spoke.

The MI6 Head was annoyed. 'And you don't think we'd have detected them moving across Europe? Or picked them up as they cross one of the busiest shipping lanes in the world?'

'We have people arriving in boats all the time,' Marko barked.

'Yes, but not these sorts of people. We also lock them up if you remember,' responded Michael. His tone failed to hide his icy contempt for the Defence Secretary.

Stewart leaned forward, interrupting the brewing argument. 'Prime Minister, you have the American President calling in three minutes.'

'Gentlemen.' Miller stood, her hands shaking slightly. 'Please, let's not start going on at each other. We're in enough shit as it is without adding to it.' She turned to Jeremy. 'Was this a foreign government?'

She thought he looked as though he was going to hedge his bets, and he didn't let her down. 'Hard to say. It has the potential to be a military unit that carried this out, they certainly had training. I'm afraid it's simply too early to tell at present, although the Americans will aim us squarely at Qatar. But then that's this year's mantra, isn't it?' He made a dismissive gesture at this last remark.

She looked him straight in the eye, the old energy returning to her for a moment. The strength she'd had in her leadership race. She saw the effect it had, and it pleased her. 'I want to know Jerry. I want to know today. I've asked Stewart…' she nodded toward the Cabinet Secretary, '…to contact every ambassador and instruct them to convene meetings with every friendly and unfriendly government we talk to. They'll all deny any knowledge, so I want you to find something. I want you to tell me who I can point our guns at. Jack…' she looked to the General. 'I want a plan for retaliation on my desk by 1800 hours. Anywhere in the world. We'll meet again at seven with Francis and Malcolm. I want RAF and Navy involvement from the start. Coordinate with Geoff, understand?' The General nodded once. 'Michael, investigate every group you can think of. I don't care if a lead takes you to the Barnet Poetry Society or Eastbourne Women's Institute, if you think it has legs, you follow it.'

'Prime Minister.' His nod was curt and formal.

'Marko, Geoff, I want military and police updates every hour. Slender will brief me herself but I want you two breathing down their necks chasing a result. I want every scrap of information for when I brief the press.'

'Prime Minister.' Their cheeks wobbled in unison as they nodded.

She fixed her face into a hard stare, head turning slowly to meet each in turn. 'Needless to say gentlemen, this stays with us until I issue the announcement. Anything on the news before then and I can assure you, you'll each be job hunting by the end of the day. I want to know who did this to us. I want to have someone I can point a missile at and blow to kingdom come. I want someone we can blame. And I want it yesterday. Understand?' They nodded. 'Thank you, gentlemen.'

They stood up and marched, strolled or wobbled from the room. She sat down heavily and let out a long, world-weary sigh while running her hand through her hair, which was starting to knot. *Was I this grey before I took office? Was I this grey this morning?*

'Prime Minister?' Her Cabinet Secretary, Stewart, the last word in upper-middle-class toff, stood close to her with a phone in his hand.

She looked up at him, feeling suddenly tired. 'Yes?'

'The US President is on line one for you Prime Minister.'

Bloody brilliant, she thought. 'Thank you, Stewart.

She turned to her Private Secretary and said, 'Michael, can I have a small one please.' He shot her a look that she read as a disappointment but moved over to the drink's cabinet without a word. Miller expelled her breath and lifted the receiver. 'Mr. President, thank you for your call...'

I Vow to Thee – William E. H. Walker

09:39

Freemark

The Fiesta Fire sped along the narrow country road. She had just passed through the hamlet of Little Tipton, where it seemed every occupant was out on the street, nestled together in intimate groups, staring toward the village peeping out over the hill ahead. Lighting her second cigarette of the trip she wound down the window a little so she wouldn't smell later, and slowed the car as she traversed the nearly single-track road.

This was her one vice, despite a pack of 20 costing nearly £20 and only being sold in petrol stations. Her jujitsu instructor constantly told her she'd have much more resilience and perseverance if she quit, but she couldn't bring herself to give it up. She loved the feeling of relief it gave her. The tingle in her arms and feeling of space inside her head as the nicotine hit. But back then smoking was still cool when she'd started, not the killer it had become today.

Rounding a tight corner, she found a polished white, blue and yellow police car with two officers stood in front of it blocking her path. One raised his arm, and she slowed to a stop as the other moved to her side of the car. She stopped the engine and wound her window down fully.

'You'll have to turn back, miss,' said the officer coming toward her. 'I'm afraid this road's unpassable at present.'

'Hi.' Freemark attempted her most engaging smile as she unclipped her seatbelt and got out of the car. 'What's happened? Is it a tree down or something? A flood?'

'I'm afraid the road's blocked, miss,' she repeated. 'Where are you heading?'

'I was heading to Lesser Worburston.' Freemark smiled at the other officer who had come over to join them.

'Do you have family there?' He looked concerned. No, pained. Almost desperate. The first officer now bore the same expression.

'No.' Something bad had happened. 'I just want to visit the place.'

A low drone could be heard gradually getting closer as the looks of concern evaporated from the faces of the two officers. 'I see, and why is that then?' asked the first officer.

Freemark thought about lying but decided it wouldn't help. 'Truth be told, I'm a reporter with the Oxford Times Online. We've had a report of a murder in the village. Is that true?'

The police officer's manner changed from pleasant to downright hostile. The low drone was nearing. They looked up as three military helicopters flew directly overhead. There was a hiatus in conversation as they waited for the noise to subside.

Must be more than just a murder, Freemark thought. 'What's happened?' she asked.

'Nothing, miss,' replied the woman. 'Just precautions being taken.'

'Precautions against what?' Freemark leaned in, conspiratorially. 'I'm going to report it anyway.'

'Nothing, miss. So you can report that. Nothing's happened, and you've nothing to report.' The male officer stepped forward. 'Now, if you'd be so kind and turn your car round in the gateway just there, we need to keep this road clear.'

'You can't give me anything? It's more than just a murder, isn't it? Was it a politician? Or a celebrity?' She scanned their faces for a hint she was right, but they remained impressively impassive.

'Back in your car please, miss.' The officers were moving slowly forward, hands outstretched, no threat, just resolve.

Freemark felt trapped. She wanted to push them for information but felt she would gain nothing from these two. They had their orders and there was nothing to be done. Plan B then. 'Okay.' She raised her hands in surrender and smiled again. 'I know when I'm beaten, I'll go.' She got back into her car and turned on the motors. Sliding it into reverse and backing into the gateway. She paused there to check her phone: no reception. 'Damn.' Waving at the two officers she drove back the way she had come, her thoughts swirling around her head as she went. 'What the hell do they need the army for if it's just a murder?' her innate curiosity was causing her blood to boil. 'You don't just call in the military for anything.' She thought back to her conversation with Frank. 'Terrorism.' She said out loud.

Slamming her foot down on the brake she brought the car to a halt on a corner in the road. 'It must be! Why else would they need the army? But in what form? Poisoning the water? Was there a military base near here?'

She drummed her fingers on the steering wheel and absentmindedly gnawed her bottom lip. Croughton was too far so it must be the village itself. Where to next? Seek a different way in? No doubt they'd all be equally impassable. Is there a footpath? She checked her phone. Still no signal. Damned countryside. How to gain access, how to gain access? As she sat there contemplating her next move, a large, military transport vehicle rounded the corner before her and swept past. She span round in her seat to watch it go and saw the soldiers lined up along the benches in the back.

'That settles it.' She said, 'In for a penny…' She put the car into drive and accelerated off back up the road.

I Vow to Thee – William E. H. Walker

11:07

Singh

Singh rubbed his eyes, had it only been three hours? He was bone-tired now. The sort of tiredness that penetrated the nerves and made you twitch at random moments. That heightened emotions and speech patterns. He'd not had this in Afghanistan. Back then he could walk for hours along roads littered with IEDs and still sit up till gone midnight doing his paperwork. These days were different. Still, only a year to go.

'Sir, the PCT has arrived. Where do you want them?' That was PC Yates, an annoying little man with an annoying little voice. The type that cuts you with every syllable. He looked like someone had tried their hand at converting a small dog into a human and hadn't quite got it right.

'The village green, Yates. I want to know as soon as we're up and running, and let Boris know will you? Tell them I want at least 5G within the hour.' Boris, the Commander of the Counter-Terrorism Unit, was currently in one of the houses with three of his officers.

'Sir,' replied Yates, snapping to attention.

And you can piss off and all! Singh thought as Yates trotted off to his task. Then he admonished himself for swearing at the man, even if it was in his head. Yates was just doing his job. He was so damn tired.

'You look exhausted, Sir.' The woman's voice was beside him.

Singh turned and smiled broadly at her. 'And I'm not sure how many more times I need to try to send you home, Maria, before you actually go.' He tried to sound friendly, aware of his manner toward Yates.

She smiled back. *She's attractive*, he thought. Not beautiful per se, but pretty. He'd not noticed it before, but then their previous meetings had been fleeting. 'I'm not sure I'd know what to do with myself if I did, Sir. I need to be useful.' She lowered her head, studying her shoes.

I Vow to Thee – William E. H. Walker

He should send her home, but he sympathised with her position, plus he needed good detectives here, and she was a particularly good detective. She had rested up with the paramedics for a couple of hours, and she seemed to have recovered somewhat.

'Singh.' The military man interrupted his thoughts. 'Are you ready to show me what you've got?'

Singh turned to the Lieutenant Colonel who stood behind him. 'Yes Paul, I'll be right with you.' Turning back to Kinsella, he said, 'Can you organise getting shifts swapped? The officers on the roads to the village need a rest. Once you've done that you could sort out getting everyone fed? Maybe some cots or something so people can rest?

'I shall do my best, Sir.' She smiled once more. *Pretty*, he thought again. *Very pretty*.

Colonel Gruder nodded toward a short thickset officer nearby. 'Captain Jameson will assist you, Detective.'

'Thank you, Sir.' Singh noted the smile Kinsella gave Jameson was guarded. He lingered briefly on it, unsure as to why.

'Right, Paul.' Turning back to the hefty bulk of a Colonel. 'Where do you want me?' They stalked off toward what had been the Head Mistress's office leaving Kinsella standing beside a map of the village.

As he walked away, he heard her shout, 'Hyde, get over here, we're going to need coffee and food. It's going to be a long day.' *She's right*, he thought, it was going to be a long day.

'Alex, I want us to work together on this.' Paul Gruder, a man as wide with muscle as he was tall, flicked his hand through the air over the virtual keyboard of his table before sinking into the creaking leather chair and gesturing for Singh to sit opposite him. His aid walked to where the small office kettle was bubbling away noisily.

Singh scratched his forehead just beneath the rim of his turban. 'I know. And, I must admit, I'm happy to see your lot here.' He smiled at the Colonel. 'If only it were under better circumstances.'

Gruder returned the smile and said, 'I've met with Boris already. He seems content to let you and me do the grunt work while he...' he made quote signs with his fingers, 'Investigates.' Singh huffed. CTU didn't want to be in the firing line when the press turned up. Paul was continuing, 'We've surrounded the village now and Captain Jameson will work with... Kinsella, was it?' Singh nodded. 'Yes, Kinsella. Anyway, they'll swap out your officers from the roadblocks. We're also to organise the removal and storage of the bodies.' He paused, accepting a steaming mug of instant coffee.

Singh received it gratefully and cupped it in his hands. He hadn't realised how cold he was. The day itself wasn't particularly nippy, but something about the atmosphere of the ghostly village sent a chill into you that was hard to shake.

He saw Paul watching him, face showing clear concern. 'Has it been tough?' he asked in a low voice.

Singh sipped his scalding coffee and put it down on the desk. 'Yes,' he said simply.

Gruder shook his head. 'Watch your officers, Singh. They're going to need help.'

Singh bristled slightly and looked to see how the advice had been meant. He saw the sincerity in the Colonel's face and sighed. 'I know. I feel for them going from house to house down there. Finding kids dead in their beds…' He trailed off thinking about it.

'Fill me in, Singh. What do we know so far?'

Singh shook his head. 'Precious little. Whoever did this seem to have left next to nothing for us to go on. As far as we can tell they went from house to house and mercilessly shot every inhabitant they found.' He paused, reflecting on all he'd seen. When he spoke again, his voice had taken a softer, troubled tone. 'Except it's more than that. They didn't smash their way in or anything. They picked the locks and shot people in their beds while they slept. They were professional, knowledgeable and ruthless. They knew which houses had pets. Every dog shot, some cats as well. Even a bloody parrot. Gave them treats to shut them up and then…' He trailed off once more. 'They knew the layout of the houses and how to bypass every alarm. They even went in the back door on some houses as they had easier locks to pick or the front creaked too badly. Even in Afghan I never saw anything like this.'

The silence lingered between them, damp and heavy with lost hope. Gruder shook himself. 'Properly planned then?'

Singh nodded. 'Expertly. Almost a military operation, I'd say, if that's not an insult.' Paul shook his head. 'We've found two patches of blood on the street. We think at least two people managed to get outside but no further. They were shot and carried back to their bed. Also, from the angle of the bloodstain, they weren't shot by the person who'd broken into the house, but by someone else on the street, which means they had people placed in the village specifically to stop anyone from escaping.'

'Jesus. That's SO training,' Paul exclaimed.

Singh nodded. 'One of the CTU officers worked it out. Boris might be as useful as a fly in your coffee, but she's switched on. Only been here 10 minutes and she worked out exactly how it was done. Hard to argue with her logic as well. She says they had people behind the houses as well to prevent anyone from running out back. It's a massive operation.'

Paul took the information in. 'Who did it? Islamic terrorists?'

Singh shrugged, running his fingers once more over his forehead. 'I couldn't say. They're not above wiping out villages, sure, but this is England, not South Sudan. Plus, as you know, their MO is AK47s, lining people up outside their houses and slaughtering them like sheep. This wasn't like that at all. This was quiet, subtle and sadistic. It even looks like they left the door open on the first house as they knew the milkman delivered to the woman who lived there. You know how many people he delivers to in this village?' Gruder shook his head but remained quiet. 'Six.' Singh's voice was a little harder now. 'Out of 97 houses. But they knew that. They somehow knew.' Singh slapped the desk, his frustrations with the day near boiling over. 'We can't find any evidence of their presence past the dead bodies and one footprint near the water pump. They've not knocked over a bowl, a vase or left mud on a carpet. Whoever they are, they're both utterly barbaric and professional. This isn't a lone wolf or half-cocked plan to blow up a tube. This would've been planned it for months, if not years.'

Paul lowered his head to his chest as though contemplating the scale of the operation. 'I don't envy you your task, my friend. We'll do what we can to help. I'll send out instructions for my team to report anything they think is worth looking at, no matter how small. In the meantime, we'll take over guard and security, free your lot up to investigate and hopefully we can catch the bastards.' He smiled at Singh and said, 'You need a rest?'

'Yes,' Singh replied honestly. 'But I can't have one yet. I need to talk to my Deputy, Wentworth and Kinsella. Reassign officers and…' His radiophone blinked into life. 'This is a test. Repeat. This is a test.' The voice came clear over the handset.

'At last,' Singh breathed as he pressed the speak button. 'This is Singh. All officers keep comms traffic to a minimum. At this point in time, military personnel are being organised to swap with you on your current assignment. Your coordinator will inform you when they're ready to swap out. When that happens, report back to the school behind the village green for reassignment.' He paused before adding. 'There's tea here, get yourself a cup when you come back.'

Paul smiled. 'You think that little teapot will do it all?'

'Found an urn in the staff kitchen,' Singh said.

'How did they cut comms by the way?' Gruder asked.

'Acid over the cell tower and distribution boxes. Dug a hole, cut and melted the fibre. Nothing sophisticated really. Could be homemade, but they knew exactly where to dig and made it an absolute pain for us to repair.'

Paul huffed, non-committedly. 'Clever though, to get them all.'

The Colonel's radio blinked, and he tapped receive. 'Sir, we've found a lady in the woods, she claims to be a reporter for the Oxford Times.'

Gruder's face twitched slightly in annoyance. 'Have her brought to the school but via the fields, don't let her into the village itself. Keep her under guard before we hand her over to the police.'

11:17

Miller

Here we go. 'Ladies and Gentlemen, thank you for waiting. I apologise for the delay. I have a brief statement to make, and I shall not be answering any questions at this time.' Miller steadied herself, ensuring her face was sufficiently stern. 'It is with immense sorrow that I inform you of a cowardly attack on our great nation. I am aware there is some speculation already and I wanted to inform you personally of everything we know so far and hold nothing back.' She paused for effect. The warm glow spread from her stomach and helped steady her nerves.

'Last night, sometime between 11.00 pm and 5.00 am this morning, the village of Lesser Worburston in Oxfordshire was the subject of a devastating terrorist attack.' She waited for the gasps of disbelief to subside. 'At this stage it appears there are no survivors, although we hold out in hope. While I am certain you can appreciate that I cannot go into specifics at this time, I can say that our emergency services, backed up by our military forces, are at the scene and investigating to ensure we catch those responsible.' The mumbling had ceased. The whole press core, deathly quiet, as though all held their breath. 'My thoughts and prayers are with the families of those we have lost. I promise them we will do all we can to bring the perpetrators to justice. I ask now for anyone who is concerned for a loved one to call the number which will be displayed on your screens and phones after this announcement.' A brief pause to draw breath and look directly into the distribution camera.

'This attack comes after many years of peace in our country. It has come after we have worked hard to destroy Islamic Jihad in South Sudan. It has come at a time when we are looking toward the distant sunlit uplands of our glorious future.' *Bit OTT that*, she thought. 'It seems that one of our enemies wasn't as broken as we thought.' Stewart had recommended her against that line, cautioning her it would lead to speculation and rumour. But she liked it so had left it in. 'We shall leave no stone unturned, no avenue unsearched, no path untrodden in our pursuit of the truth.' Another pause. Her hand was shaking slightly. She squeezed the edge of the lectern causing her knuckles to whiten. 'I will finish today by urging everyone to please give us space to investigate this atrocity. Give the families space to grieve. If you don't need to go to Lesser Worburston, please stay away.' She hoped her face had managed to form itself into a suitable expression of sincerity. 'I also ask the press to leave the families be at this time. Give them the time they need without intrusion.' One final pause. She swallowed down bile. 'Finally, I would restate my sorrow for those who will find out they have lost someone. I cannot imagine the anguish you will endure and the pain you will go through. Know your country is with you. God bless you and God bless the United Kingdom.'

She walked back into Number 10. For once, only silence pursuing her from the reporters outside.

13:46

Suss

What was wrong with this picture? To the rest of the world it was a fence. Long splintering slats of cheap wood, overlapping their way down the long thin garden like dull ripples on mucky water.

Suss saw strength. She saw the agility, the flexibility, the confidence required to manoeuvre that fence with only the slightest scratch leaving any evidence of your passing. The lightness of step and slight indentations in the soil from the back door to the fence told her this particular person was a woman. She wasn't sure how that made her feel.

She stretched her long arms up, fingers wrapping over the thin boards and ignoring the pin pricks from its rough surface. She bent her knees and pulled herself up. The air expelled itself from her lungs as she tried to haul her legs up and over, but she couldn't do it. The fence was just too high. Dropping back down, her breath raised slightly, she rubbed the scraps from her hands and stared back at the fence. *Stronger than me then*, she thought.

She moved back through the house, lost in her thoughts. This was pair nine. He had been at the front, she at the rear. He had entered the house and she had been back-up.

'You still with us?'

The gruff voice intruded into her thoughts and she pulled up sharp. Her mist of dark hair bobbing about her head as her bright eyes focused on the man who blocked her path. 'Dom? Fuck's sake, you shouldn't do that.'

His smile told her he'd enjoyed it. A smile? Really? 'You were away with the fairies again.'

She felt herself bristle; Dom had a knack for annoying her. He was too slow to understand yet too quick to conclude. Standing in Dom's shadow was his ever-present sounding board, Evan. A tall, ginger fool with the social wit of a dog treat. He was leering at her with that look in his eye. The look of the starving hunter. *They're just tits*, she thought.

'Don't tell me, you've worked this one out as well?' Dom said. Evan's eyes flicked away from her breasts long enough to give Dom a hoarse chuckle.

Fuck you two. Suss straightened up and nodded back at the house. 'This is the same pair as the last four houses. Looks like they were doing an average of six houses each. As before you've got one at the front, one at the back. He was about five seven, five eight. A busy mind, with a tendency to rush things. She was probably six foot or so. Strong, athletic, careful. This was the second house on their route so…' She pointed at the brick cottage next door. 'That's house number one for them, meaning pair 10 will have ended at that brown house just after that.'

'Bollocks!' Evan exclaimed, spittle flying from between the gap in his front teeth. 'A busy mind, do me a favour. You're making it up.'

Every fucking time she had to explain herself to these cretins. She rubbed her eyes with her delicate fingers. 'You can tell his height by looking at the angle of the entry and exit wounds. You can tell he's got a busy mind and rushes things as, unlike our friend in pair eight and assuming they all had the same level of training, this guy has had to use almost twice as many shots to do the same job, meaning he rushed things. Meaning he gets distracted, doesn't think clearly. You can tell she is more careful as the evidence of her presence is much harder to detect than, say, the heavy-arse fucker in pair seven who left smears of mud up the fence. She's tall as that last fence is six foot high and she's gotten over it like it's nothing. Meaning she's what, Evan?' The look on his face produced a warm glow in her chest as she watched him chew his lip.

Dom sneered. 'Yeah, but that's all just speculation, ain't it?!'

She could slap him right now but there was work to do and he wasn't worth the time. 'Well, why don't you two check out the first house for this pair and prove me wrong? I'll toddle off next door and start doing all our jobs there instead.'

'Jesus, you're up yourself.' Dom was shaking his head, but she saw the fear of her in his eyes. *You know I'm smarter than you, cockwomble*, she thought.

Suss met his eye and flashed him a broad smile. 'Wouldn't have to be if you two spent more time learning and less staring at me tits. Evan, fuck off.' She watched his eyes flick back up, his cheeks reddening slightly.

'You're wasting your time, Evan. She's a diver,' Dom said, nudging Evan as though this was hilarious.

Oh joy, this again. 'Yep, I'm a diver, I love to dive. Get me some muff all up in me face.' She made an exaggerated gesture with two fingers and her tongue.

Evan grinned, exposing stained teeth. 'Told you, that don't worry me.'

Her stomach churned but she brazened it out. 'I'll tell the Mrs, then. See if we can set something up. In the meantime, you two fuck off and do your fucking jobs.' She made sure her shoulder connected squarely with Dom's as she passed. Fucking nobs. Why did she let them taunt her? They were idiots, not worth her thoughts. There had been a time when they would both have paid for their teasing. Both would be lying broken on the road. But she was no longer that woman. She was this woman. A better woman.

Focus.

The white door was open. As with all the others it showed no signs of having been forced before the police had arrived. Automatic pick used as usual. She stood in the entrance, bathed in warm sunlight, her shadow stretching out into the hallway before her and turned her mind back to the previous night. Picturing the movements of the attackers. They had come to this front door. Her eyes swept the floor about her. Rug slightly out of alignment, could be nothing. She stepped inside, her head moving robotically in slow, sweeping arcs, taking in the scene.

Nothing too telling here. Her legs took her up the stairs, her eyes moving between the bannister and carpet for evidence of passing, and into the first bedroom. The bodies lay where they had died and she studied them closely. Two crimson rings covering the top half of the bed, deliberate and so similar, they could almost be art. Evidently asleep when they died. This perp was shorter than the last. The entry wounds were almost at the bridge of his nose, exit wound almost at the top of his head – 5' 5" or so maybe? Stood at the end of the bed like most of the others. Two shots, both good. Steady hand then.

Suss looked down at the floor, a pair of jeans were bunched up behind the door, almost caught. Door closed when she arrived. *Don't assume "she" yet*, Suss admonished herself.

Her eyes took in the couples' positions. They might as well still be asleep were it not for the holes in their heads. His in the forehead, hers in the temple. There was quite a gap between them, despite his size. He lay on his back, arms to the side of him, belly spreading out. It was her who caught Suss' interest. Something about the way she was positioned. It was almost as though she was clinging on to the side of the bed as she slept. Subconsciously distancing herself from him? She was tiny by comparison to his girth. Suss saw a digital photo moving in the frame. The rotund man with his slim, drawn wife. Him smiling, her looking worn and tired. Unhappy marriage. Why? She moved to the cupboard and opened the doors, stepping back to take in the interior. Her clothes, drab, dreary, lacklustre. The type you'd expect to see in a London-made fifties film about the north. Suss found herself fiddling with the sleeve of her T-shirt, a Neil Diamond one today. His clothes. Worn also, cheap also, drab and dreary also. Two people ticking off the days.

I Vow to Thee – William E. H. Walker

The small, cheap chest of drawers revealed nothing useful. Bedsheets, sensible underwear, sewing kit. The ornaments arranged on top were all cheap, bargain basement style-china. The whole room felt like its owners: unremarkable and forgotten. The drawer in the small table beside where she lay revealed an old mobile phone and, oh… Suss smiled, she knew how to look after herself anyway. Fair play.

She moved to his bedside table and tried the drawer. Locked. Interesting. From her pocket she flicked out a small knife, pressed it into the gap between the drawer and the desk, and slammed her palm into the butt of the handle. The drawer opened easily, and she peered expectantly in at the contents.

Two pens, a leaflet for a weight loss program and some rubber bands that looked older than her. Why lock this up? She jerked the drawer out fully and smiled inwardly. *What do we have on here?* she asked herself, removing the tape from around the memory stick.

Her phone buzzed in her pocket and she scowled as she removed it, then smiled in disbelief as she saw it was her parents. They couldn't wait, could they? Ah well, reassurance time. She turned from the bed to ensure there was nothing visible they shouldn't see and clicked answer. Two faces peered out at her from the screen. Him with the long grey dreads that flowed down over his back. She squat and stout, looking older than her 62 years, but with such love in her sparkling eyes. 'Hey mum, dad. You okay?' Suss fixed the smile on her face.

Her father's broad face held an expression of concern. 'Are you well, my child?'

'Yeah, dad, all good here. You two all right?' Her cheeks hurt a little with the tension of the smile.

Her mother tutted at her. 'For the love of God, take that bloody smile off your face girl before you do yourself an injury. We're not stupid, we know where you are.'

Suss let the smile drop from her face. They didn't know she was standing in a room with two dead bodies though, did they? 'I'm all right mum, seriously.'

Her mother frowned at her. 'Well, so long as you are.'

Her father rolled his eyes at her which made her smile and brought a sideways look from her mother. 'Are you busy?' he asked.

'Kinda, dad, yeah. You know, terrorist attacks and all that.'

'You always ask such stupid questions Gerry,' her mother said, hitting him gently on the arm.

'Well, I don't know what she's up to, do I?' he replied, a little defensive.

'What'd'ya think she's up to? She's running the investigation.'

Suss raised her finger. 'I'm not running the investigation, mum. Just working on it.'

I Vow to Thee – William E. H. Walker

Her mum harrumphed. 'Well, you might as well be. You're 10 times smarter than those fools you work with.'

'Now why'd you go and say a thing like that?' Her father protested. 'For all you know they're stood right there.'

Suss opened her mouth to say something but her mother cut her off. 'Well, so what? It's true. She's got the brain of Mozart while they're all running round like lost pigeons on a bouncy castle.'

Suss was still trying to make sense of that analogy when her father replied, 'I know she does. But you don't need to go sayin' it when you don't know who's there.'

Her mother waved her hand dismissively. 'Ah, what does it matter? My girls got it all under control.'

Suss stood back on her heels. These playful arguments were so commonplace she found it comforting amid all this horror. She found herself smiling as they continued.

'Now look what you done. The screen's frozen.' Her mother pointed at her.

'No mum, just waiting to see if I'd be involved in the conversation.'

14:31

Kinsella

The roads leading to Lesser Worburston were reminiscent of an end of the world film. Row upon row of news vehicles stretched away down every lane. Frantic families desperate for word of their loved ones crowded around the roadblocks like a swarm of zombies. The curious and the morbid – "grief whores" Kinsella called them – milled around the fields, testing the resilience of the soldiers' patrols. After a while, fields were opened on either side of the lanes and squaddies directed families to one side and everyone else to the other. The white noise of the crowd was such it could be heard as a distant clamour throughout the village. Cars were abandoned on verges as forlorn relatives simply took to the fields and ran straight for the village, only to be stopped and returned by soldiers or police.

The family marquee had been erected in a field just off the widest of the three roads that led into Lesser Worburston, but the sheer number of people turning up had meant a second and then third tent had to be erected on all three roads. Ignoring the request to stay away, every major news channel from across the world swarmed around the relatives like locusts until the soldiers formed a physical barrier to keep them at bay. The no-fly zone was violated continually, and it took an Apache gunship to turn back a determined FOX crew.

The news was a cacophony of nonsense and speculation. Supposed "experts" from psychologists to historians were paraded across every screen and holo-projector in the country in an increasingly desperate need to provide some sort of context, background, meaning, reason or logic to the massacre. Religious leaders from across the spectrum were filmed before screens showing a generic church or temple, condemning the violence, and sending their thoughts and prayers to the families and those affected. The leader of the Islamic Council of Britain was quizzed for hours by the BBC, ITV, Sky, Channel 4 and Channel 5 about the likelihood of this being linked to Islamic Jihad or Boko Haram. The space left by the lack of news was filled with the constant chatter of insinuation and accusation.

I Vow to Thee – William E. H. Walker

Kinsella watched it all unfold on the school staffroom TV. About her were arranged tables of food and cot beds for officers to rest on. Her work fulfilled, she watched the world go crazy before her eyes. She watched as desperate mothers and sons were displayed like hunting trophies. Each one more desperate than the last. Each one asked how they felt as though it would be a unique perspective on the situation. Each encouraged to cry, to condemn, to allow the great British public to gorge themselves on their misery.

Across social media sites like Frog, Bamboo and Twitter, "proof" started to appear as to who had carried out the atrocity, how they had done it and why. Hurriedly invented interviews with terrorists, hard-right extremists, religious radicals and political militants appeared, all claiming credit for the attack.

By 12.30 pm a video showing a supposed Real IRA leader claiming responsibility had been released, shared more than two million times and discredited. All within an hour. Boko Haram's leader was shown next to a Photoshopped map of the village. Islamic Jihad's leaders were shown cheering and celebrating in apparent joy at the success of their attack. All these films were picked up by the media and splashed across every television set in the world as a "possible" admission. Each followed a surge in tweets and posts against whichever group the user had decided warranted their scorn the most. It seemed the whole world knew who had done it, without even knowing what had really happened.

The soldiers patrolling the fields were stretched thin with what at times looked to be a continual stream of people trying to gain access to the scene. They already had 60-odd detained, sent either back to the family tents or away in police vans to Oxford or Banbury. One teenager got as far as the churchyard before being picked up and arrested. He waved cheerily to the cameras as he was led away in plasticuffs, as though this whole situation was the most fun he'd had in ages.

The whole area was quickly becoming uncontrollable when the fence finally arrived. Standing seven foot high, a wire mesh coated in slick plastic topped with razor wire, it was currently being deployed a mile from the village, closing the horror within off from the world.

By 13:45 phone footage had emerged on YouTube of Banbury Lane in Lesser Worburston. The footage showed four SOCO officers in full protective clothing exiting one house and walking into the next. It was taken down within 15 minutes of its release, but not before it had been viewed over 9 million times and shared by more than 4 million people. Quickly it became the focus of analysis and debate on the rolling 24-hour news channels, who played the footage on a near continuous loop for the remainder of the afternoon as though it were footage of the resurrection of Christ himself.

A group of frustrated family members attempted charging across a field at a group of soldiers. They were forcibly subdued and handcuffed all while being filmed by every news agency on the planet.

I Vow to Thee – William E. H. Walker

Kinsella popped a grape between her lips, enjoying the sensation of smushing it against the roof of her mouth. The sweet juice spread over her tongue as she watched a man in his seventies being tackled by two soldiers and handcuffed by a police officer.

Behind her a sergeant coughed and shifted uncomfortably on a cot while another lay still, pretending to read, biting back his tears. She'd go back in half an hour or so. Singh had told her to take some time out, so she would. She nibbled on another grape, peeling the skin off with her teeth before biting into the flesh. She should lie down for a while. It was still going to be a long day and she hadn't slept a wink last night.

15:36

Laoch

His Excellency Cohen Laoch, Bishop of Oxford, stood before his television watching the reaction to the events unfold. He sipped his coffee, vivid brown eyes absorbing every detail of the footage. His thin mouth, drawn as though by a pencil, frowning slightly. He reached down with a bony finger and pressed the button for his secretary.

The slightest of pauses before the buzzer was answered. 'Yes, Your Excellency.'

'Peter,' his northern Irish accent accentuating the "er" in Peter, 'Get the BBC on the phone, we're going to be issuing a statement.'

He didn't wait for an answer, his attention already back on the television.

18:56

Grantham

Jake Grantham sat in his kitchen, a glass of whisky listing gently in his weary hand. His eyes were closed, his head lolling slightly toward the whitewashed table.

The bright LED lights did nothing to prevent him falling into that wonderful, relaxed space before sleep takes over, where his thoughts drifted into abstractions. Where he could, by focusing his mind, make his body feel like it was tingling and vibrating as though being gently massaged by tiny needles.

He'd always enjoyed this ability to control his dreams and sensations when he desired. He knew he was fortunate to be able to do so. Frequently when he was lying in bed, he would stretch out his arms, put his head back and believe he was flying. It was almost as though he could feel the air rushing past him as he soared, twisted and banked without moving.

For now, he sent the warm feeling of tiny pinpricks down his body and relaxed. Like acupuncture for the mind. By closing his eyes and focusing he could make 10 minutes of sleep feel like five hours. It had been a wearisome day and a long night, and he needed to recharge.

Grantham was a security guard at the private industrial estate in the town of Liskeard in Cornwall. It wasn't exactly what he'd call a career, but it allowed him enough free time to indulge in his passion, watercolours. That was, after all, why he had moved down to Liskeard in the first place. After he'd been cured.

He'd visited Golitha Falls when he was a boy, his mother took him here on their one and only summer holiday together. One of her lovers had owned a house nearby and he'd remembered the place all throughout his youth and into adulthood. The freedom and beauty of the forest. The smell and feel of the cool water of the falls. The joy of being alone among the trees, away from all his pains and worries. Even then he thought how easy it would be to hide a body under the canopy of those oaks and hawthorns.

I Vow to Thee – William E. H. Walker

As soon as he'd been freed, he'd packed up what constituted his life in Oxfordshire and moved down here with the view of one day becoming a famous artist. That had been 10 years ago, and he now lived with 182 unsold paintings.

He reminded himself often that he only needed one painting to be noticed. Just one to be picked up by the right collector in the dusty church hall art sale in Truro. Just one critic to compare his work to Michelangelo, Leonardo, Donatello or Raphael, and he'd be set for life.

He'd be a millionaire on a beach somewhere. Living the high life on his yacht like that overrated charlatan Damien Hirst. He would be revered throughout history as one of the greats. One of the legends. As he would – no – *should* have been for his true love, had he not been snared by Him.

But that one wasn't allowed. Well, hadn't been allowed. The recent adventure into the darkness of his past was causing him to feel conflicted. Or was it excited? The scars on his back itched as, for the second time in two days, the intimate voice whispered inside him. It was calling to him. The true him.

Hey, you beautiful bad boy.

His words came back to him now. Now the voice had returned. *Maybe you can be free down there? Find peace and settle down, fall in love. But be ready when we call you.*

Peace? Some, maybe. But he had never found love. What the hell was love anyway? What would he do with a bitch in the house all the time? It would be like living with that whore of a mother of his, now hundreds of miles away in her shabby little cottage. Well, maybe not still. No, his paintings were his family now.

Immerse yourself in art. You will find your true self.

That's what he had achieved, or at least thought he had. He had allowed his art to take over his life. To fill the gap left by the absence of his truth. It helped that he was uniquely talented. A true generational genius.

He would spend hours adjusting his work in their frames, touching them up, moving them round the house to find the best light, or running his fingers over the canvas, reliving his genius in every stroke. He threw none away. Not even those where he'd made mistakes, dropped his paintbrush and smeared the work or when the wind had taken his easel and thrown the half-finished masterpiece into the mud and leaves. It would all be needed, wanted! Fought over when he was revered.

Maybe he was the next van Gogh? Heretic though he was. A talent unrecognised during his lifetime. Maybe it would take humanity to mature further before it recognised his presence had graced their lives? He was sure that was it and, till then, he would paint for the love of it, for the peace it gave him.

Come back to me.

He'd continue to set up a stall at the small markets in Liskeard, Truro and Plymouth while understanding that the world was going through a phase where philistines ruled. Knowing he would have to wait for the new world to be established to be granted the recognition that was his due. Not long though. Not now.

Close to sleep, closer than he'd meant to be. His mind wandered through myriad random, dreamlike thoughts. At one point, dogs were playing by a waterfall. Then children were splashing around in a pool, laughing and having fun. The next she was on her knees, her eyes bulging with fear and confusion. Then the trees in the woods behind his house spread their leaves and let the sun warm his skin as he painted.

I've missed you.

Across the room, the small DAB radio he'd bought himself for Christmas two years earlier managed to occasionally intrude and meld with his near-sleep thoughts. The voice wafting through the speakers was serious and sincere. The images of flying over Cornwall faded, and before him appeared his mother, as he had always remembered her. Drunk. To all the world she was the belle of the ball, a jewel of the stage and screen. To him she had always been the heartless bitch, forgotten and forlorn in her hovel…

You want more.

Not that she deserved less. Was it not what had she done to him all those years? Had she not left him at home for weeks on end with Irmgard, the sullen German nanny who beat him daily for any reason she could muster? Had she not pretended he hadn't existed for all those years just to protect her career? Just because she was unmarried and "famous"?

Whenever Jake remembered his childhood, which he tried not to, he remembered the beatings. The time spent alone. His mother returned to the house every few weeks with a parade of men who followed her.

It feels so good, you deserve to play.

He thought of the times when he'd fallen, grazed his knee and gone to her crying, just wanting a hug or reassurance, and found her lounging on the sofa, a glazed look in her eyes and no love for her son whom she had hidden away from the prying public eye.

Have you even relived it yet?

Bitch will rot in hell now, he thought. A smile creasing his lips, a stirring down below.

Something in the voice on the radio gradually pushed its way into his consciousness and in the haze of the half-sleep, he began to pick up words. Massacre… everyone dead… Oxfordshire borders… no reason known…' He should wake up. He should wake up, now. He blinked several times, swinging his head, his mouth opening and closing slowly like a cow chewing the cud.

'…return to our reporter, Sandra Cruson, who is with the police on the outskirts of the village. Sandra, what's the latest you have there?'

'Clive, as you know, we have seen the families of those lost being taken into a marquee near the village for what one can only imagine is the horrendous task of formally identifying their loved ones…'

Grantham sat straighter in his chair and rubbed his eyes.

'…it's becoming increasingly clear that there are likely to be no survivors from what is rumoured to be the shooting of every person living in the village. The military has erected a parameter fence a mile from the village itself, which is guarded by soldiers. This is due to the sheer number of reporters, family members and onlookers arriving by the hour. As you know, we've been shepherded into a field just outside the hamlet of Little Tipton. The whole area is surrounded by patrols of soldiers and police dog units. Gunships are enforcing the strict no-fly zone over the area and transport helicopters can be seen landing in the village itself.'

'What's the atmosphere like there Sandra?'

Well, it's a fuckin' rave Clive, Grantham thought, sarcastically.

'It's tense, Clive. Recently a third group left the marquee, erected to give them some privacy, and ran over the field attempting to break through the fence. The police and military brought them back shortly after, but you have to feel for them.'

'Indeed Sandra, over the past few hours the names of residents of the village have started to emerge online. Paul and Silvia Clement and their daughter Poppy…'

Grantham thought of the little girl called Poppy who'd not long ago been a toddler. That must have been…

'…who was 12 years old and thought to have been in their home last night. We've also had reports that the 1980s singer and star of the stage and screen Myris Grantham, known in her heyday simply as Myris, was the first victim found this morning…'

Grantham sat motionless. The corners of his mouth twitched in anticipation.

Sandra continued. '…Miss Grantham was reportedly found by her milkman shot in her bed at around 5.00 am this morning. We are told she was killed by a single gunshot wound to the head…'

Grantham sipped his whisky 'Sadly, yes. That was all it was,' he murmured.

'Many may remember that Miss Grantham had several popular albums in the late eighties including the platinum selling "Oh to Be Loved"…'

That man don't love me, he only wants me. He can't have me because I'm a lady. The familiar words wafted round inside Grantham's head like a spectre in a haunted house. No man had ever loved her. They had used her 10 times over, but no one ever genuinely loved her. Least of all him. The only joy she had ever given him was…

'…turbulent love life and several trips to rehab, Myris died alone with no family…'

'That's what you think…' Grantham said gleefully.

The reporter carried on her story, but he was no longer listening. A familiar tugging started to grow stronger in his crotch. Could he do that? They'd told him it was sinful, forbidden. The connection between that and death was too strong. He had to resist. But he had resisted. For years he had resisted. But not now, surely? They'd let him off the leash, they can allow him this? He felt the fruition of his desires grow rigid. Just this once then. They would never know.

It's a wonderful feeling, you know it is.

He lifted the whisky glass to the ceiling before placing it to his lips. The fiery liquid trickled down his throat and he felt himself fully harden. 'Bye-bye, bitch,' he said.

I Vow to Thee – William E. H. Walker

Day 2

'I cross-examined him and he double-crossed me but that's fine; I'll prosecute him one day and he'll be sentenced to life without parole. With me.'

—Natalya Vorobyova

I Vow to Thee – William E. H. Walker

04:29

Grantham

As usual, Grantham woke 30 seconds before his alarm. He listened to the news as he dressed. Loose-fitting jeans over boxers and a plain black T-shirt. Never fancy. Never draw attention to yourself.

The army of reporters surrounding the village had increased to more than 160. They were joined by several hundred family members and even more randoms. The crowd was apparently becoming belligerent. Journalists, TV, internet and radio crews from over 50 countries had descended onto a damp hill in rural England. All waiting for the inevitable gruesome details of the previous day to emerge. A ravenous public requires regular feeding.

For a while, the request to respect the privacy of the families not present at the village had been respected. But in the absence of facts, a Japanese news crew had knocked on the door of a grieving father. Broadcasting live from his doorstep, they asked him how he felt. Grantham couldn't help but laugh as the BBC news reporter commented that it seemed fair the father's fist had connected squarely with the nose of the reporter. Damn straight, he'd have done far worse had it been his family. Not that he had given two runny blood-flecked shits for his family.

It was a bright, clear morning with a fine mist spreading over the grass of his lawn and drifting between the trees of the wood behind his home. Grantham felt joyful and alive for the first time in years as he collected his half-finished canvas and paints. A sin? Surely not. A sin wouldn't feel that good. So good as to do it twice. They'd forgive him this one time. He left his house, not bothering to lock the door behind him, and took the path into the woods, energised by the sounds and smells of a peaceful world around him, ready to enjoy a few hours of relaxed painting in his quiet, still world.

That's where they found him. Brush in hand before his easel, sketching in the final details of the fallen tree as it emerged with the dawn before him. He hadn't quite got the bark right yet. It just needed... something. The continued corrections on the canvas had started to create a generally

I Vow to Thee – William E. H. Walker

unidentifiable brown smudge where once had been a half decent log. But he would persevere, it would come to him.

The two officers approached quietly from the path. The taller of the two spoke first, 'Mr. Grantham?'

'Yes.' He didn't turn, he knew why they were here.

'May we talk with you, sir?' This one had a deep, throaty voice.

'Yes.' Damn bark! The brush returned to his pallet.

'It's about your mother, sir.'

'Yes.' He dipped his brush in the water to clean it off. Maybe he should do more work on the background?

The other one this time. 'Perhaps you could stop painting for a minute?'

'I already know what you're going to say, and I don't care.' Grantham's voice snapped back causing a bird to flap away from a nearby tree. *Keep talking and I'll break your fucking neck*, he thought.

There was a pause. The taller officer took a step forward, his voice a little hesitant now. 'Mr. Grantham, I'm sorry to tell you we believe your mother was killed yesterday and—'

'I know. I don't care.' Grantham's voice raised slightly, and he closed his eyes to focus his breathing. *Keep calm, don't let the bastards get to you.* He dipped the brush into the green and raised it back to the canvas.

From the corner of his eye, he saw the officers share a look. 'Mr. Grantham, you'll need to identify your mother's body, and there are some people who will need to ask you a few questions.'

Grantham sighed. 'Dear Lord give me strength once again,' he said under his breath.

'Sir?' The man's voice was unsure. Shaking slightly. He was new at this.

'When?'

'If you can come with us, sir.'

'In a minute.' Grantham picked up his brush.

The first officer stepped into his eyeline. He was older, possibly used to dealing with the less cooperative. 'I'm afraid we must insist, sir.'

Grantham's fingers tightened around the brush, threatening to snap it in two. The old him, the true him, would have broken both men without raising his heart rate. Then, he would've found out where they lived and taken his remaining anger out on their wives and kids. But he was forbidden. That had been a version of himself before they had whipped him. Before they'd locked him away and starved him into submission. He could control it. He must control it.

You're coming back to me.

Until the previous night, he'd almost forgotten how good it felt. To feel that power and control over someone. Then his back started itching. The scars speaking to him as though He was there. *Control yourself. Control yourself.*

Grantham closed his eyes the way they'd taught him. Breathing deeply and trying to banish the thoughts of severing the shorter policeman's head from his body. He knew they were observing him, unsure how to tackle the bigger man should he refuse. But no, this was meant to be. It had to happen. He opened his eyes. 'Fine,' he said.

***

Six hours later Grantham arrived at Central Oxford Police Station. After the surprise meeting outside the station, he'd been led into reception by the two officers who had collected him in Cornwall.

He'd initially been taken to the John Radcliffe Hospital to formally identify his mother. He'd been deliberately outwardly emotionless as he looked at her corpse lying on the trolley. He'd just nodded once and turned away. Inside he was laughing. Laughing at the expression on her whore face. Laughing at his last memory of her. He'd felt himself twitch and knew he wanted to do it again. Was there a toilet around here?

Sitting in the reception area, he watched the constables who had driven him here go through a door and found himself alone. He closed his eyes and focused on his breathing. He'd slept in the car and was feeling refreshed and alert but focusing on his breathing helped keep him calm. Helped him control the urges.

I need more. I need to do it again.

'Mr. Grantham?'

He opened his eyes to see the tall redhead standing before him. She was lean rather than thin, with eyes the colour of emeralds and an inquisitive yet stern demeanour. She was nobody's fool, this one. He smiled to himself as an image of her compromised flashed before him. Not the time but worth the thought.

72

'I'm DI Kinsella, would you come with me please?' Her manner was brisk, like a stern teacher. He liked stern teachers.

Grantham stood without reply and followed her through a window-lined corridor, doors to the left and right leading to offices cramped with busy people on phones. Offices full of officers. He rolled the sentence round in his head. *Explains why they're never out on the street*, he thought to himself with a smirk. His eyes drifted over the surroundings and landed on the DI's bottom rolling gently with each step. A very nice bottom. *Spread those cheeks and...*

'In here please Mr. Grantham.' Her expression was severe. Eyes narrowed and lips drawn. She had seen him looking. He gave her a small tight smile as he deliberately brushed past her.

They entered the cramped interview room and a young-looking man stood from behind a desk and introduced himself as Detective Sergeant Nichols. Grantham didn't return the outstretched hand and sat in the proffered seat opposite him. Kinsella sat down and they each took out some paperwork. Grantham picked his nose.

Kinsella spoke first, her voice was clear and pronounced. Her accent was that of an educated woman and, he suspected, not the one she had been born into. A woman who had studied elocution. 'Mr. Grantham, I'd like to start off by saying how sorry we are for your loss.' Grantham grunted non-committedly, his eyes wandering the bare walls. He had heard no sorrow in her voice. She was professional, yes, but not in the slightest bit sorry. She continued, 'We'd like to ask you some questions about your mother if you don't mind?'

Again, a grunt.

'As you may be aware, your mother's murder was part of a much larger crime. We'd like to put together a picture of each of the victims to try to understand more about them. Would that be okay with you?'

A third grunt.

DS Nichols first asked him some general admin questions. Full name, age, address, car registration et cetera before turning to his life in Cornwall. His art, interests, hobbies. When he was done Kinsella leaned forward and met his eye. 'When did you last see your mother Mr. Grantham?'

'Nearly five years ago.' He spoke as though reading a shopping list.

'Why so long?'

'We didn't get on.' His voice was flat, almost monotone.

'When did you hear of the attack on her village?'

72

I Vow to Thee – William E. H. Walker

'Yesterday evening, on the radio.'

'Did you hear the reports of her death?'

'Yeah.' Still toneless.

'And you didn't drive up to see what had happened?'

'Like I said, we didn't get on.'

'What was she like?'

He thought for a minute how best to describe the woman who had borne him. 'She was a famous singer. She was selfish, manipulative and a whore.' A muscle in Kinsella's cheek twitched. He liked it. *You're a tasty bit of meat, aren't you?* he thought.

Her tone remained professional. 'What do you mean by that?' she asked him.

He gave an empty bark of laughter before setting her in his sights and sneering, 'What do you think I mean? She had more lovers than I've had solid bowel movements. She was a whore.' A slight rise of anger in his voice. *Provoke her, get a reaction.* 'How'd you find out about me, anyway?'

Kinsella checked the notes. 'She had your address on the back of her calendar. It's the only mention of you we found.'

Was that meant to hurt him? Try harder, love. 'Yeah, well. She didn't want me ruining her career.'

'Did she have any enemies?' Nichols again.

He shrugged. No bite there. 'I wouldn't know.'

'Was she political?' Nichols asked.

'The only person she cared about was herself.'

'Was she religious?' Kinsella again.

Grantham laughed for a second time. 'Yes, she was religious. She thought herself God.'

Kinsella's look hardened. Grantham thought she looked hot like that.

I'm going to fuck you as you die. Hehe.

Kinsella's lips tightened. 'Mr. Grantham, I'd like to remind you that we're looking at what is likely to be the worse act of terrorism committed on British soil. I would ask you to take this very seriously.'

Their eyes met across the table and a look of understanding flickered on Grantham's face. 'My mother...' he said, putting as much disgust into the word "mother" as he could, '...was not a religious woman, nor was she into politics. During the 1990s she had an affair with a Minister, a Foreign

Secretary I think, but he's dead now. But that's as much as she involved herself in anything. She didn't care enough about anyone else. Besides, she was 64 and a bit past it.'

He noted Kinsella was already shuffling the papers into a neat pile, and this seemed to take Nichols by surprise. 'I think that's all for now, Mr. Grantham. My colleague will take you back to reception and the officers who brought you up will take you home again. I'm sorry to have had to drag you up all this way for—'

Grantham interrupted. 'I have work tonight. Who's going to tell them why I'm not there?'

Kinsella looked at him coldly and he met her gaze. *Calculating*, he thought. *Cold and calculating*. He noted for the first time the small fish that hung from a chain on her neck. Then he was side-tracked by a suggestion of cleavage. He stared at her breasts and felt himself start to harden. *Not now, later. When you can picture her on her knees. Choking.*

'I'll write you up a note to give to your employers.' Her voice was like acid. 'Be so kind as to wait in reception and I'll get someone to give it to you as you leave.'

'Ta muchly.' Grinning, showing her his broken teeth. Her face didn't so much as flinch, and he followed Nichols through the door. He could feel her eyes as he left the room. He smiled to himself – she was hot for him.

Outside, he breathed in deeply and scanned the surroundings. He was delighted with his performance. He'd not lied, he'd not been asked to lie. He'd fulfilled his part. Time for a rest. Time to fulfil his passion maybe? As he scanned the car park, his eyes fell once more on the woman he'd not seen in 20 years before their brief exchange when he'd arrived at the station. He smiled broadly. This would be fun.

I Vow to Thee – William E. H. Walker

09:53

Singh

Singh stepped into yet another bedroom. Yet more bodies lay motionless. Yet more blood, yet more gore, yet more nightmares. He'd slept fitfully for an hour at about 4.00 am and knew that would be all he would get for a while.

In front of him on the floor lay the crumpled body of a girl. A dark red hole in the centre of her forehead. A pool of dried blood matting her straw-coloured hair. A yellow plastic number card standing next to her. Number four. Number three was beside her sister, who lay folded over the side of her bed like a broken puppet, two more small dark holes in her back and one soaking her blonde hair red. Awake then. Saw her killer coming. What must she have thought? What must her final moment have been like? Had she witnessed her sister being killed? He shook his head and sniffed, biting back a tear. Maybe it was better she hadn't survived? He'd met kids whose family had been murdered by the Taliban or Afghan army. They generally went one of two ways: suicidal or animal in human skin. Maybe it was better like this?

They had been identified as twins Lucy and Margret Arnold, age nine, although which was which they weren't yet sure. Singh stared at the scene, willing himself to look at the girls. As though remembering them like this would somehow make this massacre a little less terrible. The room was the smallest of the bedrooms. A bunk bed took up one wall, two small chests of drawers against the other, but still with a tsunami of skirts, trousers and socks flooding the floor. On the far wall a digital whale moved over the wallpaper, ignorant of the blood spatters it swam through.

Try as he might stop them, unbidden images of his own daughters flooded his mind. Their faces hollow and haunted like those of the twins. They were much older than these two. Adults grown and nest flown. Still his little girls though. Usha. His Sunrise, as he'd always called her, and Pia, his Beloved, were suddenly returned to his memory, reborn as children. Sweet, pudgy faces, all teeth and lopsided grins. Long black hair flowing as they ran about the garden. His son watching on, thumb in mouth,

I Vow to Thee – William E. H. Walker

forever the quiet one. Wanting to join in the game but being unsure if he'd be welcome. Singh's heart cramped and tears stung his eyes. His children before him laid out in kakaars. He caught himself welling up and rubbed his eyes. *Keep it together, it's just a lack of sleep*, he inwardly chastised. It took him a moment, but his heart rate slowed and he gathered himself. It wasn't his babies.

Singh crouched beside the bodies and closed his eyes. 'Baitat ootat sovat jaagat visar naahee toon saas giraasaa rehaao,' he whispered before standing slowly and leaving their lost lives behind.

Back on the landing he had to duck out the way as soldiers carefully took the bodies of Frederick and Teresa Amond down the stairs to the waiting van. From the room next to the girls he could hear the quiet conversation of two soldiers preparing Francis Amond's body for transportation. Then it would be Lucy and Margret's turn.

The family would be transported to the US Airforce Base at RAF Croughton before being flown to a morgue for post-mortem. Oh, for one of them to turn up something to go on. He needed something he could latch on to and investigate. They had precious little so far. Just a footprint of a size 10 military-style boot and the possibility that skin found under a victim's fingernails might belong to one of the perpetrators. But he wasn't holding out hope. They'd been clinical. The soldiers returned to the landing and he moved out of the way for them. Singh followed the girl's bodies out the house, needing to be in the fresh air and away from the crime scene.

Once outside, sunlight warming his chilled skin, he took his phone from his pocket and asked it to dial home.

'Sajan.' His wife's soft singing voice, normally so full of joy, carried a trace of concern. 'I hoped you would call. How are you?'

He couldn't tell her, he just wanted to hear her voice. That he had just pictured their children with their brains sprayed over beds and walls and needed reassurance? He couldn't tell her how close to breaking he was. She would know. He forced the thoughts away before he replied. 'I'm doing okay, how are you?'

She'd heard the catch in his voice, she knew him too well. 'We're fine, Kana has just called to ask after you, he sends his and Sari's love. They arrived in Rome this morning. He asked if he should come home and I said it was fine. They don't get many holidays. Pia is here with Mathew and the kids. She's waving at me as we speak.' A shouted 'Hi dad' from somewhere in the background. 'Usha said she would come over after work. Will we see you today?'

They were all okay. They were all safe. Singh felt some of the tension leave him and he sagged against a wall. They were okay. Of course, they'd never been in danger. He'd just needed to check. Just to be sure. 'I don't know. I'm going to London later for a meeting with the Met and a few others. I might need to come back here afterward.'

'Are the Met taking over the investigation?' Was that hope in her voice?

'I should think so. Although I've got Counter-Terror here and they've not done much so far. Some hotshot called Suss seems to be off in a world of her own, but to be fair to her she's pulled more results than the rest of them. I'll still be needed here for a while at least.'

'Did you get much sleep? Are you eating?' She was always looking after him. 'Are you taking care of your back?'

He smiled. The first time in two days. 'Yes, yes and yes. I can't be long, I just wanted to let you know about later.'

There was a pause on the line. When she spoke again her voice came as a whisper. 'Is it as bad as they say?'

For a heartbeat, he thought he might lie. Tell her the media were exaggerating, that things weren't that bleak. But he dismissed the thought as quickly as it had come; they never lied to each other. 'Yes.' He heard her whisper a short prayer.

'We love you, all of us. If you need to talk about it or just call—'

'Thanks, but…' he interrupted her. Even after 39 years of marriage, she was still just as loving. 'I can't talk about it, though.'

'We've seen the news, it's all that's on TV and the radio right now. We've had to put Netflix on for the kids. Alex, look after yourself, please?'

'Of course. Thank you. I'll be home when I can.'

'Okay, keep in contact. Always here to talk. Sat shri akaal.' She was worried about him, but she wouldn't press the subject. She knew he just needed to speak to them.

'Sat shri akaal. And thank you.' He heard his daughter call 'bye' as he hung up the phone and put it back in his pocket.

Preparing himself to go at it once again, he looked around. All about him was a buzz of activity. Every house had been opened; the bodies photographed where they lay before being prepped for transport. Those who had family already on site were taken first for formal identification. The large military transport vehicles were spread evenly down the road like a line of ants. Engines rumbling as stretcher after stretcher was carried to the gaping black loading dock at their rear.

As he turned his head, he studied a substantial red house on the corner, its bay windows bright in the morning light. The narrow front garden behind the tiny brick wall was alive with the colours of snapdragons and geraniums. The ivy snaked its way across the walls and over the top floor windows, threatening to cover the whole house if left unchecked.

He wondered about the family who'd lived there. The joy they must have experienced when they'd moved in. The children running from room to room with exclamations of wonder at their new home, squabbling about which bedroom each would get, where their beds would go, if they could have a TV in their room, a trampoline in the garden, a puppy, chickens... It was a small mercy they had slept through it all. The four kids in their beds wouldn't have known a thing.

How was it possible that someone could do that? He must have asked that question a hundred times already and still the answer wouldn't change. People are sometimes cruel to each other.

Singh remembered his parents talking about the partition of India. The violence they'd witnessed when they suddenly found themselves on the wrong side of a newly created border. How they had witnessed neighbour turn on neighbour, their desperate flight to the UK to avoid murder simply for being Sikh in the newly created Muslim country. They had not gone into details; it was too traumatic. But he imagined his feelings today would be akin to theirs. The day they'd seen their loved one's bodies and the horrific events because of the 1947 Mountbatten Plan.

'Sir?' A soldier, no more than 20, stood ashen faced before him. Singh scarcely noticed his sullen expression, his sunken eyes that gave voice to the pain of the horror he had witnessed. Everyone around here looked like that. 'The Colonel asked me to let you know we're ready to move the next lot on.' Singh nodded and turned to seek out Harry Scott.

Harry stood, iPad dangling limply in one hand, a bunch of digital toe tags in the other, watching a miserable shrouded body being placed delicately into the back of a truck. The raised section of the shroud covering the poor child was no more than a foot in length. Harry's mouth hung open like a puppet with broken strings. Singh had to call his name three times before he shuffled over to him like a zombie in a 1960s horror flick. More than one string had snapped in him. 'Sir.' His voice, no more than a whisper, had the tone of a recently tortured man. Harry had never done police work. He was an administrator, great at his job but this? Well, whose job was this?

'How are you doing?' he asked the younger man.

'I'm...' He paused, seeking out an adequate word.

'Me too,' said Singh, offering a smile. 'Have you slept?'

Harry jerked his head a little too hard, as though trying to understand the concept. 'I, I tried, but…' He bobbed his head again, the last control of the puppeteer losing its grip.

'Go home, Harry.' Singh gently took the tablet and tags from him, but Harry hardly seemed to notice. His eyes were swimming. Singh turned to face the soldier. 'Can you ask PC Bridge to take Harry home? He's in the school.' The soldier nodded understanding and with surprising gentleness slid his arm through Harry's and guided him slowly away. Singh looked down at the iPad, which detailed the travel arrangements for each household. Singh tapped his radio. 'Hammond, your convoy to RAF Croughton leaves in five minutes. I want you in the lead car and Johnson and Palmer in the rear. Two outriders to clear the roads.'

The radio hissed a response. 'Sir. Leave in five minutes to Croughton. Understood,' Hammond confirmed.

Singh tapped the iPad screen: Banbury Lane next. He stepped off the curb and crossed the street toward the small stone end of terrace. 'Corner Cottage, Banbury Lane. Mr. Symon O'Hara, 54-years-old, lived alone.' He transferred the details to the digital toe tag and handed it over to the waiting soldier. The stretcher appeared a moment later and Singh directed them toward the waiting truck. Tapping the appropriate registration next to O'Hara's name before moving on to Middle Cottage, where a second soldier stood waiting to receive the tags. 'Middle Cottage, Mr. & Mrs. Jenkins, no age yet confirmed, and their daughter, Alice, six…' The next words caught in his throat and he made himself go on, trying to not let his voice break. '…six years old and their son Phillip, three months old.' The toe tags beeped as they received the details and Singh turned away as the stretchers were carried out, preferring instead to focus on the drop-down options for the truck registrations. He didn't watch as Alice and Phillip were loaded up onto the back of the truck, but couldn't help seeing a soldier break down before being led away by his colleague.

''E's just become a dad,' explained a lieutenant who had just exited the house. A Yorkshire accent, Singh noted. He felt vomit rise in him as the images of his daughters once more flashed before his eyes. 'Here,' he said, thrusting the iPad and tags at the Lieutenant, 'You carry on, I have to get ready.'

'True the PM's comin' here?' The man looked up at him. His deep brown eyes looked clear compared to most.

'She is. Due in a little over an hour. And she'll be shaking hands and making nice, so you be sure to do the same,' he said, stomping off just to get away from it all. *Five minutes peace, please.*

Unlatching the rickety gate, he marched as though on parade, up the path next to the church that led to the school. He slowed as he approached. Many of his officers were gathered outside one of the entrances. Some smoking, others drinking tea from mugs. No one really talking. They'll all need therapy after this. How would they do the rotas now? So many officers requiring time off. He fixed his face to one of sombre command and nodded to them as he passed, receiving sparse acknowledgement from the weary faces. A little way further up he stopped beside the wall of the old schoolhouse.

The school itself was divided into three parts. The first, a proud Victorian building of sandstone, stood tall and stately. An old patinated bell in a whitewash tower in the centre of the roof. The second, bolted on to the side by way of a broad corridor, was 1960s brutalist concrete and plastic cladding. All-purpose and no design. The final part was only a few years finished and made from landfill bricks and fitted with solar tiles, water recycling and an industrial composter. The result was a muddled and confused mess of a building. A testament to the governments of investment and austerity. Standing next to the three story-high sandstone brickwork he studied the initials former students had carved into its surface. "PW 4 AH," "A.N.," "L.F 94," "M.K '87." Some were dated as far back as 1983 and 1972. Even a deeply cut set of initials from '68.

All these children passing through this school and going on to live their lives. Joining, nervous and cautious, at the age of four. Lunch boxes clutched in tiny hands, the new school uniform ironed and itching. Leaving loud and boisterous at 11. Going on to the big school, their first chapter finished.

Would there be any more? Standing here now it seems impossible there would. The only noises, the hushed conversations of damaged police officers and the sound of the latest convoy setting off with its cargo of tiny, shrouded bodies, how could this village ever be normal again? Who would want to live here now knowing what had happened? He certainly wouldn't buy here. He traced shaking fingers over a particularly deep "Z.D. 1986." Enjoying the sensation of something tangible. Something that didn't require meaning beyond its own existence.

He imagined the delight the carving of the indelible letters would have given the young Z.D. The immortality it gave them. It was unlikely they'd have been thinking of life after death. Kids tended not to think past the next week, let alone the mystical future of adulthood and distant death. At that time in their life, this would have been enough. Their initials carved into a building older than comprehension, their mark on the world.

His fingers traced over the stone, every bump and grove tingling his nerves. It was a stone in a wall. It was needed to keep the wall up. It didn't need explanation beyond that. It was simple. Singh liked simple right now. He wondered who Z.D. was and where they were now. What were their achievements, their glories? Maybe they were a scientist? Curing illness or understanding the universe. An astronaut, maybe? Working on the international space port. Had they got out? Had they made it? Were they safe?

He sighed and turned away from the wall, making his way round past the well-tended allotments with its rows of fast-growing potatoes and flowering runner beans. Bright green leaves wafting gently in the breeze.

The air was fresher here, the chill that had settled over the village seemed to lessen slightly beside the newly flowering growth. It was still spring here. Still light, bright and hopeful. Still. He caught sight of the soldiers in the next field. The blue fence just beyond them. Not all peace then.

He rounded the corner to the main school gates and found PC Abboud waiting for him. Try as he might, Singh didn't like Abboud. Not because of his heritage or his faith, those didn't matter to Singh. It was the way Abboud looked at him that Singh didn't like. There was never any emotion in those eyes. So dark as to resemble a spider. His mouth never twitched into either a smile or frown. His voice never varied from monotone. It was as though he felt nothing, and Singh couldn't trust people who felt nothing.

Abboud was standing next to the iron gates watching a platoon of soldier's march toward the village green. He snapped to attention upon seeing Singh approach. 'Sir.'

'Abboud.' Singh tried sounding pleasant. 'I thought you'd gone home?'

'I did Sir, but I came back for my shift, Sir. I wanted to help.' Singh tried to find some earnestness in his words but failed.

'Well, thank you...' He ransacked his memory for his first name. Had he ever known it? The silence stretched awkwardly until he gave up, offering Abboud a smile that went unreturned. 'We need all the help we can get. Can I ask you to go and find DCI Barns? She's in the school somewhere. She'll give you your assignment.'

'Sir,' Abboud said and marched off toward the school.

Singh watched him go. He was curious about how Abboud had managed to get a job in the force. It was much harder for immigrants and their descendants to find work in the public sector these days. Even doctors were severely scrutinised before being allowed to practice. He made a mental note to look at his file one day, just to find out a bit more about him. Those eyes, though. They frightened him.

As Abboud disappeared inside, Singh resumed his walk onto the village green. The sun shone brightly but Singh felt a shadow cast over him. The green itself was clearer than the previous day. The school taking on the role of hospital and home for the broken. Singh looked about him and saw Colonel Gruder stood with two men in elegant suits. He was pointing at the manor house and Singh overheard the end of his sentence as he approached. '...they were both in bed, same as the others. The dog was found beside the pool. It had also been shot and... ah, Singh.' He focused his attention on Singh, offering him a small smile and curious nod. 'Chief Constable Singh, this is Andrew McMillan and Joe Scott, they're from MI5.' Handshakes all round.

Oh joy, spooks, Singh thought as they both smiled thinly at him. 'We expected you earlier.'

Scott answered. He had a well-educated, Oxbridge voice. The voice of a television announcer, yet his tone was derisive. One eyebrow raised slightly as he replied, 'What would have been achieved by our coming earlier?'

Singh bristled. 'Well, maybe you could have helped us with them?' Singh waved at the stretchers and trucks.

Gruder stepped in sounding conciliatory, 'Singh has been here since the very first. He's pretty much organised the whole recovery. CTU has left him to it and done their own thing.'

McMillan responded. He, like his partner, had the tone of the privately educated. Singh suspected he'd worked hard to eliminate all trace of his Scottish roots. He was almost there but he still elongated his pronunciation of "O." 'I'm certain you've done an excellent job. I can't imagine what it's been like.' He smiled the sort of smile those born into money save for those who aren't. A mixture of genuine warmth, pity and superiority. 'We're here on specific business unless you or CTU have any evidence yet as to the perpetrators?' He cocked his head in a manner Singh suspected was meant to show interest, but instead made him look like he was asking a naughty child who'd eaten all the sweets.

'No,' Singh said, struggling slightly to maintain his professionalism. 'Whoever this was, they were exceptionally good.'

Gruder was nodding, 'I think we can conclude they had military training. A foreign power, maybe? What about from your end?'

Scott cut in immediately, 'We're not at liberty to discuss that. We're only here today about the matter we mentioned.'

'And what matter might that be?' asked Singh, beginning to feel excluded.

It was Gruder who answered him. 'Scott and McMillan want to go into the Manor House.' A pause while he turned to the two smartly suited spies. 'They won't say why.'

Singh met the eyes of the two MI5 Officers, who returned his gaze with the looks of men used to getting their own way. He wasn't prone to violence, but he could have slapped them right now. He was too tired to be tested. Thankfully, years of experience kept his voice calm and firm. 'It's been cleared, but I'd like to know why before I agree?'

'Sorry,' said McMillan, smiling again and sounding anything but. 'Need to know only.'

Need to know only? He'd been told that once before and it had annoyed him then. That had been the day Fisher had been shot in the leg in Helmand and he wasn't going to let them get off that easy. 'Mind if I check?' he asked, reaching for his radio.

'Colonel Gruder here has had his orders already,' Scott put in. Gruder nodded at this and gave Singh an apologetic look.

Singh knew he wouldn't win this, but he was damned if he would just roll over. He smiled at the men. Scott's face twitched slightly in annoyance. 'Well, given that I'm not in the army anymore, I'd like to be sure.'

McMillan placed his hand on Singh's arm. 'Alex.' The use of his first name caught Singh by surprise. 'This is a sensitive subject and the fewer people who know about it the better. We're barely going to require five minutes and then we'll be out of your hair, all right?' He managed to make the "all right" sound less a question, more an assertion.

'Fact of the matter is, you have no choice,' Scott added with a sneer that made Singh even more determined to use violence to end this. 'We're going in. This was just a courtesy.'

Singh met his smile with a stare that could melt steel. 'The fact of the matter is, I have no intention of stopping you, if...' and he held his finger up between them, 'if you have the correct authorisation to be here and have followed process. If, however, this is just another example of MI5 thinking they can stomp all over an investigation without feeling the need to confide in those charged with managing the said investigation, then we will have a problem.' He hadn't so much as raised his voice nor changed his tone, yet it was clear he had the two men now.

Singh watched them make up their minds before McMillan finally spoke. 'Do you know who lived in the Manor?'

Singh shook his head. 'Not from memory, no. We've nearly 400 dead here.'

'David Newman,' McMillan whispered, as though the words should resonate across the world.

Singh failed to keep the confusion from his face. 'Is that supposed to mean something to me?'

'David Newman was one of us.' Scott had lowered his voice also. 'Retired, but still one of us.'

Now it made sense why they hadn't wanted him to call it in. MI5 is covering their tracks. 'Retired when?' asked Singh.

'Nearly three years ago,' replied Scott.

Singh nodded. 'And you want to know what he might have left behind? Or worse, what might have been taken?'

McMillan frowned and nodded. 'Indeed, we don't know what he might have squirreled away from his time in the field. We think he may have potentially compromising information.'

Singh was feeling a little superior now. He wouldn't normally but it had been too long since he had last felt anything other than miserable. He twisted the knife. 'Do you often allow your retirees to wander off with sensitive information?'

Gruder smiled slightly while McMillan looked decidedly uncomfortable. 'Newman was, well, difficult. A splendid chap of course. Top fellow. But difficult.'

'He liked his whisky,' Scott was blunt, resigned to telling them everything. 'The man was a mess by the time he was retired. I doubt there is anything important in there but...'

'But you didn't think to check if he had anything before this?' Gruder asked.

McMillan shrugged. 'Before this, we never suspected he would be a target. He was known to be a, well, a bit of a sot.'

Singh realised his meaning. The implications made his skin crawl. 'Are you saying you think someone planned and executed nearly 400 people just to cover the murder of one former MI5 Officer?'

'Director,' McMillan corrected him, and instantly looking like he wished he hadn't spoken.

'Fuck me, if you're right...' Gruder looked stunned.

'I know.' McMillan was nodding. 'It seems unlikely but, given his department and the information he was privy to, we have to check.'

'I take it he was Counter-Terrorism?'

'Aren't we all these days?' put in Scott. 'The world is full of people who want to annihilate us.'

Singh thought he saw a sidelong glance at his turban but chose to ignore it. He aired his thoughts. 'A Counter Intelligence Director killed during a terrorist attack; I must admit it seems unlikely it's a coincidence.' He scratched his chin while he thought.

'But you don't kill an entire village to get at an easily identifiable victim. Especially when you can pull it off like these did,' Gruder said.

Singh nodded. 'You're right. But you could pick your target knowing a former MI5 Director lived there and consider being able to acquire any information he has as a bonus.'

McMillan and Scott shared a look, Scott responded first, 'I must admit that had occurred to us as well.'

'I think I need to know what you find in there.' Scott was shaking his head, but Singh was adamant. 'I want to know what you find because I don't think you're not going to find anything of value. Somehow, I suspect that if any house has been, that'll be the only one in this village that has been burgled.'

'We'll have to speak to our boss,' McMillan said. 'We can't make that call.'

'Okay. You can examine the house. I'll speak to the Commissioner and she'll contact your boss. But you don't remove anything without my say so. All right?' Scott made to protest but Singh held up his hands to still him. 'Not the detail, yet. Just the number and type of items. Files, laptops, etc. I may need to account for them later.'

'Fine,' McMillan nodded and flashed Scott a look as if to say, "decision made." Scott still looked prepared to protest but kept quiet. 'May we proceed?'

Singh nodded. 'My assistant has left for the day so come and find me when you're done. I'll be in the school.'

They agreed and Scott and McMillan walked toward the house. Singh radioed ahead to let them have access and looked to Gruder who was staring at the MI5 officer's backs.

'Do you genuinely think all this could have been carried out just because some ex-director lived here?' he asked. Something in his voice made Singh think he was hoping it wasn't true. Singh didn't know how to reply. Gruder looked at him and read the response in his eyes. He changed the subject. 'Right, we'd best get ready to greet our Lord and master… mistress?'

Singh and Gruder exchanged an amused look. He had no time for Natasha Miller. Her policies excluded people like him. Her government had continued the trend of division left by the last Prime Minister. But he was a professional and would suck it up. It was his job, and he would show her how good he was at it.

11:04

Miller

Miller sat uncomfortably in the S-76 helicopter, staring out of the window at the scene below her. The village resembled the aftermath of a military invasion. Everywhere there were trucks, soldiers and tents. People scurrying about, busy in the collection of evidence or guarding the streets and houses. In the sky about her, helicopter gunships menaced the surrounding fields.

Beside her, face set in a grim frown, large moustache twitching slightly, sat General Gwent. Old school in the extreme, but capable and surprisingly charismatic. The type of man you'd expect to be always clutching a brandy after 10.00 am, holding court in some club in Mayfair. Across from her were Martin Williams, her Private Secretary, and Metropolitan Police Commissioner Slender. Both were, like her, focused on the tableau laid out below them.

'And they've really not found anyone alive?' she heard herself ask for the third time this trip.

'No, Ma'am,' the General barked immediately, like a large dog.

Miller watched the houses pass beneath them. The church with a curious large mound behind it, a ring of earth with a huge oak in its centre. The school football field and grass running track, the well-tended gardens. Here a tennis court, there a pond. Trees were everywhere, green and luscious. Pink blossoms exploded from two bushes set before a large stone cottage, while another house was completely covered in creeping ivy. The windows peeking out from between the leaves as though hiding. She saw postcard England. The tiny village perched on the hill in Oxfordshire surrounded by a green and pleasant land.

She had been raised in just such a village. She had played with her friends in streets much like these. Spent their summers running through the fields and playing games in the woods. Riding her BMX down the hills as quickly as possible, building dens in hedges and climbing haystacks. She'd been happy then. Safe in her own little corner of the world.

She felt fortunate to have been young before the advent of computers in every pocket. Before fields were replaced by phones and games in woods with woods in games. Where everyone had known her, and she had always felt protected anywhere she went. There was always someone who would pick her up after a scraped knee or fall. Someone to keep her and her friends from getting into too much trouble, no matter how hard they tried. Happy days.

Even after the recessions and the measles pandemic, not to mention climate change and mass migration, little had changed in this world. You were polite to your neighbours, went to church at Christmas and you helped at the fete. Those were the rules of this land, and they were different from those of London, Manchester, Birmingham and the like.

'You can't have both,' her campaign manager had told her. 'You appeal to the middle income rural or wannabe rural lot, or you go for the city dwellers, but you can't have both.' She sighed, her polling numbers in the cities were still dangerously low. The country was safer ground, so she'd taken it. Well, that was being challenged now. She would have to show her strength once more. This England couldn't be allowed to fail or it would take her with it.

An image of a hologram she'd been shown on day one of her premiership flashed before her eyes and she shuddered. The one that would change their lives even more than this attack. So big, when the scientists first told her she'd laughed, or at least had tried to. Shock, she knew. It was too big. Millions would die. It was all just too much. Too much expected of her. What could she do to prevent it? Why had she done nothing to even try?

The chopper banked, lining up for landing. The three marques stood out on the horizon surrounded by a swarm of people. Vans parked higgledy-piggledy over the field below them. She could make out cameras pointing in her direction and she wondered if she should wave? No. Adopt a sombre and stern expression, she had no idea how good these cameras might be. Be implacable. The pilot's voice came through the earphones informing them to prepare for landing.

Miller shook her head clear. 'Martin, take me through it again.' She spoke into the microphone that hung by her mouth. She felt sick and wasn't sure if it was anticipation or motion related. She reached down beside her and picked up the travel mug and took a long drink. She noted Michael's expression as she indulged but ignored it. She needed it today.

He gave a slight cough, eyebrow raised, and started with the itinerary. 'In a minute we'll be greeted by Colonel Gruder of the Royal Logistic Corp and Chief Constable Singh of Thames Valley, who will take us up to the school being used as operational headquarters. They'll talk you through the operation

I Vow to Thee – William E. H. Walker

and the plans for the next few days. After that we'll take you by car to meet some of the families, they've been checked out and we've made sure to select those who are the least hysterical.'

Her cheeks flushed crimson. 'Some of them have lost their entire family Michael.'

He tried looking sheepish but failed, instead resembling a child who had dropped his ice lolly. 'Yes Ma'am, sorry.' Apology dealt with, his voice returned to its usual crisp timbre. 'That will be from 12:45 to 13:25. After that, the press conference at Marquee Two at 13:30. I have your speech ready, and the press will be briefed that you'll not be answering questions at this time.'

'Do I actually have anything to say?' she asked, failing to keep the notes of desperation from her voice.

'We're keeping it broad for the moment. Every avenue will be explored, no stone unturned, we will track down the perpetrators – the usual. It's not much, but it's important we keep you visible.'

Miller didn't feel much like being visible right now, but she nodded and returned her gaze to the world destroyed around her. They were landing at the end of a long concrete road on the outskirts of the village. On one side sat a modest bungalow, stone and slate bright and clean in the morning sun. All traces of the horror within hidden away from her. Next to them, a long paved driveway ran up to a grand redbrick house that she instantly disliked. It was overly shiny and out of place. All show and no grace like a gameshow host.

On her right, a lush green field flowed downhill to a small copse of beech trees and a low hedge. There was a broken gate down there with muddy sheep tracks running between the fallen slats. Tiny yellow and blue flowers glittered in the hedgerow, while lambs danced between the legs of their parents. Beyond the hedge the ground rose quickly, culminating in the sun-drenched white marque shining brighter than was decent next to the single-track road that ran to the hamlet just visible, nestling in trees on the next hill. She watched sparrows dart between the boughs of the trees and wished for a moment to join them. Pure freedom, just for a moment. But the helicopter bumped down and Miller felt her stomach lurch with the impact, her breakfast sloshing around inside her. She wanted out now.

A man in military fatigues ran quickly to the door and pulled it open, standing back to allow her to exit. She had to hold herself from bolting as she got out and ducked from the spinning rotors, trying not to picture her head sailing comically through the air with a mildly surprised expression on her face. Once away from the swirling blades she was met by a tall, solemn police officer who looked haggard yet still retained an air of competence and… was that disdain? Clearly nearing retirement, he was still straight-backed and thin. None of that podginess that tended to affect men as they passed 40. He shook her hand firmly, and she noted the turban. Unusual, in today's world, for a Sikh to rise so far.

The Colonel was younger by some 20 years and clearly a strong and capable man. Eyes alert and fierce, his salute precise. She had been briefed that both men had been here since the previous morning, but she would have known that by the dark bags under their eyes. 'Gentlemen, I understand I have you to thank for the exemplary way this horrific event has been dealt with thus far?' she shouted as the helicopter engines wound down.

'It's been a team effort Prime Minister. Everyone has done their utmost,' the Colonel replied. She struggled to recall his name, she'll have to ask Michael.

'I'm sure, I'm sure.' Uncomfortable and uncertain how to continue, she looked past them to where the Jaguar EE and Range Rovers were waiting. 'Well, shall we?' she said, raising her arm to signal movement. They stepped aside to allow her through and she led them to the cars, her driver opening the door for her and Michael sliding into the other side.

The Jag silently followed one of the Range Rovers down the concrete road. At the end, between a large brick garage and an old farmyard gate, they turned left toward a junction. Miller saw SOCO officers photographing a front door and dusting for fingerprints as they passed. They turned left again and along the main street. Transport trucks parked up on the left-hand side, waiting to be told to start collecting the dead. They slid quietly up a small track beside the village green where police officers and soldiers sat together in small, huddled groups. They swung into the school playground, a concrete rectangle surrounded by a high mesh fence, and exited the car. The queasy feeling in her stomach growing stronger.

The walk around was pointless in Miller's eyes. She learned nothing that hadn't already told her in London. All that she gained was the memories of the haggard and abused faces of those clearing up the carnage. She found Gruder to be a traditional English private school twit. Supremely confident in that rather overbearing almost paternal way they breed into you at the likes of Eton or Harrow, whereas Singh was precise and near monosyllabic almost to the point of rudeness. Her questions were met with blunt responses of 'Yes, Ma'am,' 'No, Ma'am' or 'We don't know yet, Prime Minister.' Though he was careful to observe the niceties, she had the distinct impression he probably wasn't her greatest supporter. She pulled her travel mug from her bag and took a quick nip, ignoring the look on Michael's face as she did so.

They'd arranged for her to meet with some of the officers, but the line was just too long. With Slender and Gruder following behind, Singh introduced her to each officer in turn. She missed every name as she racked her brains for something to say to each of them. 'Thank you for your service,' 'you've done a great job,' 'you have my full support,' 'thank you for all you've done.' It just felt so forced and hollow. Why should they care what she had to say? It's not like she could rid them of their memoires. Help them forget the sight of babies slain in their cots. Make them whole again. Slender seemed natural at it. For a woman who looked as though every feature was cast from iron, she sure did have a way of making people feel special. Miller envied her that talent. She would whisper something to each man, and they would smile or laugh. Nod their heads in appreciation and shake her warmly by the hand. How did she do it?

She was running out of platitudes by the time they made it to the Jaguar. She was grateful to return to the cocoon of the sleek, black interior of her car. As they made their way back onto the main road, the manicured cottages and old forge passing by the silent electric vehicle, Miller and Martin went over her responses to the families. It boiled down to say nothing, and she was okay with that. First rule, never say anything you don't have to. She felt sick again and reached for her travel mug.

'Maybe less... coffee, Prime Minister? Caffeine and all that.' Michael was trying to be delicate.

Miller scoffed and took a large swig. 'Coffee keeps me going, Michael,' she replied with a note of overconfidence. He reached into his pocket and handed her a mint. She scowled at it, but his eyes were almost begging her, so she snatched it from him and sucked on it as they drove out toward Marque Two.

To limit the possibility of uncomfortable questions, it had been decided that only the BBC would be permitted to accompany Miller as she met the families. The first couple were an elderly brother and sister from Newcastle who had lost their sister and brother-in-law. They were so grateful to her for coming to see them she almost felt bad for being so resentful. She assured them her government was doing all it could. Careful to ensure she faced the camera as she expressed her hope that their sister might still be found. *Because we're doing really well so far*, she thought to herself. The woman asked if Miller would pray with them and so they stood in a circle holding hands, heads bowed as the old man mumbled his way through a brief prayer for their sister. Miller tried all the while not to wonder what made the woman's hand so sticky.

Good coverage, Miller thought as she departed from them, surreptitiously wiping her hand on Michael's sleeve.

Next, the sister of a man who had lived with his wife and three kids on Hazelnut Close. The tears had flowed like vodka as she failed, through her gasps and groans, to tell Miller about how special her brother was. How lovely their kids had been, and she broke down completely when she mentioned the youngest was just six years old as she collapsed into a shivering ball at Miller's feet. Miller suddenly felt compelled to hug her, draw her in and hold her tight until her sobs subsided. Wanting to share in her loss and tell her all would be well. To promise her they would avenge her loss and smite those responsible. But no, she must be strong, stable, stoic. Always Prime Ministerial, always on show.

She patted the woman's arm weakly and called for someone to come and help her up. The woman was lifted by a volunteer and escorted away, still weeping noisily.

The third was a large man who'd clearly been here for some time or simply didn't know what a shower was. Although an old hand and pretending that there was nothing amiss when meeting people, the combination of his body odour and halitosis was almost too much for her. She attempted to disguise her disgust by feigning a slight cough. But after a couple of minutes, she realised she couldn't keep it up so ploughed on, her eyes watering slightly as his stench assaulted her.

She'd been on the verge of moving on when the tirade started. Whoever had vetted him had done a piss-poor job of it. He harangued her about how this attack was a result of her foreign policy. Her fault for the way she's treated non-British citizens, her fault the world despises us and how she was anything but a Christian. The verbal diarrhoea lasted for a full minute before Miller could extricate herself. Michael finally moving between them, speaking quietly but firmly to the irate man, distracting him long enough for her to get away.

They exited the tent and made their way back to the car to travel the three-minute journey to the next marquee and the waiting press. 'Who the hell vetted him?' she berated Michael as he joined her in the car.

'I'll look into it. I'm deeply sorry, Prime Minister.' He was already on his phone typing furiously.

'Well, thank you for getting rid of him, anyway.' She flicked her hair out of her face and searched in her bag for a mirror and lipstick.

'Shitting bollocks,' she exclaimed as the car hit a bump in the field and the lipstick slipped on to her cheek. She dropped it into her bag and fumbled for a baby wipe.

'We're here, Prime Minister,' said her driver, as she frantically tried to remove the lipstick smear from her cheek.

'Wait!' she called. But the driver, already with his door open, froze, unsure how to proceed. A photographer was standing nearby and immediately snapped several close-ups of Miller.

'Bollocks!' she exclaimed when the driver realised what was happening and closed the door. 'There's tomorrow's headline!' she fumed, wiping away the last of the lipstick. 'How do I look, Michael?'

Michael made a show of studying her. 'Excellent Prime Minister. Your speech.'

Miller took the pages from him and then reached for the travel mug, swigging back a large mouthful of the contents. She exhaled deeply and prepared herself. 'What was it the press called me when I was elected? The least rotten apple? Well, we'll show them today, Michael. We'll show them how wrong they were.' Miller missed Michael's flicker of a smirk.

She thought back to her party election win after Rupert Balmoral had resigned. The most popular Prime Minister since Churchill? Well, he'd soon fallen from grace after the great depression and she had been the one to sort it all out. She had been the one who had come up with the care package after the ice caps had melted and the polar vortex covered the country in six feet of snow for nine weeks. Well, Stewart had helped a bit, maybe, but it was she who had broken the power of the energy companies with the threat of renationalisation. She who had… well, she had more plans. No, she would not be following Balmoral into the abyss.

In many ways, this attack had been a godsend for Miller. It united the country in a way only an attack could. She would now play the role of the hero, capturing those responsible and guiding the country through its grief. All the infighting in her cabinet could go hang. If she got this right, she was secure. She could then share with them the truth she had been forced to conceal. The devastation yet to be wrought on these people. They would follow her. When the country was most at risk, she would be their saviour once again. She took a quick final nip from her coffee cup, enjoying the fiery, smoky flavours on her tongue, and knocked on the window for her diver to open the door.

The flashes of the cameras blinded her as she raised herself out of the car. She gave a small wave to the gaggle of reporters and walked slowly up to the makeshift podium against the wall of the tent. She could feel the power radiate from her. The very picture of a strong Prime Minister. Strong, stable, stoic.

Her eyes passed over the roughly 100 cameras all pointing at her. Solitary eyes like miniature black holes ready to suck her in. The single wireless microphone that connected to all the TV and radio crews loomed up at her like a striking snake. But she was more powerful than them. She was the Prime Minister. She waited for them to be still. Waited for them to shuffle themselves into position. Strong. Stable. Stoic. She opened her mouth to speak.

Her first words caught in her throat, so she sounded like she'd spent a week in the desert. 'Ladies and…' she coughed roughly. *Fuck bollocking bollocks!* she thought.

Michael was suddenly beside her, a bottle of water in hand. She smiled weakly at him and drank deeply. *Shitting wanky ballsacks!* she thought as she gulped down the cool liquid. 'Excuse me.' Her palms were sweating and she felt sick again. A couple of the reporters were smirking at her. Miller ignored them. 'Ladies and gentlemen. I'd like to start today by once again extending my deepest sympathies to all the families and friends who lost loved ones in the cowardly attack on Lesser Worburston. While I cannot yet confirm the number of those so brutally taken from us, I share your pain

I Vow to Thee – William E. H. Walker

for each and every one of them.' She paused to give a practiced look of deep regret. 'Today, I have spent time with our valiant police officers and soldiers and seen first-hand the challenges they face. I would like to thank each and every one of them for their hard work and dedication. You have all shown tremendous strength, fortitude and courage in the face of such a disaster and I know I speak for the whole nation when I give you our unadulterated thanks.'

Another pause for effect. 'The scale of this attack has left many of us wondering how such a thing is possible in today's world, with the intelligence and the military might of our country, along with that of our allies. After an event like this it is important to recognise that people want to know why and how it was possible. This is understandable and justified.' A nod of acknowledged understanding. 'However, this can lead to speculation and rumour. The result of which is always more hurt and pain for the victims of the families.' She paused, trying to work out if that was the right way round or not. *Too late now. Focus, damn it, focus.* 'Such rumours and speculations can also serve to slow the investigation as each new allegation is investigated and dismissed.' The stern teacher look. 'Therefore, I ask our friends in the media to please keep speculation to a minimum to allow our dedicated and hardworking security services to investigate thoroughly and swiftly. And let me be clear that the investigation is proceeding.' Another nod for the cameras. *Although getting nowhere...* she thought. She prepared herself for the next section. This was the rallying cry and it needed to be good.

'Stir the hearts of the nation and bring them together,' Michael had told her.

'And I make you this promise. We will capture and prosecute the perpetrators. We will find those who aided and funded them, and we will bring them all to justice in the name of those we have lost.' She turned her head slowly to each of the cameras. *This message is for you, dear viewer, personally.* 'We will use every resource and leave no stone unturned in our pursuit.' Her voice was rising with intensity now, and she was feeling ever more confident. *Sound the trumpets, here I come.* 'We, along with our friends and allies, will scour the Earth for the vile people who did this to our country and our fellow Britons. We will never let such people divide us. We are resolute in the face of their evil. We are determined in the face of the fear they try to provoke in us. We are strong in the face of their cowardly attacks. We are united in our defiance of them.' She smiled inwardly. *This is great, I am Maggie reborn.* 'We are Britain.' Her fist hit the podium. 'We are strong. We are united. And we do not surrender.' Some of the photographers actually applauded her.

Great job. Miller gave herself a moment of self-congratulation. She was feeling elated. A Boudicca calling her people to arms. *Change in emphasis now, cover all your bases.* She made her voice softer, allowed her mouth to pout slightly and her eyelids to droop, just a little. The caring, maternal Prime Minister moment. 'But we are also caring. We are kind and loving. We look after each other and support each other through all times. As such I am announcing the remainder of the week shall be a national period of mourning. We need to give people space to come to terms with this attack in their own way. Allow time for reflection and grief. This will culminate in services of remembrance across the country on Friday at 11.00 am, with a two-minute silence at 11.58 am. We will come together, in our families and communities, as one people and remember those we have lost in this terrible and cowardly attack.' Pause a moment in contemplation. 'I'd like to finish today with a prayer.' Most of those who weren't holding a camera lowered their heads, hands clasped in front of them. Miller did likewise, her eyes hooded to read the words. 'Eternal rest grant to them, O Lord, and let your perpetual light shine upon them. May the souls of all those faithfully departed through the mercy of God rest in peace. Amen.'

The crowd was still for a moment longer before the flashing started again accompanied this time by a cacophony of shouted questions. Miller stepped off the podium, and finding their path barred by metal fencing the press called after her. She struggled to keep the grin from her face as she left the tent. *This is how you lead. Resilient, resourceful and influential. I am a great leader*, she told herself. She nearly skipped as she returned to the car.

Michael joined her and they began the short trip back to the helicopter. 'The latest reports Prime Minister,' he said, bursting Miller's bubble. He was never one to offer praise for a job well done. Instead, he handed her a tablet showing a list of the latest lines of investigation and rumours from the internet, some of which were surprisingly plausible.

She took the tablet in hand while her other reached for her coffee cup. It was empty. *Damn*, she thought. 'The soldiers or police are talking,' she said as she read the report in The Mail Online of babies murdered in their cots and dogs killed to prevent their owners from being alerted. Even a hamster had apparently been killed in its cage. What was that about?

'Indeed, but if you carry on reading it's getting more disturbing.' Michael indicated a headline halfway down her list. Just after Britbart's headline: "The children were stolen and shipped out the country."

'Jesus,' Miller exclaimed. It was a Polish website, translated for her. The headline read, 'Village Population Raped after Death.' She was shaking her head slowly. 'Who the hell thinks up this shit?'

Michael shrugged. 'So long as there's money to be made… What follows is just as bad.'

A Russian site claimed China was responsible under the headline, "Chinese attack on the UK left all victims naked and mutilated." While a Chinese website claimed, "Russia & Salisbury 2 – Britain at war with Putin." Most of the western sites and online papers seemed to focus on Islamic Jihad and their potential involvement. There were reports they had claimed responsibility for the attack. That there was dancing and rejoicing in Islamic countries at the news. That the last remaining Muslim community leaders in the UK were laughing and celebrating. Several sites had videos proclaiming to show these acts of triumph. Miller wondered where they got their footage from, as the security services had nothing. 'Isn't there anything we can do about this?' Miller knew the answer even before Michael met her gaze.

'We can hope fewer people than usual believe what they read online?' His voice was monotone, they'd had this debate before. Him supporting the banning of these sites from the UK, her citing freedom of speech and thought. It had been a dead-end argument; she might only now be seeing his point of view.

Miller dropped the tablet on to the seat as the car pulled up next to the chopper. 'Oh, to be a dictator,' she said wistfully. 'Michael, I want to see my cabinet when we get back.'

'Of course, Prime Minister.' Michael instantly took to his phone to confirm the arrangements.

Miller was decided. She'd root out Islamic Jihad and make them pay. If Britain wanted to believe it was them, let them. The investigations would continue but, in the meantime she'd take the fight to Islamic Jihad. Strong, stable, stoic.

12:32

Freemark

Freemark was more than a little late for work, but Frank would understand. Hopefully. Being arrested, spending the night in a cell and not submitting a story might wind him up a bit, but she was sure he would get over it quickly enough. They'd worked together for years and she'd never let him down.

As she left Central Oxford Police Station with an official caution in her pocket, she stopped to light a cigarette and take in her surroundings. The imposing sandstone building stood bright in the midday sun. The cars passed silently by as the odd pedestrian scurried along on their way to wherever.

She watched as a police car pulled up to the curb and was surprised to see the insignia of the Devon and Cornwall Constabulary stamped onto its doors. *You're a little off patch*, she thought. Two officers stepped out and unlocked the back door, allowing a monstrous-looking man to exit.

There was something familiar about those slightly overweight features. Something in the firm set shoulders and watchful dead eyes that made her breath catch, the cigarette smoke halfway down her throat. He looked like he had once been an unusually strong man but had started to go to seed. Who was he? Their eyes met as he passed and a thin, poisonous smile spread across his face. 'Julia,' he said, his tone nonchalant like he was greeting a friendly neighbour.

Freemark found herself frozen to the spot; he'd recognised her so quickly. Who was he? How did she know him? She racked her brain and couldn't work it out. Then the freight train hit her and she felt every nerve twitch. She didn't know him; she knew a teenage version of him. The memories came back to her in a rush: 16-years-old up against the wall in the back room of the Highwayman Arms pub in Banbury. His tongue in her mouth, fingers clawing at her crotch. Unskilled fingers and a desperate, forceful desire.

She'd been half-cut and he'd been charming at first. But rough, too rough. She'd stopped him and cried out for her friend to rescue her. He'd been put out and angry. A deep anger like nothing she had seen before. Shouting at her, screaming, calling her a whore. He'd thrown a glass, missing her head by

I Vow to Thee – William E. H. Walker

millimetres, and been kicked out of the pub by the bouncers. He'd refused to leave, then spent the next 10 minutes or so on the street screaming at her, calling her every name under the sun. Finally, the police arrived and he'd legged it. She'd met him two years earlier when he'd changed schools. Why had he changed schools? Expelled. Expelled for violence. 'Jake Grantham! Shit!' The cigarette hung limply from between her lips. What the hell was he doing here? He'd clearly been dragged up from Devon or Cornwall. Had he been living there? Hiding there?

She remembered the feeling of his hand on her skin, the smell of beer on his breath. He had broken the button on her jeans to gain access to her, ignoring her muffled attempts to say no. He'd been surprisingly charming, gentlemanly even, when he'd first sat next to her. She hadn't really spoken to him much at school, they were different years and in different groups. It was only after he had leaned in to kiss her that his manner changed. At first, she thought it was because he liked her so much. But after he'd thrust her hand down to feel him and she'd tried to pull away only to find herself held there... she shivered. What had he done now? Was he handcuffed when they took him in? She didn't think so. Was he a suspect?

She stubbed out the cigarette, walked back into the police station and over to the officer on reception. 'Excuse me. My friend was just brought in, Jake Grantham? I just wanted to check if he was okay?'

She tried to smile at the officer, who looked at her as though he'd heard that very story a million times before. 'You've just left here with a caution for trespassing. Do you really think I'm going to give you information on anyone coming in?'

'But he's a friend. I only want to know if he's okay.' She tried her most winning smile and a coquettish tilt of the head.

The officer sighed. 'You're a reporter, so somewhat surprisingly my answer is no comment, and before you ask again,' he cut her off as she opened her mouth. 'No comment.'

Freemark gave him a scowl and reluctantly left the reception.

Back outside, she took her phone from her pocket and Googled Jake Grantham. As her eyes scanned the now thousands of articles about his mother, she felt cold. His mother had been killed and he'd been hauled in by the police. Had he simply been incapable of getting here any other way? Had he not wanted to come? Was he still a cold-hearted bastard? Was she biased?

Her reporter instincts kicked in and she made up her mind. He couldn't frighten her now; she had worked too hard to never be frightened again. She knew she could take him if needed, she would find out why he was here. She crossed the road and leaned against the high walls of the crown court to wait for the man who had tried to rape her.

I Vow to Thee – William E. H. Walker

An hour later, just as she was at the point of giving up, he emerged blinking from the station. Tall, straight backed and slightly potbellied, he stood and breathed in deeply. His head turning like a sentry as he took in his surroundings. As he saw her, his whole body seemed to stiffen and she thought she saw him smile.

Turning to the officers who had accompanied him, he spoke quietly to them for a moment and then crossed the road. 'Julia Freemark, you look exactly the same.' His voice was still smooth. That easy charm in his tone hadn't left him over the years. But there was no pleasure in it. No warmth.

Despite herself, she felt the nerves tingle through her. She tried to push them back down. 'Jake, how are you? I was sorry to read about your mother.' That slight twisted smile again.

'Much obliged,' he said without emotion. 'I've just been telling the police all about her.'

'You live down south now then?' She held his gaze, determined to hold her own.

His eyes never left hers. They were hard eyes, like those of a viper. 'Yeah, moved down there as soon as I turned 18. Got out of that shithole village and went somewhere where I'm appreciated. Good pubs down there as well. You can have a laugh without getting kicked out.'

A shiver went down her spine. *So, you remember it as well, fucker?* she thought.

'What is it you do?' Her mind was asking her questions. The internal monologue running in a continuous stream. *What did it matter?* she asked herself. *Why are you talking to this man? Just hit him and move on.*

'I'm an artist. I paint.' He sniffed loudly and puffed out his chest. 'Well respected, if I do say so myself.'

'Congratulations.' She was feeling uncomfortable now. The memory of that night nagging at her like an insect bite. She wanted to punch him. Smack him square in his red-veined nose and shatter it. Just one good punch was all she needed. 'Could you not get up here to see her?' she blurted out.

'Nope,' he said, regarding her, seemingly taking in every inch of her without moving his eyes.

After the silence had dragged on a moment too long Freemark felt the teenage girl inside her crying to get away. 'Well, I must be off.' She made to walk away, but he stepped in her path.

'You still happy with that husband of yours?' His voice was quizzical but assertive.

'Yes. What of it?' Her hands had tensed into fists, her knuckles white, nails digging painfully into her palms. Her instincts were still working. Her legs moved of their own accord to a more defensive stance. Right foot ready to snatch that smirk off his face with deadly force.

He took a step back, feigning nonchalance, hands raised in a mockery of defence. Chuckling a little as he replied, 'Just curious, because that's not what I hear.' He paused for a heartbeat. 'I always thought you could do better.'

She met his gaze again. Her inner teen had quietened, replaced by cold determination and bitter anger. *You are not stronger than me, fucker.* She was no longer intimidated by him; she could handle herself these days – 10 years of jujitsu had seen to that. He may have been bigger, broader and stronger than her, but she knew she could hold her own and would happily connect the heel of her trainer with his face. She stared into his eyes and held herself steady. An unspoken threat. 'I'm perfectly happy with him.'

He smiled. A broad smile showing stained and broken teeth. A wolf's smile. 'If you say so.'

They held eye contact for a moment longer, boxers before the bell. He smiled once more and made a show of moving to one side to let her pass. She was angry and frustrated. She was coiled and ready to strike for what he had done to her. For how he had managed to make her feel both then and now, but the movement to let her pass flummoxed her. She blinked, unsure how to proceed. Then she caught sight of the two officers watching them and she knew she could do nothing.

She didn't say goodbye but stomped past him down St Aldates toward Cornmarket Street. Feeling flat, as though she had let herself down. *Fuck you*, she thought. *Fuck you and your whole fucking family.*

It wasn't until she was a good 20 metres away that it dawned on her what he'd said. He had known she was married. But it was more than that, he had known they'd had issues. Although now much happier, he had known nonetheless. Frog or Bamboo might have told him she was married, but there was nothing about her husband's drinking or her unhappiness on those websites. How the hell had he known? She spun on her heels to confront him, but he was already in the car. Already pulling out of the station. Already waving to her with a large, rapist's grin on his face.

I Vow to Thee – William E. H. Walker

17:47

Laoch

Laoch sat behind his microphone and focused on his breathing while he waited for the presenter to complete the introduction. His eyes closed, he prayed silently. *God give me the strength to achieve my aims. Give them the foresight to see the righteousness of my words so that they may be saved from damnation. Amen.*

He opened his eyes as Evan Davis was saying, 'And we're now joined by His Excellency Bishop Laoch of Oxford to give us his perspective on how the local community is coping. Bishop Laoch, how has the local community reacted to this tragic event?'

Loach set himself ready to deliver his sermon, his deep Irish brogue booming out down the microphone. 'Evan, as I am sure you can imagine, my flock is devastated. The tragic murder and mutilation of the residents of Lesser Worburston by Islamic Jihad has caused a wound that may never heal. I for one—'

'I'm sorry, I must interrupt you. It hasn't been confirmed yet who carried out this attack. What evidence do you have that confirms IJ did this?'

Laoch shook his head and tutted softly. 'Evan, it's obviously Islamic Extremists. Those poor, God-fearing people murdered in their beds, just as we're starting to bring the Almighty back into His rightful place in our society.'

Evan stepped in again, 'I'm sorry Bishop, can you offer any evidence or proof that this attack was the work of Islamic Extremists?'

'It's a sign, Evan,' his voice hardened with resolve. 'Eight years ago, after the efforts to remove the illegals from infecting the streets of this country, they attacked us with the Putney Bombings. We formed the British Christian Party from the remnants of the corrupt Tories, and they drove a truck into shoppers in Reading. Then, after the election to government of the British Christian Party, the April 27 bombing in Nottingham. Now they fear the will of the people who rise to overturn the corruption that stalks this land and so they look to undermine and destroy us. The people who rise to squash the corruption at the heart of the British Christian Party.'

'Wouldn't an attack at this stage actually make people more likely to turn against ethnic minorities and non-Christian religions?'

Loach shook his head slowly. 'Muslims don't think like we do, Evan. They think that if they strike at us it will scare people away from voting for the Christian values ruling our great nation.'

Evan cut across him. 'Again though, there is no evidence this was carried out by Islamic Jihad or any other extremist group. Do you think it helps to apportion blame before there is any evidence?'

Laoch breathed in deeply, raising his voice and enunciated more clearly, 'We have to accept that, as a bastion of good Christian values in a world where it is "us versus them," we will be a target. They will try to undermine us. They will try to destroy us. They will try to slaughter us.' He let the words hang for a heartbeat. 'They fear us as we strive to bring God's word to the forefront of our everyday lives. Those who seek to destroy us must be put down.'

In the studio, Evan blinked twice before replying, 'What do you mean by "put down"?'

Loach smacked his fist into the desk, the sound reverberating in his headphones and his voice rose as though speaking from the pulpit. 'I mean put down. God has given us a chance, just one slim chance, to create something wonderful, and we must take it. They said our lives would be improved by joining the Common Market. They lied. They said we would be better off leaving the EU. They lied. They said we should live side by side with false doctrine and religion. They lied! Look at the terrorism enacted upon us once again by those proclaiming their God is greater than ours. Look at the suffering brought on us once again by those who would seek to exterminate us.'

'Bishop, you seem to be saying that everyone who doesn't believe in the Christian God is an enemy. That's simply not true.'

He uttered a small chuckle, his tone changing back to a smoother lilt. 'Not all, no. Most are misguided and can be brought back into God's love.' A tiny pause and a much harder tone. 'But most want us dead.'

Evan seemed not entirely unaffected by Laoch, but this performance wasn't for him. 'With all due respect Bishop, how can you claim that? There are over one billion Muslims in the world. If most wanted us dead, they would overwhelm us.'

'You're mistaken, Evan. They do not have the means of getting here. They do not possess the intelligence to work out what to do or how to do it. But they will, and we must be organised. Ready for the next strike once it comes. And believe me, it will come.'

Even was shaking his head slightly now. 'You sound like a general from the Crusades.'

Laoch smiled, coldly. 'The soldiers of Christ identified the threat over 1000 years ago. Since then, we have been deluded. We have underestimated their drive, their bloodlust, and they have grown stronger. We've allowed our politicians to deceive and mislead us. They've used words like equality, acceptance, integration to cow us into thinking our society is progressing when we're having our rights trampled and allowing the Devil to move us away from God's true light. The British Christian Party is now just as corrupt and incompetent as those that preceded it. Muslims are out to destroy us and—'

Even flicked a switch and said, 'I'm afraid we have to move on, thank you to His Excellency The Right Reverend Laoch, Bishop of Oxford.'

Laoch pulled off his headphones as the PM team started introducing the next segment. *Cut off*, he thought, *trying to hide from the truth*. His lips curled at the corners. It had been satisfactory, though. No, he had been excellent. He'd got his message across firmly and clearly.

Through the window dividing his booth from the presenters, he saw Evan Davis watching him. A look of naked fear in his eyes. *And you will fall with them*, he thought as he stood to leave. *Your time has come.*

I Vow to Thee – William E. H. Walker

18:35

Suss

Her left leg was jiggling and wouldn't stop. She knew why of course. A combination of an imbalance in the hypothalamic-pituitary-adrenal axis caused by lack of sleep and too much caffeine. But the knowledge didn't stop it vibrating like a cicadas' tymbals.

She hated public speaking and today was important. Understatement of the century right there. Today might well be the start of the next step in her career. A smile flitted across her lips at that thought. Her career. A few years ago, the thought of a career was laughable. Her wrist beeped twice. A message. She sought her phone from her pocket and checked it. *The best of luck baby. You'll be awesome! XOXO.*

She grinned despite her nerves. She truly didn't deserve that woman. Debs was a straight-laced, middle-class girl from Ealing. What on Earth she saw in the splintered, battered Suss from the estate she would never know. What surprised her more was how she had stayed with her even after knowing all Suss had done in her life before she had become a copper. She had forgiven it all and that was something Suss would never forget.

She itched her knee through the thin nylon of the suit trousers. Not in the least her usual style, but her boss had insisted today was the day to make an impression. 'It may be a national emergency but it's still an opportunity to progress,' he'd admonished her on the phone that afternoon. 'Can't go into a meeting with the brass looking like a reject from Boyz n the Hood.'

She wished she hadn't bothered. Deb's clothes, while in theory a good fit, always felt restricting and confined. As though they were designed to imprison you in a persona and set you on a path for life. The path to a desk and a career ladder. To security and insurance quotes. She still couldn't get her head round it, but she wanted to. For Debs.

The tablet span between her outstretched hands and she caught it before it fell. 'Don't fiddle,' had been Debs' final remark before she'd kissed her goodbye. 'You always fiddle when you're nervous.' She

I Vow to Thee – William E. H. Walker

was right, she did. Suss placed the tablet gently down next to her and let out a long breath. Her cheeks puffed out like she was smuggling golf balls. How long would they keep her here? She knew she had nothing to add beyond what she had already submitted. Why they couldn't just read that and let her get on with it was frustrating, even though she understood the theory behind it. Some learn by reading, others by talking things through. She didn't mind that, just wished it didn't have to be in front of all the top brass.

Her phone was ringing now. Bloody hell, her parents. She answered and her mother's face appeared on the screen. 'Hey mum, now's not a good time...'

'I know dear, we just wanted to wish you good luck.' Her face, round like a football, smiled out at Suss. She smiled a little impatiently, and said, 'Thanks, but I really need to get off the phone.'

'I told her not to call,' her father called from somewhere off screen.

'No you didn't, you said call if I want to, and I wanted to,' her mother replied to him.

'I said I thought it was a bad idea,' he insisted. Suss lowered the volume.

'You never.'

'Mum...' Suss tried to keep her voice down.

'I wanted to tell her we're goin' to the memorial service in London,' said her mum.

'And I told you it could wait until after her meetin',' her father replied.

'Mum!' Suss said in a harsh whisper.

'And how am I supposed to wish her luck for her meetin' after her meetin'? You know how important this is to her? She's the lead investigator.'

'Mum!' Suss was about ready to hang up.

Her mum seemed to remember she was there. 'Yes dear, what is it?'

Suss smiled, despite herself. 'Nothing, mum. Thanks for calling.'

'There, you see? I told you she would appreciate it.' She was talking off screen again.

'Mum, I need to go.'

'Well of course, dear, don't let me hold you up. We'll speak soon, love to Deborah.'

'Thanks mum, love you.' She hung up the phone and thought, *Some things never change.*

Some 10 minutes later she was still sitting there. Still waiting, now both nervous and bored, studying her surroundings. The corridor looked as though it hadn't been updated since before she was born.

Stained, flaking blue paint over wood veneer. Police union posters on a cork board informing her of the "Peace of mind found through mortgaging your home to the union" and "Never miss a day off work thanks to Revivothol. The UK's No.1 Replenishment Drug. Perfect for those 24-Hour Shifts." She snorted at that. Revivothol was simply an amphetamine that the union had shares in. Funny how it passed its MHRA tests in a week just after the last government cut the budget again.

Toward the end of the corridor was a vending machine. Suss hadn't eaten since breakfast so decided something sweet was in order. Standing, stretching like a cat waking from a six-month nap, she meandered down to the machine, tapping her wrist against it to register her account. Not much on offer here. Chocolate, or what passed for chocolate. The caramel in a Twix was more plant sweetener than sugar. Her aunt would send her real chocolate from home and she would kill for a bar right about now. Where was a Fredo when you needed one? The sandwiches looked as though they'd been there since Beethoven was a baby, while the only crisps option was ready salted flavour. Toward the bottom was an oat and cashew bar that promised to be less than terrible, so she selected it and waited for the corkscrew to unwind enough for it to plop into the bottom. She bit into it as she returned to her bench. It was not good.

The door to the meeting room opened and Commissioner Slender poked her head out. She gave what Suss suspected was meant to be a smile and came over to her. Suss, embarrassed, tried to quickly swallow the piece of disgusting snack as she approached, the result being that she looked as though she was trying to chew a live wasp.

'DI Suss, thank you for waiting. Are you well?' It was funny how she managed to make the question both completely personal and yet without any warmth. Suss could see how well the woman could manage people. She had the tone and expressions down to a tee. Had she not known the techniques herself, she would have fallen for it hook, line, etc.

She tried to reply that she was fine. That it wasn't a problem she had been kept waiting out here for an hour. That she had been perfectly happy to be left marooned on a bench with all the comfort of a block of concrete. Instead, through a visible mess of oaty mush, she mumbled something that sounded like, 'Yes, I'm blind, bank choo.'

Slender didn't react other than to reach out her hand to shake. 'They're all in there. Do you have everything you need?'

Suss painfully swallowed the last of her mouthful. 'Yes, Ma'am. Thank you.'

Slender's forehead moved independent of the rest of her face. It was almost as though she raised her eyebrows. All the muscles around rose in anticipation of the movement, yet the eyebrows themselves stayed perfectly still. Maybe it was due to her hair being tied back so tight that any additional hair moving in that direction would send the whole lot spinning off across the room? She placed a hand on Suss' arm and squeezed it. 'Try not to worry. No one is expecting all the answers from you. We just want to hear what you found in the village.'

Suss nodded a little too enthusiastically. This woman was the top police officer in the country. She was reputed to be efficient, ruthless, bold and kind in equal measures. She had risen high on a series of challenging victories and was, frankly, a hell of a woman. Suss couldn't help but admire her. Someone who had challenged all the preconceptions of policing in the 21st century and succeeded. She suddenly felt very young. 'Thank you, Ma'am. I shall do my good. I shall do my most…' *Fuckin' hell.* 'I shall do my most best.' *Brilliant. Well done you stupid fucker.*

Slender smiled her thin smile. Her eyes seemed to penetrate Suss and understand her. Green, like dew covered meadow grass. 'I know you will. Really, we're all here for you. I shall support you; I know how good you are.' She rubbed her arm once more and Suss felt a tingle over her skin as she did so.

'Yes, Ma'am.' *Seriously? What's wrong with me?*

Slender moved aside and ushered Suss into the meeting room. When she entered, expectant faces turned toward her. Frowning, serious faces. Suss swallowed and moved to the front of the room. Now or never. *Come on girl, Debs believes in you.*

19:42

Kinsella

Around the table, under the harsh light of tube bulbs housed in those bizarre slotted alcoves you only see in the tiled ceilings of cheaply built offices, Kinsella assessed the gathered. To her left sat Amelia Slender, Commissioner of the Metropolitan Police, sitting straight-backed and alert, her hair scraped into an impossibly tight ponytail. Eyes fixed on the speaker, head bobbing lightly in encouragement. Alex Singh, the Chief Constable of Thames Valley Police, leaning back slightly with a look that expressed both his exhaustion and dedication. His deputy Warren Fairfax, a middle-aged pompous bureaucrat known to be obsessed with uniform standards, clocking in times and loose women. Sarah Underhill, the Police and Crime Commissioner for Oxfordshire, elected just last year. She used to run a Sainsbury's in Didcot and was now completely out of her depth. She perched on the edge of her seat, bent over the table and tapping away on an iPad, nodding too frequently as though to express her understanding. She looked like a child eager to please.

To her right, three Assistant Commissioners of the Met, all serious and professional. Not here to contribute, but like her here to listen and be given instruction. DCI Boris Frampton from CTU, a withered old fart, possessed of the disgusting habit of scratching his balls whenever he was thinking. Here because, well... frankly she didn't know. He was a waste of space and they'd be better off when he retired.

Next to him, the Deputy Head of MI5 Christine Gout, another Oxbridge educated, entitled, privileged twit. She was methodical and a stickler for protocol, as long as it favoured MI5. Next to her the Deputy Head of GCHQ, Kinsella had missed her name, but she wasn't that worried. She was an odd-looking woman. Now in her sixties, she looked like a Play-Doh version of her former self. All distinction and definition lost, replaced with a rough, sagging version of a woman with more chins than neck.

Finally, the Deputy Head of MI6 Samuel Shawns. Had he been a woman you would have called him petite. But as a man he would be called wiry, almost boyish. He missed nothing and commented only when needed, usually with something cutting and divisive. Kinsella had to admit he was attractive. Close cropped light brown hair, a goatee, eyes the colour of sandalwood. He smelt good too. She'd caught a whiff when they'd shaken hands. Maybe in another life?

At the front of the room stood the tall and scruffy-looking DI Suss from Counterterrorism, who had apparently been at the village but Kinsella hadn't noticed her. Off doing her own "investigations" or some such. She wasn't yet 30 and was seen as a future commander. One of the best and brightest the force had to offer. Kinsella disliked her already. Younger than she by nearly 10 years, Suss was clearly operating on a different level to the rest of them. She had a reputation of being wilful and known to go off on tangents and investigations by herself rather than involving her superiors or fellow officers. A rebellious character like her being considered a future commander? What was happening to the world? She had successfully brought down a drugs ring single handily last year and had earned herself both a commendation and reprimand from her CO for it. Kinsella had to give her credit for that. But it wrangled her that this woman was her equal in rank. Was she really that good? Plus, there was the other thing as well. But she could maybe be persuaded away from that.

Kinsella shifted her weight, these hardback chairs were always so blooming uncomfortable, and sipped her water. Having interviewed Jake Grantham that morning she had jumped in her car and was in central London within two hours. 'God bless the blues and twos,' she had said

The meeting had been ongoing for about 90 minutes already and had revealed nothing of note. A lot of speculation and some ideas as to who hadn't done it. The IRA had been discounted as they had contacted MI5 through the Irish Ambassador to plead their innocence, even going so far as to offer help if the culprits were found to have made it to Ireland.

'They know what's going to happen when we find out who's done it,' Slender had noted. Frampton had mimed a bomb falling followed by an explosion. Slender didn't look impressed.

MI6 had ruled out the Chinese and the Russians. Shawns revealed MI6 possessed a mole in the Kremlin, and they were confident it hadn't come from there. Islamic Jihad had claimed responsibility, but then they did for everything and there was no evidence linking them to the plot.

Currently, they were focused on DI Suss who had taken them through a plethora of minute details that she claimed showed the various physical and mental aspects of the assailants with an accuracy that frankly astounded Kinsella. Suss was introducing them to the sixth family she had investigated. The hologram rotating over the table showed a terraced house and a green front door with the number three in brass. Suss hit a key on the controller and the picture changed to a smiling couple on their wedding day.

I Vow to Thee – William E. H. Walker

Suss' London accent made listening to her difficult without Kinsella wanting to correct her when she dropped letters, but she smiled and bit her tongue. 'Dan, not Daniel, and Jerry Martin. Married in 2016, moved to the village in October 2018. No children. Dan was the owner of a small clothin' shop in Banbury, Jerry was a software designer designin' stocktaking software. Though both were found in bed, we believe Jerry was killed in the doorway to their home. Dan had been killed by a single gunsho' wound to the head…' Suss used the laser pointer to indicate a spray of blood, '…as you can see from the blood on the pillows and wall, but there was none around Jerry.' She tapped the controller again and the hologram changed to a close up of blood splattered across the pavement. Something about the 3D rendering made Kinsella feel a little queasy. 'This patch of blood here was found directly outside the door to their house. There is also urine in the toilet bowl and stainin' the front of his boxer shorts. Soil from a plant pot across the landin' floor. We believe Mr. Martin was awake at the time of the attack and attempted to run. What is significant about this is SOCO believes he was running at the time he received a single shot to the side of the head.' She paused, looking around the room as though expecting a response. Kinsella saw a faint hint of annoyance that she was having to spell this out to them. 'It's a really difficult shot to make. A running man, in the dark and a single headshot. He was then taken back into the house – given the lack of evidence of being dragged, we can assume carried and placed in bed next to his husband. The covers were then placed over him.'

'Were they trying to make it look like he had been asleep when killed?' asked Shawns.

'We don't believe so, Sir, no. Had that been the case they would have washed off the blood from the street. We think it was more for effect.' Suss' tone was respectful.

'What effect?' Fairfax asked.

'We can't be certain of that, but I suspect it was to complete a narrative. Demonstrate their ability.'

Clearly less respect for Fairfax. No 'Sir' for him.

'How sure are we Jerry Martin wasn't involved in anything else in his line of work?' Frampton burped.

'Quite sure,' replied Gout, barely hiding her disdain for the man. 'We've been through his employment history and there is nothing to suggest he had any involvement in anything untoward. Both he and Daniel

'Dan.' Suss put in, then seemed to shrink back as she realised what she had said.

Gout raised one eyebrow toward her. Her lip curling up slightly at the right-hand side. 'Quite.' She returned her gaze to her tablet, 'As I was saying, both Jerry and Dan were generally clean. No…' She paused, checking her notes, '…unusual habits for these two at least.'

'The reason why I added them to the briefing,' Suss again, 'was to illustrate the capability of the perpetrators. Firing a shot like that would take a lot of training, particularly in the heat of the moment.'

'How long would it take to train someone to be able to shoot like that?' Slender asked.

Suss paused for a moment. 'Depends on the instructor and trainee. But I would suggest a minimum of six months' work.'

Try eight months, thought Kinsella.

'You're suggesting or know?' Slender asked before turning to one of her assistants. 'Jonathan, I want a list of all licenced gun owners and interviews with everyone who owns, operates or works in a gun range. I want to know about all their members, check into all their backgrounds, their families and political opinions.' The assistant nodded and she turned back to Suss. 'Continue.'

Kinsella watched Suss squirm uncomfortably under Slender's gaze and fumbled the clicker for the next graphic. Three new faces appeared hovering over the table, a slight blue haze to their smiling faces. 'Gerald and Susan Piper, 55 and 53. Pictured here with their grandson Harris Piper who was four years old. They were babysitting so their son and his wife could have a night away.' She pulled up a family photo taken of the couple evidently just after Harris had been born. Grandfather and grandmother smiling and staring lovingly at the baby in her arms. Their son and his wife stood close by. 'Number four, Banbury Lane. Both killed in their bed, one shot each to the head. Harris...' her words caught in her throat.

'It's all right Suss, I think we can guess,' Singh smiled at her reassuringly.

Suss gathered herself. 'As with previous houses the method of entry was an automatic laser read lock pick and no signs of a struggle once inside. On the surface, this family is much like the others in the village...'

'On the surface?' Kinsella asked.

'He was a paedophile,' interrupted Gout.

The room went still. Gout didn't seem to notice as she went on blandly. 'Suss found a flash drive in his drawer and we uncovered images and dark web search engine links on his tablet. He was also a member of a few message boards and chat rooms known to be frequented by people who specialise in the exploitation of children. It seems he was a frequent visitor and active consumer rather than physical abuser.'

'Was he on GCHQ's radar?' Singh asked.

The plasticine model wobbled her head. 'No, he was not. However, some of those he was talking to are and there is a significant investigation ongoing into their activities.'

'I think we must consider that a coincidence,' put in Slender. 'You don't wipe out a village because one resident happens to be a paedophile.'

'I agree.' Gout leaned back in her chair. 'But nonetheless it is a possible line of inquiry.'

'And Lord knows we have precious few of those,' Slender sighed.

'Except for the MI5 angle, of course,' Singh put in. There were confused faces around the table now. Kinsella sat forward slightly and noted the shift in Gout's position.

'What MI5 angle?' asked Slender, looking from Singh to Gout.

Gout coughed into her hand. 'I was going to mention this at the appropriate point but…' She paused and moistened her lips. 'It seems the owner of the manor house was one of ours. David Newman.'

'Please tell me you're joking, Gout,' Shawns propped his head in his hand and massaged his temple.

Slender's voice was a hiss between gritted teeth. 'Pray tell, what does MI5 consider to be the appropriate point?'

'This evening,' said Gout, shooting a look at Singh. 'We searched his house and while he did have one or two things that he maybe shouldn't have kept, there was no evidence they even looked for anything. He was executed in the same way as the others. In bed, with his wife. Though we don't yet know how they got round his alarm. Most likely the same program they used to disable the electronic locks. Or similar, anyway.'

Kinsella noted the looks from the others gathered around the table. A mix of anger, confusion and amusement, the last isolated to Shawns.

Gout shuffled and looked more than a little uncomfortable. 'Nothing was taken, nothing was disturbed. I don't see a link.'

'You don't think it would have been good to know about this before now? Either of you in fact?' Slender once more looked from Gout to Singh. 'Well?'

It was amazing how she could cause anyone to feel like a naughty child caught by a teacher. She possessed a knack for invariably selecting the right tone of voice for the situation. Even the deputy head of MI5 wasn't immune. 'It was deemed need to know. It was decided that, since he retired, no one needed to know where he lived. Or where he died,' she added quietly.

Singh coughed slightly, he seemed less affected than Gout but still a little sheepish. 'I looked to seek authorisation this morning for their search, but I was told it was already granted.'

'Remind me to sell you some tartan paint I've got in the garage,' Shawns said. Singh's eyes flashed annoyance to which Shawns returned a sarcastic smile.

Slender directed her gaze on the now terrified Police and Crime Commissioner who sat quivering in her seat. 'Its... erm... MI5... I thought they didn't... I mean... I thought...' She trailed off, her pen tapping out a tattoo on the table between her shaking fingers. Kinsella had to stifle a laugh.

Slender looked thoroughly put out. She eyed Singh again for a moment before slowly turning her head back to Gout, 'Well, what do you have on him?' she asked.

'I'll share it all with you later. For now, it's safe to say he retired under a bit of a cloud.'

'He was an alcoholic,' Shawns interrupted her in answer to her look, 'Of course we knew.'

Gout continued, trying to seem as though nothing had been said. 'But again, as far as we can ascertain he possessed nothing of value in his home. Save for a couple of documents which, in hindsight, it might have been better if he had handed over. But he was already three years out of the loop so...' She waved her arm as though trying to dismiss the line of conversation, clearly uncomfortable and shifting in her seat.

'Where do you find your staff?' asked Shawns, chuckling to himself.

'Anything on his computer? Phone? Tablet?' Slender asked.

'Still being analysed. He had top-notch security on all three so it's doubtful anyone would have been able to gain access.' She seemed embarrassed to be discussing this. A failure on the part of MI5.

'Top notch security on his house too though, yes?' Shawns was goading her.

'All right.' Slender's voice cut through the brewing argument. 'You get that over to us this evening, yes? And don't hold anything else back please.' She eyed Gout, who nodded reluctantly.

Kinsella watched Slender closely. She was not a young woman anymore. Her quickly greying hair fussed out of the tight ponytail. The lines round her eyes were deep and extensive, and her mouth was naturally set in a harsh straight line. No smile, no frown, just sullen and reproachful. A bullet of a woman, yet still capable of being kind, friendly, inviting, insightful. All the best qualities of a leader in one unbreakable carapace.

Slender had made a name for herself during the Westminster riots. As a DI at that time, she had successfully prevented the crowds from converging on parliament. Breaking them into small groups and kettling them, thereby limiting the damage caused and earning herself a commendation into the bargain. She had been promoted to Detective Chief Inspector and within a year she was Assistant Commissioner. Bypassing the SI roles in the process.

After the collapse of the last Tory government she'd been instrumental in keeping the Met working efficiently while the new administration was formed and fresh elections held. Then again as Deputy Commissioner during the measles pandemic she had used compassion and care to prevent worried parents from storming hospitals when the modified vaccine had been released. She was an inspiration and a useful ally. *A determined and competent politician*, Kinsella thought as she listened to her.

'...if we don't have anything else to add at this time, I suggest we each continue to focus on the elements outlined earlier. The Met will conduct searches of all properties owned or rented by known or assumed terrorist and religious radicals. In conjunction with MI5, we will arrest and detain all known persons of interest with links to firearms, terrorism and extremists. MI6 will keep us informed of all information from abroad. GCHQ will work with the CIA in monitoring all comms traffic. As you can imagine, buzzword use has skyrocketed over the past 24 hours.' There were murmurs of agreement from the table. 'Counter-Terrorism. Suss, I want you in Oxford with Singh. We'll keep you near the village so you can keep us up to date with everything that's happening there. Singh, I'm sure you can help her with that and carry on controlling the situation there?' Singh nodded his acquiescence.

Slender continued. 'The main investigation remains here with us. Boris and Counter-Terror will lead with the help of the security services. Singh, you're to continue to report to us and pursue local angles if you think it helpful. I'll be sending more officers up to Worburston, so you do what you think you need to. Don't worry about doubling up, let's explore every avenue twice and find who did this. You're to have Suss, and I'd like her to have someone to work with. She's best when she can bounce ideas off someone.' Suss smiled, looking slightly nervous. Slender turned to Kinsella, her eyes penetrating and stern. 'I understand you've asked to be attached to Counter-Terrorism for this?'

'Yes, Ma'am.' Kinsella's voice was tight and articulate.

'Why is that?' Slender asked.

Kinsella felt all eyes on her. 'The village is in my area, Ma'am. I was first on the scene, I know the locals and their habits. I want to be useful, and it's my long-term career goal.'

The room was still save for Slender's thin finger tapping against the back of her hand. Eventually she spoke. 'Singh tells me you're a good officer. Suss, any problems?'

Suss shot Kinsella a pleasant smile and shook her head. 'No, Ma'am.' Kinsella felt she may have misjudged her. But still, she was too young for the role and too headstrong. *She'll get in the way*. Why would Slender want her in the way?

'There we are then. We meet again in two days. I wouldn't be surprised if COBRA decides to focus this more tightly, but for now you continue your investigation Singh. I want to know everything you find and anything Suss and Kinsella can drag up. Thank you everyone.'

There was a scraping of chairs as they all stood to leave. Kinsella made to move toward Suss but was side-tracked watching Singh and Gout having a barely concealed whispered argument. *MI5 officer down*, she thought. *Who'd have thought it?*

20:19

Singh

Singh left the meeting room feeling annoyed. MI5 had lied to him and he'd been stupid enough to buy it. Why they couldn't just share straight away was beyond him. He supposed it was in their nature to be cagey and secretive, but it got on his nerves.

Calm down, Alex, he thought to himself. *No point in winding yourself up over this. You're not going to change anything by getting annoyed, just focus on what you can do. It's still your investigation, in part at least. They could have easily taken it from you.* He saw Kinsella hovering near the vending machine as she appeared to be pondering her choice as he walked over to join her.

'A healthy dinner then?' He got a smile back, but Kinsella's expression was distant. 'You okay?'

'Yeah.' She seemed to mentally shake herself. 'Just wondering what else MI5 is holding back from us.' She pressed the button and a Mars Bar rolled down into the drawer. Retrieving it, she tore off the paper packaging and bit into a large chunk. 'Not as good since they got rid of the plastic,' she said through a mouthful of synthetic caramel and nougat.

'Nor since they went sugar-free,' he added, and she nodded while she chewed. 'Are you pleased to be working with CTU?' Singh couldn't help but watch her masticate. She had a pretty mouth.

'Yes, Sir. Thank you for that,' Kinsella tried a smile but with the chocolate in her mouth it didn't really come off. She swallowed. 'I won't let you down,' she smiled again, chocolate on her teeth.

'I know. You did well on that college murder case a couple of months ago. I think you're ready for the move.' He nodded his head toward Suss, standing awkwardly in the corridor seeming unsure where to go. 'What do you think of her?'

She considered her response and Singh wondered at the delay. 'We've met before at a conference last year. She seems switched on. Unconventional, sure, but smart.'

Singh nodded, wondering if she didn't like her. 'I've not met her before today, though I know her partner DS Stone.' Singh noticed the look, a flash of emotion over Kinsella's face at the mention of DS Stone. He wasn't sure if it was anger or suspicion. 'Do you know her partner?'

Kinsella's eyes focused on him. 'DS Stone? No.' Her tone was pleasant, but he was sure he'd seen that momentary flash of... something. Some emotion he couldn't quite pin down.

'Apparently Suss is seen as a highflyer.' A moment's pause. 'As are you,' Singh added and she smiled, clearly a little embarrassed but thankful he'd thought to include her.

'You're quite different though, you'll either complement or grate on each other. I suspect that'll be for you to decide. She's argumentative apparently, but then she's also usually right and you don't like to be wrong.' He tried to make it sound like a compliment. She shifted slightly and returned his smile.

'I'll do my best, Sir. Any advice on where we should start? The manor house maybe?'

Singh shook his head. 'No, MI5 haven't finished with it yet. Continue with the SOCO reports.' She made to respond but he cut her off. 'Yes, I know there are hundreds of them and I'm not sure they'll be useful or we'd probably have heard it by now, but they all need reading. Plus, you'll get a better idea of the victims. As we've seen today, Suss has already turned in some potentially interesting information. See if SOCO can expand on that? Check if there's anyone else like our MI5 Director in there.' He studied her face as she looked deep in thought. 'Do you think this might all be due to David Newman? he asked.

Kinsella shook her head as she replied, 'I don't think so Sir. Given that MI6 didn't seem to know he was there, who would know he lived in the village? And if you did know and were capable of carrying out an operation like this leaving so little evidence, you'd simply kill him. Why kill everyone?'

Singh nodded his agreement. 'I agree, but it will need looking into anyway. It could be that they were looking for a village to attack and picked this one because they knew he lived there.'

She nodded, thinking. 'That's a possibility, I suppose. I'll get on it.'

He checked his watch. 'I best be getting on, see if I can get home before my wife goes to bed. I could do with a night at home. I expect you could as well. Spend some time with your husband and—'

'My husband is away,' she cut him off, her voice flat and a little defensive.

'But your own bed at least?' He tried to make it sound like a gift, but her eyes had acquired a vacant expression.

'Yes, Sir.' *Something wrong at home?* he wondered.

He smiled at her, trying to keep things pleasant. 'Well, keep me informed. And good luck, Kinsella.'

He shook her hand and they parted. As he walked to the car, he thought about assigning her to CTU. She was good at her job and the investigation would need all the help it could get. She'd be fine and he suspected her and Suss would get along okay. Then he remembered that moment when he'd mentioned DS Stone. There had been something there. Did they know each other? Some previous misdemeanours between them? Suss seemed happy enough to be working with Kinsella so if there was a problem it was something she was unaware of. Kinsella didn't strike him as the type to take issue with Suss and Stone. What could it be?

DAY 3

'They lose the day in expectation of the night, and the night in fear of the dawn.'

—Seneca

I Vow to Thee – William E. H. Walker

03:46

The woman woke up screaming. The child's blood-soaked face, the broken skull and vacant eyes were etched into her mind, indelible and visceral as though she had wrought the injuries on her own body.

Jerked awake by her cries, her husband instinctively wrapped her in his arms.

She was crying and shaking, eyes wide and unfocused. He held her tight, comforting her. Stroking her hair, whispering softly to her, 'It was only a dream. It was only a dream.'

Gradually her tears subsided and her body stilled. He held her close to him, noting how frail she felt. How drained. The bones in her back standing proud against her sweat-soaked nightgown.

In a small voice, hoarse from crying, she apologised and told him she didn't know what had happened. She moved away from him, wiping her eyes and nose. She was okay, he needn't worry, it was over, just a dream, go back to sleep. He tried to resist but she insisted. She was all better now. She would take a pill and it would be okay. She wasn't going back to where she had been. No more scars added to her wrists. He kissed her on her forehead, squeezed her arm and rolled over to pretend to sleep.

She reached into the drawer in her bedside table and withdrew a pill packet with Luvox printed on it. She swallowed three and lay back down, her head resting on her sweaty pillow. She couldn't tell him about her dream. Couldn't tell him what she had seen. Couldn't tell him what she'd done. What she had been a part of. What she was still meant to do. She could never tell him. She was alone now. And the dreams continued to haunt her.

You'll be fine. You're strong. You'll get through this. I believe in you.

She knew now that He had lied to her.

I Vow to Thee – William E. H. Walker

06:43

Freemark

Freemark lay on her back in her king-size bed, eyes on the ceiling, fingers twisting the sheet into knots. She'd hardly slept a wink last night and was feeling wired.

Having submitted her report to her editor she'd returned to the village and stood with the crowds of onlookers. She had spoken with locals, other journalists and police until Stephen had called wondering why she was still out at 10.00 pm.

Still no facts to go on. Still no truth told. Rumours and stories grew, circulated, proved false, dropped and then re-emerged in slightly different packaging. Panic, fear and mistrust bred from each other like cancer. She had felt them all from those gathered around the outskirts of what was now one of the most secure militarised zones in Europe.

Resolved to the fact that it was morning and she wasn't going to get any more sleep, she rolled over and picked up her phone. Already there were over 20 breaking news notifications in the past half hour.

From downstairs, the sound of her daughters' laughter wafted up to her with the smell of breakfast her husband was preparing. She grinned; Maddie always made her smile. Just her presence in the world was enough to make Freemark's heart brighten.

She thumbed through the notifications and clicked on one from a website called 'New Christian News.' The notification read "PROOF: Islamic Jihad Claim Responsibility!!" Scrolling through, the article claimed that Islamic Jihad's leader Sa'ad Essa had been overheard congratulating his followers on their attack. There was no video footage, no witness statements, just pure speculation with a clickbait headline.

Whaddaloaddabollocks, she thought, affecting an East End London accent in her mind and dropping her phone on the duvet. She rubbed her eyes, uncoiled like a spring and bounced out of bed, ready to hit the day.

Her 30 minutes of exercises consisted of sit-ups, press-ups and crunches followed by a quick battle with the punch bag and a cold shower. She was beginning to feel more human again as she headed downstairs. She needed to find some time to push herself, to get her heart rate up a bit. The morning routine was a little tame.

She caught the tail end of a story Maddie was telling her father about a chicken farm she'd visited with school the previous day and smiled again at the sound of her daughter's animated voice. Thank the world for Stephen and Maddie.

At school Stephen was always too cool and too old to notice her. He'd been the modern equivalent of Danny in Grease. Minus the leather jacket, but with just as much hair gel. Always slick and stylish, sexy and confident. Every girl had fancied him, and he'd known it.

But then after college they'd met up at a barbeque and hit it off right away. 'The sparks weren't just coming from the charcoal,' her friend Sian had told her. They'd gone on a first date to the cinema and ended up on a boat to France and spent the remainder of the weekend in a small hotel on the coast in Brittany. From there they'd hardly been apart. They'd talk constantly. Even at work they'd text each other. It was as though every word in the English language was theirs to share alone. They'd not planned to move in together, but after their return from France – baguettes, wine and garlic in hand – he'd slept at her flat and just never left. Eventually, when a friend had asked why Stephen seemed to own nothing in their home, they'd made it official and he moved in. It hadn't taken him long to propose and they'd spent the next year scrimping and saving to have the perfect wedding. A castle in Gloucestershire, 200 guests and a beautiful sunny summer's day.

Shortly after the wedding, Stephen got a big promotion so they had moved to London and lived the high life. Although he worked long hours, they had filled every moment together with activity. Evenings were spent in the theatre or at dinner or parties with friends. Weekends were brunches, lunches and concerts in the park all accessed from their company-supplied penthouse flat in Mayfair. It had been a dream. A wonderful, thrilling, dream. At least at first.

She'd first suspected he had an issue when they'd invited two friends over and somehow made it through four bottles of wine even though she'd only had a couple of glasses. That's when she'd thought it through. How slowly it had happened. How easy it had been to miss.

He'd gone from one or two beers an evening when they first met to one or two bottles of wine after a "hard day" to beers with lunch because he was entertaining clients to wine with lunch because… Greggs had a queue. She'd not spoken up until it was almost too late.

His personality had changed as well. He had been the light of her life and all her blessings. Her joy in human form. The alcohol had created a sullen and moody man who would spend his evenings staring into space and ignoring her. Not because he wasn't listening, but because he'd effectively switched off and shut down. No drive left but to drink. His work was suffering, which made him angry, which led to more drinking and outbursts of rage.

They'd nearly not made it. She'd begged and pleaded with him to cut back but he'd been unable to handle life without the alcohol.

There had been good times. Times which had persuaded her to stay. Like the time he'd surprised her with tickets to Paris. A weekend of art and romance. They'd visited the Louvre and climbed the Eiffel Tower, dinner in a Michelin star restaurant before snuggling up together in a little hotel in Saint-Germain-des-Prés in the 6th arrondissement. That's where Maddie had been conceived and where he'd promised her he would seek help.

For a while, he'd tried. But then after he'd crashed their car on the M4 and was banned from driving for two years, he'd lost his job and, tearful and dejected, he'd agreed to move back to Oxford where he would get sober and become a full-time dad to their new-born daughter.

Now, four years on, they had regained their contentment. He was sober and happy and working again, albeit in a much less senior role. Freemark thought he was brilliant. Just brilliant.

'…there were hundreds of them, daddy. But this one only had one wing and when I asked the farmer about it, he said it was because of a fight it had had with another chicken, so I asked why he had let them fight and he said it was in… in…'

'Inevitable?' prompted Stephen.

'In-ever-table. Yes!' Maddie looked up at her, her face radiating love and happiness. 'Mummy! Daddy made me soldiers!'

Freemark kissed her daughter on the head. 'Mmmmm I love soldiers.' She reached for one and Maddie put her arms around her plate giving her mum a toothy grin. Freemark smiled back and gratefully accepted a cup of coffee from her husband.

'Rough night?' he asked.

She nodded but didn't reply. Sipping her warm coffee and leaning on the kitchen side, watching Maddie telling her soldier that he was going to get his head wet in the egg but that it was okay, it was meant to happen.

Stephen stroked her arm and smiled. 'Grandma is going to come and see you this evening, isn't she Maddie?'

'Yeah! Grandma and me are going to play board games,' she said between mouthfuls of toast.

'Swallow first, Monkey.' Freemark ruffled her hair and looked at her husband. 'When did you arrange this?'

'Yesterday evening. What with everything that's happened I assumed you'd be having another long day today and I have to go through the company's evacuation and...' He paused looking at his daughter. '...if this happens again... plans. We've already got contractors listed to add additional CCTV and security measures.'

She put her coffee down and gave him a hug. He kissed her forehead and held her close. He smelt of shower gel with a hint of masculinity. She breathed in deeply and closed her eyes, a warm feeling spreading through her body. 'Thank you,' she breathed.

He gave her a gentle squeeze before looking at her with mock seriousness. 'No heroics today though, okay?'

She laughed, lightly. 'No. I'm done being heroic. Investigation from my desk today.' The previous day's encounter came back to her. 'Do you remember Jake Grantham from school?'

Stephen scrunched up his face in thought. 'Name rings a bell...' he said as he loaded dirty plates and pans into the dishwasher. 'Was he my year or yours?'

'In between, though I don't know by how much. He joined in year nine after being expelled from his previous school.'

Recognition flashed across Stephen's face. 'Big lad, smarmy? Always dressed like he was on a night out?'

'I don't remember that, but yes, too big and smarmy.'

'He was a bit of a...' he nodded toward their daughter. 'Aubergine emoji if I remember right. Used to pick fights and thought the world owed him something. Famous parent. Mother, I think.'

Freemark nodded. 'His mother, yes, she was in the village. I saw him yesterday at the police station.'

He raised his eyebrows, a "is he guilty?" look.

Freemark shook her head. 'No, I don't think it was that.' The image of his sweating, desperate face pressed against hers flashed before her.

She must have shown her feelings as he put down the pan he was holding and crossed to her. 'All okay?' His voice was all love and concern.

She gathered herself and nodded. 'Oh, fine, fine. I was just surprised to see him there.' She had not told Stephen about that night. He couldn't do anything about it so what was the point? All it would do is make him feel angry and impotent. She'd had enough of that living with him in London.

'They think he's involved though?' he asked, a look of keen interest on his face.

She bit her lip while she thought about it, absently watching Maddie dunking soldiers into her egg and arranging them on her plate. Happily lost in her own little world. 'I don't know. There was… it just didn't feel right.'

'You think he…' He surreptitiously made a slitting throat motion. 'His mother?'

She looked at him disapprovingly and shook her head. 'I don't think so. I don't know. But I think he hadn't come up willingly from Cornwall. He was dropped off by a police car, escort and everything. Plus, he didn't exactly look like he was grieving. Seemed almost like he didn't give a toss.' She sipped her coffee, watching Maddie apologise to a soldier for dunking him before biting off the top half and smiling as she chewed. 'Remember anything else about him?'

Stephen picked up the saucepan again and opened the bin, scraping off some grease before placing it in the dishwasher. 'I don't think he was overly popular at school. At least not with the boys. He was a good-looking bloke though and I think some of the girls fancied him.' Freemark thought of her button being broken. Stephen continued, 'He could be charming but there was always something off about him. Something that just said go away, leave me to it. We pretty much did. Do you remember Francesca Moss? Lived in Middleton. She went out with him for a while.' He washed his hands and dried them. 'But surely if Jake's mother was, you know… in the village, maybe he couldn't get up here?'

'Maybe,' she said, thinking about Francesca Moss who had lived in Middleton. She shook herself back to the present and downed the last of her coffee. 'Right little miss naughty monkey, time to get you ready for school.' She tickled her daughter, causing her to giggle and drop eggshell on the floor. 'Come on,' she said, escorting her wonderful daughter upstairs to help her get ready. She needed to be out soon, she had someone to investigate.

09:28

Kinsella

Kinsella sat opposite to Suss in a stuffy office in Thames Valley HQ in Kidlington, reading the SOCO reports on the first 100 victims. There were 12 officers assigned to the task and she had wanted to leave them to it, but Singh had declared the task important and Kinsella hadn't wanted to disagree. They had been at it for an hour already and the files had started to blend together. Kinsella had stopped a few times having to go back to see if the person she was reading about was a 15-year-old boy or a 40-year-old woman, before realising this was a 65-year-old man killed in bed next to his wife. She sighed heavily, placing the pad down and rubbing her eyes.

Suss gave a small smile. 'They startin' to merge together yeah?'

Kinsella nodded, stretching her arms and back.

Suss still had half a muesli bar in her mouth and crumbs spilled out as she spoke. 'Is it just me, or are SOCO basically sayin' they got fuck-all?'

Kinsella smiled indulgently. She'd been surprised by Suss, the woman had been affable and considerate to her ever since she'd arrived in Kidlington that morning. She'd treated Kinsella like a seasoned member of CTU rather than an unwanted add-on. Despite her age, she carried herself well. She could dress like a teenager, speak like a woman of learning when she needed to and think like a veteran cop. And she was a DI at 29. In CTU no less. Kinsella herself was still considered quite young for the post, but Suss put her completely in the shade.

A morning spent reading through the details of each person's death was taking its toll on them both, even with a constant supply of fresh coffee and snacks. Kinsella paused and raised her eyebrows. 'Well, nothing more than we knew already.' She took a sip of water from the paper cup on the table.

Suss grinned. 'They've not left us anything as they're too well trained for that.'

Kinsella regarded Suss, wanting to know the woman's mind. 'Do you think this was a terrorist group or military operation?'

Suss tore open the wrapper of a second muesli bar. 'Terrorists trained by a government. Someone like Argentina having a pop at us via an organised group.'

'Argentina?' Kinsella couldn't help sounding sceptical.

'Maybe? These guys were clearly well trained. Not just to the same level as the military – soldiers aren't trained to worry about footprints and DNA evidence. They had Special Forces training, no doubt. Now, I'd guess something like Mossad, Navy SEALs or someone like that. Maybe the SAS?' She bit into her snack.

Kinsella looked at her, eyebrows raised. Meeting her calm gaze, unsure whether to take her seriously or not. 'SAS? Are you saying you think our government could have done this?'

'Yeah, it's not that farfetched if you think about it. Governments have done this sort of thing to their own people before.' She popped the last of the muesli bar into her mouth and spoke while she ate. 'I'm not sayin' it's the most likely theory, but it's something we must consider. Look at their attitude to immigrants, to non-Christians and people who don't… look British.' She subconsciously touched her dark skin.

Kinsella noted the gesture but decided to ignore it. 'But surely that lends itself to a foreign power being responsible? A government who takes issue with our country's stance on these things?'

Suss shrugged, resting her elbows on the corner of the desk. 'Like I said, it's not likely but Miller is losing popularity and seats. An event like this brings the country together and presents her – if she can claim to find the culprits – as the saviour.'

'I'm not sure that's likely.' Kinsella shook her head, wondered if this was a serious chain of thought or just a flight of fancy. Intriguing, but not accurate.

'You're probably right. Like I said, it's a consideration.' She lapsed into silence for a moment, flopping back against her chair. 'More likely religion-based, but I don't think it's IJ who did it.'

'No?' Kinsella was curious. Something about this woman was fascinating. She was currently lounging, legs apart, with one foot resting on a chair. Tight ThunderCats vest top showing off her slim stomach and pert breasts. Equally tight jeans ripped at the knees and thigh, fluorescent socks under scuffed trainers. Her dark hair a cloud around her, smooth skin the colour of ochre. She wouldn't have looked out of place on a park bench surrounded by unruly teenagers. Yet here she was, a Detective

Inspector, proposing ideas most officers might have overlooked. She was a contradiction. She spoke like a common street rat but with the authority of a judge.

She was shaking her head now. 'No, I think it's more likely an extremist religious faction from the UK.' She sounded so matter of fact, yet her words took Kinsella by surprise and she tried to hide it.

'Really? A homegrown Islamic terrorist group?' Kinsella thought to reach for her water but changed her mind.

Suss eyed her through her long lashes. 'I never said Islamic terrorists. I said religious terrorists. Could be Christian, Jewish, Islamic, not sure. I just think it's most likely a religious group.'

Kinsella felt herself fluster a little, but she hid it well. 'What makes you say that? We don't have any religious symbols or literature or anything like that left at the scene.'

'I know, I'm just thinking.' She squeezed her nostrils and sniffed. 'To get people to do what they did in that village they need to be driven by more than just political ideologies. Look at all the worst atrocities in history – all of them carried out in the name of religion.'

Kinsella felt her ardour rise in her chest. She adjusted herself in her seat as though considering her response. 'Most I'd agree. The Holocaust wasn't driven by religion.'

'Anti-religion is still religion. And it could be argued that Hitler was tryin' to present Nazism as a new form of religion. One which framed himself as God.'

Kinsella wasn't in the mood for a discussion about the nature of Nazi theology, so she tried to bend the conversation round to simpler ground. 'But look at all the good religion does as well.'

Suss held up her hands in a show of surrender, clearly seeing the desire to move on. 'I'm not sayin' all religion is bad. I take no issue with it either way. Just sayin' that it's easier to drive people to do things they would never normally do if you give them a holy reward rather than an earthly one. Look at all those poor kids who've blown themselves up for honour or a misguided sense of altruism. I think we need to look at radical Christian groups.'

'Why Christian specifically?' Kinsella took her water and sipped it, watching Suss over the rim of the paper cup.

'Stands to reason don' it? For years Christians have been making inroads into politics and mainstream life, but the message ain't got through yet. We've still got all the same issues as we did before but now politicians thank God for it all. It's like we've gone halfway toward becoming a Christian state and stopped. Maybe one group had enough of waiting?' Kinsella didn't reply. 'I don't know, I'm spitballin'.' Suss grinned at her. 'Ignore me.'

I Vow to Thee – William E. H. Walker

Kinsella could see she was just working things through in her mind. No real direction to the thoughts, no firm theory she wanted to explore. She decided to change the subject. She returned Suss' smile and flicked a page over on her pad. 'How's your wife?'

Suss didn't seem to mind the change of subject. She grinned at the mention of Deborah. 'Awesome, as ever. She's workin' on this from London. Lookin' into the ballistics.'

Suss' skin seemed to glow as she spoke of her wife and Kinsella couldn't help but feel a little jealous. 'How did you two meet?'

Suss chuckled. 'It's a bit embarrassing really.' She scratched the back of her neck. 'She nicked me.'

Kinsella snorted a laugh. 'Arrested you? For what?'

Suss blushed, looking suddenly shy and noticeably young. 'I was stealing from Tesco.' Kinsella remained quiet until she continued. Suss pulled at her ear and ran her finger over her eye before continuing, 'My parents didn't have much money. Dad was unemployed, mum worked three jobs to support us. I was just tryin' to get us some dinner.'

Kinsella squirmed, uncomfortable in her chair. 'How old were you?'

'I was 19. She should've charged me, but she let me off with a warnin'. I was so grateful I asked for her number. She gave it to me and...' She was smiling again now but there was still a little nervousness in her eyes.

Kinsella moved on. 'Your mum sounds like a heck of a woman.'

Suss brightened. 'She is. Really she is. She never gave up on me. Worked her whole life. Dad as well. He worked as a cleaner in an office in the City for 40 years until they closed it and he was laid off. Struggled to find a job after that, was considered too old.'

'How old was he?' Kinsella asked.

'Just 55. They were old when they had me. Well, older than average anyways.'

Kinsella felt awkward. 'Sorry, I don't mean to pry...'

'It's all good. Mum was an assistant in an accounts firm but got laid off when I was 17. She worked her arse off after that. Dad, well, he went downhill for a while after losing his job. Depression and all that. He tried to top himself when I was 18. Then again when I was 22. He's all right now though, mostly. They won some money on the lottery, not a lot but enough to get a decent mortgage on a house and get outta London. Livin' in a village now. Retired and that.' That shy look again. Kinsella found it endearing. 'Sorry, didn't mean to go on...'

Kinsella found herself shaking her head and reaching out to rest her fingers on Suss' arm. 'No, no. It's fine. Thank you for sharing.' She stroked her soft skin with the ball of her thumb and smiled weakly at her. 'I didn't know.'

Suss shrugged. 'It's fine. It's been a good few years now. Plus, I've got Debs and she's awesome.' She tried a grin, but the light had faded from her face.

Kinsella felt compelled to hug her but resisted. She gave Suss' arm a squeeze and sat back, uncomfortable. Unsure how to continue. Safe ground. 'Shall we look at the crime scenes?'

Suss gave her a distant smile and picked up her tablet.

08:30

Shanks

'I don't think I'm being disloyal at all. I think it's perfectly obvious the Prime Minister has lost control of parliament, her cabinet and the country. Of course she has, after all she's a career politician and we all know what they stand for: themselves.' His expression suggested this was the most obvious thing in the world.

'But aren't you a career politician as well?' asked the interviewer.

Shanks smiled warmly and tutted. 'No Mishal, no. I was persuaded to run in the by-election by my constituents who were sick to the back teeth with the lies and corruption they saw from parliament. I had no desire to be thrust into the political limelight. But equally I could not stand idly by while we, the great British public, were lied to repeatedly by this self-serving corrupt government.'

'But you're part of the BCP, your Party is in government, why join them if you're at odds with them?'

He made a show of looking disappointed. 'Because the BCP was founded on principles that I wholeheartedly agree with. We had a charter that was laid out at the formation of our Party and which I support 100 percent. It was simple in its message but strong in meaning: "To create a fair society with true Christian values".' He let the words hang for a moment before continuing. 'But the current Prime Minister has corrupted that message, bent and twisted it until it is now unrecognisable. What we need now, more than ever at this time of national crisis, is strong leadership. A stable government led by someone who can guide us through these choppy waters and into a bright new future.'

'Someone like you, you mean?'

A small laugh and shake of the head. 'No, I have no desires in that direction. I am here to serve my constituents and the British people. They are the ones who should decide our next Prime Minister. Our

I Vow to Thee – William E. H. Walker

great Party members should vote for who they believe is best. I'm sure they will make the right choice when the time comes.'

'So, if there was a leadership race tomorrow you wouldn't stand?'

'Let me be absolutely clear on this.' He leaned forward and met Mishal Husain's eye. 'I am here to serve the people of this great nation. I will do whatever it takes to ensure they have the country they deserve, the future they deserve and the government they deserve. As I said before, our Party is founded on the principle that we build a fair society. Now, I believe we are not even close to that. How can we be when one man can earn a billion a year while his neighbour is starving? When hard working people must choose between paying rent and heating? When a group of extremists can murder hundreds of our citizens and get away with it? No, we do not live in a fair Britain, but I believe there is a way to get there. We just need to have faith and be strong.'

'That's not a no…'

'Mishal, I am not going to go into hypotheticals with you—'

The interviewer interrupted, 'It's not that hard to answer if there was a leadership contest tomorrow. Would you run, yes or no?'

He spread his arms as though the answer was obvious. 'Mishal, I will do what the British people ask me to do. But I have no desire to be anything more than a humble representative of this great nation fighting each day for what's best for my constituents and the population of this wonderful country.' He smiled broadly. Warm and inviting.

'I suppose that's as good as we're going to get. Thank you, Mark Shanks, MP for North Oxfordshire. Next, we have Joanne Simpson, MP for Sussex East in our radio car…'

Leaving the studio, he checked his phone. One message from the Chief Whip. "No more unauthorised interviews!" He smiled to himself, heading to his car. *Tough*, he thought.

I Vow to Thee – William E. H. Walker

10:45

Freemark

Sitting at her desk, Freemark typed "Francesca Moss" into the Frog search engine. A smiling woman of a similar age to Freemark appeared instantly on the screen. Her profile picture showing her in her garden with three kids aged between about two and 10, all piling in around her in joyous union. According to the listing she and Francesca had several mutual friends.

She clicked on the tab and brought up her profile. She was listed now with the surname Mason, married some 12 years, living in Banbury and working as an accountant. Freemark scrolled down her wall. Photos of the kids, funny anecdotes, pictures and holograms, the occasional night out. Nothing out of the ordinary. Freemark clicked the friend request button. A box appeared asking her if she'd like to send a message with her request. Freemark thought for a moment before typing.

"Hi, Francesca. Not sure if you remember me, we went to school together. I'm investigating the village attack and wondered if we could meet up?" She wondered if she should mention Grantham, then bit the bullet. "I wanted to talk specifically about Jake Grantham. Hope we can meet?"

She read it back to herself before clicking send. The box disappeared and she sat back in her chair. Was she barking up the wrong tree here? Was his treatment of her all those years ago clouding her judgment and making her look for things that were not there? Or could he really be involved somehow just because he was a bastard? She saw his smile when he spoke to her. Cold, reptilian. Not a hint of sorrow for the loss of his mother, just the merciless glower of a predator. It made her shiver.

She rose quickly and made her way outside. Standing in the car park she lit a cigarette and drew on it, the nicotine hitting her brain with a warming, fuzzy glow. Leaning on a car charge point, she watched a pigeon pecking at a fast food box, bits of chip flying in all directions as it did so.

She stood in deliberate stillness, watching the world, focusing on the details that caught her eye. The bright leaves in the tree, the deep green insulation moss on the opposite wall, the crack in the pavement out of which busy ants scurried. She was calm and in control. She was in charge.

Her phone intruded on her with a ping. Taking it from her pocket she read the message. Her eyebrows raised toward her hair line as she did: "Francesca Mason has blocked you."

She's blocked me? What the hell! It must have been his name. She had to speak to her. Where did her profile say she worked? Accountant at… Denvers & Cotters? No! Danvers & Cotters. Stubbing out the cigarette she returned to her desk and searched for the company. The address appeared instantly and she tapped her phone to the computer to transfer it before grabbing her bag. Was this connected or was she just going to drag up old wounds for no reason other than the satisfaction of knowing Jake Grantham was a bastard? *It must be connected*, she told herself before heading for the door.

Around 40 minutes later she parked across the street from the small, redbrick building bearing the logo Danvers & Cotters Chartered Accountants. She bit her lip and wished they hadn't banned chewing gum. Instead, she fished in her bag for her cigarettes.

Her left hand played on the steering wheel while the right brought the cigarette to and from her mouth with mindless regularity. What was she going to say to this woman? "Hi, I'm the woman you just blocked on Frog, I'm here to pester you about… something, I just don't know what?" No. she'd have to act like she knew what she was talking about. Like she had more information than she did. She pulled down the visor and looked at herself in the mirror. 'You've got this, you've got this,' she intoned. She opened the car door and dropped the cigarette butt on the ground, crossed the road, head held high, willing confidence into her stride and opened the door to the office.

A plump woman in a flowery summer dress sat behind the reception desk. Bobbed hair cut just a little too short, large eyes peering up at Freemark behind fluttering eyelashes, wide mouth extending into a well-practiced smile. 'Good morning, Miss. Welcome to Danvers & Cotters, how may I help you?'

'And an exceptionally good morning to you,' replied Freemark, going for approachable and friendly. 'I'm here to see Mrs. Mason.' Freemark smiled her most charming smile at the receptionist who, taking her name, looked at a computer screen. A look of slight concern on her face.

'I don't see an appointment. May I ask what this is concerning, and I'll call through?' The plump bottom lip folded itself under its upper twin. The large eyes scrunched themselves up as though this was a huge problem.

Freemark thought quickly and decided honesty was the best policy. 'I'd like to talk to her about Mr. Grantham.'

'Mr. Grantham?' asked the receptionist, eyelashes fluttering like a butterfly taking flight. Freemark nodded and she tapped a few numbers into the phone by her side. After a second's delay, she said, 'I have a Mrs. Freemark here for you. To discuss Mr. Grantham.' There was silence and her face grew grave. 'I shall,' she said, and tapped a button to end the call. 'I'm sorry but Mrs. Mason is in a meeting currently—'

'I'll wait,' Freemark interrupted her.

'She didn't say when she'll be free.' The receptionist looked annoyed now. 'She'll be busy all day.'

'Fine.' Freemark perched on the seat by the window and picked up a company brochure, deliberately avoiding the receptionist's stern eye and pretending to read. She heard her typing something into her phone before she went back to working on her computer.

After 20 minutes Freemark was starting to wonder if this had been a mistake. She might have somehow annoyed Francesca enough that she might now never speak to her. Plus, she could do with a cigarette.

She was about to stand when a flustered looking woman in a typical office suit violently pushed open the doors from the offices. She marched over to Freemark and stared down at her, hazel eyes burning, skin the colour of ripening tomatoes. 'I've nothing to say to you,' she snapped. 'Please leave now.'

Freemark stood, though she was a good few inches taller than this woman the anger and determination she exhumed almost overwhelmed her. Such rage, but also fear.

'Mrs. Mason, I'm sorry to—' she started.

'I said I have nothing to say to you.' She hissed the words and was visibly shaking.

Freemark raised a hand. 'Please, I'm on your side and—'

'Leave!' Francesca flung out her arm to point at the door. It also shook with rage. 'Now!'

The receptionist looked from one woman to the other, then moved to pick up the phone. 'I'll call the police,' she said.

'No, wait.' Freemark was thinking quickly now. 'Mrs. Mason, please, I don't want to upset you. I need to know about—'

'That man is dead to me.' The words were spat out between her teeth. She glared at Freemark, her eyes bulging. 'I will never speak of him again.' She turned on her heels and headed toward the door back to the office. Freemark and the receptionist starred after her, her finger hovering over the third nine.

I Vow to Thee – William E. H. Walker

Freemark had to do something, she racked her brain and then just as Francesca opened the office door said, 'He did it to me as well.' She blurted the words out. Francesca froze but didn't turn around. 'When I was 16,' Freemark continued. 'In a pub here in town.'

Francesca stayed perfectly rigid for a good few seconds, her back to Freemark and the now troubled and confused receptionist. When she spoke, her voice was like a trap snapping shut. 'Follow me,' she said and marched through the door. Freemark followed eagerly, leaving a bewildered receptionist to replace the receiver on the phone.

The office was like a million others. Beige walls, grey carpet, polystyrene ceiling tiles, rubber plants and cheap artwork in frames. Freemark was reminded why she had never wanted a job like this. It would kill her to be stuck inside somewhere so devoid of life. These places felt like graves.

They marched quickly through a small open-plan area festooned with paperwork. Freemark knew that accountancy was exempt from the paper limits other firms had to contend with. No matter how advanced computers became, no matter how infallible software was proven to be or how much storage you could compress into a hard drive, the government and lawyers still insisted on having proof of their electronic money on tangible old-fashioned paper. Banknotes might have gone the way of the dinosaur, but money on paper was as important as ever.

Francesca held open a door for her and she stepped inside, finding herself in a small meeting room. 'Sit anywhere.' Freemark settled nervously into her seat on the far side of the hexagonal table while Francesca folded into the chair nearest the door, just in case escape was needed.

Freemark tried a smile again. Francesca returned it with a look of malevolence and mistrust. 'You have five minutes,' she said curtly.

Freemark gathered herself. 'I need to know about your relationship with Jake Grantham.'

'Why?' Her eyes never wavered from Freemark's.

Why did she need to know? Could she say, "I think he's involved in the killing of several hundred people?" Then it came to her. 'I think he's done it again.' Her voice was soft, quiet, confiding.

Francesca replied instantly, her tone the growl of a guard dog. 'Done what?'

Freemark leaned forward, hands held together as if praying. 'Mrs. Mason, when I was 16 Jake Grantham assaulted me in a pub in town. He pushed me up against a wall and…' She faltered. 'Broke my jeans and hurt me.' She gathered herself. 'I believe he was your boyfriend for some time, and I wanted to know if you can tell me anything about him? What did he do to you?'

Francesca's eyes were welling up. Her lip trembled and she wrapped her arms about herself. Her head shook slowly as she stared at nothing. It was a good minute before she replied. 'Do you know how hard I've tried to forget that man? The…' She wiped a tear from her eye. Freemark could see the battle going on within her. Her desire to break down and cry, reliving the memories, with the need to be strong and in control. 'The man is a bastard.' She spat the words out. 'A complete and utter bastard!'

'I'm sorry to ask you to talk about him but it's really important I understand. I think he's involved in something.' She leaned over the table, imploring her. 'Something terrible.'

Francesca stood suddenly and walked over to a water jug on a side table and poured herself a glass, not offering one to Freemark. She downed it and poured a second. Freemark gave her the space to reply. When she eventually did, her voice came in gasps, as though forced from punctured lungs. 'We were together for nearly a year. I was 17, he was 18. He was so charming and nice when we met. Could sweet talk birds from trees. Always complimenting me on my looks, clothing and stuff. Laughing at my jokes and interested in me for me, you know?' Another tear quickly wiped away.

'What changed?' asked Freemark.

She turned back to face Freemark. 'When we first got together, I'd never… you know…' Freemark nodded her understanding, not wanting to speak and interrupt her now. 'He was so gentle. He went slowly with me and helped me enjoy it. It was like that at first. He was my teacher, and he enjoyed the role. But then…' She shuddered, remembering. Small droplets of water spilling onto the cheap tangerine coloured carpet. 'He wanted more. He wanted to try more things and I started to get uncomfortable.'

'What sort of things?' Freemark felt her skin crawl but knew she needed to press.

'Initially it was, you know, stuff you see in films.' She looked embarrassed, willing Freemark to understand without the need for her to say it. 'Handcuffs and that.' Freemark nodded again to encourage her. Francesca returned to her seat and put the glass on the table between them. 'Then after a while I didn't want to do it, so I said no. He said it was okay and I'd get used to it and learn to enjoy it. But it just hurt.' She looked at Freemark for an agreement that this was wrong.

Freemark leaned forward again and asked, quietly, 'Did he hit you?' She nodded. 'Worse?' She nodded.

'Beaten?' she nodded again. Freemark let out her breath. She couldn't help but think she'd dodged a bullet.

Francesca wasn't done though. 'When I said no, he pretended it was okay, but he didn't let it go.' She was close to tears now. 'Once, when I'd fallen asleep he handcuffed me… he… he… I woke up and he was inside…' She reached into her pocket for a handkerchief and wiped her eyes. Sniffing loudly as she drew thick smears in her foundation. She was shaking with the effort to remain in control. 'I kicked him off me. Told him I didn't want to see him anymore. I struggled as best I could, but my hands were bound and he was too strong and he got violent.' Her hands locked into fists, vibrating near her face. 'Then one night I woke up to him...' Her body was lurching as she fought the desire to succumb to grief. 'He was holding a knife...' The tears were running freely down her cheeks. 'He'd cut my clothes away.' Her hands were moving toward her stomach but she didn't seem aware of the movement. 'I tried to cry out, I really did, but he stuffed something in my mouth...' She wrapped one arm over her mouth to stifle a cry.

Freemark moved round to place her hand on her shoulder. Gripping her tight as though she could take some of the anguish from her. It took another two minutes before Francesca could speak again. When she did, the words stuttered out between racking sobs. 'He... he...' but she didn't finish her sentence. Her shaking hands moved down to the hem of her shirt, lifting it with trembling hands to just below her breasts.

Freemark's mouth fell open as she took in Jake Grantham's work. The scars were inches long and ragged, like they'd been allowed to heal without medical intervention. Some as thick as a thumb, while others thin and precise. Some swirled in patterns while others were slashed into the flesh in brutal jagged lines. As Freemark looked on, Francesca pulled her shoulders back and sniffed loudly. Her head twitched, eyes ablaze in defiance as she fought for control. She was tough, this woman. 'He said it was, he said it was to remember him. So I'd never forget him.' Francesca had stopped crying now, her ferocity returning. 'The bastard wanted me to remember him, so he cut me while he raped me.'

Her words echoed about them as though the room itself couldn't comprehend the meaning. Freemark stared at her stomach. The lines crossed over each other from rib cage to pelvis, mingling with the stretch marks of childbirth. She's never seen anything like it. Francesca dropped her shirt, which broke the spell. 'I had to bandage myself up. Took a week off school claiming sickness. Mum was suspicious but I put a thermometer in a cup of tea to persuade her I was ill. He said if I told anyone he'd kill me. I couldn't,' she sniffed and wiped her cheek. 'I couldn't risk it.'

Freemark's throat had closed as though she'd swallowed glass. Gathering her thoughts was not an option. 'I'm so sorry. I had no idea, I'm so sorry. I wouldn't have come had I...' She trailed off. Tears of her own stung at her eyes. She flopped into a seat, her mind numb. The cruelty, the brutality.

Francesca rubbed her eyes and nose. The tears had ended. Control restored. She looked at Freemark with blood-red eyes. 'You say he's done this again?'

It took a minute for Freemark to remember her lie. Time to be truthful. This woman deserved it. 'Actually,' Freemark replied, drawing in a deep breath, 'I think he may have done something worse.'

I Vow to Thee – William E. H. Walker

138

I Vow to Thee – William E. H. Walker

10:54

Grantham

Grantham ran his hands under the warm water, squeezing soap bubbles out from between his fingers. His mind was awash with images. Memories he would take with him to the grave. Her face. Her beautiful face.

You little beauty, you!

He knew this was bad, knew that it was wrong to feel this way. They had told him so many times. Beaten and whipped him until he stopped wanting it. But the energy it gave him. The thrill. God, he loved this. It made him who he was. It made him closer to God.

You've done a wonderful thing.

He looked out of his kitchen window at the freshly turned earth. *She's deep enough; no fox is going to dig that up*, he thought. There would be potatoes there soon enough. Beans and carrots too. His body tingled, his mind ablaze with pure unbridled joy and he felt more alive now than at any other time of his life.

Fuck closer. He wasn't closer!

I am a fucking GOD!

I Vow to Thee – William E. H. Walker

11:06

Miller

Miller stood before the TV screen. Matt Parsons, her Deputy PM, was giving an interview to Sky News. After the headlines that morning, she needed some good coverage and was hoping Matt would deliver. From the minute she'd left the village, the online press had been awash with the images of her in the car, her cheek smeared with lipstick.

Within half an hour the picture was being used as both a comparison for her premiership and a meme for everything from "Bad day at the office" to "When the monkeys steal your makeup…"

Combine that with the wall-to-wall coverage of that raging Lesser Worburston nutter blaming her for everything currently wrong with the world, the attacks from the opposition as to why she'd met so few of the families and spent such a short amount of time at the village, along with her own ministers leaking and giving off-the-record press conferences about her ineptitude… she was starting to get desperate.

Matt was her best – and maybe last – hope to repair the damage done today. The lack of any evidence or intelligence as to what the hell had happened up there in Oxfordshire was like a 10-tonne weight dangling precariously over her head by a gnat's pubic hair.

All anyone could tell her was it was possibly Islamic Jihad or possibly someone else. A fat lot of good "possibly" was. She had to do something, any action of some sort.

The answer was simple, or so the US ambassador had told her. Ask Qatar to arrest the leader of IJ, known to be hiding in their country, detain him and deliver him to the UK or face the consequences. If not, declare war. Simple. Strong. Decisive. But could she really do it? Would Qatar listen to her? Could she really start yet another war in the Middle East? It's not like they could win these days. Not with every soldier's death paraded on the news like a national tragedy instead of them just doing their job. What was a soldier's job if not to die for their country? What was the point of them if all a country was meant to do is ensure they don't die? You can't win a war like that.

I Vow to Thee – William E. H. Walker

No, she would beat this yet. On the other side she'd be a national hero. An unstoppable force of will, able to sweep through all those changes she had wanted to make at the start of her premiership. The lives she had wanted to improve. A bold new direction for Britain.

She sipped her drink. On screen, Matt was being questioned about the speculation flooding the internet regarding the attack. He battered the most absurd rumours away with an easy charm and discussed why the more reasonable were being investigated but were as yet unproven, but at no point would they prejudice the investigation. He was doing very well. A firm and reasonable voice on her side promoting her views, thoughts and feelings.

Matt had come through the old boy's network like the rest of them, but he wasn't quite as annoying. Yes, his manners were those of an aristocrat. Yes, his voice was deep and serious with that slight hint of privilege the public were conditioned to find reassuring. Yes, he had a handshake that was distinctly Masonic and pronounced the word "plastic" with an "r" next to the "a." But he wasn't one of the silly-arse Etonians who were only in government due to daddy's money and connections. Matt was a serious politician who, like her, believed they were there to make the country better. To improve the lives of the little people and help those who needed it. For some reason Miller's brain chose this moment to think back to the reports on the growth in homelessness over the past year, but she shook it off. A 23 percent rise was obviously an exaggeration.

In the meeting that morning they had gone over the plan. Negotiations with Qatar with a view of bringing pressure on them from the United Nations, but all to be kept hush-hush to save Qatar face. Sure, they were harbouring a terrorist, but they seemed to not actually know where he was hiding and had claimed to have been working for a few years searching for him. Therefore, it was important – given their military was almost as powerful as the UK's – not to piss them off. Even if America was promoting bombing them. They only wanted to do that as the President was in trouble himself. No, keep it civil, keep it low-key.

The conversation on the TV had turned to her. Matt's voice had become forceful.

'I disagree, I don't think Prime Minister Miller came across as agitated. No, what we saw yesterday was a woman who cares deeply for every one of the people in this great country of ours.'

God bless you Matt, Miller thought.

The off-screen presenter cut across him. 'But we're now on day three and we don't seem to be any closer to finding out who did this. Your government is in meltdown, isn't it Deputy Prime Minister?'

Matt shook his head. 'That is simply not true. The government and cabinet are united in their condemnation and determination to carry on with the business of running the country. We are together like never before in our drive to succeed. Our intelligence services are working tirelessly to uncover the truth about who did this, and I can tell you now they've made great progress.'

'Wind it back Matt,' Miller said out loud. 'Wind it back in.'

'Deputy Prime Minister, are you saying that the government knows who did this?'

Matt paused and gave a small, elegant smile. 'I believe I can say we do.'

'Bollocks Matt!' Miller shouted so loudly her Principal Private Secretary, Michael, sitting just behind her spilled tea over his tie. 'What are you playing at?' she said.

'Can you tell us who it is?' asked the now clearly excited presenter.

'Shut up, Matt!' She started to pace. They'd all agreed not an hour before to keep this schtum. Why was he doing this? Why?

'I'm afraid not, no. But we are working on bringing them to justice as we speak.'

Was he going to blame her? Miller wanted to tear the plug out of the wall. It didn't matter that it was powered wirelessly, she just wanted something to tear out.

'Why can't you tell us who you believe it was?'

'Get him off the air!' she screamed at her PPS.

'How?' he replied, looking perplexed.

The PM has decided we shouldn't tell people yet.' A serious expression, a slight shake of his head.

'Fuck you! Fuck you! Fuck you! You backstabbing little Etonian shit!' Miller was beside herself. He had betrayed her. He had screwed her right over and he knew it. Now everyone would be asking why she has decided not to reveal the murderers of nearly 400 people to the grieving families. There would be questions of a cover-up.

As though reading her thoughts, the Sky presenter asked, 'Is this a cover-up?'

Matt looked grave. 'No, Andrew, certainly not. She just doesn't think it's the right time to let the public know who and why. She thinks it's best to keep this from them at this point in time.'

That hurt! That one really fucking hurt. Now she was a monster who didn't want to offer succour to the British people in their hour of need.

'I take it you disagree with her?'

He held out his hands in a sign of resignation. 'I do as I am instructed, although I must admit this time it is particularly tough.'

He was trying to destroy her. He wanted to replace her and he was making his move. She'd be slaughtered in the press, she'd be destroyed by the opposition and her cabinet would run rampant. She was finished.

'I want to hear from Commissioner Slender within the hour on the progress of the investigation,' Miller shrieked at Michael.

'She reported in this morning, Prime Minister, she said they are making progress but they have no definite leads as yet.'

'Well tell her to get her shitting arse in gear or I'll find someone who can!' Miller spun on her heels. Bollocks to Slender. And shitting bloody bollocking arsewipes to Matt for turning on her.

Miller pounded over to the crystal decanters and poured herself a large brandy. She could see Michael watching her in a mirror, a look of – was that pity? – as she downed her drink and poured a second as her mind searched for an angle of revenge. She would have Matt's balls in a vice and squeeze the shit out of them. Then she remembered her first day as PM and the report she'd seen and barked a hollow, slightly manic laugh. Michael looked at her, clearly a little disturbed. *Fuck you, Matt Parsons. If you think you're taking me down, I'm taking you with me.*

I Vow to Thee – William E. H. Walker

14:23

The Man moved as silently as possible, although the chances of being heard here were pretty much slim to none. The mask over his face itched but he didn't touch it. There was nothing toxic here, they had checked for all known gasses, but he had no desire to smell that which currently sloshed around the ankles of his tall rubber boots.

He had been told to allow 64 minutes to complete his task and he was only 49 minutes in with three down and only one to go. It had been easier than he remembered from the training. Getting the barrier set up, making his way down under the road, the map memorised. He had been ignored by the public, just another hi-vis worker fixing a problem they didn't care to know about.

He crept forward slowly, ignoring the sensation of unknown things bumping against his legs and stopped under a short manhole. Looking up he saw the slight ring of light filtering through the fine gaps in the metal cover. The ladder was in place against the wall just like it had been for the others.

He turned and pulled on the rope at his waist and the small inflatable bumped gently up against him. He picked up the angle grinder and attached it to his belt. Up the ladder and into the manhole tunnel that would, had he chosen to, take him up and out onto the crowded streets. From above came the noise of cars moving slowly through traffic, people walking and talking. The distinct white noise of a city.

He ignored it; he was focused. He placed the angle grinder against the brickwork and turned it on. It made short work of the grouting, a stream of dirty grey powder falling into the filth below him. He'd not need to worry about the noise, no one paid attention to anything but themselves in the city.

When he had worked his way around a square section of brickwork, he knocked the eight bricks out and let them fall with gloopy splashes into the darkness.

Stepping back down the ladder he put the angle grinder back on to the inflatable raft and picked up the strap of the box, easing it gently over his shoulder. He made an effort to keep it level, though it didn't need to be. He'd trained for this for months, yet he still felt nervous holding it. It was made of acrylic, hermetically sealed and everything inside was bolted in place. Nothing could go wrong with it. He could

I Vow to Thee – William E. H. Walker

knock it against the wall or drop it into the river of filth below and it would be fine. Yet he still handled it gingerly.

He placed the box against his waist and returned to the ladder. He took each step slowly; his breath slow and regular as he placed each hand and foot carefully on the rungs before him until his head was touching the cover to the street. Lifting the box, he placed it gently in the hole, removed the strap and tied it in a knot around his belt. He then opened the small panel on the front of the box. Inside was a switch and a tiny LCD screen. A gloved finger flicked the switch and the LCD glowed softly. The Man watched as the readout showed three small blinking dots. He held his breath until the readout changed. "WIFI CONNECTED." He breathed out into the mask, *Just one last thing to do*.

He returned to the inflatable, moving quicker now, feeling relieved and excited, and picked up the cover. These had been well made. They looked just like a square of bricks but were 3D printed. The same rough finish as you would expect from the real thing.

He strapped it to his belt and collected the sealant. Back up the ladder, he slotted the cover over the hole he had made and sealed it in with the glue. This bonding agent had been designed to dry almost instantly on contact with air so it would be effective even if it had been raining. He almost dropped back down before remembering what he'd be landing in. Instead, he held himself there. It was done. They'd foreseen and planned for the memorial service; it was a standard response from the government and they would take advantage of it.

The Man breathed in deeply, held it for four seconds and released. He was ready to go. She'd be waiting for him. Checking his watch, he had six minutes to get back. Just enough time. They'd probably check down here given the crowds they were expecting for Friday, but if he had done his job right, then they'll never find them. Not until it was too late.

I Vow to Thee – William E. H. Walker

15:06

Miller

'He's on line two, Prime Minister,' Michael called through from the adjoining room.

Miller switched off the reporter interviewing that annoying tick Mark Shanks and threw the remote down on the nearest chair. Another viper in her nest. *Why couldn't he just sod off?* she thought. He had a game, she knew it, but she didn't yet fully understand what it was. At some point, he would come for her and she'd have to be ready. But what did she really know about him? There was nothing helpful in his MI5 file. As far as they were concerned, he was the very picture of propriety. She'd get to him later. For now, she had a clear target. Someone she did have dirt on, and such wonderful dirt it was.

'Put him through,' Miller smiled coldly to herself and lifted the phone to her ear. 'Herbert,' she said brightly. 'How's the wife and kids?'

'Not bad, Natasha, thank you. How's your husband?' She could almost hear the smirk in his gruff smoker's voice. It was an open secret Natasha and John had been living in separate locations for a while now.

'Good thanks, he's away fishing currently. Though he's offered to come back,' she added quickly.

'Fishing, huh, is that what we're calling it now?'

Smarmy little git! Natasha thought to herself. 'Very droll Herbert, I was actually calling you for a reason. How would you like an exclusive?'

A snort on the end of the line. 'Not like the PM herself to offer something like this, don't you usually get a civil servant to leak on your behalf?'

Miller gave a short, clearly false laugh. 'This isn't a leak, it's an opportunity.'

'For you or me?' A hacking cough and then the sound of a lighter clicking once, twice.

Miller felt a little queasy. 'Where are you right now? Would you care for some tea?'

'I'm currently in Belgravia. I can be with you in about half an hour?' he said, drawing noisily on his cigarette.

'I'll add you to the list.' She put the phone down. No pleasantries for him, The Sun had been at the forefront of stories speculating marriage problems in No.10, but they were still useful for some things.

She picked up the phone again. 'Michael, would you invite Charles Brinkworth to tea in an hour? Tell him it's urgent.'

'Charles Brinkworth, one hour. Certainly, Prime Minister,' came the punctilious reply.

She opened the file on her desk. At the top of the page were the words "MI5 Background Report." Below that was the name "Mathew Jeremy Montgomery Parsons." He'd know who leaked this, but it was worth it to ensure he would never replace her. Just to know she had been the one to finish his career would be enough.

Since his appearance on Sky that morning the internet was awash with articles accusing her of cowardice, betrayal, even treason at her refusal to reveal who had carried out the attacks on the UK.

The calls for her replacement had suddenly become a shout, with Matt being praised for his bravery at defying the Whip and informing the public of the progress of the investigation. Matt himself had appeared on the BBC shortly after where he'd been "persuaded" to reveal that the evidence pointed toward Islamic Jihad as the perpetrators. There was no evidence of this, Matt was lying, and she knew now that he must have been in discussions with the US and persuaded to attack Qatar if he was able to replace her. Well, she'd show the little shit who was in charge.

Half an hour later Herbert Strange sat opposite her, a glass of Sherry in hand and Matt Parsons MI5 file spread out on his lap. He whistled through his teeth, the leer on his face akin to that of a hyena. 'It says here there are photos?'

Miller nodded, swirling her own drink around its glass. 'Page 15.'

Herbert flicked through and held out the copies of the photos as a sickly chuckle rumbled from his chest. 'Jesus. He looks good in heels, don't he?'

'I think it's the hair.' Miller returned his appreciation with a thin smile and sipped her Sherry.

'He'll know this was you, won't he?' Miller wondered how such a petite man could have such a deep and gravelly voice. Must be 20-plus years of smoking, she supposed.

She shrugged. 'What was me? Someone left his file out and you stumbled upon it. Of course, you can't take it with you.' Herbert looked confused. 'Well,' Miller continued, smiling at him. 'Maybe just page 15.'

I Vow to Thee – William E. H. Walker

Herbert laughed loudly, which turned into a hacking, wrenching cough. It took him a minute to recover. 'He thought he had you beat but you've got him.' He shook his head looking at another photo. 'This'll end him, you know that, right?'

Miller's eyes were hard. 'We're in the middle of a national crisis and he's playing politics. He deserves everything he gets.'

'Yeah, but this is politics, pure and simple.' He waved the photo out for her. 'Any truth in what he's said? About Islamic Jihad?'

Miller held his gaze. 'In my keeping secrets from the nation? No. In the possibility it's Islamic Jihad? It's too soon to be sure. But they're certainly at the top of the list of suspects. And it's a very, very short list.' She took another sip of Sherry before topping up her glass and passing the decanter over. 'When will you have that out?' She nodded at the picture.

'Within the next couple of hours. I'll send it to him for comment once I'm back in the office. It'll be up on the website by five. He's gonna go nuts, you know that, right? He'll likely to say anything to divert attention.'

'It's going to take something special to distract from that negligee,' Miller replied over her glass.

Again, Herbert laughed and studied the picture. 'He's not a bad looking lad, is he?'

She sniffed and flicked her wrist. 'Not my type. Anyway…' she downed her Sherry, 'I have another meeting and you have a story to write.'

They shook hands and the editor departed while pulling out his phone before he'd even left the room to start the process of destroying a Deputy Prime Minister's career. Miller sat back down in her chair and sighed heavily. *Fuck me, I'll fuck you harder.* She laughed as she thought it and poured herself another Sherry.

There was a knock on the door and Michael entered. 'The US Ambassador, Prime Minister.'

Miller stood as the middle-aged, smooth-talking lawyer entered. She held out her hand and he made to hug her. It took her a little by surprise, but she recovered quickly enough. 'Charles.' She returned his embrace, noticing Michael's look of disapproval as she did.

'Natasha, you look as stunning as the day I first met you.' He kissed her on each cheek, holding her hips just a little too tight and close to his body. They'd first met at Oxford 24 years ago while both studying law. *It had been an exciting four years*, Natasha thought. He was still strong, charming and handsome. The rugged, hard jawline of a cowboy. Great teeth. He still smelled good too. They released each other and stood slightly apart, grinning. 'To what do I owe the honour?' he asked.

'I wanted to talk to you about Qatar.' She watched his grin broaden and took his arm, leading him toward the drink's cabinet, smiling and simpering like a teenager. *I'm not there yet Charles, but I might be persuaded to let you give me what I want*, she thought.

19:02

Freemark

Freemark ran her hands through her hair. What a day. So much to digest. She sipped her tea, running everything she knew through her mind. Jacob Salvador Grantham, what a name! Born February 25th, 1986 at Oxford John Radcliffe Hospital to the singer Myris Heather Grantham and an unknown father. Raised in Lesser Worburston by his mother. No known reason for her moving there. She would still have been touring, frequently away and for long periods. Who had been with him then? The father, maybe?

He'd attended Lesser Worburston primary followed by a Broughton boys school from where he had been expelled for an unknown reason at some point in his second year. Joined Middleton Secondary in year nine and stayed there until he was 18.

School records were patchy, it seems he hadn't set the world alight at any institution. So far, she'd found a photo of him standing in a group of three kids at roughly eight years of age wearing a dressing gown with a paper crown on his head. A typical primary school nativity scene. A picture taken by a local newspaper of the school rugby team with a sullen Grantham standing, arms folded, at the back of the group. And a picture of him tagged on Frog. A pub, a group of grinning lads, clearly underage, drinking pints almost as big as their heads. In all three, Grantham's expression was flat verging on villainous. As though even back then all pleasurable emotions had been sucked from him by some unknown force.

She knew he'd had a relationship with Francesca Moss, during which he had gradually attempted to groom her into S&M. When that had failed, he had tortured and raped her. No other girlfriends identified yet. Thankfully, she supposed.

It was then he must have moved away, presumably directly to Cornwall to hide from the heat that would have been raised after Francesca's brutal assault, although she had revealed that she didn't involve the police. Freemark's heart had gone out to her then, a young girl terrified of what the world would say about her. Would they accuse her of leading him on? Had she invited him to do it? Wanted

I Vow to Thee – William E. H. Walker

him to, even? It was sick, but Freemark could see it happening. It was all too common. And that warning. The threat to kill. If, at 18, he was already capable of such threats, what would he be capable of now?

Francesca had kept silent. Bandaging her stomach up herself and letting it heal without intervention. Changing her bandages daily and cleaning the wounds. Imagine if the cuts had got infected? Freemark shuddered at the thought. But if it wasn't because of Francesca, why had Grantham gone to ground? He couldn't have known the police weren't involved. He must have assumed they would be.

Anyway, he'd moved to Cornwall and taken up painting. She looked at the computer screen where Grantham's website lay open. The work was terrible. Freemark was by no means a connoisseur, yet even she knew enough to recognise there was no talent there. Work? No idea, but it seemed unlikely the paintings were his main source of income. Married? God, she hoped not. Kids? She shuddered.

Overall, she knew precious little more than when she'd started out. Except to have it confirmed to her what he was capable of and how lucky she had been when he'd tried to assault her in the pub. *Nicotine please*, asked her brain. She checked the time. If she had a cigarette now that would leave enough time for the smell to dissipate before she got home. She stood up and walked outside.

The evening air was warm and still, the setting sun sending long shadows across the small car park and illuminating the light sandstone that made Oxford, Oxford. Try as she might, the image of Francesca's stomach kept coming back to her. Those scars, crisscrossed and ragged. Inflicted by the same man who had tried to rape her. What would he have done to her had he got her alone? A man who could do that to a 17-year-old girl could easily kill someone. Was it such a stretch to think he could be part of this? His mother had been killed there. His famous mother. Could there have been some neglect or abuse?

Could he be angry at her? Hate her? Hate all women? She'd need to dig and find out more about his mother. She was finding it hard to imagine what sort of person could join a plot to kill that many people. It didn't make sense. If he hated women, leading him to attack women and maybe even kill women, then it would make sense if she were investigating the death of a woman, but not this. Not an act of terrorism. So why couldn't she let it go? Was it just due to seeing him after all this time?

Her phone pinged and she took it from her pocket. A video message. Her smiling daughter sitting on her bed next to her husband waving at the camera he held out. 'Night-night mummy!' She put her whole hand to her mouth and made a kissing noise, throwing her arm out almost hitting Stephen. Freemark laughed. Her beautiful daughter would be asleep by the time she was home. Stephen would be sipping wine watching some police drama on TV, a lukewarm dinner left for her in the oven.

She stubbed out the cigarette and turned toward the door of her office. Home time. She wanted Maddie. She wanted the smell of her hair, the feel of her skin against her cheek, the sound of her breathing as she slept. Freemark felt the familiar squeezing sensation in her chest as she thought of her daughter. The most precious thing in the world. All hers. Born to the man she loved more than life itself and simply perfect in every way. Home time. Home to her family.

Maybe it was a coincidence that his mother had been one of those killed? So many were murdered it was entirely possible. She wouldn't be surprised if she knew some of the victims. It was so close to her. She'd been to school not 10 miles away from there. *Leave it be*, she thought to herself. *Leave him be.*

23:07

He sat in his living room, fingers curled around the arms of the chair, gripping so hard his nails were white. 'I didn't… I didn't say nuffink… not to no one… I wouldn't…'

The Man pulled the rope tighter around his waist. His legs and arms were bound already, but it was good to be sure.

'Please! I would never say a word… why would I?' The tears ran swiftly but there was no reply to his pleas. 'Ya've gotta believe me… I'm one of ya, I'm wiv ya all the way! Please, ya gotta believe me…'

The Man pulled out a mobile phone and held it out for him to see. On the screen was the social media site Frog showing his page. The status update in the centre of the screen read: "Knackered today. Didn't sleep a wink last night. But what a night!" It was dated three days earlier.

He struggled against his bonds, head shaking wildly, sweat thrown from his sodden brow. 'But… but… that's not… it don't mean, it don't mean nuffink.' His pleading eyes met the sharp, cold and pitiless eyes of the Man. They were dark, like burnt wood. He knew those eyes.

The Man dropped the phone into his lap, stuffed a piece of cloth into his mouth and left the room. Although now effectively gagged he tried to scream. He screamed until his face turned purple. Screamed until his lungs refused to exhale any longer. His tied legs jiggled against the restraints, the mad dance of a hanged man. The muscles in his arms stood proud as he fought against the rope around his wrists. He bucked and jerked, then suddenly he was falling. Tipping backward in his chair, head smashing hard against the tiled floor. Sparks slashing through his brain, numbing his thoughts. He didn't hear the Man turning on the gas on his cooker, leaving the frying pan of oil, a glass cylinder the size of a boiled sweet, in its centre, warming on the hob.

He didn't hear him leave. He heard the explosion though. The fire tore through the house, devouring his world as it went. He saw the flames approaching. Saw the house dissolve around him. Heard the cracking, tearing sound of his life ending. Within minutes the living room was ablaze. The ropes caught fire, they burned quickly as they were designed to do so. But it wasn't quick enough. He was ablaze when the rope finally broke, but there were no more screams.

Day 4

'The proud person always wants to do the right thing. The great thing. But because he wants to do it in his own strength, he is fighting not with man, but with God.'

—*Soren Kierkegaard*

06:44

Laoch

Laoch didn't usually read *The Daily Mail*, finding it too puerile and sensationalist for his liking. But the headline "Bishop of Britain" was cause enough for him to make an exception. He'd met the reporter the previous afternoon. Sitting in the warm spring sun in the roof garden of the exclusive Michelin Star restaurant in Mayfair, he'd expanded on his view that it was only logical that Islamists were to blame for the massacre. 'You have to understand,' he'd said, taking a tiny Victoria sponge cake from the delicate afternoon tea selection on the immaculate linen-covered table between them. 'For them, there are no innocents, no children yet to sin, there is only them and us. They consider themselves above us, better than us. They do not yet understand how wrong they are. The Devil works through them making them believe they're doing the Lord's work. Though, of course, they can't be as we all know that Mohammed was nothing more than an agent of Satan.'

The reporter had made a note on the tablet while gulping down a second glass of the Bordeaux Château Lafite 2009. 'Your Eminence…'

'Excellency,' Laoch corrected him for the fourth time, more than a hint of annoyance in his voice.

'Excellency. What can the British public do to defend themselves against these extremists?'

Laoch sat back in his chair, smiling warmly and opening his arms wide. 'Nothing.'

'Nothing?' The reporter looked shocked.

'Nothing if they carry on as they are. But if they come to God?' He left the message hanging in the air before continuing. 'Only through God can we beat back the tide of hatred and ignorance that seeks to destroy us.'

'You mean pray?' the reporter smirked.

'Of course pray,' Loach answered, sitting forward and focusing all his will on the squat man sitting before him. 'And fight back.'

156

The squat man was not unmoved by the force of the reply, but he tried to hide it by taking another sip of wine. 'Fight back? You mean physically?'

Loach snorted. 'Good Lord no.' He tutted as though this question was profoundly stupid. 'I find violence abhorrent. No, fight back through actions. Fight back through words. What we choose to not accept.' He had made sure to emphasise the "not." 'Our government is leading us down the garden path. I'll admit they've made some headway with the fightback against extremists and perverts over the years, but we're not there yet. Our politicians pay lip service to the Lord, but they don't honestly believe their words. They don't accept Jesus into their hearts. We are still far too liberal, far too accepting of perversion and the work of the Devil. We will not be free and equal until we truly accept the Lord into our hearts and stand against the perversions our government wants us to accept. It is not an option to accept homosexuality as normality when God tells us it's not. It is not reasonable to accept abortion as a human right when it is not a human right. God does not tell us to murder children. It is not acceptable the way some women flash their semi-naked bodies in the name of fashion. God taught us modesty. These are sins, as God has taught us.' He sipped his wine and waited for the reporter to finish digesting his words and swallow the tiny cucumber sandwich.

'Should we allow others the freedom to practice their religions?' asked the reporter, stuffing a tiny jam tart into his mouth and masticating loudly, flecks of pastry falling to join their brethren already on his shirt.

Laoch took a second to appear to consider his answer. 'In their own countries, away from us? Of course. It is not for us to tell others how to live their lives, they must come to God in their own time. But here? In God's chosen country?' He shook his head slowly and deliberately. 'No, they should be brought to God or leave us in peace. Once they have gone, we will be free of their influence and we can begin to grow our country again. We will be free of the problems they cause. The rape gangs in York last year, a horrible incident. All those young Christian girls and boys abused like that.' Laoch made a show of screwing up his face and shuddering. 'Then there's the terrorism and fear they have inflicted upon us just this week. Not to mention all the other acts of terrorism enacted on English soil by those we sought to offer refuge.' Laoch was struggling to remember exactly which one of the incidents so he hurried on. 'Measles is not a British disease. It was imported here by them.'

'Measles isn't a British disease?' The reporter's eyebrows were raised, he looked almost amused at the idea.

'Well of course not. It was first diagnosed in Scotland and we all know what they're like. Best thing we ever did was grant them independence.' The reporter tried to hide a smirk but Laoch caught it and continued. 'Once they're gone, we won't have to live in fear for our families. We will be free to live in

156

I Vow to Thee – William E. H. Walker

157

peace. Or, if they choose to stay and have accepted Jesus into their hearts, we will be a great nation once again. Those who are unable to turn to Christ must accept that this is not their country. This is not their home.' He sipped his wine, an exceptionally good vintage.

'For many, this is their country, their home. They were born here, grew up here, contribute to the economy, surely that's a good thing?' The reporter paused to thank a waiter who had refilled his glass for the third time.

Laoch eyed the man with suspicion, he was meant to be friendly. Had they not picked him specifically for his sympathies? Was that not why they were treating him to this lavish tea? Yet here he was, smirking and asking stupid questions. He frustrated Laoch. He kept his smile, although it didn't reach his eyes, dismissing the remarks with a flourish of his hand. 'Many believed that Facebook was a good thing, look how wrong they turned out to be. Or a Labour-Lib Dem Coalition.' He gave a small laugh. 'The fact that these people don't realise they have just been staying here, rather than living here, doesn't make them right. God invited them here to show them his love, but many have chosen to reject it. It's why you have so much more violence and crime in immigrant communities. They're having to constantly fight against God's love.'

The reporter looked quizzical and maybe just slightly drunk. 'You don't think there might be a link between the poverty of immigrant areas and the crime level?'

'On the contrary,' replied Laoch, feeling satisfied now, an answer ready for this question. 'I do. By rejecting the Good Word, they have left themselves destitute in both life and soul. They are poor because they are without God. They are criminals and rapists, thieves and murderers because they are without God. They were given the privilege of coming here to find God and they have rejected him. We must now reject them for the sake of our fellow countrymen.' Maybe an egg sandwich this time? His thin fingers snaked out and selected a tiny rectangular morsel from the display. He bit into it, enjoying the feeling of soft, seasoned egg spreading through his mouth. He swallowed before continuing. 'Some may seem to be living a life of comfort in nice houses with jobs of privilege and security, but they are poor in their hearts and souls. They know they do not belong here, and they must be helped to understand and accept that. We must gather together and encourage them to either return to their homes or welcome God into their hearts.'

'What is it you actually want?' The reporter sounded belligerent. He was definitely a little drunk now.

Laoch frowned. 'What do I want?'

'Yeah, I mean…' he paused to drink more wine, gulping rather than sipping. 'Are you running for government or are you just wanting to tighten up the laws? Start a revolution or riots? I mean, didn't

I Vow to Thee – William E. H. Walker

they do enough when they banned the burqa or prayers in the workplace? Do you think turbans and…'
he looked blank for a second '…those twiddly bits of hair Jews have?'

'Payot,' said Laoch, testily.

'Right, paylots. Well, do you want those banned as well? Should we restrict the right to worship other Gods even further? What's going to improve the country by banning more things?'

This wasn't the game he'd signed up for. Maybe next time they could choose someone who could handle their drink. 'I don't want to ban anything of the Sikh and Jewish religions. God will bring them to the fold in time. But the Muslim is different. Muslims are dangerous. They have proven themselves thus. By their actions shalt ye know them.' He tapped the side of his skull with his long index finger. 'Have they not been bombing us constantly since 2001? Have they not sent their young and frail to die in pain taking our beloved brothers and sisters with them? Have they not killed nearly 400 of our brothers and sisters just this week? Babies in their beds and whole families wiped from the face of God's Green Earth. Do you not think this is a sign from the Almighty that we must expunge the Muslim threat from the face of the planet?'

The reporter sat back, chewing on another strawberry tart, the flakes of pastry now half-covering his chin and shirt, almost as though a second skin was growing over his clothes. A lizard shedding its skin. Loach wondered if he'd gone too far with him, but the message needed to get out. 'Yeah, erm… I think I have everything I need.' He started to rise before seeming to remember something. 'One last thing.' He slurred the words. 'You're from Northern Ireland, so can you really still claim to be British?

Laoch's face grew puce, his blood boiled like magma. When he spoke, his voice could have burned the building to the ground. 'Northern Ireland was stolen from Britain. The heathen Catholics robbed us of our future when they stole our country from us. Believe me, Northern Ireland is Britain.'

'But didn't Northern Ireland vote to interg—'

'NORTHERN IRELAND WAS STOLEN. AND GOD SHALL RETURN IT TO US!' Laoch was on his feet now, his finger stretched out rigid toward the nose of the reporter. He had used what he called his "sinners" voice. The one he reserved for the more "smitey" sermons. He stayed there for a moment, enjoying the fear in his interrogator's eyes, before sitting back down and pouring tea from a fine china pot into a fine china cup, seemingly oblivious to the now-silent dining room. All eyes on him. Not even the light tinkle of a fork on a plate to break his spell.

'Well… erm… right. Thank you for your time and the food and wine. I'll write this up and it should be online tomorrow morning.' His voice was faltering, sweat glistening on his brow.

I Vow to Thee – William E. H. Walker

Laoch stood, giving him a warm smile, all animosity forgotten and shook his hand, a hard, strong grip for such a thin man. 'It was my pleasure, thank you so much for your time. I'm sure you will do a wonderful job.'

***

Loach finished reading the article and tapped the side of the pad in thought. It had been watered down, as was to be expected. Since *The Mail* had been dragged through the courts for the whole Lord Brokenshire wrongly accused paedophile and child murderer thing, they'd been a little more cautious than in the old days. Still, it would serve a purpose.

He dropped the tablet onto the sculpted mahogany side table and allowed himself a satisfied smile. Frog had already blown up with the report. The hologram he'd posted to coincide with the article's release had been shared over 2 million times already, and it was still early. There were the usual haters, of course. The "intellectuals," entertainers, left-wing comedians, homosexuals, perverts and suchlike condemning him as racist and an extremist, but that was also to be expected. He didn't really understand the psychology but apparently it strengthened his position. That's what they'd told him, anyway. The more visceral the responses to his holograms, the more people attacked him with facts, figures and wit, the more his base grew. And it had grown significantly in the past four days. According to his PA, his Froglets now numbered near 16 million. Froglets. Such a fitting name for the unwashed masses spending their lives squelching through the mud in the hope of finding a lily pad to climb onto and bathe themselves in the sun. His sun. And Laoch would lead them there. He would storm parliament and install himself as their leader. And they would follow him. They would follow him anywhere.

He stood from the antique wingback chair, padded over to the Louis XVI table and poured a large Balvenie 25-year-old Doublewood into the Norlan tumbler. He'd been unsure when he'd been approached by the woman as to whether she could keep to all she had promised him. When she'd told him he'd have the Bishop's position inside a year, he'd laughed. When she'd told him he'd become the voice of the Christian revolution – the Bishop of the People – he'd told her she was mad. But it was all coming true. It was all coming true, for him.

He sighed a relaxed and triumphant sigh. From rejected and despondent village vicar to Bishop of Oxford, to the voice of the next great revolution for Britain. The Voice of Freedom. The Voice of God. All inside six years. He almost laughed. He had been transformed from run-down and dejected to wise and glorious. His words touched the hearts of millions and he was loved. And this was just the beginning. He would stir the populous into such a tumult they would do whatever was required of them. And in partnership with the group, he would rise as high as any Royal. Maybe even higher still? Emperor? Too much to hope for?

His fantasy was interrupted by a knock on the large oak door. Peter, his PA, entered. A particular young man, no older than 25, always groomed to the extreme. He was slight with long legs and high cheekbones. Soft, wavy hair that traced itself over his forehead. Full lips and bright, interested eyes. He'd become invaluable to Laoch in so many ways.

His voice was gentle, like a summer breeze. It made Laoch's heart flutter. 'Your Excellency, she's here.'

Laoch smiled and put down the untouched whisky. 'Excellent, excellent! Show her in!' He was ready for his accolades today. Peter's pert bottom wiggled across to the door with Laoch's eyes following it.

Peter held the door as the woman entered. She didn't glance at him as she moved, almost silently, into the room. Laoch was still smiling as she took his hand, her own smile distinctly absent. He felt the corners of his mouth falter. She still made him nervous, but then he knew what she was capable of. Without preamble, she said, 'I trust you're ready for your next appointment?'

He nodded; her luscious green eyes flashed in the sunlight as they regarded each other. She seemed to be able to see into his soul. Laoch felt a little afraid. 'I am ready. I have no fear, I shall do as required.'

08:16

Miller

Parson's resignation letter, written on expensive cream linen paper, lay on her desk. Miller allowed herself a moment of self-congratulation. It was all rather dull, save the second to last line which, had he resigned for a less damning reason, might have been hurtful to her.

'It has become clear to me, in a world where even our Prime Minister leaks stories to the press, that we are facing a constitutional crisis hitherto unseen in our Great Nation.'

The story had appeared on The Sun's website by 4.45 pm and she had noted his refusal to comment. The pictures, particularly the one in the corset, had been shared countless times and spread across all social media and news outlets worldwide within an hour. Matt had resigned by six that evening and was reportedly already back home in Somerset.

Don't play with me. I'll bloody well have you. Miller's internal voice was very satisfied today. She stood and walked to the window that looked out over the courtyard behind No.10. She swung her arms to loosen them up, enjoying the tingling sensation as the blood flowed down to her fingertips. All her enemies would fall. Parsons was gone; Margret Durrage, that northern cow who'd kept making speeches against her, was bent to her will; Shanks would crumble. What was he to her anyway? Just some jumped-up backbencher trying to make a name for himself. He would sink into ignominy with the rest, then she would be left in charge and without competition. She deserved to be here, she deserved to be Prime Minister.

There was a knock at the door and Stewart entered carrying a large stack of papers. 'Good morning Prime Minister. I have the latest on the investigation and preparations for tomorrow's memorial service for us to discuss.'

Brought back to reality, Miller sighed and picked up her cup of tea. It tasted bitter and for a second she wondered what was different. Then she spied the decanters and realised it lacked substance. *Maybe wait a little longer*, she thought. She smiled at Stewart. 'How many are we expecting now?'

He puffed out his cheeks as he sat in the large chair opposite her desk. 'In the Abbey? 2000. A full house.' He checked his notes. 'The Americans are sending the VP, the Russian ambassador has now confirmed, as have the ambassadors of Guatemala, Iran, Belgium and Argentina.'

'Argentina?' Miller sat down behind her desk, putting her cup down on a parliamentary memo from the foreign office. It left a brown ring that slowly spread outward, smudging the report of Qatar's determined resistance to the notion Sa'ad Essa still resided in their country. 'They're not going to try to use this as an excuse to talk about the bloody Falklands, are they?'

Stewart smiled, indulgently. 'Most likely, yes. But we needed to invite them to talk about the problems in Peru. If we can put pressure on them to stop interfering with the election there…' he cocked his head and raised his eyebrows as though to suggest it was an unlikely outcome.

'Not much chance of that.' The Peru situation annoyed Miller. The Argentines, since reverting to a de facto dictatorship, had been trying to install a far-right government in Peru to form a coalition of like-minded governments across South America, creating a power block that could take on the US and Europe. With Brazil still getting over the civil war caused by the assassination of its president, Peru was an ideal target for the Argentines. With them onside they could potentially launch an attack on the Falklands, something they'd been threatening since the near continent-size lakes of crude oil were confirmed there 10 years ago.

Britain had signed up to the "Zero from Fossils Accord" in Oslo in 2026 so had volunteered to leave the oil in the ground in exchange for 10 years of financial incentives from the other 187 countries who had signed up. This was something the country needed far more than oil. These would, the accord said, come in the form of tariff-free trade and tax breaks for UK companies. So far, only France and Germany had officially agreed to start the compensation scheme and Miller wasn't sure any of the others would be quick to oblige her. Despite the dire warnings and predictions for the next few years, things were moving all too slowly. Too late, most likely, given the reports she'd had when she first came to No.10. She really should get on that soon, but not today. Today was taken. Tomorrow she would deal with the other thing. Well, maybe Saturday. She brought herself back to the present. 'We'll have to ensure to sit them beside our American friend, won't we?' She smiled at Stewart who showed he appreciated the joke.

'Outside the Abbey, we're expecting somewhere between 300,000 and 500,000 people to turn up. Commissioner Slender and her team have chosen to use the route from Marble Arch down to Parliament

Square and large screens are being placed at equal points along the route today. The security services are doing sweeps of the area as we speak, all police leave has been cancelled and, as per your instruction, we have an additional 2000 soldiers to line the streets and Parliament Square itself.'

'Dress uniform mind Stewart, they're to at least look like they're an honour guard.' She pushed out a finger to emphasise her point.

He nodded readily and turned the page. 'Indeed, Prime Minister. The King's Guard will parade at Horse Guards and Buckingham Palace. We're expecting some tourists there of course, but the majority will go with the crowd.'

'Any threat warnings so far?' She was feeling good today, buoyant even. Her head was clear and she felt alert and in control, back on her game. She'd even ignored the drinks trolley for a few hours and had promised herself she would do so for a few more.

Stewart sorted through the pages until he found a small selection bound in blue and handed them to Miller. 'Intelligence Services reports. To summarise, they're all hedging their bets. After their collective failure this week they're keen to cover their own, as it were, thus they are all completely clear in their uncertainty as to whether there may or may not be a threat.' He held out his arms and his smile seemed to say "Obviously."

Miller thought, not for the first time, how Stewart reminded her of Sir Humphrey Appleby of Yes Minister fame. He was much younger than Nigel Hawthorne had been, but there was something about how he conducted himself, how he constructed sentences. It had been said at the time how politicians had claimed to recognise the Civil Service in the charming and devious Humphrey. Maybe that's why she found Stewart so similar?

He had worked for her predecessor and would work for her successor. He was totally secure and would do what he thought best, rather than always what she asked. Yet he did it all with a smile and civility that could unnerve you if you let it. Had this been the 18th century, he'd have been the aristocracy, playing cards and drinking in clubs. In the 21st century, he was a civil servant, unelected and untouchable. The true power.

Miller flicked through the pages. 'So if they're saying nothing helpful, is it even intelligence?'

Another indulging smile from Stewart. 'They do say that the likelihood of an attack, given the precautions we're taking, is low but present. As head of GCHQ, Sir Randolph has said he believes the event should be postponed or cancelled, although it should be noted he accepted his invitation to the service.'

Miller snorted. 'You're not serious?'

'Credo quia absurdum est,' intoned Stewart. He caught Miller's look of confusion. 'I believe because it is absurd.'

Sir Humphrey indeed, Miller thought. 'Anyway, we're not cancelling it.' She picked the page out of Stewart's hands and read. 'See, we've got the dogs out today, metal detectors, microbe and gas detection, even radiation readings. Bins are being emptied and removed, the mobile phone signals will be cut, sewers checked, buildings searched, a no-fly zone established, a no-drone zone, snipers, soldiers, police everywhere – what else can we do?'

Stewart thought for a minute. 'May I suggest we have a look at the arrangements for the reception here afterward? How might we manage the discussion between the US Ambassador and our European partners?'

Miller knew what he was getting at: her change of heart over Qatar. 'I'm not sure we have to yet, other than to bring them in on the idea of evidence pointing to Islamic Jihad. What have our American friends got for us?'

'So far?' Stewart again flicked through the pages and produced a single sheet. 'They have recorded conversations between leaders and lieutenants commenting on the success of the attack, they are actively monitoring web and dark web chatter, they have a confession tape from a captured leader—'

This excited Miller. 'A captured leader? Where did they capture him?'

'I think it is best not to ask that particular question, Prime Minister.' Stewart looked down his nose at her in a disdainful way. 'The Americans don't always respect borders in their pursuit of terrorists.' Miller acquiesced and Stewart continued. 'They also have footage of people they claim are Islamic Jihad fighters moving what seem to be silenced rifles into a box for what the Americans claim is transport to the UK.'

'Is that enough?' Miller asked. She needed it to be for her plan to work.

Stewart pondered the question. 'For the British public and press? Most likely. The mood is such that we could probably point the finger at France and the public would bite.'

It was Miller's turn to look disdainfully at Stewart. 'Poor taste, Stewart.'

'I'm merely attempting to point out that our own people are not the problem. I must confess to being doubtful as to whether this evidence will pass muster with our allies, let alone the UN. It is tenuous at best and does not, I fear, justify the American proposal. Particularly when you consider that just yesterday the Qatari ambassador gave a speech in the UN condemning the attack on Lesser Worburston in the strongest possible terms and pledging to do all they can to both support us and find Sa'ad Essa, should the rumours prove true and he is hiding in their country. Though equally, they maintain they no longer believe he is. I fear that we will find ourselves isolated in a way we've not seen since Brexit, the invasion of Iraq or the COVID outbreak.'

Miller stood and paced behind her desk. He wasn't wrong. 'Well, we'll need more then. What do we have?'

Stewart picked out another sheet. 'Nothing of note Prime Minister. We have an arrest in Derby on Tuesday of a man claiming to be an Islamic Jihad lieutenant and mastermind of the attack.'

'Well, that sounds encouraging.' Miller gripped the back of her chair. Something was pricking at the base of her neck. Nerves? A fly, maybe? Would it look odd if she reached behind and scratched?

'Not really, Prime Minister.' Stewart spoke slowly as though to a child. 'He's also claimed responsibility for the Bakerloo tube attack, the 2017 London Bridge attack and the assassination of Pope John Paul the Third.'

Miller screwed up her face. 'I didn't think there was a John Paul the Third?'

Stewart looked slightly exasperated. 'Exactly, Prime Minister.' He returned his gaze to the paper. 'Other than that, there's some noise picked up by GCHQ between two supposed fighters discussing how they wish they had taken part in the attack.'

Miller slapped her chair. 'We can claim that's linked. Their colleagues were involved and they wished they were.' There was a hint of desperation and frustration in her voice.

'I think that's called doctoring the evidence, Prime Minister.' He dropped the pages down on the desk. 'Suffice to say that I do not believe this plan is viable or, indeed, the correct action to take at this point in time. I believe it would be more prudent to review our options as and when more evidence has been collected. Then we can move forward with purpose rather than blunder into another unwinnable war that lasts for 10 years or more.'

His frankness surprised her, but she was resolved. 'It's my only option.' Miller's voice was firm. 'If we don't, then we're finished.'

'Incorrect, Prime Minister. Unprovoked attacks on sovereign nations tend to go down rather badly with the UN. At worst, what happens if we don't attack them is you lose the next election. If you do attack them, we might lose our place in the world.'

Miller's jaw dropped and she stared at him wide-eyed. The carefully tailored suit, the £400 shirt and silk tie. Nails manicured and hair immaculate. His skin moisturised and unwrinkled save for a few fine lines around his bright, clear eyes. He was the very definition of a civil servant. Although eight years her senior, he looked equal to her in age thanks to a careful diet, exercise and the best private healthcare the Great British public could pay for.

'They attacked us first.' She realised too late she was pleading.

Stewart's voice remained impassive. 'The evidence says otherwise, Prime Minister.'

'*Some* of the evidence says otherwise. But much of it points directly at them.' She felt like a child arguing to stay up past her bedtime.

'With respect, Prime Minister, it does not. Some of the evidence, such as it is, points toward the Islamic Jihad group committing the attack. None of the evidence points to Qatar.'

'They're aiding them.' Miller heard the petulance in her voice, but she couldn't stop herself.

'I don't think you really believe that, Prime Minister.' Stewart's voice was incredulous.

Miller suddenly felt very tired. She turned away from him to look out the window at the half acre of manicured garden. She knew what she was planning was wrong, but she saw no other way to save her premiership. As it stood, even with Matt gone she knew she'd be out inside a month. Once the press was over his cross-dressing antics, they'd return to badgering her with accusations of incompetence and secrecy. Her Party wouldn't stand for it and she'd be ousted. Probably replaced with Roger-bloody-Boldermore with his perfect smile and quick, likable wit. Or, God forbid, Susan. Susan, who had opposed every one of her reforms and would reverse everything she'd done since coming to power. Not that that was a lot, she reflected. She'd been stymied and beaten all too often. Bugger the lot of them, she'd be the one to save this country if it were the last thing she did. 'Actually, I do believe it,' she replied in a voice that lacked conviction. She tried again. 'I do believe it!' She turned on her heels to face him, the fire returning to her. They locked eyes. 'And if I order it, I expect my orders to be followed to the letter.'

Stewart sat still for a moment before his face broke and he smiled broadly. The paternal figure. 'But of course, Prime Minister. I am here to do as instructed. I shall serve the country at all times.'

Miller didn't like the way he said "country" rather than "Prime Minister" or "you," but she accepted it and sat down. 'Right, what's next on the agenda?'

Stewart collected up the papers and replaced them carefully in the file. When he spoke, it was as though no hint of anger or frustration had passed between them. 'Naval patrols to guard the fisheries, Prime Minister. The budget needs approval and I hear the Chancellor isn't keen on it.'

Miller rubbed her eyes with the balls of her thumbs. *Another contender for my replacement*, she thought, taking the pages from Stewart.

I Vow to Thee – William E. H. Walker

09:46

Freemark

Freemark put the last crisp in her mouth and bit down. It was a little crunchy, but mostly chewy. She'd wanted Walkers but the exorbitant price tag thanks to the plastic replacement packaging meant she chose the Cleavers paper-bagged option instead. They weren't as good, but they did the job of giving her a much-needed salt fix.

She clicked "finalise" on her article about the memorial service due to take place in Banbury church the next day, coordinated to coincide with larger services to be held in Westminster Abbey, Edinburgh, Belfast, Dublin, across the Commonwealth. Lesser Worburston itself would be isolated for a private service for the families of the bereaved and service personnel who had attended the scene. Even Sydney was holding a two-minute silence in the middle of the night to coincide with the UK's. It seemed the whole world was coming together to remember those killed in their sleep in a tiny village in Oxfordshire.

She'd asked to go to London to report on the memorial service there, but Frank had said that the local angle should be a priority so she was going to Banbury. Fun, glorious, run-down Banbury. The market town that time forgot.

She remembered shopping there as a kid. All her clothes had come from Next, Gap, Debenhams, M&S and Top Shop in the shopping centre. Stores now closed to online competition. These days the shopping centre was just home to £2 shops, tattoo parlours, 4D sex shops and grubby hair salons.

When the M40 extension opened in 1991, Banbury had exploded outward with both housing estates and warehouses. It had been home to distribution companies aplenty and seemed to be a town on the up. But the ever-increasing cost of fuel had put a stop to that. Although electric trucks were now commonplace, Banbury hadn't survived the first fuel crisis. The town had effectively shut up shop. It was now home only to those too poor, sick or lazy to leave.

An attempt by the Symone Black Government as part of her "Rejuvenated Britain" project to advertise Banbury as a new commuter hub, with trains to London and Birmingham every 15 minutes at rush hour for only £58 a day on the "New All-Electric National Rail," had fallen flat once people had started to visit the town and saw the state it was in. A few speculative and curious commuters had purchased, hoping for a return on their investment, but not nearly enough. An Oxfordshire council incentive scheme that offered 25 percent off the cost of a house had attracted a few more, but neither scheme ever really took off. When the new estate in Oxford had been approved, the incentive scheme was scrapped with those who had purchased finding themselves unable to now sell their home.

Since then, with Bicester Garden City continuing to grow steadily, Banbury had been forgotten. Its once-vibrant streets, with the ornate sandstone shops and cobbled alleys, left to wither like a flower fallen in the mud.

Screwing up the crisp packet, she added it to her paper bin and opened her email. Attaching the article, she typed up a quick message to Frank suggesting pictures of the Eiffel Tower and Brandenburg Gate lit up in the colours of the Union Flag to accompany it. She hit send and made to stand to go outside.

Her phone pinged with a notification. The Sun headline, "Deputy Drag Queen Resignation Letter in Full." She read the article, not quite sure how much to believe, but the photos were there: Parsons resplendent in full S&M drag, Parsons in a pink floral number. Another Minister in disgrace, Miller's government in a nutshell.

Tony the intern, a short stocky lad who for someone so confident in his own abilities really should use deodorant, was walking toward her holding out a letter. 'Just arrived Jules,' he said, smiling. 'Secret admirer?'

Puzzled, she took the letter. The envelope felt like silk. A soft, delicate pink. Expensive and possibly homemade. Certainly the maker was a craftsman.

Freemark was unsure how to deal with this. Stephen wouldn't send a card. Flowers, maybe, but his idea of a suitable card was a three-quid job from the garage. 'I don't… who sent it?' She looked at the grinning Tony, who shrugged.

'Guess you'll have to open it and find out.'

She turned the envelope over in her hands. Her name on the front. The handwriting small, neat, eloquent even. She tore open the back, watching the tiny strands of silk split apart as she ran her finger along the seam. The card was almost warm as she removed it.

I Vow to Thee – William E. H. Walker

The picture on the front was a watercolour of a small bay. White sands and grey rocks leading to a gentle sea. It was beautifully painted. The sun nestled among clouds sent a shard of light down to the sandy beach. Small waves rolled gently toward the shore. It was a truly lovely picture. With tentative fingers she opened the card. Four words in the middle of the blank page. Four words in the same eloquent and neat hand. Four words that turned her expression from curious to confused to furious. Eyes bulging and four-letter words rising unbidden to her lips. Her limbs tensed and she wanted to scream across the room. She threw the card in the paper bin and ran her hands through her hair, gripping it together behind her head.

Tony laughed, clearly not reading her expression. 'Not someone you fancy then?'

'When did you get this?' she snapped. He looked put out, suddenly surprised by her reaction.

'Post just arrived, didn't it. Couldn't miss it, it was the only thing that wasn't junk.'

'Fuck's sake. Fucking fuck fuck. The fucking little fucking shit.' She was pacing now. What was his game? Was he trying to wind her up? Did he know about her visit to Francesca? Why the fuck was he writing to her?

'Great to see you.' Tony had retrieved the card from the bin. 'So, it is an admirer then?' He was smiling again, everything a sodding joke to him.

'Get rid of it.' She wasn't thinking straight, and she knew it. 'No.' She snatched it off him and dropped it on her desk, opened a drawer and rummaged through, pulling out a small paper bag.

Carefully, now touching only the corner, she placed the card and envelope in the bag. Tony watched her, his face resembling a confused puppy. She took some tape and sealed the bag then put it back in her drawer.

'What are you doing?' asked a now thoroughly confused Tony.

'The bastard who sent me that is a rapist. He… we… we knew each other in school. His mother lived in the village.'

Tony didn't know how to respond. His mouth opened and closed, the words spluttering out. 'A rapist? You mean… you?'

'No,' she said testily. *Though not for want of trying*, she thought. 'But he's a nasty piece of work.'

'Why'd he send you a card?' She could see Tony had no understanding of how to react.

'We bumped into each other at the police station. He was there to… well, I'm assuming to talk about his mum.' She bit her lip. Why was he writing her cards?

'Should you contact the police? Given everything that's happened?' Tony asked, all traces of humour gone.

She thought about it, beginning to regain her composure. Her reaction, she realised, had been extreme and she started to calm herself. She had no need to be afraid as she could wipe the floor with him. She had no reason to be angry, he could not touch her. She breathed deeply for a moment and considered what to do. Tony stood by her, unsure of how to help, mouth hanging open like a fish sucking in plankton. After a minute she realised he was right and that he'd borne the brunt of her reaction. She tried a small smile at him and he responded uneasily. 'Tony, you're right. Thank you. It might be just a sick joke of his or he might genuinely think this is some sort of romantic gesture. Either way, I'm not letting the fucker get one over on me.'

'You want me to come with you?' Tony moved closer to her.

Freemark smiled at his change of tone, almost protective now. Not a bad kid. 'Thank you, but no. As far as I know he's in Cornwall so there's no risk. My cars charged; I'll drive over to Kidlington.' *I need a cigarette*, she thought. 'Thanks again Tony, I'm sorry for freaking out there a bit.'

He smiled softly, seeming happy to have regained her good graces. 'No worries. If you need anything, let me know, yeah?'

She picked up her bag, retrieved the card from the drawer and left. In the car, she thought about calling Stephen. Partly just to hear his voice, partly to let him know what had happened. But how could she explain all this? What would he think of her?

At the station, she fortified herself with a third cigarette before walking into reception. The officer at the desk told her to wait while she got someone to help her, and after a couple of minutes she was taken through to an interview room by a friendly constable. He asked her to wait there for someone to come and take her statement and offered her a coffee before leaving. Freemark sat behind the standard brown pine desk, looking at the small camera and voice recorder.

After a minute, the constable returned with a small paper cup of coffee and a tall woman in an expensive suit.

'Mrs. Freemark?' she asked. Freemark nodded as the striking redhead in the immaculate suit sat down opposite her and smiled. Her sparkling green eyes reminding Freemark of emeralds.

'I'm DI Kinsella. I'm here to listen to your complaint.'

10:12

Kinsella

Kinsella slammed down the phone. *Piss off*, she thought, then regretted it and apologised while touching the fish pendant at her throat.

'Another dead end?' asked James Collins, a DS who sat opposite her in the office.

Kinsella nodded, wanting to pick up the phone again and scream down the receiver. 'It's like anyone who works for MI5 or MI6 just thinks they are better than us and doesn't need to share what they know.'

She growled in annoyance. 'Seriously, what's the problem? Either you know where the guns came from or you don't, so just tell me. Don't keep me dancing on a string with the whole...' She mimicked a very posh Oxford voice '...we're currently reviewing our findings and shall get back to you if and when we have something we think should be shared with you.'

James laughed. 'You realise you didn't sound any different then, right?'

She gave him an exasperated look and put her head in her hands. 'I swear it's like they're reading from a script.' She rubbed her eyes.

'You had breakfast yet?' James asked.

She raised her head and studied him, trying to decide if he was being nice or if he was trying to chat her up again. She'd known for some time he was interested in her. More than once she'd caught him staring down her shirt or at her bottom. He'd tried not to show it, but he was too attentive and just a little too quick to interact with her, even when he had nothing to contribute.

'I've not, no.' She kept her voice neutral.

He reached down and produced a paper bag that he held up, smiling. 'Pain au chocolat, me lady?' He pronounced it pain-o-choc-o-late.

Kinsella smiled and her stomach growled a little. It was a sweet gesture and she had meant to make breakfast before leaving that morning but hadn't quite got round to it. There had been a voicemail from her husband. He'd been called to Switzerland on urgent business and wasn't going to make it home for at least a week. She'd not recognised how she felt at first, but now she knew it was almost happy.

James handed a slightly squashed pain au chocolat over the desk and she accepted it gratefully. He was a few years younger than her, a good looking lad as well. Strong, with big hands. *Just hands…? Stop it!*

Caring, it seems as well. 'Oh Lord, am I so easily tempted?' She groaned to herself and thought, *It has been a long time since my husband has shown me care, must I be strong? Can I not indulge myself just a little?*

A PC walked over to James and interrupted him as he was about to offer her his coffee. Kinsella couldn't help but hear the conversation. 'DS Collins,' he said. 'Sorry to intrude, we have a Mrs. Freemark at the desk with a complaint, I'm wondering if you could see her?'

James flicked a look at the man. A change had come over him, he was authoritative. Kinsella liked it. 'A complaint about what?'

'It seems she's received a card, which has her scared something rotten. She said it was sent by a gentleman who she used to know and bumped into here at the station the other day. Mr. Grantham.' Kinsella's ears pricked up.

James was nodding. 'Okay, no worries. Can you put her in room three and I'll be in shortly?' The PC nodded and moved away.

Kinsella's mind was racing. Grantham had sent a letter to someone locally. Why would he do that? James was rising and moving to go, she needed to know. 'James,' Kinsella said, giving him a winning smile, 'I'll take this one.'

He looked surprised. 'Don't you have your hands full?'

She held her smile and his eye, trying to set her expression to "lusty temptresses" although in truth it had been so long she wasn't sure she pulled it off. 'To be honest it would relax me a bit, you know: dealing with something unrelated to the village. Would do me some good just to talk about something else, even for half an hour.' She moved around their desks to stand beside him. Close to him. She noticed his arms had started to rise as though to hold her, but he withdrew them quickly, face flushed a little. She continued to speak, 'Besides, I need you to go and find out who's doing what at the memorial service.' He was almost ready to capitulate. Kinsella rested her hand on his arm and felt him shiver slightly. Was he so inexperienced with women, she wondered? Could she train him? 'Go on now, you're doing me a favour.'

He looked down at her hand then up to her eyes. He looked almost ready to lean in. 'Of course,' he said quickly. 'No problem.' He looked embarrassed and grinned, his pearly white teeth gleaming.

'Thank you.' She removed her hand from his arm, but James continued to stare at her. 'Off you trot then,' she said gently.

'Right!' he said, gathering his phone and keys before stumbling quickly away while looking back over his shoulder at her like a puppy sent to his basket.

Kinsella watched him go. *'A sweet boy, but a bit stupid*, she said to herself. He'd be just for fun.

She walked through the office and out into the corridor where the constable who had come to see James was walking toward her carrying a cup of coffee. 'For her inside,' he said by way of explanation.

'I'm taking this one,' she said, moving aside to let him enter first. She closed her eyes for a second, took a deep breath, held it, released and followed him in.

'Mrs. Freemark?' She smiled warmly, nerves fluttering a little. 'I'm DI Kinsella, pleased to meet you. I'm here to listen to your complaint.' She shook the woman's hand, a firm grip from a strong-looking woman, not an ounce of fat on her. Tall and lean, clearly she worked out, although she looked frightened as well. Face twitching as she held it set. *Strong physically, maybe not mentally?* she thought. Kinsella sat and motioned for Freemark to do the same. 'Why don't we start at the beginning. What happened?'

Freemark bit her lip before speaking. 'Two days ago, I was arrested for entering the village after the cordon had gone up.'

Kinsella recalled the incident. 'You're the reporter for The Oxford Times.' Freemark nodded. 'I remember seeing you being put into the police car. That wasn't the smartest thing to do.'

Freemark looked annoyed at the reprimand. 'Maybe not, but I spent the night in the cells and got an official caution for my troubles.'

Kinsella tapped her pen against her iPad. 'So, this is related to that incident?'

Her manner changed again, the more fearful woman this time. 'Not exactly. As I was being released, I saw someone I used to know arrive in a Cornish police car, Jake Grantham. He's the son of one of the victims of the village.'

Kinsella made a show of writing the name down on her pad. 'And how do you know Mr. Grantham?' she asked, keeping her voice level.

'We were at school together. Middleton Secondary. But I didn't really know him then. It was…' She paused and bit her lip again. 'It was in a pub in Banbury. He, he tried to force himself on me.'

Kinsella looked up from her notes. "Forced," an interesting word. Ensuring her tone was pure professionalism, she asked, 'Force? What do you mean by force?'

Freemark rubbed her index fingers against her thumbs. 'We met; we were chatting for a while. I was a 16-year-old kid and he seemed… nice.' Again, she bit her lip. *An annoying habit*, Kinsella thought. 'We kissed and then he tried to push his hand down my jeans. He… broke them.'

Kinsella thought about the man she had seen just two days earlier. He had menace in his eye and she could see him doing this. 'He tried to force his hand where? I'm sorry, I have to be thorough.' She smiled, trying to appear sympathetic while inside, her stomach churned.

Freemark sipped her drink and her cup shook slightly. 'Down into my knickers to touch me between my legs.' It came out in a rush. 'I stopped him and he became angry. He was chucked out by the bouncers.'

'Did you report this at the time?' Freemark shook her head. 'May I ask why?'

Freemark looked at her. 'It's not really rape, it's assault. It's also my word against his and that never goes anywhere.' There was fire in there after all Kinsella realised.

'When did this happen?'

'Er… 20 years ago.' Freemark replied quietly.

Kinsella held her next question for a moment. 'Forgive me, but what has made you decide to come forward with this now?'

Freemark's head seemed to twist as though affected by a twitch. 'I saw him again recently.'

'Recently? When are we talking about, outside the station or before that?'

'Outside the police station the day after the attack. He was being escorted in. At first, I didn't recognise him, but he recognised me, then I remembered. I hung around to see if it really was him and he saw me. He came over and asked me how I was. He knew stuff about me.'

'Like what?' Kinsella was eager to know more but hiding it. Her face a picture of the conscientious police officer.

'Well, he knew I was married. Which yeah, he probably found out online. But…' She paused. 'A few years back my husband was drinking too much. He was working in the City and it was all work and parties, and we didn't handle it well. It was a rough time.'

I Vow to Thee – William E. H. Walker

'I'm sorry to hear that.' Kinsella's brain was quickly making the connections while her own husband's near-permanent absence seeped into her mind.

'Anyway, Jake seemed to know about that, which makes no sense as I didn't put anything online about it. Nor did Stephen, my husband.' She clarified, 'I didn't want to advertise our troubles to the world.' She trailed off. 'We nearly split up. If it hadn't been for Maddie, our daughter, we would have. But she saved us in many ways. Kept us going.'

Kinsella noted the pain in Freemark's voice. *Old wounds heal slowly*, she thought. Her hand subconsciously touching her midriff. 'Mrs. Freemark, what was it that Mr. Grantham said to you that led you to believe he knew about this?'

Freemark was clearly brought back from long-forgotten memories by her question. 'He asked if I was still happily married, I said yes, and he said, "that's not what I hear".'

Kinsella could see she was still pondering the words herself. *What does that mean? How could he have heard that? From whom?* She interrupted Freemark's thoughts again. 'You don't think it could be that he was pretending to have heard something? You say he lives in Cornwall now, so how could he have heard?'

Freemark's eyes rose to the ceiling in thought. 'I suppose he might have been, but then this arrived.' She pulled the paper bag out of her handbag with a shaking hand and slid it over to Kinsella. 'I've put it in there in case you needed forensics on it.' She smiled, shyly. 'I doubt there's enough to go on and obviously I touched it, but…' She trailed off.

Kinsella took the small brown bag and removed the card from inside, forensic testing possibilities ignored. The soft, silky envelope, the neat writing on the front, the beautiful scene on the card itself and the four words written inside "Great to see you." She must admit her reaction to this card would probably be similar to Freemark's. There was something innately creepy about it. You could read so much into those four words, but she couldn't say that to this reporter. She couldn't let her know. 'Mrs. Freemark.' She paused as she placed it back in the bag and put it under her pad. *Out of sight*, she thought. 'There's nothing illegal in sending someone a card, provided it's not threatening or offensive.' She smiled to soften her words. 'If it is this…' She looked down at her pad, '…Mr. Grantham, or whoever it may be, they can claim that they were genuinely trying to express their happiness at seeing you. I don't think there's anything actionable here.'

Freemark visibly composed herself before replying. Like she had been about to argue but thought better of it. 'I take your point. I think I just wanted to get this on record, just in case.' She paused, finding the end of the sentence, '…in case I find myself confronted by him again.'

I Vow to Thee – William E. H. Walker

Kinsella nodded understandingly, remembering Grantham's sneer and reptilian eyes. 'Of course. Well, at this stage, unless you have anything else I'm afraid I must be getting on.' She rose and Freemark, taking the hint, stood up with her.

'Of course, thank you.' She smiled and looked relieved to have spoken to someone.

Kinsella stopped and fished in her pocket, producing a card. 'Look, here's my number. If you get anything else or if anything happens, give me a call.' She put her arm out to guide Freemark through the door and into reception.

'I will, thank you again.' They shook hands.

'Not a problem, bye now.' She watched Freemark leave the building before reaching for her phone. She scrolled through her list of contacts until she found the name "Nan" and selected a message.

She wrote, "I hear Uncle John is feeling unwell, send him my love," and clicked send.

I Vow to Thee – William E. H. Walker

14:05

Grantham

The sound of his phone cut through his dream. He'd been fantasising about her. The woman who'd humiliated him 20 years ago. He'd been in control of the dream and she'd been in the process of choking as he'd pushed himself deeper into her mouth. The interruption annoyed him.

Who the fuck do they think they are?

Sunlight cut through a crack in the curtain and he rolled over to check the time. Still six hours till his shift, who the hell wanted him now? He scratched his crotch and realised he was hard. The bitch was still in his thoughts, was he wrong to think of her? He'd been taught to resist, taught that it was sinful to act on such urges, but he wanted her. Wanted to make her pay for humiliating him. He remembered his dream and felt himself twitch.

His phone pinged again and he swore at the empty room. 'Siri, read message.' There was another beep before the woman's voice chirped from the speaker, 'Uncle John is sick. Call me. Love, Nan.'

What the actual fuck? He felt his anger rise within him; Uncle John is not sick. All thoughts of vengeance on Freemark gone, he threw back the covers and rose from the bed. He pulled on a pair of jeans and slipped into his trainers. Uncle John is perfectly fucking fine, thank you.

They don't know you like I do.

He slammed the door behind him and marched up into the woods behind the house, his eyes moving through the undergrowth to check he wasn't being followed. It was a habit; there was no one around to follow him.

He arrived at the fallen tree and paused, scanning the vicinity for movement. All was still except for the soft flutter of birds, the gentle low buzz of a nearby bee and the rustle of leaves in the breeze. He reached into the hole he'd chiselled from the log and pulled out the Ziploc-bagged phone from inside. It

I Vow to Thee – William E. H. Walker

scanned his face, he entered the passcode and it unlocked. He punched in the number and pressed dial. The phone was answered on the second ring.

'Yes?' said the voice.

'Unwell?' he snapped back.

'Yes. Sending letters to journalists seems to be an indication of that.'

Grantham's voice spat from between his teeth. 'What the fuck are you talking about?'

'Do. Not. Swear. At. Me.' The voice was pure venom. Grantham found his anger poleaxed by the power and the fury in that voice. Memories of what it was capable of, what it had done to him, flooded his head like an ocean rising to engulf a continent. For a moment, he was that broken man again. Drenched in his own blood on the floor, begging for forgiveness.

'I'm sorry,' he stammered.

'Why did you do it?' Calm now, almost melodic.

He struggled to find the answer. 'I've… missed her.'

There was a long pause. 'She went to the police with it. She reported you. You know what that could mean?'

Grantham hadn't thought of that. He'd just wanted to mess with her head. 'They won't do anything. I didn't say anything. It was a nice card.'

'She spoke with DI Kinsella in Oxford.'

Grantham was surprised and the thought of Kinsella's arse popped into his head. He shook it off. 'So, we're good then? That bird's useless. She interviewed me and missed everything.'

Another pause. 'No, we're not good. We're at a critical point. No further indulgences or infractions will be tolerated. Do I make myself clear?'

They don't get you. They don't understand you. They're holding you back.

Grantham ground his teeth and gripped the log tightly.

When he didn't reply the man's voice continued, 'I'm telling you now, you're not to indulge in this fantasy anymore. Remember what I taught you? You cannot reach forward while you are looking back. The demon inside you is not your master. You are stronger than any man I know, but you have disappointed me.'

The words hurt Grantham more than he expected. He remembered the day he'd shared all his longings, his sexual experiences and desires. How they'd helped him control them and use them. They had stripped him naked and whipped him, poured iced water over him until he'd nearly drowned, then talked through his issues until he was ready to be useful. Ready to be a servant. A soldier. He owed them so much. They were the reason he wasn't in jail. They were the reason he had his house, his paintings, his life. They were right to be angry now, weren't they? His inner self was screaming at him. He wanted more. They had stripped him of his identity. Made him weak. Like the sheeple who flock to work in the cities. Just another man. 'Sure. I'm sorry,' he said, not entirely convinced he meant it.

'You're better than this. You know that, yet you choose not to listen to yourself. Instead you choose the demon. Tell me it's true.'

He sighed, remembering the dream he'd been having before he woke. He bit his lip and breathed in deeply. 'I'm better than this.' He repeated it three times. The image of Freemark's eyes begging him to stop as he pounded her into the bed came to the front of his mind.

'You're thinking of her now, aren't you?'

How did He always know? 'I am.'

'Do you remember how to handle it? When the urges come on you like this?' His voice was soft and lyrical now. Comforting, calming, as his inner voice receded.

He sighed, feeling a little embarrassed. 'I do, yes. I will do it when I get home.' From within him, a now smaller voice screeched like a banshee.

'Good. So Uncle John is no longer sick?'

The power He had over him was immense. The inner voice faded to nothing and he was left bereft. 'Yes. He's better, I promise.'

'Good. I'm truly pleased. We all need you; we all love you. You know that, don't you?'

He sagged against the log. 'Yes. I love you all too. Very much.'

'You remember your training? These instincts can be controlled, they don't have to own you if you don't want them to.'

'I know. It was a knee-jerk reaction.' Freemark's image was still there but fading quickly.

'How did you know about their marriage problems?'

Grantham was taken aback for a second, then remembered his conversation with Freemark. 'I bumped into a mutual friend about six years ago… when you let me out for a while. She was a gossip and talked about everyone she knew from school.' He paused before continuing. 'I didn't mean to cause issues.'

'I believe you, but you must control it. For the greater good.' The voice was full of love and forgiveness.

He felt ashamed now, he had betrayed them. 'I know. I'm really sorry.'

'Good man, we will speak soon.' The call clicked off.

Grantham felt drained. He'd let them all down and they were right to punish him. His back ached as he thought of what he was about to do.

As he walked back to the house his eyes flitted over to the freshly dug vegetable patch. He didn't know everything then. Just what Kinsella had told Him. He wasn't infallible after all. He wasn't infallible. The memory of Kinsella's cleavage popped into his head and he felt himself harden slightly. From within him there was a tiny whisper.

Both together?

Now there they were, both together with him. One pleasuring the other as he took his time with them. He was lost in the thoughts as he entered his house.

He took the knotted rope from the chest under the window and looked at it. He saw it curl around Kinsella's throat. Saw her eyes bulge as he pulled it taut. 'Might as well, I'm going to have to punish myself anyway.' He went upstairs and into his bedroom. He removed his trousers and lay on the bed, the rope wrapped tightly around his hand as he pictured Kinsella and Freemark in the bed with him, pleasuring him while he beat them.

He'd make up for this later. Maybe.

15:47

Suss

'What's this?' Suss said, picking up the pink piece of paper in the plastic bag from Kinsella's desk.

DS Collins looked up from his computer, crumbs of mixed nuts spilling from his mouth as he replied, 'A woman brought it in, Kinsella dealt with it. How's you?'

'All good, sexy, how's you?' she commented, receiving a look of flustered embarrassment from him in return followed by a mumbled reply she couldn't quite make out. She winked at him before returning her attention to the card. 'Great to see you', Suss read. 'What was the problem?' she asked James.

James shrugged. 'No idea. Cookie?'

Suss smirked. 'You give me the nicest pet names. Do you ever not have snacks?'

'Never!' he grinned, holding out the bag.

Suss broke off half a chocolate chip. Kinsella was walking toward her desk, but Suss couldn't read her expression. 'You okay?' She looked pensive, agitated maybe? Suss was sure her eyes were focussed on the pink page in her hand.

'Yeah.' The smile looked a little forced. 'What are you doing with that?' She nodded at the page.

'Nothing. Saw the pink on your desk, got curious. Surprised you'd take on something new right now.' Suss bit into the cookie.

'No, nothing like that. I thought there was a possibility it was connected given that it's a local thing, but I was wrong. Seems a woman has a stalker, but she doesn't know who. Probably nothing but young love gone wrong.'

She's quite posh, Suss thought. She knew Kinsella lived in a massive house in Summertown with a rich husband, but not much more than that. But she was quite posh. Why did she have a feeling Kinsella was lying? James's expression was odd as well. It had changed when Kinsella had explained the card, he looked confused like something was wrong with her reply. He fancied her though, that was obvious. Maybe just a bit of the ol' sexual tension? Suss dismissed her fears and smiled. 'Fairy muff, I got a lead. Well, I got us someone to talk to.' She dropped the page back on Kinsella's desk and noted how quickly she made it disappear back into the pile of papers.

'Excellent, who?' Kinsella returned the smile, seeming to relax.

'A fella in Greater Worburston says he thinks he saw some Middle Eastern blokes acting funny a few days back. I was gonna ask you if I could send your sexy DS here?' She gave him a playful punch on the arm, and he laughed, his face reddening.

'Sure, no problem.' Kinsella turned to James and asked, 'You happy to go?'

'No problem.' He stood as though electrocuted and tapped his phone to Suss' to accept the address from her.

'Thanks, fit boy!' Suss grinned at him as he fumbled the device back into his pocket and walked out of the room.

'Must you flirt with him?' Kinsella asked her, a note of exasperation in her voice.

'What? He's a cute lad! Not my type, granted, but still. Though I think he has someone else in his sights?' She looked down her nose at Kinsella, who reddened.

'I don't know what you mean,' she replied briskly, but Suss could see she already knew. 'What's our plan?' Kinsella asked to change the subject.

Suss decided to leave it. 'Well, the London team has been sieving through all car purchases over the past six months. They've come to the same conclusion as us: electric-only because noise an' all that. Had a chat with the boss this morning and we're lookin' at least 20 cars needed for the job. So we got talkin' about where you'd buy them, and they've been interviewing owners at the dodgier end of the market to see if they can find anything. And I said we'd be interested in helping out.' She shot Kinsella a wide grin, showing off her chocolate-stained teeth.

'Sounds good, we should get the list off them.'

'Way ahead of you there, girlfriend,' Suss beamed, handing over the tablet. 'There you go.'

She watched as Kinsella scrolled down the list. 'There's got to be a couple of hundred here…'

'It's 246.' Suss popped the last of the cookie in her mouth, 'But…' She moved to perch on the edge of the desk and lean closer to Kinsella, noting that she seemed a little uneasy at being so close, but that didn't bother Suss. 'I've got a system, see?' She clicked on the corner of the tablet and flicked the screen over to a much smaller list. 'These dealers are all within a 50-mile radius and known to be a bit funky.'

She gave Kinsella another grin as she said it. 'They've sold cars to criminals in the past and fudged the paperwork. Now…' She flicked the screen again, '…these dealers are proper dodgy. Organised crime mob. I'm thinking we start with them and see if they can give us anything.'

Kinsella was studying the list. She looked as though something had caught her attention. 'You think these guys will give up their contacts?'

Suss shrugged. 'These guys sell to criminals, sure. But I doubt many of them would be happy with their cars being used for terrorism against their own country. Boss agrees with me. They've been toutin' the same thing.'

Kinsella was nodding. 'I think you might be right. Where do you want to start?'

Suss pointed at the list. 'There's one right here in Oxford and one in High Wycombe, toss you for it?'

Kinsella laughed, a slightly strained laugh in Suss' opinion. 'It's all right, I'll go to High Wycombe, you can do the easy one.'

'Awesome!' She stood and smiled at Kinsella. 'I'll race ya.' They left the office and walked out into the bright sunshine toward their cars. 'Any plans for the weekend?' Kinsella asked.

'Yep, gonna see me folks.' She'd been looking forward to the visit.

'That'll be lovely.' Kinsella was smiling at her; she could see that she meant it.

'Yeah, I'm just gonna chill out and try to forget some of this shite.' She smiled at the thought. 'How about you? You're off Saturday, aren't ya? Gonna go and see your mum and dad?'

Kinsella shook her head, a momentary look of sadness on her face. 'No, no. I lost my parents when I was a kid. No family at all, actually.'

Suss felt terrible. She reached out, took Kinsella's arm and said, 'Oh, God.' She saw Kinsella wince. 'I'm so sorry, I didn't—'

'It's okay, long time ago and all that.' Suss watched her, and she looked uncomfortable. She released her grip and changed the conversation as they walked. 'I'm betting at least one of the cars was brought in Oxford.'

'I don't gamble,' Kinsella replied. She seemed distant, lost in thought. From her expression, Suss suspected regret. Kinsella saw Suss watching her and attempted enthusiasm. 'But if any turn out to be from around here I'll be happy we've made some sort of progress.'

They stopped by Kinsella's car and she unlocked the door. 'Good luck on your end. I'll see you later then,' Suss said.

Kinsella smiled thinly at her and closed the door. Suss watched her drive off then walked over to her own vehicle, feeling shitty that she'd mentioned her parents. She'd not known Kinsella was an orphan, it must've been hard for her growing up alone.

She clicked the console to DAB and selected Ballad Radio. Céline Dion's voice broke into the cab, and Suss started to sing along: 'Let beauty come out of ashes, and when I pray to God all I ask is can beauty come out of ashes?'

She saw a couple of constables staring at her as she pulled out onto The Boulevard, a huge grin on her face and the music blaring out. She gave them a wave and laughed at their expressions. *Fuck 'em.* She needed to feel happy while dealing with this relentless shit.

She took the Banbury Road into town with the music still blaring, voice raised in song until she got to Hythe Bridge Street when she switched the radio off and brought up the map on the screen.

She knew the car dealer was just past Osney Island, but she wasn't really sure where. Turned out to be just off the Botley Road close to Pets at Home.

Around 10 minutes later she pulled up and took in her surroundings. The area felt unloved, grey and forgotten. Warehouse-sized dull metal and plastic retail units, abandoned as the businesses went under, stretched out over a cracked and weed-pocked car park. Faded signs of successes long past still sat over doorways, home now only to flying rats and their nests. Suss hated pigeons.

The unit she was interested in had once sold sofas. The old and stained sign still held precariously in place by a few wires that had once served to light it. Had it not been for the rows of shiny new BMWs, Mercs, Jags and Porsches outside, she might have not realised the car dealership was here at all. Although she suspected that people like Simon Turnball didn't need to advertise like most businesses.

She got out of her Beemer and walked casually toward the building, being careful to check out the marques and look like a potential buyer. When she was five metres from the doors, they opened with a well-oiled swoosh and a slim man in an immaculate black suit strolled toward her, smiling broadly. Not a hair out of place, fingernails manicured and Oxfords polished to a high shine, he wasn't what she had expected. She had thought the owner of a car showroom that specialised in selling to criminals would be a sullen degenerate. This man looked like he'd just stepped out of the most fashionable restaurant in Milan.

When he spoke, his voice carried a hint of a Newcastle lilt in it but polished by years of practice. 'Good afternoon officer, how may I help you on this fine and beautiful day?'

Suss was a little surprised by his calm demeanour but covered it up quickly. She made the decision to be civil, fixed her expression with a large grin and shook the proffered hand, which was both smooth and moisturised. 'What gave me away?'

His smile broadened. 'Oh, nothing really. Just your car – you can see the blue lights in the grill and it's a police number plate.'

Suss gave a little laugh. 'Shouldn't be surprised you know your cars, should I?' *Play this on the level. Get him onside*, she thought.

'No.' He released her hand. 'Simon Turnball.'

'DI Suss.' She flashed her badge and he gestured her toward the building. She walked with him, admiring a Porsche 959 as they passed.

'Now, I suspect you're not here for a new car?' He was smooth, like a lounge singer. She could imagine women finding him attractive.

'I'm looking for your help.' *Be honest. He's not a suspect.*

He shot her a look, a mix of amusement and surprise. 'Well, first time for everything I suppose.'

They stepped inside the vast old showroom. It was cool compared to the day outside but had an air of rejection and decomposition. He had made no effort to decorate the place. Faded and tattered "Closing Down, Everything Must Go" posters still adorned the walls beside torn pictures of beautiful, smiling staff members in immaculate uniforms advertising the latest in three-seater comfort.

The floor space itself was home to a select few of his pricier models. A McLaren 470 CTS stood gleaming beside a brand new Mercedes S Class EI. Suss' eyebrows shot up as they passed a new Tesla Model Z and she gave him a look of incredulity. 'That thing can do 250mph, right?'

'So they say,' he replied nonchalantly. 'Though I've only ever had it up to 80, of course.'

She couldn't help but laugh, finding it hard not to like him. 'If you ever want someone to test it for you...'

It was his turn to laugh. 'I'll be sure to get in touch.'

He ushered her into a smaller side room. Inside, beige ruled – everything was clearly the remnants from its past life when it had been a shop. A flatpack desk, two plastic chairs, a rubber plant, two filing cabinets and a solitary picture on the wall.

Simon gestured for her to sit and slotted himself behind his desk, adjusting his jacket as he did so. 'Now, what can I do for you Detective Inspector?'

'Suss,' she replied.

'Suss,' he repeated, leaning back, the chair giving a slight creak as he did. 'Like suspicious??' A cheeky smile.

She returned it. 'No, like with a double O. It means sweet in German.'

'A fitting name.' He nodded, joining his hands in his lap.

They sat and faced each other. She noted the scars through his eyebrow and over his top lip. *Glass or fist?* she wondered. She kept her tone conversational, not wanting him to clam up. 'I wanted to know about the Merc you sold a couple of weeks back to a Mrs. A Bramble?'

He made a show of looking thoughtful. 'I'm not sure I remember exactly which car you mean?'

Suss took out her phone and flicked the screen. 'Let me be specific: Merc E Class 360, 400bhp all elec. Licence plate WF25 BXT, sold on the 18th of April to Ms Alice Bramble, 9 Church Road, Sandford-on-Thames for £55,000. That would be about £40k less than the retail price, wouldn't it?'

He smiled, a little thinly. 'Oh right, I remember. Such a sweet old lady.'

Suss sat forward and met his eye. 'Thing is mate, Mrs. Bramble is bollocks. She don't exist.' She fixed him with a stare, but his expression didn't change. Still calm and relaxed, a man in control. She suspected he was probably more than capable of withstanding prolonged questioning.

After a moment, he shrugged. 'Mrs. Bramble was the name she gave me. I uploaded her driving licence to my computer.' He waved his hand at a battered old scanner that must have been 10 years old. 'I did everything I could to ensure the sale was legit; I can't be held responsible.'

Suss sat back. 'I'm sure you did.' She scratched her nose. 'The reason I'm asking, Mr. Turnball, is what if Mrs. Bramble used that car to murder a village full of people?'

She saw the flicker on his face. Was it annoyance or intrigue? He took his time answering and Suss kept quiet. When he replied, his words came slowly, deliberate. 'I can assure you DI Suss, Mrs. Bramble is not the type of lady to do something like that. She is not a violent person. Her interests, I believe, lie in a more recreational area.'

A drug dealer then, Suss thought. 'Really? But I thought you didn't really remember much about her?'

He rested his arms on his desk, the easy smile playing across his face. 'I remember her as being a gentle lady, not capable of such an act in my opinion.'

'I'd like to see her information,' she shot back.

'You have a warrant?'

She laughed. 'Nah.'

'Then, no.' The conversation had been quick, as though they'd rehearsed it. Each knew their part, each playing their role with the ease of a seasoned professional.

Suss considered her angles and the man before her. He knew the law; he knew how to skirt it. There would be nothing here that would give away Mrs. Bramble's true identity. The copy of the driver's licence would be good enough to clear him of any responsibility. There was no point in threatening him.

'You got kids?' she asked lightly.

This change of tack didn't seem to surprise him. 'Two,' he replied smoothly. 'Boys, six and four. You?'

She ignored the question. 'There were kids in Lesser Worburston.' He looked annoyed again, and Suss suspected he'd worked out where she was going.

'Indeed, so I hear. Poor kids.'

Genuine? she wondered. 'Mrs. Bramble might hold the key?'

He shook his head and sighed. 'Look, I can assure you Mrs. Bramble had nothing to do with that. He…' Simon's cheek twitched at the slip, 'She is not capable of that.'

Suss kept the amusement his mistake gave her from her face. 'What about any of the other little old ladies you've sold cars to?'

He seemed to consider the question for a second. 'Why do you ask me, specifically?'

'You're one of a couple, but your rep precedes you.'

He looked incredulous and his voice grew harsher. 'You think I'd sell to someone who was going to do… that?'

Now she was sure that was genuine anger. 'Not deliberately, no.'

His face had grown tight, lines etched into his cheeks. 'I don't sell to people I don't know or without recommendation. No one I know would associate with scum like that.' The veneer had slipped, and she saw the man beneath the manicure. The hard street brawler he'd worked so hard to leave behind. She saw something else there as well – real indignation that she could think him involved.

'You really wouldn't do it, would you?' She registered the flash in his eyes and realised she'd judged him correctly.

I Vow to Thee – William E. H. Walker

'Of course not. Do you think me an animal? Cunts like that deserve to be strung up.' His Newcastle accent was coming through strongly and he fought to calm himself. 'Excuse the language.'

'No worries, I happen to agree.' She smiled at him and some of the tension lifted.

'Was it a Merc E Class they used?' He looked slightly worried that it might be true.

She shrugged. 'Not sure. Truth be told we're lookin' at several cars probably brought recently from establishments like yours.'

'Not like mine!' he corrected her sternly, and she held her hands up in apology.

'Not like yours, but establishments who sell to the Mrs. Brambles of this world. At least one of your fellow traders might not have been so reluctant to sell to them. Or might not have known they had until it was too late.' She paused and worded her next sentence carefully. 'Selling to the people who murdered babies in their beds. That takes a special kind of cunt, wouldn't you say?'

She noted his expression, a look of disgust quickly hidden behind the restored veneer. 'I'm afraid I can't help you. I didn't sell to anyone capable of that. Sure, I can admit there's been a couple of people in here over the years who, let's say, have interesting histories and tastes, but they've been recommended to me. I wouldn't have seen someone like that without recommendation from someone I trust.'

No, you need to know they're not going to squeal on you when you fudge the paperwork, Suss thought. She needed to press him; he was truly angered by what had happened. 'You could ask about? Other car garages? Your colleagues or friends? Unlikely they brought all the cars they used from the same place, but it could've been, like, five at once maybe. That Merc you sold Mrs. Bramble has silent autopilot. Something like that would be hella useful for an attack. Maybe someone new in the past few months?' She could tell he was mulling it over, so she leaned over the desk toward him. 'Kids, Simon. They murdered babies in their cots.'

He seemed to come to a conclusion. 'I could…what do I get?'

Always the merchant. She thought about what she could do. 'Left alone to sell dodgy motors to the Mrs. Brambles of this world?'

He looked tempted. She twisted the knife. 'Plus you'll get to help us find the fuckers who kill kids like yours.'

That swung it. 'I make no promises.' He put out his hand for her to shake it, ready for her to leave. She took it, gripping it tightly and sealing the deal.

'Thanks. I'll leave you my card.' She made to get it from her pocket but he shook his head.

'No, I don't want that here. If I find anything I'll find you.'

'Okay, and thanks.' She smiled, relieved, and turned to leave. Simon would help, she was sure of it. If he could, at any rate. He'd been truly angered by what had happened.

She'd call Kinsella in a bit and find out how she'd got on. She had to travel to High Wycombe, so she'd probably still be on the road. Nice of her to let Suss take the nearest one, she didn't have to do that. It turned out to be a productive meeting as well. Suss smiled to herself. She felt like a little progress might have been made, although there was still the Christian angle to work on. Maybe she should visit a church? She'd not been in one since she was…nine? 12? She couldn't remember wasn't. She needed to know about the different Christian congregations in the country. Jewish as well. See which ones were considered radical and check if they had form. Couldn't hurt to look into it. The worst that could happen is she closes off that particular avenue.

She took her phone from her pocket and looked up the Bishop of Oxford. Articles and a Wiki page on Bishop Laoch appeared. Suss screwed up her face. *That bastard, of course. Bishop of Oxford.*

She clicked on the first article from the Times. "Bishop Calls For Action Against Islam." She skimmed through, feeling a little sick at his rhetoric. "All Muslims should be sent home or convert to Christianity…"; "…the only way we can prevent further attacks is to select a government that is working for the people through the Word of Christ…"; "…the British Christian Party has lost its way – a leader should be selected who is working for us. Not for the so-called ethnic minorities who have flooded our country…" He was a nasty piece of work, no doubt about it. She wouldn't put it past him to start something like this.

She headed out of the car park and back onto the Botley Road, her brain joining dots on a path somewhere she was to know. He'd have backing, someone to ensure his success. A radical group maybe? Who would know? Church officials? Where was he before Oxford?

Suss realised she was driving out toward Botley rather than back into town. She'd been so lost in thought she was on autopilot. She pulled into a side road and swung the car around. She'd have to investigate him. See what life had given him before his elevation to the post of Bishop.

The car's central console bleeped into life and displayed a message: "Status Zero on Trinity Street. All available units to attend."

She cursed her luck and clicked the message, replacing it with a map showing her route and required position. She was CTU, she wasn't meant to be involved in this sort of thing. She flicked on the car's lights and siren and took off back into town, thoughts of Laoch pushed to the back of her mind.

22:37

Kinsella

Pulling up outside her house in Summertown, Kinsella listened to the silence of the night around her. The gentle breeze rustling the leaves, the slight creeks and scrapes that spook the darkness. She was too tired to be nervous of the dark. Too long in the tooth as a police officer to fear the unknown. Too distracted to worry about what may or not be lurking in the shadows. She sat in her car and stared at the house she had meant to call home. Her eyes skimmed over the large beechwood windows, the solid red brickwork, the soft glow from the lamp left on in the living room spreading its light over the ceiling and undrawn heavy curtains and felt nothing but resentment. What was this week's excuse? She had almost forgotten. Oh yes, Switzerland. Another lie, she was sure. He'd be in the flat he thought she didn't know about. The one she'd followed him to three years ago from his office to the rendezvous with... her.

The realisation that they weren't going to work had seeped through her gradually, like a cancer. Eating away at her, unnoticed at first, taking her spirit bite by bite until bitterness was all that remained. Their marriage, not yet six years old, had never been a fairy tale. It was like being sold a shiny new job only to find out you had to do it naked, exposed for all to see. Yet this exposure was different. It was personal. She had to see it for herself.

The marriage day itself, a beautifully sunny Saturday in July with the village church decked out in roses and lilies, family and friends smiling lovingly as she walked down the aisle, was so atypical it could have been an advert. He had looked majestic in his morning suit, top hat perched on his head, cravat shining at his bride-to-be waiting for her. Watching her approach down the aisle as he stood at the altar with the self-confident smile of a predator. His eyes aglow as he took in her slim form as she stepped carefully between the rows of beaming guests. She had been radiant in her ivory silk strapless dress, a demure smile on her delicate face behind the gossamer veil.

Afterward, their reception: a marquee set out on the lawn of the local hall, three-course meal and speeches from all the usual suspects while the kids ran riot outside. The traditional swing band playing

I Vow to Thee – William E. H. Walker

into the evening before the guy claiming to be a DJ, but in reality charging £200 to select tracks from an online music service, encouraged them to dance till midnight before they were whisked away in the hired Rolls to spend the night in the one and only four-star hotel within a 40-mile radius. He'd been too drunk to perform; maybe that was the first sign?

Once the two weeks in the Caribbean in the five-star resort honeymoon was over, the presents all opened, the thank-you cards sent, every permutation of every conversation about the day given breath, reality had set in. And reality really wasn't what the wedding brochures and estate agents had claimed it to be.

The tall, sporty husband. The Project Funding and Procurement Specialist had been emotionally and physically absent from the start. His marriage was to hotels in Japan, the US, China, Europe. Golfing holidays in Portugal, Spain, Singapore, the US. Her marriage was a meal for one and an empty bed.

When they'd been introduced by a friend of a friend, he'd been on the cusp of getting his own department specialising in, she still didn't know what. She was a DS stalled in a holding pattern. He'd played rugby during the winter and cricket in the summer. She swam in the local pool and had girls' nights out with her friends. Activities she'd not participated in for nearly five years.

After just three months dating, the charming, sexy man had popped the question with a three-carat diamond. When they married just three months after that, he was a successful manager and being paid a million a year, but she was still an undervalued DS.

They'd purchased the six-bedroom monolith in Summertown, thanks in part to the government controls on house prices at that time. The estate agent who had shown them around, an overweight young man with a too-tight suit, slightly greasy hair and overly white teeth, took them to a beautiful, airy room with a high ceiling and open fireplace. He painted pictures of cribs and play mats, books and toys spread over a cream carpet. Wallpaper depicting scenes from nature to aid sleep and learning. He described a dream future of kids running around the large garden, helping bake cakes in the kitchen or cosying up by the fire in front of the Christmas tree singing carols. They'd been so captivated they had agreed to pay the asking price on the spot.

The mortgage had been just about double his annual income, which is why she thought he'd suggested he just get the mortgage in his name so that she didn't have to worry. She'd been so invested in him she had readily agreed. The sale had gone through smoothly and they had drafted in an interior designer who'd shown them drawings of their new home in all its potential splendour. From where the new kitchen island would go in their new "old oak" kitchen that boasted such wondrous features as a built-in rubbish sorter and composter, a state-of-the-art laser oven and waterless sonic washing machine.

I Vow to Thee – William E. H. Walker

The living room would have the very latest QCrystal wallpaper with pre-programmed seasonal changes and voice control.

The furniture was by the designer "Salot" and although neither of them watched TV, they'd agreed to installing the new 3D projection tech that implanted a virtual screen and eight projectors around the room. When used in unison, they created a slightly see-through life-size holographic representation of the show you were watching in the centre of your room.

She'd been devastated when she found out he was using it for cam girls. Their new joint account credit card was used to buy holographic sex with online whores. That was one month after they'd moved in and she had cried for a week. In secret. He must never know.

But the real damage came when she found out they couldn't have kids. The bespoke nursery lay dormant, gathering dust as they'd tried everything short of intervention for six months with no luck before finally getting themselves tested.

It had nearly broken them when they found out he was the reason why they couldn't. Even with the advances in sperm analysis and genetic sequencing, it was highly unlikely it would happen for them. There had been a brief conversation about adoption, but he was adamant he didn't want to raise someone else's kid. She remembered he'd slammed their bedroom door on her and thrown furniture across the room. She suspected, though he never said it, that it was his pride preventing him from agreeing to the idea so she had vowed to work on him. To persuade him.

She'd left the iPad open on adoption pages but had stopped when she had come home to find it smashed. Shards of glass and circuit boards spread over the oak hallway floor. She had messaged his oldest friend to find out if the idea was a dead end and it seemed it was. He had come home drunk and screamed at her for involving his mate in their private affairs. Chucked his beer bottle at the wall and stormed out of the house. She'd tried to cajole him, to fuss over him, to make him happy again, but he was distant and nothing she could do could bring him back to her.

He started to spend more and more time out of the house, either in London or meeting his friends. Then she'd found the card for a massage parlour in town that specialised in "happy endings" and resigned herself to having lost him. They'd drifted apart after that. She'd thrown herself into work and was a DI by the end of their second year of marriage. Thanks, in part, to the untimely death of her predecessor. He'd done the same and continued to build his reputation. They avoided each other, found excuses to be late home so the other would be in bed. Or sleeping on the sofa with the excuse of not wanting to disturb. "I came home late, I didn't want to wake you"; "I'd had a drink, I thought it would be for the best."

She hadn't noticed it at first, but her mood changed. She stopped seeing friends, put on weight and drank more than she used to. She found it difficult to smile and sleep. It wasn't until He found her that she had realised how much she was suffering.

One night, having read a message from him that he would "stay at Tim's" and knowing full well he didn't know anyone called Tim, she had stood in their ridiculously expensive kitchen, so tense she could be used as a bow string, and screamed. She screamed until her lungs felt raw. Screamed until she had no voice left to scream. Screamed until the only sound left in her was a hollow, painful crackle that tore at her throat like blades. She hadn't slept that night and resolved to leave him. To be done with this sham of a marriage and walk out. The suitcase was packed, the wedding band left on the table in the hall, the house abandoned, the car unlocked with the driver's door open, when she saw the Man standing quietly in the driveway.

She hadn't recognised him at first, her tears blurring her vision. Had almost shouted for help when she'd seen him. He was a ghost. A spectre. A memory.

From then on her life changed. She had returned home, knowing He was there to comfort and protect her. He showed her why she mattered, how she could make a difference, how she could be someone. Someone who could change the world. Someone important. She would be forever thankful for that. He saved her. He had helped her remember where she had come from.

Now, nearly three years later, she sat outside the large empty house wondering if there was a reason to go inside. Her life wasn't in there anyway. She decided to go and get a take-out. A mushroom and algae beef burger maybe? Comfort food. Starting the car, she pulled out onto the street trying to not think about her husband in the arms of another woman. Tried instead to remember what He had told her about why her mind did this. Why it gave her pictures of another woman pleasing her husband. They were there to remind her. To remind her how much better she was than them. How she mattered and how they would pay when the time came.

She would cry when it was over, she knew that. But not because it was over, but because it released her and she'd be able to move on. To live the life she had once had. To be free.

I Vow to Thee – William E. H. Walker

22:38

Shanks

The moderator checked the screen in front of him. 'Our next question comes from Robert Hammer, Robert?'

A man of about 50 with a rotund figure put his arm up. The microphone swung to hover above him. 'Thank you. Prime Minister Miller has been accused of failing to react appropriately after the horrendous attack this week. Do you still have confidence in her or are we now at a point when we need a general election?'

'Thank you, Robert. Mr. Shanks?'

He sat up in his chair and smiled briefly at the man called Robert before setting his face in a grave expression. 'The political classes are ruining this country. They take us for fools and are happy to lie to us on a daily basis without shame or fear of consequence. We've had scandal after scandal after scandal and now, once again, we're in the grip of a despot who's clinging on to power long after it was the right time for her to go. Corrupting the country with her indecision and incompetence.' He waited for the applause to die down. 'I for one am ready for a change. I for one have had enough of flitting between Labour and what is essentially Conservative under a different branding. The BCP was supposed to be a step-change in our political landscape, we were supposed to be the fair ones, the courageous, the ambitious. But we've slipped back into our old ways of conservatism. Squashing the average Briton and bleeding our public services dry. And what's the alternative? Labour?' He pointed at the Shadow Chancellor sitting opposite him on the panel. 'Labour has been in government four times since 1974. Now, I don't remember the seventies...' a small laugh from the audience, '...but we've all learned about the Winter of Discontent that followed their shambolic time in office. Then came Thatcher and Major who took too much from the people, so they voted in Blair and Brown, who blindly led us into the depression of 2008. Another great overspend that nearly bankrupted our country.'

'That's not true, the problems came from the US—' the Shadow Chancellor was shouting over him.

'Excuse me,' he kept his voice calm and low, holding the eyes of his opponent. 'In normal society, we wait for someone to finish before speaking.' The audience laughed loudly and cheered; the Shadow Chancellor was steaming. Shanks waited for it to subside. 'As I was saying, after 08 the nation swung back to the conservatives of Cameron, May and Johnson who gave us 15 years of austerity and corruption.' He gave time for the grumbles to be picked up on the audio. 'Then again Labour in power again ending with another recession that the BCP was trying to find a way out of when Miller came into Number 10 and ruined it.'

'Thank you for the history lesson.' Fiona Bruce found a second to cut in. 'Do you have a point?'

'The point is, we keep seesawing from one side of the political spectrum to the other, from boom to bust, from save our schools to save our banks, and the only people who always continuously suffer are the normal, everyday hardworking citizens of this great nation and I for one have had enough.' His words were met with thunderous applause from the audience. He sat back in his chair and gave them a small wave of recognition.

Fiona Bruce gave the audience time to calm down before turning to the stout man beside her. 'Charles Manderley?'

Charles pushed his spectacles back up his nose. 'I find myself agreeing with Mr. Shanks on a number of points. The country has been see-sawing between Tories and Labour for too long, and the BCP is indeed just Toryism under a different name. The country does need a new direction and I believe it is one only the Liberal Democrats can offer.' Several audience members started shouting and booing at this.

Shanks leaned forward. 'May I ask you a question?'

Charles looked put out. 'I think we've all heard enough of your leadership election shtick, Mark.'

Shanks fixed his face into one of outrage. 'Excuse me? I merely wanted to ask you why you think we normal people can believe a word you say when just last month we paid for you to have £10,000 of renovation done to your flat in Soho?' The audience's shouts of anger grew louder to the point where Fiona Bruce had to ask them to be quiet.

Charles sneered at Shanks. 'Don't libel me, sir. You know full well that those repairs were done to prevent the building subsiding.'

Shanks' eyes narrowed as he answered. 'They may well have been. But that's not an excuse as to why we…' and he pointed at himself and the audience, '…had to pay for it. Would you pay for my house to be done up?' The audience cheered again. Shanks was enjoying this.

Day 5

'Without darkness nothing comes to birth, as without light nothing flowers.'

—*May Sarton*

08:42

Suss

Suss had arrived at the station early. Today was the memorial service and she'd need to be at Lesser Worburston for 10.30 at the latest. She was using the time to catch up with reports – the boring part of the job she'd had hammered into her by her supervisor when she was a DC: "Reports may be dull, but they will always have your back. They're your defence that you have done your job properly."

Her phone was ringing and showing a withheld number. *Who the hell are you?* She plugged it into her computer and within two seconds the number was on her screen. Not registered to anyone but calling from an industrial estate in Oxford. Suss knew who it was. Tapping the phone, she smiled as she answered it. 'Mr. Turnball?' she said and was rewarded with a grunt of surprise.

'You know you're only meant to trace numbers if you suspect a crime has been committed, right?' She couldn't tell if he was smiling or scowling.

'What can I say? I don't like withheld information; it makes me think someone's hiding something from me.' She was careful to keep her voice friendly. 'Did you find anything out?'

'As it happens, I think I might have. A pal of mine in Bedford sold six Volkswagen Silente to a couple he didn't know about six weeks back. They claimed they were exporting them to Ireland, but he didn't believe it.'

Suss sat up a little straighter, excitement brewing. 'Got a name?'

'Yeah, but you know it's going to be fake. I've got a description though. He's not willing to give me his CCTV.' Suss felt her skin prickle at the mention of potential video footage. 'Told him I thought they might be the same two who tried to rip me off a few weeks ago. Anyway, he was fairly short, mid-sixties, long flowing white hair. She was in her fifties, brown to red hair going grey. And fit.'

She noted it down, pausing at the last word. 'Fit?'

He laughed. 'As in hot. Don't shoot the messenger, I think it was all he noticed about her.'

I Vow to Thee – William E. H. Walker

'Do these cars have tracking?' *Please let them have tracking*, she thought.

'Yeah, but won't do you any good, they were, to quote him, "damaged in an accident".' She could hear the sarcasm in his voice. 'Might be able to get you the plates though. Will take a while. He's funny about that sort of thing. Understandably.'

'You think telling him what you're really up to will help?'

'You're joking, right?' He sounded incredulous.

'Of course,' she reassured him, a broad smile on her face.

'I just thought it was a bit odd. Buying that many cars, you know?'

'I know. Look, I've gotta go but thanks for this Simon. I think it might be helpful.' She made sure to sound grateful.

'No worries, I'll let you know about the number plates. In the meantime if you're free ton—'

She put the phone down, not wanting to hear his proposal for the evening. Six VW Silente. She pulled up the specs online.

'All-Electric, 0-60mph in 2.8 seconds. Autodrive, silent running mode.' *Silent Running mode?*

She clicked the link: "Volkswagen's silent running mode allows the occupants to relax in almost total silence. The car's motors are designed to emit no noise and, when combined with the latest Volkswagen Air Sprung Suspension and Bridgestone tyres, you'll hardly even notice you're moving."

Sounds like the perfect car to carry out a raid to me, she thought. Her phone beeped a reminder: "Memorial Service." If she didn't leave now she was going to be late.

She raced out of the office to her car. A man in his sixties and a woman in her fifties. It seems an odd couple to be terrorists, but why would they want six cars? She'd have to tell Kinsella what she'd found out. See if they can dig up who they might be. She'd keep her fingers crossed for the number plates, although she suspected they'd have changed them for the attack as they may have driven them before the day. But it was a chance at least.

She drummed her fingers on the steering wheel as she drove, pondering the problem.

I Vow to Thee – William E. H. Walker

10:45

Kinsella

She listened to Singh giving out the orders for the day. He was his usual punctilious self as he doled out the locations and duties to the constables who stood around him. Singh had been in the force for nigh on 40 years, a lifetime dedicated to protecting a country that was gradually rejecting him.

These days there was no central ground in politics. As such, Singh had needed to be exceptional in his work, for every failure would be jumped on as an excuse to get rid of him. She reflected that even now, a maximum of four years from retirement, he was still every bit as dedicated and fastidious as when she had first met him. Kinsella suspected he wouldn't have even made sergeant had he joined the force today. That quiet mistrust of people of a certain colour was all too imbedded in the force in recent times.

When he was done and had dismissed the officers to fulfil their duties, he turned to Kinsella. 'How are you feeling?' His voice was full of concern.

'Yeah, okay.' Her eyes wandered over his dummala. Such a deep, vibrant blue it seemed to shimmer in the sun. 'Just thinking today might bring back memories.'

He nodded. 'Indeed, for all of us. All those people in London, they didn't actually see it, but…' He paused, waving his arm to encompass all the officers walking to their posts, '…we did.'

They stood together and watched as the officers formed in a wide square in the centre of the field. The soldiers and police who were involved in the aftermath were having what was meant to be a private service of remembrance just outside Lesser Worburston itself. Only the families of those lost had been invited to join them. This hadn't stopped several hundred civilians and TV crews from turning up to surround the field like vultures around a carcass.

Already present were two regiments of the Oxfordshire & Buckinghamshire Light Infantry, their Union flag standing before them. The white background with the proud Red Cross and dragon standing tall in the summer sun. The fire and rescue service, ambulance and Thames Valley police force, along

I Vow to Thee – William E. H. Walker

with the SOCO units, stood shoulder to shoulder in the peaceful countryside. In a little over an hour Singh would bring them all to attention for the two-minute silence of remembrance. It made Kinsella shiver.

After the remembrance, the Mayor of Banbury was due to thank Singh and the military commanders for their hard work by presenting them with the Key to the City. Kinsella wondered if that was a key anyone really wanted. Before then, the Vicar of Lesser Worburston, The Right Reverend Colebatch, would lead them in a service.

'Why isn't Bishop Laoch here again?' DI Suss asked, joining Kinsella and Singh to watch the preparations. For once she was dressed smartly. Her dress uniform suited her.

'He's conducting a private prayer for the dead. Apparently.' Singh's voice portrayed his true feelings for the Bishop of Oxford. 'I dare say we'll be fine without him.' He fiddled with his tie before nodding as though he was ready. 'Right, we should get to our places. Service starts in five.'

Kinsella's pocket vibrated and a soft pinging tune floated out. Despite herself, her face flushed. 'Give me a second.' Kinsella made a "just need to check something" motion with her arm and took a step back. 'Probably my Nan…'

'Be quick,' Singh called as he and Suss walked to the line of waiting soldiers and police.

Kinsella turned from the crowd, walked back a few steps and took her phone from her pocket. The locked screen showed a "One new message" notification. It recognised her face and fingerprint and opened for her. The message read, "Grandad is ready to go, we'll see you soon." Kinsella paused for a second before replying, her fingers quivering as she did so. "That's good, send him all my love." The phone went back into her pocket and she breathed in deeply, held it for four seconds, relaxed. Then turned and went to stand next to Suss.

***

Reverend Colebatch stood at the microphone and led the congregation in the hymn, How Great Thou Art, the military band providing the music. Kinsella sang quietly without glancing at her hymn sheet. She knew it off by heart although she'd not sung it in years. She'd been told a while back that it was blasphemous because of the line "When Christ shall come with shouts of acclamation." Christ was already here. Already walking the Earth and working through us.

I Vow to Thee – William E. H. Walker

She noted Singh standing to her left with the Regimental Colonel and his Assistant Chief Constable, singing along as loud as the next man. Hypocrisy or diplomacy, she wondered? Suss was moving her mouth but Kinsella couldn't hear anything coming from it. From across the square and from the crowd gathered around it, the singing rose to praise the Lord.

It was odd, Kinsella thought, that singing like this somehow always managed to sound bored. As a young child, she'd only been taken to church for Easter and Christmas. Sitting at the back because the rich and influential families sat at the front. Listening to, what was clear to her even then, the sound of the moneyed classes of England paying lip service to God. 'Nothing quite like 40 rich white men to ruin a hymn,' she remembered her mother saying once as they left a Christmas service.

The hymn ended and the Vicar Colebatch raised his voice in prayer. 'Dear Lord, as Jesus healed the sick and the lame, so I ask you today to help heal the people of this great country struggling in the darkness of grief…'

Kinsella had an itchy leg. Her inside left thigh felt prickly as though electricity was running through it and she needed to scratch. The crowd had their heads bowed in silent prayer as the vicar droned on. Glancing about her to ensure she wasn't being watched, she itched her leg quickly and violently. Suss smirked and winked at her; Kinsella had the sense to look embarrassed.

Another hymn: Abide with Me. Somewhat predictable, Kinsella thought. But even after 60 years, it was still a favourite and brought people together, which was the whole point of this charade. People pretending to care. People pretending they empathised and sympathised with the families when, in secret, they were just grateful it wasn't them. They weren't here through a shared sense of remorse, but relief. Or simply to be able to say for the remainder of their lives, "I was there." It made her sick. She eyed the faces of the crowd, picking out the reasons for coming from their expressions. Here a fat man with his countenance locked into a neutral expression. "I was there." Here a woman with her arm around a child, holding on tightly and dabbing her cheek with a silk hanky. "It wasn't me." There a woman with a veil over her face should a TV camera happen to drift through the crowd. "I was there." Once again it was proven true – nothing brings a nation together quite like the desire to be involved and share their collective grief, although all too quickly it becomes stale. The reflected glory fades and suddenly being "there" isn't enough to sustain your deluded sense of self. Soon you need something else to latch on to. Something else to prop up your dwindling sense of pride in your non-existent life. "I was there." Well, I was there.

As the hymn ended Colebatch asked the crowd to join him in the Lord's Prayer.

I Vow to Thee – William E. H. Walker

The sun was rising high in the clear blue sky as Colonel Gruder began his walk to the microphone. Walking wasn't the word; he was marching the way only someone who'd spent nearly 20 years perfecting their art can do. That slow and deliberate step, arms and legs high, face set and severe. Every inch the soldier, just as Singh was every inch the police officer. Both men stern, determined and dedicated.

Singh looked after his troops; he expected a lot from them. Professional dedication in everything they did, but he accepted they made mistakes sometimes and would support them when needed. She'd only seen his anger once. It had seemed to boil up from somewhere deep within him and erupt like a volcano. The laver spewing from his mouth and eyes, and gestures to burn all those caught in it to cinders. She had watched him tear apart a colleague of hers for sleeping with the victim of a crime. It had been reported in the papers after she had sold her side of the "Cop Cops Off With Victim" story to the Daily Mirror. Singh had sat there, calmly listening to the excuses – his sorry tale of love lost, divorce, loneliness and depression, before ripping him to shreds in a tirade so violent that Kinsella had heard it from two office's away. She, like many others, had rushed to see what was happening and witnessed her colleague running from the room in disgrace. The corner of Kinsella's mouth twitched upward at the memory, but she caught it and reset her expression before anyone noticed.

The Colonel stood tall as he began to read the names. Each of the victims cited and remembered individually, as though somehow that honoured them. His voice carried clear across the assembly, each syllable deliberate and solemn. This part of the service was expected to take 20 minutes and they had to stand throughout.

Kinsella remained motionless at attention, but her eyes wandered once more through the crowd. Some were weeping openly, others stoic and still. Some were hugging loved ones or small children. "I was there"; "I wept openly"; "It was so well done, a beautiful tribute." Cheeks glistened wet in the sunshine from some of the officers unwilling to move to wipe tears away. Determined to remain still and to attention, to show respect to those lost. They, at least, had reason.

She knew that this exercise was being repeated up and down the country. From London to Edinburgh, the names of the fallen were being read out by local dignitaries and officials. In Westminster Abbey it was the Duke of Wessex. In Scotland it was Prime Minister McCloud. Between 11.37 am and 11.58 am the names of the 396 men, women and children killed were being listed and remembered by everyone from loved ones to total strangers. "I was there."

In London it was reported that nearly 400,000 had turned up to pay tribute. In Edinburgh it was close to 200,000. Glasgow another 100,000. Belfast, 50,000. Even though the union had broken up, the upsurge of grief and relief felt across this close-knit group of islands was palpable.

I Vow to Thee – William E. H. Walker

The UK had suffered terrorism of one sort or another for countless years, but it had always been bombings or shootings in cities. No one had ever thought to do this. Rip the heart out and the body falls.

Back when there was still a Northern Ireland they had suffered murders of individual families and groups and more bombings and killings than anyone else. These had been reported on the national news and people had sympathised with them, but this was different and everyone felt it. The country had changed.

Practically all businesses had decided to close to allow their employees the time to mourn. Weatherspoon's were holding what they were laughably calling "Great Britain Day" in their pubs, with the special offer of a pint of Heineken for 99p to "Remember the Fallen." Kinsella had almost laughed out loud when she'd seen it was a Dutch brand. All the major religions were hosting services in their temples to remember the dead. The schools were all closed, public transport was suspended for the hour between 11.00 am and 12.00 pm, every internet and TV channel were showing at least one of the services. No doubt all would have their pictures fade gracefully between Westminster, their local city and this circus here. The attack had touched every facet of British life. It had shaken them in a way no bombing of a tube or bus or building could. This memory would last… for at least the next few minutes.

This wasn't a corrupted teenager with homemade explosives blowing up a bus. This had been precise, ruthless and without mercy. Little England didn't suffer the way London or Belfast had. Things like this didn't happen here. They were the safe ones, hidden away on their little protected vistas, limiting their access to the outside world and it to them. Driving into the local town for the supermarket, but otherwise living out their lives in the carefully selected and peaceful recluse. Never thinking that it was this that made them so vulnerable. So easily picked off when the planning was right. All it took was 40 people with an unshakeable belief and dedication to effectively end the village's existence and terrify the country like never before.

In the past four days, news outlets had reported on some of the measures people were now taking to protect themselves. "Burglar Alarm Sales Skyrocket"; "Steel Window Shutters Come to the UK"; "CCTV Cameras and Laser Tripwires." There had even been that guy in… she thought Lancashire but it might have been Yorkshire… who'd had armed police surround his house after a neighbour had reported him for trying to rig up a shotgun to automatically fire if he had any unwelcome visitors.

This was how you shock Britain today. London had suffered the effects of terrorism for well over 200 years. From the Suffragettes, IRA, Al Qaeda and ISIS, to Islamic Jihad, the Reformed IRA and various homegrown nutters. Terrorists had bombed buses, mowed down pedestrians with their cars, shot, stabbed and battered people for longer than most could remember. It was expected and mostly ignored. A bomb in London provoked an afternoon of focused news coverage, then people got on with their lives.

I Vow to Thee – William E. H. Walker

She remembered 7/7, although she was still young, and recalled watching the news unfold in the aftermath of those explosions. Then the next day she'd been on a bus heading to Marble Arch to meet her mother. Even when Islamic Jihad had remotely detonated two massive car bombs by the Tower of London and killed over 400 people, the very next day she had watched reporters talking about how "Britain refuses to bow down to terror"; "the tourists were out and about"; and "Londoners getting on with their day," and she'd thought at the time, *What does it take?*

London would require something more, something different to frighten it into submission. In a city of 10 million people, the death of 400 went pretty much unnoticed. What was required for London was something bigger, something devastating and broadcasted live to the world. A real showstopper.

Her nose itched now but she remained still. She thought about how the world hadn't bounced back as it had before. The sheer audacity had hit them hard, the way it had been carried out so precisely had shaken them to their core. Now they would remember. They wouldn't be allowed to forget it. She'd heard the village would be kept as a memorial and no doubt soon to be a tourist attraction for the morbid, but that was still in debate. Another memorial to the dead. Another reminder of our inability to deal with our problems. Still more to come. The world was full of memorials to terror, yet people never learned from them. Over time they simply fade and become a stopping point on a tour. A paragraph in a guidebook: "Here are the wire poles erected to remember those who died in the attack on the docks. Next, the home of Sir Isaac Newton."

The Colonel finished the list of names and took a step back from the podium. Reverend Colebatch inched forward and spoke a few words of prayer that ended with the audience joining him in an "Amen." Singh's commanding voice brought all to attention, and the bugler raised the brass to his lips and the forlorn notes of the Last Post wafted through the warm early-summer air.

As the last note died, a stillness descended. Birds stopped singing, the wind died down, not even a baby murmured. The whole world around them seemed to stop to remember those lost to bring about peace. Kinsella remembered a quote she had once heard: "For one priceless moment, all people on this Earth are truly one."

Then, at 12.00 pm, quietly at first but spreading quickly like a pathogen, the panic started.

11:06

Miller

'Please be seated.' The Bishop of Westminster's voice rang loud and clear through the speakers secreted in the Abbey's high walls. He stood at High Altar, hands held aloft in prayer, visible only to a few of the 2000 who had filed in over the past hour to pay homage to the fallen.

Miller sat in the front row, a look of what she hoped was dignified grief on her face, head bowed as she listened to the Bishop's prayers. From the corner of her eye she noted the camera pointing directly at her. She tried to be still under its gaze. She knew from her lessons back when just a junior minister, 'The temptation when one realises one is on camera...' her old Permanent Secretary, a fearsome-looking man of 60 with tufts of white fur-like hair sprouting from his head, nose and ears, had told her on her first day in the post of Housing Minister, '...is to act like one is a puppet on a string and gambol about as though one is suffering a fit.'

She remembered sitting behind her desk like a small child in school being demolished by a brutal maths teacher. 'One must conduct oneself with dignity and finesse.' He'd demonstrated this to her with graceful, almost ballerina-like movements of his arms, slow and particular. 'Small movements are exposed to the camera and emphasised. Arms should remain still, features controlled.' Here he had stood almost to attention, arms to his side and face still as stone. 'Thanks to Blair we spent many a year with politician's thinking they had to go about doing "normal things" such as going on a fairground ride, eating bacon rolls, dancing or...' A look of complete disdain, '...juggling.' He had sat down opposite her, his eyes boring into her. 'The public doesn't want to be ruled by their equals, they want their politicians to appear strong, stable, stoic. Politicians are meant to be admired and respected, therefore you must project that image every time you appear in public. Strong, stable, stoic.' He had looked down his nose at her and she had shrunk back into her chair at his gaze.

It had been clear from the off that he had been in charge. She had done as she was told and survived to be promoted. She had never forgotten his words and, though her first few appearances on television had been quite stunted and, as one commentator had commented, robotic, she'd found her flow and garnered some praise for her ability on screen. Now, on the biggest performance of her career to date, she held herself still, head bowed, hands clasped in front of her. Strong, mostly stable, stoic.

Beside her stood Marcus Thomas Eloquence Sanders, Vice President of the United States, smelling of expensive aftershave. He was a good foot taller than Miller's five foot seven inches. A giant in both stature and politics, he was rumoured to be the favourite to replace President McAstly when his second term ended in three years.

Miller had once heard a story about him that she couldn't help but believe. At a fundraising event, while he was running for VP, he'd overheard a man commenting on his name. Laughing about it and wondering what sort of parents would call their child Eloquence. Once he had been elected that man had found his assets frozen and himself on a plane to India within 24 hours without a penny to his name.

Marcus was what Americans now called a Modern-Day Puritan. A few years back in a pre-Trump America, his views might have been considered extreme and even racist. But after the assassination attempt nine years ago where Muslim extremists were wrongly blamed, the right-leaning US had taken a fair old leap into almost total fascism.

President Flanders had succeeded in banning all immigration from the Middle East and South America and installed religious teaching in all schools. President McAstley had banned the preaching of Islam and created the Expulsion and Liberation Program. In six intense months, more than half of those born outside of the US had been expelled from the country. By the end of McAstley's first year, attempts to immigrate to the US had fallen by 95 percent.

Over 21 million people were "relocated" home. A program so massive no commercial flights took off or landed in the US for its duration and reportedly cost the US over $1 trillion. Evangelical churches reported a rise in attendance of over 200 percent, and the politicians spoke openly of their disdain for non-western cultures and other religions.

There had been reports of people never making it back to their country, but these rumours were quashed and denied. The United Nations protested as the USA swung further and further toward extremist ideologies. But these protests were all but ignored as the US continued its drive for puritanism.

They eventually tried to appear to cooperate. They investigated the missing and sent teams to interview those expelled, but nothing happened. No conclusions were drawn and no penalties exacted. The US military was still the largest in the world, and with an aging Putin now in his sixth term as Russian president and turning his sights on Eastern Europe after completing the annexation of Georgia, they needed the US in the club too much to protest too loudly.

I Vow to Thee – William E. H. Walker

Now, standing beside her, his face set to a sombre and stern expression, he whispered 'Amen' at the end of the prayer and turned to smile down on her, a surprisingly joyful twinkle in his eyes. Miller didn't like him; he was too extreme for her. In many ways British politics had been saved by the reintroduction of God, but nothing like what they had done.

Finding themselves competing with the once fringe elements such as the Reform Party, the Tories and Labour had to react. The Labour leader Connor Franklin introduced the "Christian Britain Bill" to parliament proposing to change the rules requiring all schools in England and Wales to teach only Christian theology and British values.

The Reform Party leader was forced to support the bill despite not wanting to show support for the government and despite their leadership being mostly atheists. All the opinion polls showed huge support and thus it had sailed through the Commons and Lords and had entered into law inside two months.

After that, politicians gradually started to talk about their trust in God, asking the Almighty to bless the country and support their endeavours. Over time this became the norm to the point where these days no minister or politician could even think about finishing any speech without thanking God for something, even if the link was tenuous at best. God was thanked for the good harvest, for the hard work of charity workers and the quality of pheasants at a shoot.

Attending church became part of the routine for all in the political sphere and many debates or deals were worked out during the sermon. Soon parliament reintroduced prayers at the start and end of each session and filled the House of Lords with bishops and priests. One year on from the law passing, Christianity was firmly entrenched in the language of British politics. Just not quite in the heart.

Getting God into the general populace proved relatively simple. In an attempt to show they were the ones truly responsible for the Christian Britain Bill, the Reform Party created the "British Education & Understanding Initiative" with a mandate to educate the public in a way that didn't disrupt their everyday lives.

The initiative worked on three fronts: social media was harnessed to promote the anti-Islamic agenda. Pages and articles created that showed so-called rape gangs and religions rioters in blurry video footage. Youths assaulting people supposedly because they were British or Christian, old men talking to young girls in apparent grooming attempts. Carefully crafted to be just enough to convince the watcher without giving away the truth of the footage.

TV documentaries were commissioned to show how the rise in crime in the UK was linked to the rise in immigration.

Newspapers, now on their last legs, were given information for raids on brothels and drug dens to report, in graphic detail, how the perpetrators were from Eastern Europe or the Middle East. Photographs of drug-addled white women were splashed across the pages next to bearded sullen-looking men with headlines such as "This Is Why They Come Here!" and "Look At What They Do To Us!" Anti-Islamic feelings in the country were at their highest recorded level ever.

Noting the success of BEUI, the Labour-Lib Dem coalition decided to copy it. They changed the anti-Islamic message to one more centrist and Christian leaning. Now social media pages carried headlines such as "Why Being Kind Can Help You Live Longer"; "Christianity Saved By Baby"; and "Paying Taxes Makes You Sexy To Women." The initial response to the changes was poor and the initiative was dropped after just six months. It was reinitialised by the British Christian Party, who once again changed the focus to overtly Christian, but with a heavy emphasis on nationalism.

Thanks to the experience of former Reform Party members, the new Christian clickbait filled social media. "Lose 20 Pounds Through Prayer"; "Christianity Cured my Depression"; "British Christians Are The Sexiest Men On Earth Says Model." Again, TV shows were utilised with the creation of new comedy and documentaries expounding on the virtues of being a British Christian. How being Christian was a mandatory element of being a "True British Citizen."

By the time Miller was elected the view had moved into the mainstream, with many teenagers competing to be the first to "come out" as Christian. Suddenly Netflix, Amazon, Google and their ilk were trying to appeal to Christian audiences. ITV's reality TV show "Sex Shop" was picketed by over 3000 teenagers outraged that it went against Christian teachings.

Christian music was downloaded in increasing numbers. Celebrities started sharing stories online about how pious they were. Videos of wannabe TV and music stars praying or ranting against Islam became commonplace. Vlogs and blogs on everything from bible knowledge and the essence of Christianity to how to get rich through God flowed through the internet like a tidal wave.

Still, it was nothing compared to the US where it was now illegal to practice anything other than Christianity and Judaism. Over there, women could be arrested for dressing provocatively or for disobeying their husband.

True, it was harder these days for non-white British people to progress in business or public office, although no specific laws prevented this. In the US those of Asian or Middle Eastern descent needed to carry a chip in their arm to prove they had the right to be there. If the chip were damaged or unreadable, they could be removed from the country without notice.

Gangs of youths would make sport of attacking people of colour and attempting to break their chips to get them sent home, even if they were born in the US. Just last year a gang of 12- to 15-year-old boys had attacked and raped a girl of 13 on her way back from school. She had been found by a neighbour and taken to hospital. When it was discovered her chip was broken, she was refused treatment and died of her injuries.

What remained of left-wing power in the US protested most strongly but, outside of California, there was little resistance and publicity. This was one of the catalysts for California's current efforts to secede from the Union.

***

The service progressed all too slowly for Miller and she was finding it difficult to remain focused. She'd had a rough night's sleep and was feeling a little light-headed. The small nip before the service was wearing off and she felt herself shiver slightly. They finished the last line of the Lord's Prayer and Prince George, Duke of Wessex, rose from his pew and stepped forward to stand at the lectern.

He was to read out the names of all those who had lost their lives. Those in attendance were expected to remain standing while he did and then for the two minutes silence that was to follow. Miller's feet were already sore. Definitely the wrong day to wear high heels, but she had liked the way they finished her look.

In his soft melodious voice, the Prince spoke each name slowly and carefully. He was always a good public speaker despite his young age. His father stood to her left and Miller, glancing at him, thought she saw pride in his downcast eyes. She knew from her weekly meetings with the King that the Royal Family had concerns over the direction the country was taking but that they would not interfere directly with her plans.

Since the death of the Queen, there had been a slow but steady reduction in warm feelings toward the Royal Family which Miller had tried to help reverse. Appointed by God they may be, but they'd never really recovered from her death and the vacuum it left. There were high hopes for the Prince when he came to his throne, but that still seemed to be some way off.

Miller's legs were aching by the time the Prince called out the last name of the list, took one pace back and lowered his head in prayer. She shifted slightly, adjusting her weight as the bugle rang out. It was going to be a long day, with a discussion on everything from war to trade to peace treaties in Africa

I Vow to Thee – William E. H. Walker

and hopes of goodwill in South America. Miller was so lost in thought she hardly noticed as the last note faded away. The whole Abbey stilled and settled into silence.

The distant drone of the vast crowd outside, which had permeated every moment of quiet of the service thus far, had vanished. From all about the vaulted space came the light noises of small movement. The shifting of feet, a sword nudging a belt, order papers being shuffled between fingers. Across the world, people had stopped to remember. To pray, to hope for a better world.

Then she heard the explosion, and everything went to hell.

11:42

Laoch

The 400,000-strong crowd of the sanctimonious, self-righteous grief whores filled every crevice from Marble Arch to Parliament Square like sewer rats. The vermin climbed over each other, pushed and cajoled, squeezed into every pocket of space, squashed in closer and closer so they could hear the pathetic crowing of the oversized Bishop of Westminster through the huge speakers next to the massive screens.

They were here to be seen, not because they care about those who died. It's that strange mix of fear and sexual frisson that brings them together. Like being choked by a lover. You know they're going to stop, but the excitement is not knowing when. You're helpless, but you love it.

Laoch knew that a part of them wanted it to have been them. To know that their family was gathered around crying over their lost life. Their names read out in the churches and memorial services up and down the country before being indelibly carved into the stone or metal of a memorial. That at least would give their pathetic little lives some meaning. They'd be remembered for something rather than just disappearing off into nothing after the deaths of their grandchildren. Who remembers their great grandparents? No one. His history teacher had once told him, "We each live three lives. The lives we live today, the memories we give to our children and the mentions they make of us to their children. Beyond that, we are forgotten." This had terrified the boy Laoch. It had been meant as a prompt to do something with their lives, to ensure they would live on past those who knew them. But it had done nothing but scare the living piss out of his six-year-old self. For a long time, life had been too much for Laoch – he had run scared from its inevitability, hating its finality and frailty. He had buried himself in his attempts to hide from it. The truth was that he'd only joined the church to find some meaning to life. To find something that mattered. But even that failed. He'd found himself washed up, alone and more frightened than ever. But that was then. He had meaning now. He would be remembered now.

He sipped his whisky as he watched them pass by beneath his Mayfair flat before checking the time.

I Vow to Thee – William E. H. Walker

His watch said 22 minutes. The service was being broadcast across the world so that all may come together in a great mutual embrace of self-congratulation at their own goodness and godliness disguised as grief. Pathetic. The TV was giving a thankfully muted close-up of the Bishop standing by the High Altar reading a prayer. Even with the sound off, he knew what it was.

'Lord, do not abandon us in our desolation. Keep us safe in the midst of trouble and complete your purpose for us, through your steadfast love and faithfulness, in Jesus Christ our Saviour. Amen'

It seems a bit pointless to ask for God to keep you safe to complete your purpose when your purpose was to die to start a revolution. He downed what was left in his glass and poured himself another. *One last one*, he said to himself. He'd need the courage today. Today was going to hurt. 'For the greater good,' he said out loud, toasting the air and downing the whisky in one. The fiery liquid warmed him from his lips to the pit of his stomach.

His watch said 18 minutes.

Prince George stood at the lectern, evidently reading the names of the dead.

Okay, maybe one more. He poured himself another, larger whisky and held it just short of his lips. 'Lord, what we do today we do for you. We do this to give you a better world. We do this to rid your blessed country of Britain of the heathen bloodsuckers that infest your land. I know you believe in what we do. Please keep me safe today. Amen.' He downed the whisky.

The time said 10 minutes.

He was pacing now. Outside the sound of the crowd, though muted by the thick triple glazing, was incessant. The white noise of insects. On the TV the Prince had a sombre expression as he read out each name.

Why had he burned the instructions this morning? Why hadn't he waited until now so he could double-check? Did he have to stand four paces from the window or five? He slowed his breathing. *Calm down, you know it's five. Five paces back and two to the left.*

Without thinking, he walked over to the wall beside the window. Apparently, according to the green-eyed woman, there was a large steel girder running right up through that section, but to all intents and purposes it was just another bit of wall. What if they'd made a mistake? What if they had the wrong plans? He tapped the wall and there was a dull thud. He crossed the room and tapped the wall there. The same dull thud. What if they were wrong?

Six minutes.

I Vow to Thee – William E. H. Walker

He closed his eyes and calmed himself. These people, or at least this woman, had managed to get him here with no apparent difficulties. She had been right in everything she had said so far. She'd shown him the plans, walked through it all with him and he was going to be fine. He opened his eyes and took another deep breath, held it for four then released slowly. Another. And another. Not helping. Maybe one more drink.

Four minutes

He poured the glass halfway to the top before he realised what he was doing and stopped. His hand was starting to shake. On the TV the Prince turned a page and the camera panned to a bugler, who placed the instrument to his lips. Last Post time. Shit.

Three minutes.

He should get ready; he should be in position. He walked over to the window looking out over Hyde Park Corner. Outside 100,000 people waited for their turn to trudge slowly through to Parliament Square. There to stand and do what? What do they do when they get there? Mill around for a minute and then go to the pub? What was the point in all the walking?

His eyes focused on a mother with two girls. The children were grinning up at her, clearly loving the crowd around them and having no clue as to why they were there. Following them was a man with a young boy on his shoulders, the boy holding his father's hands tightly as they moved slowly down the road. An elderly woman holding on tight to her walking frame, a look of determination on her face. A group of teenagers sitting on a wall, vaping and watching the big screen set up to show the service. Wellington Arch surrounded by picnicking families. An aging black couple walking hand in hand, looking sincere and sorrowful. Her, frumpy and round, carrying a bouquet of flowers. Him, tall and straight-backed with dreads flowing down passed his arse. *Fucking immigrants*, he thought.

Across the city, bells rang out three times. Everywhere people stopped what they were doing. They put down their shopping, turned down their radio, readying themselves for the two minutes' silence.

Two minutes.

The world was mute. The world was still. He walked back to stand before the TV. The pictures slowly faded between the crowd, dignitaries and Royals, all stood with bowed heads of prayer. They showed London, Edinburgh, Cardiff and Lesser Worburston itself. Now the Sydney Opera House, the Eiffel Tower, Brandenburg Gate, and The White House all lit in the colours of the British flag. He stood watching the pictures change, showing those at home that the whole world stood with them. That they weren't alone.

I Vow to Thee – William E. H. Walker

Shit. He should be in position. He half-ran to the window, jerking to a halt, eyes locked with the centre of the cross that separated the panes of glass. Taking one last look at the mass of scum outside, he spun round 180 degrees to face the room. He moved too quickly, causing his head to spin. Maybe one too many?

Carefully, he took four paces before twisting like a drunken soldier, 90 degrees and taking two paces to his right. Then he turned 90 degrees again and stopped, facing the wall. The whisky jiggling in his hand and a silent prayer in his head.

One minute.

He stared at the wall. He didn't see the slight indentations in the wallpaper, the patterns created by the light reflecting around the room. He simply starred like a cow before slaughter. And he was sweating. A thick ribbon of moisture ran down his spine, gluing his robe to his back and making it itch.

Surely it's time now? Surely it must be? He wanted to look at the TV, but it was behind him and he had not the will to move.

Had he taken five paces or four? Was it meant to be five paces or four? Or six? No, five. Or four. Shit!

It must be time.

Outside the world was still silent.

It must be time now. It must be.

A balloon flew past his window. Or was it a pigeon?

Had something gone wrong? Had they failed? They must have done; they must have failed.

He lifted the glass to his lips, almost relieved. He'd not wanted to be hurt, not wanted to do this even though he saw how it would benefit him. How he could achieve so much more with just a little sacrifice. But something had gone wrong and he'd not have to go through with it. Thank God.

Then, far off in the distance, he heard Big Ben chime once. Then he heard a pop. Just a soft pop really, but a pop nonetheless. It seemed, somehow, insignificant. Like when a bubble gum bubble bursts.

Then he heard a bang and realised the pop was a bang but just further away.

Lord keep me safe, he thought as a third, much louder bang reverberated through the building, shaking the floor beneath him. Outside the screaming had started. The mass blind unthinking panic of the crowd.

I Vow to Thee – William E. H. Walker

He made to raise the whisky to his lips but at that moment the glass in all the windows blew into the building, the pressure of the explosion flung him backward as glass and brick tore at his skin. Dust billowed into the room, blinding him, driving its way up his nose and down his throat.

He hit the back wall with a sickening crack and collapsed into a ball, all the air expelled from his lungs. He lay where he'd fallen, unable to comprehend and process the noise and movement around him. His vision was nothing but sparks of white, like fireworks exploding in his pupils. His world was reduced to the sensations of the choking dust, the fragments landing on him, the ringing in his ears, torn skin and clothing and his total lack of ability to do anything about any of it.

The noise seemed to go on for a lifetime. From his left he heard creaking, which grew into a rumble and then a roar. He opened his watering eyes as the wall on the far side of the room simply disappeared in a curtain of dust and grime taking part of the floor, along with the grand piano and bar with it. He saw it all, his mouth open in a silent scream.

Get out of here, his mind yelled at him. *Move or die.*

He tried to stand but his legs were jelly. Slowly, he stretched out his bleeding arms and dragged himself forward. Belly to the floor, he scraped his way across the debris, fingertip by bloody fingertip to the door, and tried to rise to reach the door handle. It took all his effort, but he eventually made it and opened the door a fraction, just enough to squeeze himself through. The corridor outside was a sea of shattered glass and brick. A woman, a neighbour he thought, sat on the floor, a large fragment of glass protruding from her neck, blood soaking her Louis Vuitton top. His mouth opened and closed by itself as his eyes met the cold, dead stare. He hardly noticed the urine staining his crotch.

He coughed and wheezed and tried to pull himself over the debris, small murmurs escaping his lips as the glass cut into his arms, legs and torso. He tried to move but he could feel his body giving up, could feel oblivion about to overwhelm him. He needed to leave, to get free of the smoke and dust, to be the hero he was meant to be. The one who survived. It was God's will. God's task. But instead he choked and spluttered and gagged and weakened, his muscles gave in and he flopped to the floor, blood welling about him from hundreds of cuts. His head sank onto the carpet. *God's plan.* He closed his eyes.

I Vow to Thee – William E. H. Walker

12:02

Freemark

They were running. She was scared and panicked and running. Everyone was. The news of the explosions in London had come through not 30 seconds ago and infected the crowd of about 2000 who had gathered outside St Mary's Church in Banbury to hear the vicar administer prayers for the victims.

Now she was running, and she was frightened. Beside her, a man pushed a woman into the wall of the church as he fled. She hit the solid stone hard and fell to the ground, blood flowing from a cut in her forehead. Freemark stopped to help her and was immediately put to the floor by another man desperate to escape. She hit her head, blinding her, scraping her arm and making her bite her tongue. Someone stood on her leg and she cried out, blood welling in her mouth from her wounded tongue. Then there were hands about her, lifting her up high. A tall, broad man was hauling her onto his shoulder and carrying her through the crowd. She saw a second man lift the other woman and carry her behind them. Freemark was in a daze as she was carried, helpless through the panicked throng. He held her there as they made their way through the graveyard, down the alley and onto the high street.

He pushed his way through the crowd of running, screaming, terrified people and into the doorway of Cash Converters. There he took her from his shoulder and deposited her gently on her feet. 'You all right love?' he asked. His voice surprisingly gentle for such a big man.

She nodded. Her head, arm and leg were sore, but she was okay. 'Thank you.' She managed to fumble out the word.

'Best we stay here, love. You wait behind me, it's a little crazy out there right now.' He moved between her and the crowd who continued to stream past.

Freemark shook her head clear and looked at her arm. Her top was torn and there was blood from a scrape. Her trouser leg had the perfect print of a large boot on it. It would bruise but it felt okay. She watched from behind the big man as the crowd started to thin.

I Vow to Thee – William E. H. Walker

He turned to her. 'You need a hospital love?' His face was the type you'd expect to see on a retired cage fighter, more scar than skin, but the look in his eyes was of genuine concern and care.

She shook her head. 'No, I'll be fine. Thank you though, I think you might have saved my life.'

He grinned. 'Nah.' He sounded slightly embarrassed. 'You sure you all right though?'

She nodded again. 'Just scraped a bit, I'll be fine. My car's only up the road.'

He nodded at her and looked down the street. 'Right, well, if you're okay I'm going to go find my lads. We got split up.'

She thanked him again and he left, heading up the road toward Banbury Cross. She looked for her phone in her bag. The screen was cracked and some of the OLED had leaked out, but it was still working. She found her husband's number and put the phone to her ear. Three small beeps and then nothing. Confused, she checked the screen. No signal. *FUCK.*

A drop of water hit the screen. Rain? But it was clear skies and warm. It wasn't raining, she was crying. The realisation took her by surprise, and she slumped against the door of the closed shop, weeping uncontrollably, her chest heaving as her breath caught in her throat. She stayed there for some time, huddled over, lost in a world of trampling feet, fear and death so near it terrified her.

As she regained control, she struggled shakily to her feet. Wiping the tears from her face, she sniffed back snot and ran her sleeve over her nose. Maddie, she needed to see Maddie. Now. She half-ran, half-stumbled down the street toward the Fresh 'N' Frozen car park, constantly checking her phone as she went. Still no signal.

The door handle failed to recognise her fingerprint and she realised her hand was muddy. She spat on it and wiped it against her trousers. The door opened. She pressed the start button and switched on the radio.

'…very little information as to what sort of devices these were but they were clearly immensely powerful and will have caused many casualties, as well as widespread damage to nearby buildings. No word yet on the safety of the Prime Minister or Royal Family but we can tell you that Westminster Abbey was not caught in the explosions.'

'Jesus,' she said out loud.

'In case you're just joining us, there have been four large explosions in London, all focused on the crowd who came out today for the memorial for the attack on Lesser Worburston. These explosions appear to be bombs aimed at causing maximum casualties on those who attended the public service to mourn this week's terrorist attack. They don't seem to be aimed at political figures but at civilians. On

I Vow to Thee – William E. H. Walker

families and friends. Ordinary people who had come to London today to show their support and mourn, now finding themselves the victims of another senseless and violent attack on our nation by, we might assume, the same group who carried out the first attack on Lesser Worburston…'

Freemark slumped back, stunned. The news there had been a bomb in London had caused panic at the church, but she didn't realise it was four. And aimed at the mourners in the street rather than the politicians and Royalty in Westminster. Her journalist instincts kicked in. *Easy target*, she thought.

Surely there would have been precautions? There would have been police, dogs, cameras, helicopters. How did they manage to do this? The broadcast continued.

'We've just had word that King Charles has arrived safely back at Buckingham Palace and is said to be unhurt. Also, news coming in now that Prime Minister Millar is safe and has been taken to a strategic location to coordinate the response. Just to describe what we're looking at, the first explosion occurred in Trafalgar square just as the two-minute silence was ending. Nelson's Column remains standing but the buildings around the square have lost all their glass, although Canada House and the National Gallery seem unaffected. The second explosion was just seconds later on Pall Mall outside the Reform Club and opposite St. James's Square. The front of the Reform Club has been taken off by the force of the explosion, which seems to have torn a hole in the roadway though it's difficult to see through the large plume of smoke and dust raised by the blast. The third was outside Green Park Tube Station where again there is a large crater left in the road. The building over the station has half-collapsed and flames can be seen from within. The last and biggest explosion was on Park Lane. Here you can clearly see the damage caused to the road and surrounding buildings. There is a block of flats next to where the bomb went off, the front of which has been destroyed, so clearly there will be casualties there also. Emergency services were quickly at the scene of each explosion, but the sheer scale of this attack must surely be causing them problems. I think we can expect the death toll to be in the thousands, if not high thousands. It has been estimated up to 400,000 were in London today, it is simply unbelievable that this can happen to u—' She clicked off the radio.

Maddie! She needed her daughter. She needed to hold her, feel the life within her. She rammed the car into reverse, spun it around and then thumped it into drive and out of the car park.

Police cars, ambulances and fire engines were already gathered outside the church as she hit 70 down the Southam Road toward Oxford, and home.

She arrived outside their house in Botley 40 minutes later having broken every speed limit and had several near-misses with other clearly panicked drivers.

Leaving the car in their driveway with its door open, she ran to the house. Maddie was playing with her robot dog in the living room, attempting to show it what rolling over looked like. She glanced up as Freemark entered.

'Mummy hurt?' She looked so pained.

Freemark swept her daughter up into her arms and held her tight to her chest. The little girl responded by wrapping her arms and legs around her mother so tight she threatened to cut off her circulation.

Stephen came in from the kitchen, saw the cuts on Freemark's face and moved quickly to her. She was crying softly. He took them both in his arms and kissed his wife's cheek. She was home. Safe. She was home. She sobbed quietly in Stephen's arms; her wonderful daughter's face buried in her neck. Safe.

12:06

Kinsella

She watched the Colonel barking out orders to his troops, watched them run to the helicopters powering up their rotors in the next field, watched them disappear south toward London. Beside her Singh was speaking urgently into his phone, trying to get more information on what had happened. Suss was sitting in the car next to them, shaking her head slightly in utter disbelief as she listened to the radio presenter describe the four massive explosions that had ripped through the crowds in London.

Singh hung up the phone. 'We've got to get these people dispersed carefully, then most of us will return to Oxford to monitor the situation.' His eyes scanned the angry crowd. 'The Prime Minister will no doubt declare a National Emergency and they'll most likely put a travel ban in place. Hillingham!' The stocky, balding Superintendent jogged over to join them. 'We'll need officers to cover the motorway slip roads, Oxford Airport and all the train stations if they do decide to put a ban in place, sort that will you?' Hillingham nodded briskly and walked away, calling officers to him.

'Jones!'

A tall, willowy Superintendent stopped dead in her tracks. 'Sir.'

'You're in charge of crowd dispersal,' Singh barked at her.

'Yes, Sir,' she replied, marching off in the direction of a group of officers.

Kinsella wondered what duties he'd have for her. He did look impressive at times like this, calm and determined, like she assumed Moses would have been in front of the Pharos. Except Singh was Sikh, but that wasn't his fault.

He turned to face her; eyes set. 'Kinsella, Suss... Suss! Turn that crap off!' Suss rushed to obey and stood, nervous, before him.

'I want you two back in Oxford in the control room with DCI Wentworth while I finish up here, I'll join you shortly. I want to make sure panic doesn't spread and there are no other...' A pause. 'Incidents.'

I Vow to Thee – William E. H. Walker

A PC ran over to him. 'Sir, reports from Banbury say the crowd at St Mary's panicked at the news, there have been a number of injuries.'

Without pause, Singh Turned back to Suss. 'Fine, you go to Banbury and see what's needed there. Kinsella, you're to Oxford.' He waited for a second and neither woman moved. 'Now, if you please.'

They realised his meaning and hurried off. Suss jumped into her car and turned the stereo back on before firing up the siren and lights and speeding off.

Kinsella got into her car and followed more slowly. Once out the field she turned on her lights and accelerated down the tiny country road. No stereo for her, she already knew what had happened.

She was focused on her breathing: in for four, hold for four, back out again. Keep calm, remain focused. She kept this up till she felt a little light-headed and was overtaking cars on the B road to the M40 junction at Banbury.

As she crested a hill, she made out Suss' car in the low ground ahead of her overtaking on an S-bend. She was going for it. Kinsella knew they could track her car, so she kept the speed up and sirens on as she joined the M40 heading south.

In her pocket, she heard her phone go off. Moving into the outside lane she enabled autopilot and retrieved the handset. A notification informing her she had a message from Nan. The phone recognised her eye and fingerprint and opened. "Grandad thanks you for your well wishes. He'd like to know what you're up to these days. Can you come and see him anytime soon?" She took a minute to digest the meaning and then replied, "Of course, I'm staying in Kidlington today. I'll message you later." Replacing the phone in her pocket she increased her speed to 120mph.

The tires skidded slightly as she arrived at the station in Kidlington. Once inside she made straight for the major incident control room where she found DCI Wentworth chewing through what appeared to be, based on the pile of wrappers beside him, at least his 10th nicotine gummy sweet.

He looked surprised to see her. 'Singh send you?' he asked without preamble.

She nodded. 'Yes, boss. Wanted an update.'

'We're fucked,' he replied simply, pointing to the TV mounted on the wall. It showed drone footage of four plumes of smoke climbing into the clear blue sky above central London.

'Wow.' Kinsella breathed the word. The sight was enough to take anyone's breath away.

'Indeed.' DCI Wentworth popped another nicotine sweet into his mouth. 'We've got everyone coming in already, but the damage is done. There's been a stampede at the memorial service in town, a few hospitalised – including a small girl who was trampled. High Wycombe, Milton Keynes, Banbury,

Swindon and Reading all saw something similar but on a smaller scale, no major injuries there so far as we've heard. The military is flying into London to control the situation there.' He wiped the beads of sweat from his brow. 'We've had over 100 calls about suspicious people and packages, which we have to investigate, but most of the officers were out at the events either on duty or attending a service. We've called them all up and anyone with a warrant badge on them is out looking into all these reports or on crowd control.' The list came out in a rush. He picked the sweet out of his mouth and looked at it, holding it out like it was pure evil. 'And this shite is fuckin' awful! Someone give me a fag!' A sergeant leaned over the desk and offered him one from his packet.

'Walk with me Kinsella.' He raised his voice, head turning to take in the room. 'You lot, any more calls about packages give them to one of the teams based on their postcode. Ensure the message gets out on local radio, all businesses are too close for the remainder of the day, including taxis. Anything urgent, I'm right outside.'

Kinsella followed him out of the building where he lit the cigarette and drew on it gratefully. 'And they say these things will kill me.'

'How bad was it?' Kinsella declined the proffered cigarette.

'As bad as the village. More casualties probably but…' He shook his head, uncomprehending. 'Bombs in the crowd, big enough they took the front off buildings.'

Kinsella raised her eyebrows. 'How?'

'Fuck knows. Hidden on people? In bins? We've not got a clue if I'm honest. Well, not out here in the sticks anyway, we've just got to deal with the issues it's caused us. I'm going to need your help.' It was an order, not a request, she knew, but he always liked to make it sound like it was a favour.

'Of course, anything I can do.' She smiled softly. He was a good-looking man, although vain. It was said he was forever in the toilets checking himself in the mirrors. She knew he had started dying his hair, trying to hide the encroaching grey. His skin was smooth though, like polished mahogany, and he wore expensive aftershave.

'You can head into town and deal with the shutting down of shops. There aren't many that have chosen to stay open, but the pubs were planning on a roaring trade after the service, and the fucking Weatherspoons are full of pissed up idiots who'll be spoiling for a fight. Given that this attack's come so quick after the last I'm worried about riots or revenge. We need to shut the whole sodding town down and get through the night without some twat committing a murder. Can you organise that?'

She nodded. 'Sure. Do we really have no information as to how this was done?'

'Northing coming through to me, I'm too fucking low in the food chain, but there's been no warnings about what to look out for so I'm guessing they've not got a scooby.'

Kinsella nodded, her body tingling. 'Fine, well, if I need to know to look out for anything, in particular, you'll let me know, right?'

'Do I look like it's my first day?' He held his arms open.

She smiled apologetically at that. 'Sorry, boss. Oh, and please can you call Singh? He'll be on his way back here now but will want to be briefed before he gets here.'

'They seek him here…' It was an old joke of Wentworth's and Kinsella smiled dutifully at it as she walked back to her car, still unsure what the actual joke was.

'Can I get military backup if needed?' she called to him.

'Haven't a clue, I'll let you know,' he called back, stubbing out his cigarette and heading inside.

She climbed back into her car and pulled her phone from her pocket. She opened a new message to Nan and entered "If I'm honest, I'm not up to much really. X" She clicked send and then deleted the message chain before starting the motors and heading into Oxford.

12:15

Suss

Her car overtook an old petrol Focus on an S-bend and she cursed the driver for not paying more attention. She was in shock, she knew it, but as usual she surprised herself by how calm she was.

When she was six, growing up in the Sumner Estate in Peckham, she'd found herself cornered by three older kids who wanted her skateboard. One of the boys had pushed her, causing her to scrape the skin from her palm and replacing it with stinging specks of grit, her vision hadn't blurred with tears, her lip hadn't quivered. Her brow had set, her vision cleared, her pulse slowed. With deliberate, calculated movements, she'd kicked the boy hard in the balls before she'd even risen from the floor. She remembered picking up the skateboard and holding it like a baseball bat, daring them to approach. They'd backed away calling her names. They had not tried it again. Her parents always told her to turn the other cheek or run away, but she could never seem to bring herself to do it.

She was so lucky to have them, she'd not been the easiest of teens to live with. She had found it difficult to fit in at school. On reflection she knew this was partly due to her unwillingness to accept the truth about her sexuality. School had been both stupidly easy and frustratingly slow. The classes, too large and too long, understaffed, teachers underpaid and undervalued, pupils too interested in their social status and social media. In a class of 40 kids, Suss found herself isolated in an environment where educational attainment wasn't as important as who followed you on Instagram. Where kids spent more time on selfies than homework. She hadn't known how to fit in so had tried everything. At first, the good student, hand up first, always with the right answer. Then, after hearing the girls taking the piss out of her, she'd started acting up. Correcting the teachers came first, then turning up late, then not at all. When she had still found herself alone, she'd made efforts to get in with the pretty girls. The "Look-I've-got-200-likes-on-my-bikini-pic" girls. Tamara, Zahra and Abeda. The three most popular girls she knew.

She'd watched hours and hours of YouTube videos on contouring, eyeshadow, hair styling and fashion. Her wardrobe changed from comfortable to risqué. She had developed her online profile. Spent

I Vow to Thee – William E. H. Walker

her evenings snapping hundreds of selfies to find just the right one to share on her feed. At the weekend she would visit the tourist hotspots with her friends, spending the day snapping photos of each other with this week's haircut, this week's dress or this week's makeup. Her cosmetics and clothes collection grew steadily until her mother asked her how she was affording it all. She had lied, telling her it was all from charity shops or her friends. She'd got better at hiding it after that.

The competition between the group of friends grew with the stockpile of clothing. Each trying to outdo the other with the number and enthusiasm of their followers. Sharing how many likes they had was suddenly not enough. "I've had 20 dick pics this week"; "This 50-year-old guy contacted me." She was not immune to it all. At 15 she was overjoyed to be able to tell her friends about her new 20-year-old boyfriend. The man she'd lost her virginity to. The man who had left her in the car park after they'd done it. The man who abandoned her 10 miles from home with no way of getting back. That was the beginning of the end. The long, tedious walk home in the rain, wondering if it was all worth it? The final nails had been the change from selfies in bikinis to naked selfies on Snapchat, to naked selfies with the hashtag "cumtribute." She couldn't work herself up to doing it and her supposed friends had all laughed at her and called her names. To keep them onside she had agreed to let them take photos of her in her underwear. She hadn't realised until too late that they'd sent them to every number in her phone. The memory of her mother's tears stung to this day, although her father's cold silence was worse. He hadn't said a word, just closed the living room door to her, leaving her alone in the hall. She had cried all night. The following morning the clothes and makeup were gone. The friends, well, that was a different story. Abeda she caught on her own outside the local Co-op. She'd punched her until her nose broke and her lips bled.

Tamara's parents received the photos she posted online. Screenshots of the conversation's she'd had with a plethora of men, most twice her age. They'd move out shortly after that. Zahra she followed to the shopping centre, waited until she had shoplifted clothing and makeup, then called the police on her. Still, it hadn't made her feel better. Her father still wasn't speaking to her.

She threw herself into her schooling and left with 11 GCSEs at grade nine. Her mother had practically squeezed the life out of her when she'd told them. Her father had hugged her for the first time in months. She hadn't been able to help herself, she'd cried at his warm touch.

She had missed the chance to apply for college so she went off to find work. Her new persona, the ripped jeans and vintage T-shirts, hadn't gone down well with prospective employers so she'd found herself working on the checkout in the local Aldi. The job was dull, the people sullen and resentful, her manager bossy and frustrating. One colleague made life difficult, his inability to take no for an answer ending with her knee in his bollocks and his nose bloodied. Her mother's reaction to the news of her sacking had surprised her, she had been almost proud.

With no reference to call on, her father got her a job with a friend of his at the local kebab shop. It was sweaty, greasy work, but she had to admit she enjoyed it. Dan, the son of the owner, helped, their secret rendezvous adding a thrill to the daily grind.

Life had changed after her father had lost his job. His withdrawal from the world and loss of income had made life harder for all of them.

That's when the thieving started again. Small items, initially. Tea bags, a loaf of bread, things they needed. Before long though, she was trying new ideas. She started working short cons such as "ringing in the changes" and enlisted a friend for the lost dog routine. She told her parents she was working at an office in the City, but each day she would go into town and work the punters. She hid most of the money in two shoe boxes in her bedroom, careful to only spend roughly what she would have made for a bottom-of-the-ladder job in an office. She worked all day at the cons but still couldn't resist the supposed easy target for theft. And that's where she met her. Debs had been off duty, shopping in Tesco when she'd spotted Suss slipping a loaf of bread into her bag. She'd followed up through the supermarket and arrested her just after payment.

The connection was instant, for Suss at least. She told her everything. Her life, her father's problems, her hopes, her criminal history – it all spilled out to the kind, sparkly-eyed stunner in the Tesco manager's office.

To her amazement, Debs had let her off. She'd taken her from the store and driven her home. She'd gone up to the flat with her and met her parents. But she hadn't told them what Suss had done. She'd just introduced herself as a friend and pretended nothing had happened. Suss could have kissed her for that.

They'd started meeting up on a regular basis for drinks or a meal. Never describing them as dates, but never shying away from the possibility. Suss found herself helpless, falling so hard and so fast yet totally unafraid. To her, it was as though they were just meant to be together. It was simply fate.

On the evening of their fifth non-date date, Debs had surprised her with a proposition. The Labour-Lib Dem Coalition had a program designed to attract the best and brightest of the "BAME" community into the police force and Debs encouraged her to apply. Suss found her fascinating. As smart as her, but with the added bonus of confidence and experience. Never condescending or patronising. Always kind.

That evening they had discussed how her life would go if she continued down the path she was on. Suss saw that she was right. She was clever, but far too impulsive. She would eventually be caught again and this time probably end up in prison. She was surprised to find so much appeal in the idea of police work. It wasn't until Debs had asked her to picture her mother's face when she saw her in handcuffs that Suss was totally swayed. It was as if Debs knew that would decide it for her as he'd always tell her she was making her parents proud. She'd signed up the next day and finished top of her class in training.

Her last criminal act was to persuade a friend to visit her parents claiming to be from the postcode lottery and informing them they'd won £55,000. They had been so overjoyed they'd accepted his assurance it was legitimate and took the money in two shoe boxes. Debs had raised her eyebrows but said nothing as they sold their house and moved out of town.

The police, it transpired, was a perfect environment for Suss. A natural inquisitiveness and an eye for details, she rose quickly through the ranks. Debs helped her progress and nudged her over to anti-terrorism after just four years in the job.

By this point they were happily living together. A love nest in Putney. Just the two of them whiling away their evenings playing games or talking nonsense. It was the happiest time of her life and she owed it all to Debs. When she had proposed, Suss had literally shouted it from the balcony before calling her parents, their friends, her boss, the local pizzeria. The wedding was small but sweet: 20 guests in The Boathouse pub before a week away in windy Wales. Nothing could spoil their love. Life was perfect.

Now, after seven years in the force, she was a Detective Inspector, a promotion that had brought her mother to sobs louder even than when she'd got married.

They'd moved out of London to live in the quiet village idyll and Suss wasn't sure they'd like it as much as they thought they would. Gloucester was BCP heartland, and her parents weren't exactly their core demographic being the children of Caribbean immigrants. She supported them in every way she could. They'd stuck by her through everything and she'd decided she would never let them down again.

Even if that meant changing the whole world for them.

The car lurched over the mini-roundabout at Middleton Cheney and sped along the road toward Banbury. Inside, Suss processed the events of that morning. It had been a rush from the off. They'd talked for half an hour that morning, Debs needing to leave early. She was to be stationed in Croydon and needed to be there for the preparations. Suss wanted to call her but knew she'd be busy. Plus, GCHQ would probably have taken the phone signal down by now. Suss had got in early to the station, been side-tracked and had to drive quickly from Kidlington to be on time but had made it. Just.

She'd arrived at the family centre, the less formal name for Marquee One, at 10.40. She'd parked up, spoken with a couple of officers she'd met during the investigation, then joined Singh and Kinsella just before the service started. They'd chatted briefly before Singh had called them to position. Kinsella had remained in the periphery. Waved them off and hung back. Why had she done that? Kinsella had

I Vow to Thee – William E. H. Walker

received a text. She seemed quite furtive when it came through, walking away from them and turning to view it. Who'd she say it was from? Had she? She couldn't remember.

The tyres squeaked and skidded beneath her as she took the roundabout at 55mph and sped down the outside lane of the dual carriageway, rounding the corner and bringing the panorama of Banbury into view. Marked in its centre by the green-tiled factory that ensured the town enjoyed a permanent and permeating smell of stale coffee.

Why was she suspicious of Kinsella? She'd never been anything but nice to her, outright friendly even. Which, given her age, intelligence, position, colour and orientation, was increasingly rare in the UK today. Was it the God thing? She'd seen Kinsella wince when she'd sworn and guessed she was religious, then saw the fish that hung on the chain at her neck and put two and two together. That in itself didn't bother her, although she thought of herself as agnostic at best. Was it just that? She took the motorway roundabout at 70 and sped down past the hotel, overtaking the cars that pushed each other to get out of her way.

Did she even really know Kinsella? They'd only met properly four days ago, and despite the friendly manner she'd struck Suss as holding something back. There was something else. Suss swore at a Min-E that wouldn't move out her way and took Bridge Street into town where she realised she was the only person traveling towards the town. *Fleeing the scene*, she thought. She pulled up hard outside the church where a few police cars and two ambulances were treating the wounded. She got out and nodded a greeting to the nearest paramedic. 'How is it?'

He nodded back. 'Not too bad, few broken bones and concussions, no fatalities. Could've been a lot worse.'

It suddenly hit her that she wasn't going to see her parents this weekend after all. A moment of guilt wrapped itself around her chest. She'd missed the last two times she was meant to go because of work. She knew they'd understand, but it didn't help.

She took in the street around her. Down the road stood the Banbury Cross with its statue nearby depicting the lady in the poem. She watched a small Ford screech out of the high street, around the cross and up the road toward Oxford. Blind panic in the face of the unknown. The desperate need to get home to the family, maybe?

She twisted back to look at the church. The vicar was picking his way through the crowd of emergency service personnel toward her and she didn't have time for him, she needed to restore calm. Kinsella was all but forgotten as she called two constables from where they were talking with a man in an ambulance and instructed them to close the road. There wasn't much going on now, the majority of

I Vow to Thee – William E. H. Walker

those who had attended were already on their way home, but it would be good to show the police were in charge. Priority one: calm the town. But in her subconscious mind, suspicion brewed.

13:16

Miller

'How many?' Her voice was shrill, a note of hysteria cutting through as she fought to keep control of her emotions and paced around the cabinet table.

'From the little we know thus far, the size and location of the explosions…' He checked his notes, 'Looks like it could be as many as 10,000 to 15,000 dead and an equal number injured.'

'What the fuck?' Miller felt ice run through her spine. Another major terrorist attack on her watch. More bodies, more lists of the dead and dying. More grieving families paraded on TV, more blame on her fucking desk.

She saw the dead in her mind, blasted apart in a sea of blood. She saw the children, limp and lifeless. Flotsam in the ocean of death the press would say she had let happen. They would ask how it was possible. How could she have let this happen? Social media would crucify her. Spread her arms wide, nail her to a cross and watch her slowly die. Every country on Earth would be showing wall-to-bloody-wall coverage of her failure.

A spasm of pain shot through her, causing her head to twist sideways and lock with a shudder. She'd failed them, the 10,000 to 15,000 who had been invited to London to commiserate with her. She'd invited them to their death. It was too much.

'How Stewart? How?' Even she heard the panic in her voice.

He spoke with his usual tone, as though today was nothing out of the ordinary. Had he been born poor, he'd have been a salesman, the sort in the cheap suit and home whitened teeth. The sort who was never phased by any question or predicament. An engine may explode on a test drive, but they'd still smile at you and ask how much you wanted to pay. But he'd had the privilege to be born rich, and thus had those qualities that in the salesmen were smarmy and unctuous, he had been polished and refined. Honed to ensure he fulfilled his destiny as Head of the Civil Service. 'MI5 is compiling a report for you as we speak, Prime Minister. May I suggest we focus on the response? Military deployment?' Miller's brain failed to connect the dots. Stewart smiled gently in that annoying superior manner of his. 'Deploying the military to support the emergency services with search and rescue? Maybe imposing a travel ban and curfew? Perhaps even closing the border?'

Miller, with all her pent-up frustration, anger and fear, wanted to punch him in his Etonian smile. But he was right. She turned to Michael. 'General Sinclair. Get me General Sinclair.'

He held out a phone for her. 'He's already on the phone, Prime Minister.'

She hated them both now. Both highly educated, both totally immune to the trials and tribulations of politics. They had their jobs until the day they retired, whereas she was likely to be out by the end of the week. She snatched the phone without comment. 'General, I need your troops in London now to aid the emergency services in the search and rescue. How long do you need?'

There was a pause before the gruff General's voice. 'First troops on the ground in 15 minutes, Prime Minister.'

'Good. I also want troops deployed at all major air and seaports and a national shut down of the transport network by 2.00 pm and a curfew in place for seven tonight.' She handed the phone back to Michael and ran her hand through her hair. 'A brandy please, Michael.'

Stewart sidestepped into her peripheral vision and she snapped her head round to glare at him. 'Prime Minister, I'm not sure that's…'

'Stewart, I'm about to be held responsible for the deaths of up to 15,000 people. I think I can be forgiven for having a little brandy, don't you?' Her eyebrows raised, head cocked, she eyed him with disdain and he sighed.

'Very well, Prime Minister.' He waited as she downed the drink Michael had given her and thrust the glass back to him for another. Michael obliged and she drank the second just as quickly.

Stewart rubbed his eyes with his thumb and forefinger. 'Now you have some Dutch courage, may I suggest we draft a response? COBRA must be called, of course – what time would you like to meet them?'

Miller was only half-listening. Her mind conjured images of the dead raising themselves from their broken piles, twisting their battered bodies to face her. Their faces, masks of blood and gore. Many were children, women and the elderly. One was heavily pregnant, the unborn child clearly visible with half her body blown clean away. All were pointing at her, all were screaming. She could hear them, so loud were the screams inside her head she screwed up her eyes and gripped the glass tightly as a small girl would her teddy after a nightmare. A child, no more than three, materialised before her, her head severed but for a thin strip of skin. Miller wanted to run. Wanted to curl up somewhere small and dark where no one could find her.

'Prime Minister.' Stewart's voice, loud and insistent. The screams faded as the brandy began to enter her bloodstream. The child's bloody visage became smoke drifting away before her. With a huge effort of will, she dragged her thoughts back to the present. She opened her eyes and found herself against the wall of her office, her body drenched in sweat. Stewart stood impassive before her. Was that concern in his eyes? If it was, she doubted it was for her. She walked, shaking slightly, over to the brandy and poured herself another. She downed it and breathed deeply. She had to control herself, had to win. She could do this. Was she not the woman who had finalised the sale of over 30 hospitals? Was she not the Minister who had overseen the creation of the new English Church Schools? She was the Prime Minister. She would not go down like this. She slammed down the glass. She would act. Firm, decisive action.

'Michael, where is the US Ambassador?' She saw the surprise on his face.

Michael answered, hesitantly. 'He'll be back at the embassy, Prime Minister.'

'I want him on the phone, now.' He didn't move. 'Michael, now.'

Stewart again cut in; she could see he'd read her mind. 'Prime Minister, now is not the time to think of war.'

'We're already at war!' Her strength was returning to her. The fire in her belly, the thrill of the fight. 'We've been attacked twice and we're losing. We need to respond, and we need to respond now. Michael. The Ambassador. Now!'

Michael still didn't move, he was watching Stewart, waiting for the older man's response. She met Stewart's cold calculating gaze, she was shaking and sweating, but she met his eye. They stared at each other for some time before his head dropped loosely and he sighed. 'Prime Minister, I must advise you in the strongest possible terms—'

'I want the US Ambassador, now.' Each word was spat. Each word enunciated to the extreme. 'You,' she pointed a shaky finger at Stewart, 'do not run this country.' The finger thrust itself hard into her chest. 'I. Do.'

Stewart hesitated a moment longer before slowly shaking his head, fingers rubbing his eyes. 'Of course, Prime Minister. We can but advise and will carry out your wishes in the national interest.'

I Vow to Thee – William E. H. Walker

Michael was already dialling as she turned away from them and headed back to the drinks trolley. She heard the door close and saw that Stewart had left the room. Michael was talking quietly into the handset. 'Prime Minister, he'd like a face to face.'

She downed the brandy and turned to look at him. 'One minute.' She fussed at her hair, trying to get it under control. Rubbed her cheeks, wiped her eyes and brow clear of sweat, before sitting down on the ancient leather and mahogany chair. She squeezed her nose between her fingers and sniffed loudly. When she was sure she looked better, the picture of a Prime Minister in total control, she nodded to Michael.

The Ambassador's face appeared hovering over the desk in front of her, lit from the tiny box beneath. 'Prime Minister.' His voice was as smooth as ever. 'May I begin by passing on my government's condolences and offer you any and all support we can.'

Miller forced her voice to be calm. 'Thank you, Mr. Ambassador. May I ask after the welfare of your Vice President?' She knew the Vice President had been extracted even quicker than her.

'He's doing well, thank you. How can I help you, Prime Minister? I understand our intelligence services are already in discussion.'

'Charles…' She paused and braced herself for this. 'I've decided… I've decided to join you in the offensive.' The words came out in more of a rush than she had meant it to.

The image before her smiled slightly. 'I am sure our President will be delighted to hear it. Our Vice President will want to meet you to discuss this further, he was due to fly back to the US in half an hour but this might persuade him to delay his departure.'

'Ensure it does.' Her hands were shaking again. 'I'll meet him tonight if he's free?' The Ambassador was smiling openly now.

'I'm sure that can be arranged, I shall have my secretary contact yours.' He paused. 'Once again, Prime Minister, you have my sincere condolences for this horrendous loss of life.' The face disappeared.

Miller sagged back in her chair, all her energy drained. After a few minutes she looked up. Michael was waiting for her. She raised her glass and noted his look of annoyance. There was a knock at the door and Stewart entered. 'Prime Minister, the Head of MI5 for you.'

Miller was bone-tired and a little light-headed, but she waved him in. She was the Prime Minister; she had a country to run. A country that was about to be at war.

15:06

Shanks

He looked up and saw the cameraman running toward him. The reporter picking his way through the debris, just behind his crew. He knew how he must look, he had practically rolled in the dust, rubbed it into his arms and sprinkled it into his hair. Not too much on his face though, he still wanted to be recognised.

'Mr. Shanks, Mr. Shanks, are you okay?' The man was panting and sweaty, the camera pointing directly at him.

Shanks chose to bark at the man. 'Okay? Look around you, of course I'm not okay.'

'Are you hurt, sir?' Despite clearly still in reporter mode, the man's expression showed concern.

A wave of dismissal. 'I am fine in that regard, thank you. I wasn't here when it happened.'

The reporter looked confused. 'So, why are you here now?'

Shanks chose a look of incredulity and waved his arms in a wide arc. 'Look around you man, we've been attacked! People are hurt and need help; it is our duty to tend to them in any way we can. Even if that is just helping the injured or providing water for the thirsty.'

The reporter looked stunned at the reply. 'Shouldn't you have been taken somewhere safe?'

'Safe?' He made his voice rise higher like the question was utterly ridiculous. 'You think any of us are safe? Look what our government let happen. Look what our Prime Minister let happen to us.' He spotted a man sitting dazed on a pile of rubble and moved over to him. He knelt, the camera following his every movement, the reporter leaning in to try to catch his words. 'Sir, sir, are you hurt?' Shanks kept his voice low, affecting the air of a caring nurse. The man was clearly in shock and said nothing. 'I'm going to check your legs to make sure nothing's broken sir, okay?' Again, no response. He patted his legs gently, watching his face for signs of distress but there was none. 'I'm going to take you to an ambulance, okay?' The man seemed to become more aware of his presence as he hooked his arm under

I Vow to Thee – William E. H. Walker

his shoulder and lifted him slowly to his feet. He turned and made a show of remembering the presence of the reporter. 'I'm going to take this man to an ambulance. If you've any sense of decency, you'll stop recording and see who you can help.'

The reporter looked genuinely shocked by what he was seeing – no politician had ever acted like this in front of him before. He stammered out his question, 'Anything to say on the events of today?'

Shanks paused, holding the man up while he appeared to ponder the question. 'I am deeply, deeply saddened by today's events. I cannot even begin to imagine the pain and suffering of the families and friends of those we have lost today. My heart and prayers go out to them, I trust they are with God now.'

He started to move off then stopped as though he was remembering something. He turned to face the camera and looked directly down the lens. 'I should also apologise. I'm truly sorry that I am a member of a parliament that allowed our government to let this happen.' A tear rolled down his cheek. 'I am truly, most humbly sorry. I hope you can forgive us for failing you.' He turned from the camera and walked away with the traumatised man leaning against him and a smile in his heart.

22:14

The Man sat in his flat and raised his glass to the footage playing on a loop on the TV. The smoke and fire of London spilled from his screen into the filthy room, his 12th beer of the evening spilling onto the cigarette-scarred carpet. After three years sober, he'd been given permission to get drunk and he was making the most of it.

There was a soft knock at his door. He turned to face the sound, annoyed at the interruption to his evening's pleasures. 'Who the fuck are ya?' he challenged.

'It's me,' came the quieter response.

He grinned broadly and stumbled to his feet, dropping his cigarette in the ashtray next to his chair and sending empty cans skidding across the floor. He opened the door with a flourish and bowed. 'Welcome to my 'umble apartment, me lady. I trust you are well?' He finished his speech with a hiccup.

'Quite, thank you.' The voice was laughing. 'And it's a lovely place you have here.' She entered and swept past him. He caught her perfume as she went, sweet and spicy.

With slightly blurred vision he watched her arse as she passed, feeling like his evening was about to get even better. 'I didn't know you was comin' or I would 'ave baked a cake.' He grinned showing his missing front teeth.

'Oh, I just thought I'd pop by and see how you were enjoying your evening.' She picked up an empty can. 'Quite a bit, I see?'

He laughed, his bloated belly shaking. 'Well, yeah. I 'aven't drunk in three years so I thought I'd treat meself.' He burped loudly and slapped his midriff. 'Not going to carry on mind, nor putting the weight back on, just doing as instruct... instructed.'

'Indeed,' she replied, her voice light and mellifluous.

Her legs were long and thin, her knee-length skirt tight to her thighs, showing the curves of her buttocks. Her white blouse was open to her cleavage, the hint of a lace bra showing at the edges. *Fuck me, is that what she's here for? Well, bring it on,* he thought as he picked up a dirty glass from the kitchen side that was awash with pizza boxes and half-finished kebabs.

I Vow to Thee – William E. H. Walker

'You, you wanna drink?' he asked her, noting how her skirt rose slightly as she sat on the seat next to his.

'Please.'

'Beer all right?'

'Fine, thank you.'

He opened the fridge and pulled out a can of Hop House 13 and poured it carefully into the glass.

'Forked out for the good stuff, didn't I,' he said, proudly showing her the now empty can.

'Only the best, you've earned it,' she smiled at him. He wanted her.

He opened his arms wide in what was meant to be a show of gratitude. It sent half the glass of beer splashing onto the carpet. 'I've just done my bit. All I 'ad to do was climb down into a sewer and drill a bit. Nothin' I ain't done before.' He returned to the seat next to her, handing the glass to her, before twisting to collect his smouldering cigarette from the ashtray on the floor. 'You can take your gloves off, love. It's a grand evening. Plus…' he waved toward the TV, '…we've pulled off a masterpiece 'ere.'

She smiled again. 'You're right, we have. May I suggest a toast?' She raised her glass.

His shaking hands collected his can from the table between them. 'Aye. Aye, a fuckin' toast!' He grinned at her. *Then we fuck like rabbits*, he thought.

They clinked glass to can and he downed his in one. He didn't see her put hers down without touching it.

He smacked his lips and crushed the can in his hand.

'Fuck me, I've missed this.' He threw the can down and appraised her with a wonky gaze. 'Don't get me wrong, I appri… appreciate what you did for me. Getting me fit and sober and all that. Giving me purpose and everything but…' He stared at the can on the floor. 'I have missed this…'

She smiled indulgently at him, her eyes reflecting the light from the television.

'So, what's brought you 'ere tonight then?' He reached out and ran his fingers over her exposed calf. Her skin was soft and warm, but she didn't move. Encouraged, he moved his hand upward to the hem of her skirt. 'You want a little bit of old Johnny then do ya?' He looked up at her, but she wasn't smiling anymore.

The pain started in his stomach. It burned like hot coal against his ribs. He clutched his hand to his chest and lurched over, coughing and choking. His mind raced – something was very wrong here. 'What the fuck 'ave you done to me?' he bellowed at her. She remained perfectly still.

I Vow to Thee – William E. H. Walker

The burning pain was spreading up through his chest to his heart. It was like a thousand needles puncturing his every nerve. He tried to stand but collapsed to the floor in agony, every nerve ending ablaze, his eyes trying to focus on the crushed can inches from his face. *Has she poisoned me…?* His mind tried to process what had happened.

'You were useful, Johnny…' her voice was soft, kindly, '…but there's no room for you in the New England.'

He felt like his chest was exploding, the pain too much to bear. Spittle gushed from his mouth onto his chin and cheeks as he tried to speak. Then, just when he thought the pain could get no worse, it ended. His lifeless eyes stared up at her, scared, disbelieving.

She stood, stepped lightly over the body, walked quickly to the front door and left without looking back. Old Johnny had been useful. And now he was done.

Day 6

'The quickest way of ending a war is to lose it.'

—George Orwell

09:30

Miller

Miller stepped out the door of Number 10 to be instantly blinded by the flashes of 100 cameras and she felt her stomach knot itself inside her. The previous afternoon had been a constant stream of meetings covering all aspects of the bombing. She'd met with the heads of MI5 and MI6, then with COBRA and Commissioner Slender. Then the Defence Secretary and Head of Armed Forces to instruct them to draw up yet another attack plan in the Middle East with the Americans, followed by a cabinet meeting to fill them in on her plans to join the Americans in the invasion of Qatar. Surprisingly, there had been little resistance. Harry Harper, the Health Secretary, had requested to go on record as being opposed to the war, but he'd not actually voted against it. It seems they had recognised the need to retaliate, to do something – anything. Then a brief speech of condolences to the press, followed by dinner with the Vice President to finalise the agreement.

The dinner had gone exactly as expected. The VP, all confidence and smarm, had passed over the evidence of Islamic Jihad's involvement in the attacks on Lesser Worburston and London and promised their support in selling it to the UN. As expected, it wasn't much. Snippets of conversations between IJ fighters talking about the Lesser Worburston attack, photos of Sa'ad Essa in what the Americans were claiming was a suburb of Doha but could have been anywhere.

The memory stick, which the VP had slid across the table, eyes flitting from side to side like a spy in a bad film, had contained a video of Sa'ad Essa personally briefing his men on the particulars of the attack. The VP had told her it had been gathered just two days before the bombing but that the intelligence officer who had filmed it had been unable to get it to the US in time to prevent the massacre.

Miller had held the small USB drive in her hand like it would explode. 'Are you telling me that one of your agents knew this was going to happen and didn't tell you?'

The VP had smiled and drawn on his cigar. It struck Miller again how odd it was that someone who, just last week, had spoken about the dangers of smoking cannabis could sit there and puff on the huge Cuban without seeing the irony. Britain had followed the US in the legalisation of cannabis, but unlike the US they hadn't rowed back on the position. Miller agreed with the Civil Service – it mellowed the population and kept them at home.

'It shows exactly what we need it to show,' he'd said. 'That Sa'ad planned the attack on your country from his safe house in Doha.'

Miller looked up at him, conscious of what he hadn't said. 'Is this real?'

Again, that sickening smile, like a rapist approaching his victim. 'It's real footage, yes.' A dismissive wave of the cigar. 'We've had to improve the audio quality due to the distance it was filmed at, which meant we had to guess at some of the words but—'

'So you made it up?' Miller was getting worried.

A light laugh and open arms, a lecherous grin. 'Not at all. We've just taken elements of what he's said previously and included them in the film to give a fluidity to the speech.' A sip of brandy as Miller's face fell, knowing she had no choice.

Miller groaned and downed her third brandy. It was either this or lose power. Either this or lose herself. Now all she had to do was sell it. First to the country, then the UN, but first to herself. The latter made her feel a little queasy.

Upon her return from dinner, Stewart had asked to see the footage. She had snatched it away from him like a child hoarding sweets. His initially slightly startled response had again been to exercise caution but by that point she had become argumentative and simply told him where to go. Her apology this morning had been met with a studious statement of understanding of the strain she was under, but she still regretted it.

Walking to the podium she felt bile rise in her throat. Last night she had mixed wine, port, brandy and whisky, and was now regretting it. A dizzy feeling like you'd just exited an out-of-control fairground ride. A deep breath during which she tasted stale alcohol. A weak smile that hurt her cheeks. *Don't vomit. Do not vomit.* She stared, doe eyed into the distribution camera and felt herself wobble. *Don't vomit.* 'Good morning to you all, and may God bless you this morning. This morning…' Three mornings in 10 seconds? Off to a great start. *Don't vomit,* '…we wake to the aftermath of the worst terrorist attack this, or any nation, has ever had to endure. One which comes so soon after the horrific events in Lesser Worburston last week. My prayers are with the families of those lost, I know their souls are with God.' *Don't vomit.* 'It is clear to me now that this country is fighting an enemy determined to destroy us. An

I Vow to Thee – William E. H. Walker

enemy who is against everything we stand for. An enemy who will stop at nothing to achieve its goals.' *That's a better flow. Don't think of flowing.* 'This morning I can announce that, through the hard work of our intelligence services in partnership with our American friends and allies, we now have irrefutable evidence that these attacks were planned and carried out by Islamic Jihad under the direct instruction of their leader Sa'ad Essa.' A murmur ran through the crowd of reporters. 'At 8.30 this morning I sent a message, via our embassy in Doha, to the Emir of Qatar demanding they surrender Sa'ad Essa to the United Kingdom within 24 hours or face the consequences. We are currently awaiting their response. Our friends in the US have given us their assurance that they will join us should military intervention be necessary.' Miller tried to look grave, although she suspected she just looked unwell. 'Now, that is the last thing we want, but we will do everything necessary to defend ourselves against further attack. The world will know that you cannot attack us without consequences. We will avenge ourselves on Islamic Jihad and ensure that Sa'ad Essa is brought to justice, either through the courts or by the sword.' Her fist slammed into the podium and a sharp pain ran up her arm. Her lip twisted, but the pain was a useful distraction. *Maybe I'm not going to vomit?* 'Britain has suffered, her people have suffered and we will suffer no longer.' That was good. 'Qatar will give us justice or we will take justice to Qatar.' A pause for effect, then, 'God Bless the United Kingdom'. Another pause. *Not bad, not bad at all.* 'I shall now take some questions.' She looked out at the slightly blurred raised hands of the reporters 'Jenny, BBC.'

'Prime Minister, what is the evidence we have and why has it only come to light now?'

A standard question, she had prepped for this. If only she could remember the answer. Ah, yes. There it is. 'We have footage of Sa'ad Essa planning the attack, it will be released to the media once I have presented it to the UN. We also have recordings of IJ fighters discussing the attacks and photographic evidence of IJ fighters transporting the explosives used in yesterday's attack. We also believe we have DNA evidence taken from near one of the bomb sites yesterday which seems to match a known IJ sympathiser here in the UK. The video footage was filmed prior to the Lesser Worburston attack but sadly took time to get to us. The agent who filmed it was killed in Qatar and the footage wasn't found until yesterday. Matt?' *Was that too quick? It felt too quick. Slow down.*

'Thank you, Prime Minister. Does this evidence show Islamic Jihad is responsible for both attacks?'

Miller nodded. 'Yes, the recordings show IJ fighters discussing the attacks on Lesser Worburston.'

His face contorted. 'But not London?'

Miller nodded a little too enthusiastically. *Damn it, forgot London.* 'The Sa'ad Essa video includes London, yes. One more? Jon?' Hang on, did the video show that? She couldn't be sure now, but it was too late.

I Vow to Thee – William E. H. Walker

'Thank you, Prime Minister. Do you have any reply to the comments made by Mark Shanks yesterday holding you personally responsible for the two attacks?'

Miller felt a chill run down her spine as though someone had dropped the entire continent of Antarctica down her back. Mark-fucking-Shanks. She maintained her demeanour, but her left eye twitched. 'No. Mark Shanks seems to have made his mind up, despite not being in government and therefore not seeing any of the evidence we have. I'll admit, his actions yesterday were admirable in the aftermath of the bombing, but he is not positioned to comment on that which he does not understand. Derik?' She realised she couldn't finish on that question.

A portly man leaned forward 'Thank you, Prime Minister. Do you see any similarities between your presentation of this evidence, which we have yet to see, and the so-called "dodgy dossier" which led to the post 9/11 attack on Afghanistan and then Iraq? Are we going to be involved in another 20 years of war costing thousands of lives and tens of billions of pounds but ultimately leading to nothing?'

Fucking Guardian, Miller thought. Why had she picked him? She stiffened and instant regret followed that as her belly churned like a washing machine on spin, so she ploughed on. 'No,' she said forcefully. 'I'm sure you can appreciate that at this stage I'm not willing to show our hand in terms of evidence. But I shall do at a suitable juncture.' She twisted her neck a little too hard, sending a shooting pain up the side of her head. *Like fuck I will*, she thought. 'Also, I'm not willing at this point to go through our plans should Qatar refuse to hand over Sa'ad Essa, but I can assure you that, should it be necessary, we will ensure any campaign is limited and direct with clear purpose. We don't want or require regime change. We'd love to work with the Qatari government to resolve this peacefully, but we are prepared to do whatever it takes to bring him to justice.' She adjusted her collar, feeling a little dizzy again. Time to end it swiftly. 'Thank you everyone.' She turned her back to the storm of questions and tried to seem confident as she walked back into No.10. Heels were not her friend today. She needed a drink.

Despite her warnings to him via the Whips Office, Shanks would be giving an interview on Channel 4 shortly and she needed to know what he was going to say. His appearance during the aftermath of the bombing yesterday had been a master stroke and she was beginning to worry about him. He was more politically astute than she had first assumed. He was trending on social media as a hero, but the only person to create heroism out of this situation was to be her. She would win this, not bloody Mark Shanks. Miller! She would be the one to save the country, bring down Islamic Jihad and send Mark-sodding-piss-stain-Shanks back to the shithole he came from. She reached out to push the door, but it opened before her and she stumbled inside.

I Vow to Thee – William E. H. Walker

10:53

Shanks

'I meant every word of it, my heart bleeds for those who have once again, as a direct result of the failures of our government, been left bereft. Left alone and left undone from the needless violence unleashed upon us by our enemies. I take responsibility for this tragedy. I am part of this government, therefore I am responsible.'

'How can you be responsible, Mr. Shanks? You're not in the cabinet or indeed any of the select committees. You don't oversee the intelligence services. How can you hold yourself responsible?'

'John, you're right. I don't sit in cabinet, nor do I see the intelligence service reports that, I suspect, would have shown extensive evidence of planning for something like this. But I must still hold myself to account and let the public decide if I am guilty. We all must do so. From the Prime Minister down to the lowly backbenchers like myself, we must each analyse ourselves and submit to the judgement of the Great British people.' He kept his expression grave as he spoke.

John leaned back in his chair. 'Do you think now is the right time for electioneering?'

'Electioneering?' He let a note of anger rise in his voice. His mouth sneered, his head shaking slowly, his eyes widening slightly, teeth gritted. 'Electioneering? John, yesterday we suffered the worst terrorist attack in our history just five days after what was arguably the most savage attack Britain has ever known, and you have the guile to call my pleas for our government to accept responsibility and ownership of this and to do all it can to support those affected by these horrendous attacks and ensure nothing like this can ever happen again, electioneering? I take offense at that. Grave offence.' He looked the presenter squarely in the eyes and saw him flinch.

'I meant no offence Mr. Shanks…' He wasn't backing down though, '…but all your speeches over the past six months could be seen as a drive for power.'

I Vow to Thee – William E. H. Walker

'I desire no power.' His tone was unequivocal. 'I'm struggling to see why you're choosing to make this conversation about politics the day after such a horrendous attack, when we should all simply be taking a moment to reflect, spend time with our loved ones or visit a neighbour to pray together.'

John wasn't satisfied. 'So you're saying you won't run for the leadership should Miller step down?'

Shanks narrowed his eyes. 'I serve where I am wanted. I serve at the calling of the people and it is my privilege to do so. But this is not the time—'

'That's not a no.' John raised his eyebrows.

Shanks didn't smile. 'This is not the time for electioneering,' he replied coldly. 'As I said, I hold Miller's government responsible for these attacks and she should consider her position, but I am not going to start sparring to replace her the day after such a vicious attack.'

'Mr. Shanks, MP for North Oxfordshire, thank you very much.'

A woman's voice, 'Now, the first forensic reports of the bomb sites show RDX was used...

12:50

Singh

'You should put your feet up Sajan. You deserve it.'

He'd loved her smile for as long as he could remember, and he would love it until the day he died. 'Thank you Makhna, but I still have work to do. I'm just taking 10 minutes to myself.' They'd not called each other by their names in years. Makhna, his love. Sajan, her sweetheart. He shifted his legs, the laptop warm on his thighs. She gave his arm a squeeze, her hand comforting. He felt some of his stress leak out to be absorbed by her, like she was drawing it from him though her touch like a sponge.

He'd needed some time at home, some time with his wife. He'd spent much of his day sitting in their conservatory surrounded by their fruit trees. They'd been something his wife had insisted on. 'I'm not going to miss out on fruit just because you can't get it in the supermarkets,' she'd insisted. His eyes focused on the small but luscious green trees, breathing in the scent of oranges, lemons, mangos and bananas, her hand resting on his arm and he felt the world lifting from him.

Since Monday morning he'd worked an average of 16 hours a day. Always in the village, always surrounded by the dead. Even after all the bodies had been removed he had felt their presence. Every room told their stories. Every bloodstain a testament to their violent end. He'd never felt so stressed, so wired and so lost. Even during the war, when he'd lost three of his men to an IED and seen their limbs flying through the air, their bodies disappearing in a pink mist, he'd been able to understand it. Understand the realities of war. But this was different, there was no explanation for what had been done, his brain just couldn't join the dots logically.

And then the bombing followed by a day and a night standing in the major incident room in HQ directing the operations to close the counties of Buckingham, Oxfordshire and Berkshire. In many ways, the bombing made more sense to him – it was conventional warfare. You bombed your enemies, that's how war worked.

I Vow to Thee – William E. H. Walker

Too tired, he was just too tired. He looked up into the eyes of his beautiful wife. 'You are so good to me.' He smiled at her, reaching up and taking her hand in his.

'And you work too hard,' she hit his arm playfully. 'Now, I must get on with dinner. Will you be here?'

'That depends, what are we having?' he grinned playfully.

'Kadhi pakora. And some sattu if you're lucky.'

He licked his lips. 'Mmmmm, my favourite! I shall definitely be here.' She laughed at him, leaning down to plant a kiss on his forehead before leaving to tend to the dinner.

'Thank you Makhna,' Singh called after her.

He returned to his laptop, wondering how to finish the report on the several racially motivated attacks they'd dealt with in Oxford, Aylesbury and Newbury the previous day. The case he was listing – a young Somalian woman beaten half to death in an alley just off Kingsbury in Aylesbury – made his skin crawl. The officers had dragged a group of boys of 16 and 17 into the station. Unrepentant, violent, spouting slogans such as, "Laoch for PM" and "Niggers go home!" He'd met the type before over his career, but these lads were middle-class students, not the usual skinhead idiots you'd find falling for this sort of thing. It made him fearful, like the country was returning to a darker time.

It was his experience that people often glorified the past as if there was a bygone age where everyone was polite, friendly and helpful to each other. Where the sun shone brightly and the cities were clean. Where there was never any crime and the world was in a state of perpetual peace. He happened to know that the world had only experienced 25 days of actual peace since 1914. But still, Britain today seemed haunted by a past they wished they'd lived. Interesting, he'd thought, "they" rather than "we," he'd never done that before.

'How're you feelin' dad?' his daughter Pia asked from the door.

'All good, my beloved.' He waved her round so he could see her, too tired to turn his head. She came and sat on the stool opposite him. He studied his daughter. She'd grown into such a strong and capable woman. A doctorate in psychology from Cambridge, her own practise in York, two great kids and a loving husband. He'd often told her how proud he was of her, but his words had never done his feelings justice.

They had been told of her dyslexia diagnosis at the age of eight. He remembered that night lying in bed worrying if she would cope. Would she find herself excluded or thought stupid as she struggled with her spelling? He hadn't needed to worry. Pia had a fire in her belly that scorched anyone who tried to put her down. She wasn't a fighter; she didn't get angry. She would just set her face and work at the problem until she'd beaten it, be it maths, spelling, sport or whatever.

He'd once found her, aged 10, out in the garden throwing a tennis ball in the air and hitting it with a rounder's bat that, it transpired upon investigation, she had "borrowed" from school. He'd asked her what she was doing and she'd confided in him. They'd played rounders that day in school and she'd missed each time she'd been up to bat. A boy in her class had laughed at her so she had brought the bat home to practice. She threw the ball in the air, swung the bat and sent the ball scurrying along the ground toward the fence. He'd congratulated her and complimented her on how much she had evidently improved. She smiled her toothy grin and ran to get the ball.

He had thought she must be done but she'd repeated the process over and over, sending the ball bouncing across the lawn. He'd asked her why she was still practicing, and her answer had summed up her life to come. 'I'm going to be able to hit every ball over the fence. Until I can, I'm not done.' And that's exactly what she had done: spent her life working to hit every ball over the fence. For the most part she had succeeded.

And now here she sat, nibbling on the roasted seeds his wife had left for him, looking out over their garden in contented silence, a woman he could be and was proud of.

'How are you, dad?' She didn't take her eyes from the garden.

He considered his response for a moment. 'I'm doing okay. How about you?'

'Fine.' Her response was automatic; this wasn't about her. 'Matt will be back with the kids soon so just having some quiet time.' Her husband had taken the children to the cinema for some escapism from the horrors about them. They sat for a moment in near silence, the only sound the soft cracking of seeds in her mouth. 'You must have seen them, the bodies I mean.' Her tone hadn't changed, and he realised she was in professional mode. She'd not come here as his daughter; she'd come here as a doctor.

'I did.' He never lied to her.

'What was it like?' She was sieving out the sunflower seeds to eat first, as she had done since she was a toddler.

He saw the twins in their bedroom, the baby in his cot, the teenager with his blood on his pillow. 'It was tough, really tough. I've not seen anything like that since Afghanistan.'

'How did you respond?'

He sighed. 'Are you my daughter or my shrink?'

She turned and met his eyes. 'You need to talk about this dad, you need to work it all out in your head. If not me, then someone.'

He saw the pain in her face. The naked concern for his wellbeing, and he relented. 'I cried. Often and a lot. I...' He faltered, the faces of the dead crowding his mind's eye. 'I saw a three-month-old baby in his cot. His head was... gone.' He felt the tears welling up again, but his daughter didn't move. 'Whole families wiped out. They were everywhere. And now London...' He wiped his eyes with the balls of his palms. He didn't want to lose it in front of his daughter.

'Why did you cry?' She was watching him closely.

The question surprised him. 'It was horrible. The blood, the death.'

'But you've seen all that before.'

'Yes.'

'Did you cry then?'

'No...'

'So why did you cry?' She wanted him to realise something, something he'd not actually stopped to consider. Why had this affected him so strongly when he had seen men, women and children killed many times before?

'I suppose it was different. They were just people. In Afghanistan we found a village that had been torched. The residents had been burned alive in their huts. It was horrible.'

'But you didn't cry?'

His mind returned to that day in Helmand. Pulling open the blocked doors and finding the charred remains of families trapped by the flames. He'd been professional then. Dealing calmly with the situation.

'No. It was terrible, but it was different.'

'How?'

He considered his response. 'They were in a war zone. It was different. They didn't deserve to die of course, but it was war. The village is...'

'Home?'

She was right. The village was home. It might as well have been here. His family. He had pictured them there among the dead. 'Yes, home. They attacked my home.'

'And your kids?'

His response caught in his throat. He recalled the twins in their room, his vivid images of his daughters and their blood-soaked faces. She leaned closer to him, willing him to understand. 'Did you see us there?' She was looking directly at him now, her expression grave. The tears welled up again. He nodded his response. 'In all the kids?' She kept her voice gentle, reassuring.

'Yes.' His voice was hoarse, tears running freely down his cheeks.

She crossed the small distance between them and crouched before him, lifted his hand and placed it against her cheek. She was warm, her skin soft like silk. She nuzzled against his palm. 'Dad.' She was looking up at him, deep into his eyes. 'We're okay dad. It wasn't us. It wasn't us.'

He couldn't speak. He reached forward and they embraced. He held her close and she squeezed him tight. He breathed her in, rejuvenated by the scent of his daughter. Her life and strength a part of him.

They stayed like that for some time. At last he pulled away from her reluctantly and kissed her forehead. 'You are wonderful my beloved Pia. Thank you.'

'You're pretty good yourself dad.' She grinned at him.

From the far side of the house came the sounds of screaming excited children. She rolled her eyes and he laughed. 'Looks like I'm mum again.' She stood and stretched a little, surreptitiously wiping a tear from the corner of her eye. 'You going to be okay?'

He nodded again and gripped her hand tightly. 'Yes. Thank you.'

She smiled. 'You need to talk things through, dad. I'm here if you need me.' She squeezed his arm and left him.

He wiped down his cheeks with a tissue and gathered himself. He'd not realised he had needed that, but his daughter had sensed it. Seen the trauma within him and had, in the space of a couple of seconds, worked out exactly what needed to be said. She always did. She was wonderful like that.

19:50

Shanks

'It's an abortion. That's what it is: an abortion. She's taking us for fools and hoping we won't notice but I for one will not stand for it. No longer will we, the great British people, be taken for mugs by a Prime Minister who is so far out of her depth she's drowning.' He made sure he sounded angry. 'Don't get me wrong, I have great sympathy for her and she's found herself in an impossible position. But what does she do?' Shanks looked around as though inviting an answer. 'Instead of asking for help from her colleagues, or even the other political parties, she's drowning and dragging us all down with her.' *Nice metaphor*, he thought.

'What would you be doing in her stead?'

'It's not for me to say.' He held up his hands as though defeated. 'I would start by stopping the march to war she's set us on. We know it was Islamic Jihad, that much is clear, but there are other ways to prevent them from hurting us. I would reason with Qatar. They might be an Islamic country, but they're a sovereign nation state, and didn't we – not so long ago – vote to regain our own sovereignty? We must respect that and work with them despite their faults.'

'You don't agree we should do all we can to prevent further attacks?' The TalkRadio host leaned forward in anticipation.

'Don't put words in my mouth, Julie. Of course we should, but invasion is not the answer. No one wants a war and I personally doubt the evidence is even that persuasive.'

A look of confusion on Julie's face. 'If I'm hearing you correctly, you're in no doubt it was Islamic Jihad who attacked us, but that the evidence saying it was them is false? How can you reconcile that?'

'It's really quite simple. Islamic Jihad are the only group who have the means and motive to carry out such an attack, and they do it all the time in Sudan and Syria. They're animals. I think it's obvious they're behind these attacks and they're set to carry out more. Which is why, instead of invading another country, we should focus on home and protect ourselves here. Improve our police forces and homeland security. Crack down on extremist ideologies that go against the word of God.'

'Doesn't every ideology that's not Christian go against the word of God?' Julie flicked her hair from her face. *She really is an awful woman*, Shanks thought.

He smiled. 'I'm going to answer that with a question. Do you remember back in the early 2000s how tough life was?' A heartbeat pause. 'How we were overrun with illegal immigrants and eastern Europeans? How we were constantly told to respect other people's religions, sexualities, genders but never our own?' He leaned forward and continued before Julie could interrupt him. 'Do you remember then how we were told we'd be able to begin to bring this country back to where it should be? After the botched job of Brexit, we were able to regain power over our own destiny and send those who would seek to divide us back home. But what did we do? We capitulated and failed in our mission. We had the opportunity to reintroduce Christian teachings to our children and cleanse the land of those who would hurt us. We've started but we're nowhere near finished. Now we are at a crossroads in that journey.' He made a cross with his hands. 'On the left, we have the powerful and the rich.' Here he struck his elbow. 'They want to keep us ignorant and afraid. Drugged up and spending money.' He clenched his right fist. 'To the right, we have the liberals who would have us godless and overrun with immigrants and refugees. They are the most dangerous. They seek to remove our identity and bring us all down. But!' Here he stretched the fingers of his hand out before him, vibrating with the power of his words. 'Ahead of us, if we can rid ourselves of the last of those who seek to undermine us, who pay lip service to God while holding secrets that will destroy us… if we can overcome those who would destroy our great nation, then we will find ourselves on the open road to glory and to a peace that lasts a lifetime. We can rebuild this country from the ashes. We can burn away the old and reinvent ourselves. We are the only nation on Earth that can, for we are Britain! And we will never surrender to the tyranny of this Prime Minister.' He hammered his fists down on the arms of his chair.

Julie looked slightly stunned but stumbled on. 'Well, thank you for joining us today, my guests were June White, MP for Hounslow, Karen Collins, the Editor of Metro Online, and Mark Shanks, MP for North Oxfordshire. Thank you for listening, hopefully you can join us again next week – goodbye.'

'We're clear,' said a voice from the darkness behind the camera.

Shanks stood quickly, he needed to be away. He had some campaigning to do.

'Well, she's going to love you,' June said as she shot a thin smile at him. 'You've just thrown her under the bus.'

I Vow to Thee – William E. H. Walker

Shanks didn't smile. 'She's already under the bus, all I did was not stop driving. How's your Party reacting to all this?'

She shrugged. 'The usual. No one has a clue what's going on as we crash into yet another war no one wants.' She gave him a quizzical look 'Do you believe the evidence is real?'

'No,' he replied without emotion or guilt. 'No, I think the Americans have cooked it up to get us to go to war with them. I think it's as real as unicorns.'

She gave a mirthless laugh. 'I'm inclined to agree. Why do you think Islamic Jihad did it if you think the evidence is false?'

He had been surprised to find he liked this woman. A Labour MP she may be, but she was smart. She may look like a mix between a Teletubby and Uncle Fester, but she was switched on. Just a shame she was a woman really. 'Who else could it have been? As I said, they're animals.'

She was shaking her head. 'Well, I'm going to need more convincing than that before I agree with you. Are you voting on Monday?'

A motion of no confidence was rumoured to be on the cards for Monday morning. The Leader of the Opposition had discussed the option within 10 minutes of the Prime Minister's announcement. Seems the rumour was about to become fact.

He nodded 'Yes, but I won't be supporting it.'

She smiled at that. 'I'd be surprised if you were. Good night.' And with that, she left.

He took his phone out of his pocket: 11 missed calls and 16 unread messages. Four calls from the Whips' office, two from the PM's Office and the rest from reporters. The messages were much the same, a few from his close colleagues congratulating him for his stance and offering their support, a couple of requests for interviews, the Chief Whip asking him what the fuck he thought he was doing. He smiled at that; he knew exactly what he was doing.

19:32

He watched her from the window in the empty house opposite hers. Noted her wounds and wondered how she'd come by them. Watched her playing with her daughter. Watched the family eat dinner, talking and laughing at the table. Watched her put her daughter to bed, read her a story and kiss her goodnight. Watched her relaxing with her husband, a close cuddle on the sofa and a glass of wine. Watched her get undressed and into bed. Watched her read sitting up in bed, just a light T-shirt covering her slim form. Watched her turn out the light. Pictured her choking by his hand. He didn't notice that four hours passed by as he watched her.

He left his seed on the windowsill.

I Vow to Thee – William E. H. Walker

Day 7

'The chief beauty about time is that you cannot waste it in advance.'

—Arnold Bennett

07:32

BBC 1

'We cannot accept this evidence as fact based on the word of a Prime Minister who is known to be liberal with the truth.' Helen Botas, the Labour MP for Newcastle, leaned forward in her chair as she spoke. 'If we are to go to war, then it must be with firm, irrefutable evidence and the backing of parliament, and not as a kneejerk reaction to a horrendous tragedy.'

Naga Munchetty responded, 'Why not accept the evidence as presented? We must have trust in our system, no? If our Prime Minister says there is evidence and is willing to present that to the UN, then it would hardly be likely to be false.'

'Because there has been no evidence presented, and until such time as it is we must exercise caution. Look at what happened the last three times the UK has gone to war in the Middle East. We had the Afghan war, which lasted 21 years. The invasion of Iraq, which the evidence for that decision was discovered to be false so there is precedent. The bombing of Syria against IS, which turned into a proxy war between the US and Russia, and then the invasion of Syria to stop Islamic Jihad that, we were told at the time, would be a year in situ at most and ended up lasting for six and included our bombing South Sudan.' She shook her head and pursed her lips. 'We cannot pursue another war in the Middle East unless it is the only – and I do mean only – way to prevent further death at home and there is strong, irrefutable evidence presented to and then voted on by parliament.'

'Let's bring in the Foreign Secretary, Joseph Hobbs. Mr. Hobbs, why is your government hiding this evidence from the people?'

'Good morning Naga. Firstly, we're not hiding the evidence, we're presenting it today to the United Nations as the Prime Minister promised she would.'

'But you're not showing it to the British People?'

'At this point it was decided that we would not share what we know with the wider world as there is currently an ongoing investigation into both the attack on Lesser Worburston and the London bombings, which might be prejudiced by the release of this evidence.'

'But the Prime Minister has already said what she has. In the press conference yesterday, she said you have recordings of conversations, photographs etc., so why withhold it?'

'As I said there is an ongoing investigation…'

'Have you seen it?'

'I have seen the evidence, and I—'

Naga cut him off. 'And you think it's enough to justify war?'

'If you'll let me finish, I have seen the evidence and I am convinced that it shows Islamic Jihad are behind the attacks we've seen on this great nation over the past seven days.'

'But does that justify war?'

'We're not talking about war here. What I'm saying is—'

'No. I'm sorry minister, but yesterday the Prime Minister spoke directly of war. Are you saying it won't be a war?'

'What I'm saying is, we don't want to go to war anywhere and we will do all that we can to prevent it, but if the Qatari government continues to refuse to give up Essa Sa'ad then we will do all that is necessary to bring him and his organisation to justice for the crimes they have committed.'

'Minister, we received a report this morning that the Prime Minister is an alcoholic. Can you shed any light on these rumours?'

His surprise was evident. 'I… I don't think that's fair…'

'But she does like a drink?'

His eyes bulged. 'No, I mean we all like a little tipple of an evening but I don't think it's right to accuse her of being an alcoholic.'

'What about if she likes "a little tipple," as you put it, at 9.00 am?'

'I really don't think you should listen to rumours put out to damage the reputation of a Prime Minister who's currently doing an outstanding job under extremely difficult circumstances.'

'So, you've not known her to drink at 9.00 am?' Naga's tone implied she knew the answer.

The minister's lips trembled slightly. 'Well, no, I don't recall ever—'

'Had she been drinking when she made the decision to attack Qatar?' Again, the tone was almost conversational, but implied knowledge.

'No, I mean, I wasn't in the meeting when—'

'What about during the COBRA meeting? Or the cabinet meeting, was she drinking then?'

'Well, I mean, we had a Sherry afterward but—'

'But she's not an alcoholic?'

'No, well… I don't think so.' He looked like he wanted to run and hide.

'Mr. Joseph Hobbs, Foreign Secretary, and Helen Botas, MP for Newcastle, thank you both very much.'

07:40

Suss

She stopped crying at about 3.00 am but hadn't slept. She had made herself some toast, but it had been left, forgotten, to go cold in the toaster. She had drunk the tea she'd made, although it was cold by the time she had remembered it. Now she sat on their sofa, the empty cup in her hands as she stared at the blank television.

Debs wrapped a blanket around her and squeezed her shoulder. 'You okay?'

'Yeah.' What else could she say?

'Do you want anything to eat?'

Suss shook her head.

'Some more tea?'

'No,' she murmured, unconsciously lifting her cup. Debs took it and walked out to the kitchen. Suss wrapped the blanket tight around her and drew her knees in to her chest, leaning on the arm of the sofa.

When she'd found out her parents were caught in the blast her mind had gone into meltdown. There was no conscious thought. She'd just crumbled, her mouth hanging open, unable to breathe. The tears had come later, running down her cheeks in a river as wide as the Nile as the sobs racked her body.

When they had brought her home, she had clung to Debs so tight it must have hurt. She had cried harder and longer than she would have thought possible, past the point where she actually made noise. Cried until her throat closed, her mouth froze open and drool ran down her chin as her silent scream tore through the world like Armageddon. Deep into the first night when the tears had ended, she was still unable to think, still unable to process the news. She had lain in her bed, her head on Deb's shoulder, mindless in her grief.

It had come in waves. They would be talking about something innocuous, some subject Debs had suggested, and she would just break and bellow and allow herself to be held like a sickly babe. By morning she figured she was too tired to cry but too numb to sleep or think properly.

She wanted nothing more than to cuddle her mum. To feel her skin against her cheek and to be a child again in the ever-loving circumference of her warm arms. She felt the sting in her eyes and wiped it away. She would never hear her mother's voice again. Would never hold her father. Never be told off for being late to dinner or play hide and seek with him in their tiny flat. Never again be told how proud he was of her. Never again have him call her "my child."

The wail that tore from her throat brought Debs running back in from the kitchen. She fell beside her and scooped her into her embrace. She held her firmly, kissing her hair and stroking her back until the tears passed. Until her body stopped shaking.

When Suss raised her head, Debs was smiling kindly down at her. She gave her a kiss on her forehead. There was no judgement in her eyes, just love and sadness and her own pain and loss. Suss knew Debs loved her parents almost as much as she did.

When Debs had come out, her own parents had rejected her. 'It's bad enough for you to fancy women but does it have to be her?' her middle-class, middle-England, well-to-do father had said. Debs had held Suss' hand tight and told her father where to go. That had been the last time she'd seen them. Seven years and counting since Debs had chosen Suss over her own family.

Suss' parents had instead welcomed Debs with open arms. When they found out what had happened, they'd invited her to live with them until they found a place. For six months they'd lived in that house and Debs had ended up calling them "mama and papa" out of both respect and love. Now Suss could see Debs hid her own grief to comfort her and it made her love her even more. She needed to act. Needed to be useful. She should be better, or at least active. 'I need to get up,' she said, feeling as weak as a newborn.

'Okay, what would you like to do?' Debs stood and held her hands out to Suss, who took them and stood, swaying slightly.

'I…I…' *What day is it? What time is it? Should I go to work?* She had the funerals to arrange, a coffin to buy and… she realised she had no idea what went into planning a funeral.

Debs seemed to read her mind. 'It's Sunday, it's about 8.00 am, I've already called Wentworth and told him what's happened, he sends his love. Our DCI knows as well, so you're off work till you're ready.' Suss looked at her in total bewilderment. 'We can do whatever you like, my love.' Debs gave her that soft smile again.

I Vow to Thee – William E. H. Walker

Sunday? Was it Sunday? Two days since… The drive went out of her, the momentum lost. Suss slumped back on the sofa. 'I, er, don't know.'

Debs rested on the arm of the sofa and played with Suss' hair. 'Why don't we have a cup of tea then we can make a decision?' Suss nodded. 'Would you like the telly on?' Again, Suss nodded. 'TV on – E4.' Debs said clearly to the room. The TV switched on to E4, which was showing a repeat of the comedy Big Babes, and she gave Suss another kiss before leaving the room.

Suss wrapped herself back up in the blanket and lay down. Mindlessly staring at the two women on the screen for a few minutes before she remembered she hated this show. 'TV – BBC 1.' The screen changed to the morning news. Suss couldn't take much in but she stared at the reports of the explosions that had killed her parents.

She'd spent the Friday afternoon in Banbury, clearing up the last of the mess left by the crowd who'd panicked and run at the news. At 4.00 pm she'd received the call to curfew the town. She'd issued the orders and they'd locked Banbury down by seven. Not a soul on the street as she had patrolled through the night.

In the morning she'd been relieved and had driven to the hotel in Oxford where she was staying during the investigation and had slept right through till 6.00 pm.

When she'd woken up she'd called her parents. No answer, so she'd left a message. She'd brushed her teeth, had a shower, singing "Girls Kick Ass" while she was in there, dried herself off and got dressed.

Once on the road to Kidlington Police Station she'd tried her parents' house again and the phone had been answered by a voice she didn't recognise. He told her he was a constable in the Gloucester police. Told her parent's bag had been found near the bomb that had taken the front off the Mayfair flats. Told her he was deeply sorry for her loss.

The car was travelling at 45 miles an hour when she stopped steering. The car's autodrive and driver monitoring systems had kicked in and within three seconds the software had registered she was unconscious, put its hazard lights on, started to drive itself to the side of the road and called an ambulance. She'd woken in the back of it with the crew bent over her. She'd been brought home that evening and found Debs on the doorstep, tears in her eyes and her arms open wide.

The voice of the news reader slipped in and out of her mind like water. The sights and sounds of London aflame caused not a stir in her eyes.

Debs returned with two more cups of tea, placed Suss' on the stool by her head and perched on the arm of the sofa, resting her hand on Suss' leg, her finger stroking her gently through the blanket. Suss glanced up and mumbled her thanks. She'd been crying again but had taken care to wipe the tears away before leaving the kitchen. The thin, vivid red rings around her eyes though, those she couldn't hide. Suss reached out and squeezed her hand and tried a smile. Debs returned it and squeezed her hand back, hope beckoning in her tired eyes.

Turning back to the television, they watched as the camera zoomed in on Trafalgar Square. The 8K resolution clearly picked out the dismembered limbs and bloody bodies strewn over the flagstones. It wasn't even 9.00 am for God's sake. Dust and debris covered the whole area, the glass in every window save those of the National Gallery and Canada House, had been blown out. Bomb proofing proving its worth.

It was reported that, despite the efforts made, many of the paintings in the gallery had been damaged by the dust billowing in through the open doors from the street. The screen switched to a live feed and the camera panned across the scene as the reporter talked of the effort the emergency services and military were making to find survivors. It zoomed in on a group of soldiers with search and rescue dogs, all stood in a tight circle receiving orders from a tall Major. Suss thought she looked a bit like Kinsella.

For a second, she envied Kinsella. She was an orphan and would never have to experience the pain she felt now. A nagging feeling interrupted her grief. It was unwelcome, like a blister on your heel when you're halfway up a mountain. She wanted to wallow, wanted to cry and live in her pain. Wear it like a warm jumper and lose herself to it. But this nagging thought interrupted her, burrowed into her like a tapeworm and laid eggs. Kinsella must remember her parents, must have experienced something like this when they died. Had her grandmother told her? Then it hit her. It hit her with the force of a nuclear explosion, and she sat bolt upright causing Debs to spill her tea and swear involuntarily. She reached out to comfort her but Suss shook herself free. 'She's an orphan,' she said out loud, her eyes flashing.

'Who is, love?' Debs asked, a note of concern in her voice.

'She said she had no family.' Suss' mind was racing, paths snaking out from abstract, disconnected thoughts to questions she needed answering. 'But she got a text from her Nan!' She was nearly shouting now. She lurched to her feet and grabbed a Poddington Peas T-shirt drying on the airer, staggering around hurriedly dressing to head into work.

Debs looked at her, totally lost. 'Babe, what is it?'

'She got a text from her bloody NAN!' That was a shout of triumph, for suddenly things were starting to make sense.

08:16

Miller

'I want him gone; do you hear me? Gone! Today! Now!' She was so angry she was shaking. Even for her it was still too early for a drink, but she was tempted and needed one.

'He's not a minister, Prime Minister, so we can't sack him. And expelling him from the Party will only serve to give credence to his accusations,' Nick Temple, her Chief Whip, implored her.

'Then find something to smear him with! I want everyone to know you can't go on television and rubbish me… our government like that without consequences.' She felt hot. Was it hot? Sweat glistened on her brow, the familiar morning feeling of sickness strong in her belly.

Nick wrung his hands together. 'I don't have anything to smear him with, Prime Minister. He's only been an MP for six months, he's claimed no expenses, he's a regular churchgoer, he's single but with no hint of impropriety, he doesn't smoke, drink, gamble. He's as clean as they come.'

Miller slammed her fists down on the table in frustration. The MI5 file on Mark Shanks had said pretty much the same thing. So far as it could tell, the man didn't even watch porn. Even she watched porn! What sort of person didn't watch porn? There was nothing negative in there. He'd been elected in a by-election after the sudden death of his predecessor – a gas leak in the house if she remembered correctly. He'd kept his nose clean and appeared to just be another new MP learning the ropes, then this. This tirade of abuse hurled at her over the past few weeks. What had she done to him to deserve it? Nothing. She couldn't even remember meeting the man, although a lot of her evenings were like that recently.

'There must be something,' she said, the note of desperation in her voice once again.

'Nothing that we can find.' Nick sounded apologetic. She liked him; he was supportive.

'Maybe I should meet him?' she wondered out loud. 'Smooth the road?'

I Vow to Thee – William E. H. Walker

Nick shook his head. 'I'm not sure that's the best idea, Natasha.' He always used her first name, she let him when she wouldn't tolerate the same from others. 'Since his appearances last night, he's garnered praise from the left, the right and the church for speaking out against war, not to mention the swell in online support. His colleagues on the back benches are rallying to his cry. If you were to meet him it might appear as though you're scared.'

She thought about it for a second and nodded. 'You're right, I won't legitimise him. He can stew on the back benches, but I want you to find something I can use on him, Nick – any indiscretion, however slight.'

He stood, nodding like an over eager puppy. 'I shall get right on it.' He turned to leave just as Michael came into the room. 'Excuse me Prime Minister, but I thought you'd want to see this.' He handed her a tablet, and she took it in weary hands. As she read the headline her head started to swim. Nick leaned over her to read.

The headline stood out against the bring screen: "NATASHA DRINKS MILLERS AT 9.00 AM."

What the fuck? Who told them? She read the opening paragraph.

"Sources close to the Prime Minister report that Natasha Miller has developed a drinking problem. It is widely known in Number 10 and throughout her cabinet but has been hidden from the press until now. One source said, 'She'll already be on to her second or third brandy by 10.00 am, we can't stop her. She's out of control.' In response to requests for an interview, no ministers were available and we have yet to receive a response from the Prime Minister's Office."

'A response?' Miller was frantic. 'To what?' Michael held out the page of A4, which she took and scanned the contents. 'When did this come in?'

'About 20 minutes ago, Prime Minister. It's the usual tactic, it goes down much better with the readers if they're able to say we've not responded.'

Miller shook her head like a child facing a firing squad. 'Can we deny it?' She felt suddenly claustrophobic, the room closing in on her. Nick, just a bit too close despite the large desk between them.

Nick looked up at Michael, who replied calmly, 'Of course Prime Minister, we are already in the process of doing so.'

'Who leaked it?' she asked Nick in a small, pathetic voice. She wanted nothing more than to shrink back into her chair.

His mouth was opening and closing seemingly without reason. 'I… I don't know Natasha, I'm sorry.'

I Vow to Thee – William E. H. Walker

'Well, find out for fuck's sake!' she squeaked at him, rising from her chair. 'Who's doing this to me?' She made to get herself a brandy, but stopped and sank back into her chair like a rag doll. They nodded once and scurried toward the door. 'Michael.' He turned and smiled at her. A smile she could have torn from his face had she had the strength. 'I want Stewart. I want him right now.'

'Certainly, Prime Minister.' He bowed from the neck and left her alone.

She reread the article, the headline stung her eyes and she realised she was crying. When had this happened to her? She'd been so strong, so confident, so capable. Now she was a washed-up wreck with a drink problem. What had happened over the past six months to make her like this?

There was a knock on the door and Stewart entered. His face was grave and set. 'Prime Minister, the American Ambassador is on the phone. He wants the final go ahead from you.'

She gathered herself together. Sniffing loudly, running her hands through her hair, she said, 'Yes, Stewart,' trying to sound serious and in control.

He advanced right up to the edge of her desk. 'Prime Minister, I beg you – please don't do this.' He was wringing his hands; it was the first time she'd seen true emotion in him. 'At least wait for the UN to report on the evidence we've presented to them. Don't just react because things are bad right now.'

For a second she wanted to listen to him. Wanted to stop the violence before it began. Then her eyes flitted down to the headline emblazoned over the tablet and her stomach twisted. She turned from him, chin held high, hand outstretched. 'The phone please Stewart.' He gave a world-weary sigh, lifted the receiver and handed it to her. She could still win this. She could still survive. She sniffed back tears and cleared her throat.

'Mr. Ambassador, good morning. We are go.'

12:47

Freemark

The pale pink envelope was waiting for her when she arrived at work. She'd spent the morning interviewing local bin men about the further changes to recycling in the area. From July, all hemp products must be placed in a different box to all wood-based products, the latter gradually going the way of plastic and confined to the pages of history.

Yesterday had been exactly what was needed: a day at home playing in the garden with Maddie. It had been another day of high temperatures and they'd taken the opportunity, at Stephen's suggestion, to get the paddling pool out and try to forget about the world and its problems. She had kept the news on in the background, but her day had been filled with the joyful shrieks of her daughter splashing around in the pool. The cut to her head she'd received in Banbury wasn't bad, the type you get as a kid and brush off before carrying on playing. It's funny how as an adult they seemed scarier. Understanding brings fear the way no monster under the bed ever could. The car radio brought news of the first air strikes on Qatar as she was on her way back to work. She wondered when this would end, unsure she could remember a time when the country wasn't bombing someone.

She filled Frank in with more details on what had happened to her in the Banbury panic, accepted his awkward hug and promised to tell him if she felt like she needed more time to recover. She'd felt okay that morning, having gone for a good 10 mile run, had a decent breakfast and spent some more time with Maddie. She was looking forward to writing up the bin men's comments for her article, then she saw the envelope, identical to the one she had received before.

'What the fuck?' she said out loud, causing several of her colleagues to turn to peer quizzically at her. 'Who left this here?' she called out to the room. 'Who left this on my desk?' She held up the envelope like she was holding a sewer rat.

I Vow to Thee – William E. H. Walker

Herb, the American expat who'd moved over here when the puritans had taken over, raised his hand. 'I did, it was just sitting on the mat when I arrived this morning.' He looked nervous. 'Did I do something wrong?'

She acted as though he'd not spoken. Her eyes wide and her hand shaking slightly as she noted the big difference between this card and the last. This one had no postage stamp. This one had been delivered by hand.

She dropped it like it would bite her, opened the top drawer and fished out the card for DI Kinsella. She punched the numbers into her phone and waited, her eyes never leaving the envelope. Cautious, as though it could somehow leap up and grab her by the throat. After three rings the phone was answered, 'DS Maguire,' said a thick Welsh accent.

'DI Kinsella please.' Her voice tremulous.

'I'm afraid she's out of the office, Miss. May I take a message?'

'Please tell her Julia Freemark called and I've had another letter. She'll know what it's about.'

'I shall indeed, Miss. Have you reported this to her already?'

No, you muppet, I'm calling you because my gran sent me a lovely cheery note. 'Yes, I saw her five days ago.'

'Righty-ho then, keep it safe for us please if it's important. I'll pass your message on to DI Kinsella as soon as she's back in the office.'

'Thank you. Bye.' She hung up as he was saying goodbye to her.

Freemark sidestepped to her right as though readying to box and felt her initial fear begin to subside, instead replaced with a burning anger. The fucking bastard was at it again. What was this one? Should she open it? 'No! Bollocks to him, I'm not going to give him the satisfaction. The police can do it.' She sat down at her desk and attempted to focus on the story about the bin men, but her brain kept wandering off thinking about what he had decided to write to her this time. Just as she had reached the limit of curiosity, the phone rang. 'Freemark,' she said, curtly.

'Mrs. Freemark, DI Kinsella. I understand you've received another note?' Her tone was clipped, polite and with professional detachment.

'Yes. Yes, thank you for calling me back. I have – same envelope, same handwriting, everything. I'm sure it's from him again. Though this one wasn't posted, it was delivered by hand.'

There was a pause on the line. 'By hand you say. How do you know?' Kinsella's voice had turned curious.

'There's no stamp.'

'I see, but you said he was in Cornwall, the man you believe is behind this?'

'I thought he was, I saw him leaving your station in a Cornish police car,' she said. *Did I say that, or did you?* she thought.

'Yes, I remember you saying a...' The sound of tapping, '...Mr. Grantham.'

'That's him.'

'Well, when can you come in with the letter?'

Freemark was eager to get something done. 'Now, if you're free?'

Another pause. 'Can you give me half an hour?'

'Sure.'

'Incidentally, what does this one say?'

'I've not opened it yet.' She looked back at the note, it whispered "read me" to her, like she'd gone down the rabbit hole.

Another pause. 'Well, you have better powers of resistance than I do. Come in and we can open it together.'

Half an hour later Freemark had shook Kinsella's hand and told her about how she'd managed to get hurt, receiving a standard dose of sympathy in return. She was guided past the office and toward the same interview room they'd used previously. Freemark noticed the striking black woman burst through a set of double doors. She was wide-eyed, scruffily dressed and with an explosion of hair. She stared at Freemark from across the room. Freemark smiled at her but didn't receive anything back, just a quizzical look mixed with nightmarish horror.

Kinsella closed the door, gesturing for Freemark to sit. She produced a paper bag from her pocket and held it up. 'I didn't know if you'd want to do fingerprints on it?'

DI Kinsella smiled at her. Freemark didn't really like that smile, it seemed a little strained, but the woman seemed efficient and intelligent enough. 'Good thinking. Though, as I said to you last time, the writing of a card – so long as there's nothing offensive or threatening in it – doesn't usually constitute a crime.'

Freemark nodded. 'I realise that but, well, with what I told you about what he did to me, and that other woman...'

'I know, but as I'm sure you know, since he was not charged with either offense…' She left that hanging in the air for a moment. 'It might be that if this continues you could have a case for harassment, but we also have to prove it's the man you're accusing.' Her eyes were steady as she met Freemark's gaze. They were cold eyes, Freemark thought. There's no love there. But then this woman must have had a hell of a week along with the rest of the police. Maybe she was tired.

'Shall I open it then?' Kinsella asked.

Freemark nodded and Kinsella removed the envelope from the bag and carefully opened it along the seam. From within she withdrew a card identical to the first. The beautiful beach scene surrounded by a white border. Kinsella paused for a moment studying the picture, then opened the card and read out the message. Just three words this time: "Hope you're okay." Freemark suddenly felt a little sick. 'How the hell did he know I got hurt?' she asked, a note of fear in her voice.

Kinsella was studying the card. 'Are you sure it's from this man you spoke of?'

Freemark was confused now, she had been so sure it had been him. It couldn't have been a coincidence that the first card had arrived the day after she'd seen him and bore the message "good to see you." But how would he know she'd been hurt? 'Are you sure he returned to Cornwall?' she asked.

Kinsella nodded, consulting a pad she had with her. 'Apparently after he'd been interviewed he was taken home by the same officers who brought him up here. Either he's returned or it's someone else?'

Freemark's mind was racing. *If not him then who?* 'Is there any way to check if he's still in Cornwall?'

Kinsella looked momentarily annoyed but hid it quickly. 'Given what you claim about this man, and if it will put your mind at rest, I can ask some colleagues in Cornwall to check on his whereabouts. But it will take some time. Until then, maybe think about who else this could possibly be from? Someone local perhaps? It might be that this is a rather poor attempt at a romantic gesture?'

Freemark screwed up her face. 'A piss poor one if it is.'

Kinsella smiled again, a little warmer this time, maybe? 'Well, I must say I've known some men who would think it was. But either way, you have a think about who else it might be and I'll follow up with my colleagues in Cornwall.' She rose from her chair and Freemark realised their time was over.

She stood as well, feeling a little rushed. Was Kinsella trying to get rid of her? She didn't really have much to go on. Two cards, both unsigned and with seemingly innocuous messages inside. What did she expect her to do? Fly down to Cornwall and arrest him? Throw him in jail for writing a card?

Kinsella was leading her through the office and back into reception. 'Have a think and let me know if anything comes to mind. Once I have an answer for you from the Devon and Cornwall Police I'll let you know, but do bear in mind they cover an enormous area. ' She smiled that cold smile again and showed Freemark out.

After she had gone, Freemark realised why she didn't like her smile. It didn't reach her eyes. She must have been of a similar age to Freemark, yet she held herself better. She was a woman in total control, Freemark thought. You don't fuck with her.

She crossed to her car and got in. Maybe this was someone else after all? Maybe an admirer? A weird, reclusive admirer? No, that was bollocks – it was him and she knew it. Why was Kinsella trying to persuade her it wasn't? Or had she imagined that?

There was a sudden tap on her car window making her jump. The striking black woman stood looking down at her. Her expression wild, almost unhinged. Freemark took a moment to gather herself and pushed the button to lower the window.

When she spoke, her voice carried a thick London accent and more than a little desperation. 'Hey, sorry to bother you. I'm a colleague of DI Kinsella's and I wondered if I could ask you a couple of questions?' Her eyes flitted from side to side, as though she didn't want to be seen.

This woman didn't look like a copper. Torn jeans and a T-shirt. 'Sorry? I've just been interviewed by DI Kinsella, I've told her everything I—'

'What did you talk about?' Her words were rushed, she was clearly agitated about something. She leaned down into the window, her face only centimetres from Freemark's. She smelt of stress and sweat.

'Sorry?' Freemark was confused. 'Who are you?'

She flashed a police badge. Freemark barely had time to register it before it was gone. 'I'm a DI in CTU. I need to know what you told my colleague.' She was clearly becoming annoyed at having to repeat herself.

Freemark was starting to feel a little trapped in her car. 'Erm… right. Well, I've been getting sent these cards from someone I used to know. They've been scaring me. It's a guy I went to school with. Grantham.' Something flicked across the woman's eyes. Recognition? Triumph maybe?

'What did they say? What did Kinsella say? It's imperative I know. Hold on.' She practically ran round to the passenger's side and got in before Freemark had a chance to object. 'Please. I need to know.'

There was something earnest in her expression.

I Vow to Thee – William E. H. Walker

Trust. She could trust her, Freemark thought. Something in the strange woman's face told her this. She told her everything. About the cards, Francesca Moss and Kinsella's response. When she was done, the woman's expression seemed to cloud over, like she had drifted off somewhere private. Freemark just stared at her, unsure how to react.

After a couple of seconds, she shook her head as though waking, her cloud of hair catching the light and sparking, her expression severe. 'Thank you, Mrs. Freemark. You've been a great help.'

She got out, closing the door softly behind her. Freemark pressed start and pulled out of the car park, still unsure what had just happened. As she moved on to the street, the beginnings of a thought nagged at her, just out of reach from her conscious mind. There was something amiss, although what she had yet to realise.

12:46

Suss

'Nigel, how are you?' She tried to smile warmly at his image on the screen and received a look of pity in return that, despite their friendship, made her want to punch him. It was the look those who had never known loss thought appropriate. The slight head tilt and gentle nod. She knew he meant well; he wasn't the target of her anger.

'Suss? I thought you were off. I was sorry to hear about your parents.' Her stomach knotted.

'Thanks. Look, I've a favour to ask. Can you pull me a serving officer's file?'

There was a hiss of breath. 'Erm... Suss, I'm not sure I can, not without authorisation.'

'Nige, I really need this.' She was practically squirming.

'Can I ask what it's about?'

'It's to do with the bombing but I can't say anymore.'

'Suss, you know I love you, but I don't think it's good for you to investigate this, you're too close.'

'For fuck's sake Nigel, my parents died in that fucking bombing.' Her voice was like a knife's edge. Her grief came to the fore. 'I need to know if this... person was involved.' She closed her eyes and squeezed her wrist with her hand, breathing deeply. 'I'm sorry Nigel.'

He was shaking his head, brow furrowed with concern. 'You don't need to apologise to me. I can't imagine what you're going through.' His voice was quiet and calming. There was a pause and another release of breath. 'What's the name?'

'Thank you!' She pumped the air. 'It's Detective Inspector Maria Kinsella of Thames Valley.'

He threw his arms in the air. 'Jesus Suss! I didn't expect that, I thought it would be a constable or sommit?'

'Nigel please, I really, really need this.'

He tutted a few times before replying. 'Fine. Give me a couple of hours to finish up what I'm doing and I'll email it to you, okay?'

'You're a wonderful friend Nige, thank you.' She felt herself relax a little for the first time since she'd heard of her parent's death.

'Of course, anything you need just ask, okay? Debs looking after you?'

She smiled a little at the thought of her partner. 'Yeah, she's been amazing.'

'Well, I'm sending you both my love. Let me know when the funeral is, yeah?'

She felt a sudden pang of guilt as she'd not started arranging anything yet. The undertakers had called but she'd not been able to deal with it. Now she was running around on a flight of fancy. Was it a flight of fancy? 'Yeah, and thanks again. Bye' She ended the call and expelled the breath from her lungs, turning everything she knew over in her mind.

Kinsella. Orphan. Nan. And now Grantham. There was a connection there.

The office buzzed around her, but she heard none of it. Her eyes were closed as she thought things through. She needed to see the file, she needed to be sure. If Kinsella's grandparents were alive, all was well. If not, she didn't want to think about it yet. Get the file first. 'Once I have that, I'll know if I can trust her.' Her anger burning through the grief.

14:56

Laoch

When he opened his eyes, Laoch blinked slowly at the daffodil-yellow ceiling, heard the beeps and hum of hospital equipment, felt the mask over his mouth and nose. His throat was parched, as though he'd spent a week in the desert eating nothing but sand. His eyes stung as though nesting wasps. His head held a jackhammer and there was an urgent ringing in his ears like a church had lodged itself in his mind. He tried to rise but pain shot up his arm and he slumped back down. Finding himself stuck, staring at the ceiling, he groped around him until he found what felt like a button and pressed it. A soft "bong" sounded somewhere nearby and from the corner of his eye he saw a nurse rise from behind a desk and approach his bed. She smiled as she reached him. 'Reverend Loach, you're awake. How are you feeling?'

He bridled slightly at the mispronunciation of his name and tried to speak. 'What day…' His voice, scarcely more than a whisper, was hoarse and painful, the words catching and grating.

'It's Sunday, Reverend. You've been in and out of consciousness since you were brought in on Friday.' Her Welsh accent was kind and gentle. She was checking the readouts on the screen beside his bed against a chart. 'Doctor will be along to see you shortly. Can I get you a drink of water?'

He nodded, slowly, his neck, stiffer than steel. 'Pe… Pe… ter,' he croaked.

She shook her head. 'No one here at present, a young lad visited but he left a few hours ago.' She smiled again and walked away, returning a couple of minutes later with a small paper cup of water. 'I'm going to raise the bed; this might hurt a little, okay?'

He nodded again and she reached down and pressed a button. As the top half of his body was raised, he became aware of the bandages that covered his arms, legs and across his chest. His eyes widened; she must have noticed as she gently placed her hand on his arm.

I Vow to Thee – William E. H. Walker

'It looks worse than it is, dearie.' She smiled again reassuringly, took the mask from over his mouth and lifted the cup to his lips. The water felt like nothing he had ever experienced before. It was as though God himself was washing his mouth out with holy eau-de-vie. Then his throat contracted and he coughed, his lungs trying to wrench themselves free of his body. 'It's all right dearie, it's all right,' she cooed, patting and rubbing his back.

A short, dumpy woman in a long white tunic appeared before him. She seemed brisk and efficient. From her tightly cropped hair to her sensible shoes, she looked like she never sat down, never slept, just closed her eyes and recharged. Always too busy but so used to it the strain didn't even show. 'Reverend Laoch.' An obligatory smile. 'How are we?' she asked as she picked up his chart.

Laoch croaked at her, 'What happened?'

'Reverend, you were injured in an explosion on Friday in Mayfair, do you remember? You've been here for two days and have been slipping in and out of consciousness.'

The memory hit him like a punch to the face. They'd hit the memorial march. He'd been in the flat. They told him he'd be safe, no more than cuts and bruises, nothing serious or life threatening. Not that he'd end up in hospital unconscious for two days. The bastards had lied to him!

He became aware the doctor was speaking and brought himself back to the present. '…broken in two places but that will heal. We'll keep you on oxygen for the time being due to the smoke inhalation and to monitor you. But, luckily, overall you came out of this okay. Far better than many.' Her voice was low and reflective. She shook her head and rallied herself. 'Long story short, you're on the mend but it will be a few more days before you're using your arm again. I think God must have been looking out for you, no?'

Laoch struggled to digest all she had said. This must have shown in his expression as the doctor's expression looked grave. 'Do you understand me Reverend? Is my Polish accent too thick for you?' Laoch blinked in surprise at her tone. Without waiting for a response, she turned to the nurse. 'I need you in bay three. Full range of bloods please.' The nurse nodded, smiled at Laoch again – although a little strained this time – and left. The doctor followed but Laoch reached out for her.

'The news.' Each word a blade in the throat. 'Please, the news?'

She sighed, seemingly tired of life. 'Four large explosions in the crowd, roughly 10,000 dead but maybe more. No one really knows for sure.'

He blinked and thought, *10,000 dead?! They'd said it would make a statement.* 'Who?'

She gave a harsh bark of laughter. 'That's the 64 million dollar question, isn't it?' A small shrug. 'I don't know, but Miller blamed Islamic Jihad.' Her expression was one of pure sadness. 'All I can tell you is that at half past nine this morning we started bombing Qatar.'

He stared at her, uncomprehending. She gave her obligatory smile again and left. He lay in his bed, oblivious to the noises of the busy hospital around him. He wasn't sure how he should feel now. They'd told him he wouldn't be hurt, yet here he lay. A broken arm, stitches in his face, head and stomach. A throat so parched Cecil B. DeMille could use it as a film set. They'd lied to him.

He reached for the cup left on the over bed table, took off his mask and poured the little remaining water down his throat. It was glorious.

They said he'd be fine. They lied. Lied to *him*! How could they? He was meant to be their leader, the voice of the revolution. He looked down at his broken and battered body. The bruising seemed to cover most of his torso, or at least those parts not bandaged. His legs black and blue. They'd nearly killed him. HIM! Bastards!

The anger boiled up from within, filling his chest. His breathing hitched, there was a sudden pain and he retched. Coughing and spluttering as his body went into spasm. Doubled over he choked uncontrollably. The movements sent arcs of pain over every inch of his broken form. Suddenly there were arms on his shoulders pushing him backward, a soft hand placing the mask over his mouth. A voice telling him to breathe slowly, focus on his breathing. The face of the nurse hovering over him, speaking softly and holding him down. The pain began to subside and his breathing came easier as the oxygen did its work. After a minute or so he was able to speak. 'Thank you,' he whispered.

She smiled and patted his good arm. 'That's okay, dearie. You just need to keep your mask on and try not to move too much. I'll get you some more water. When you want a drink, use the bed to lift yourself up, sip and then replace your mask, understand?' He nodded gingerly. 'Rest now dear, nothing you can do but get better.'

He raised his finger to point at the small television perched at the end of his bed. She nodded and moved the remote onto the bed beside him. She looked sad for a second then left him to his thoughts.

He had a lot to think about. A lot to work through. He needed to decide his next move, but despite his best efforts he slipped quietly back into sleep.

I Vow to Thee – William E. H. Walker

18:46

Grantham

"If you don't know me by now, you will never, never, never know me. Ooooooh no you won't!"

The volume from the radio was turned up high as Grantham stood before his hob frying onions to go on the mushroom sausages, mash and gravy. He mumbled along as he added a little tabasco sauce to the onions and moved them round the pan. He was in a great mood. He'd woken up an hour earlier and was dressed in his uniform ready for his shift. The six-hour drive the previous night hadn't taxed him. He felt exhilarated. For the first time in years he was happy, and this was different to what they'd done to him. This was better than being cured.

We're back baby.

He had to admit that when he'd left them last year for the quiet time before the start he had felt at peace with himself. A renewed sense of purpose and meaning to the world. A life beyond the pain he had known. He recognised now that what he had felt then was a lie. Like cheap paint, it was a thin veneer over his true self. And like rising damp, his true personality had surfaced to rot the covering away.

He knew society would call him a monster, but he didn't care. He knew society said it was wrong to enjoy causing pain, but how can it be when it gives such joy? He knew they thought it evil to rape and strangle those women. They'd taught him that. Beaten it into him. Strung him up and tortured him to erase this desire.

But right then, as he stood basking in the memories of the whore he'd picked up on the way home, he didn't believe them. He remembered dragging her unconscious body into his car and driving her home. Remembered the pleading in her eyes as he ran his knife over her skin before she screamed as he cut her. The life fading from her eyes as he choked her. He was himself again. How can something that makes him feel so good be wrong?

It can't. It just can't. You're better than them.

Had it not been for the time he was caught when he'd decided to ambush that slut on the Banbury Road after her night out, he might have been able to enjoy the last decade without feeling guilty. Without having to hide himself away in the arse-end of nowhere painting. Granted, he loved painting and he knew it would make him world famous, but he'd much rather have enjoyed his other art form. His raison d'être. The cold voice inside him that wanted more, wanted to have some fun.

You love me, I love you. We go together like two plus two.

When they'd first told him the plan, after he'd been "cured," his inner self – his demon as they'd called it – he had been overcome with the news that he would be let loose on the world after so long. It had screamed to be released, clawed at his insides like a rabid wolf. It needed to be fed, to be sated. And they'd made him wait for it, yearn for it, before finally, snarling, they had let him loose. Freedom. But they'd had to catch him first. Subdue him.

He'd realised he was being watched while strangling that bitch, knife in his free hand ready to slice her open. After that they'd dragged him away from the churchyard and locked him up. After they'd stripped him of his clothes and shut him away in the cage, he'd been frightened – an unusual experience for him as an adult. He thought they wanted revenge, but they hadn't – they wanted him. Or at least, that's what they'd said. First they'd have to cure him.

That's when the beatings had started. The food and sleep deprivation, 24-hour music and the abuse screamed at him through the bars of his cage. He had pleaded with them, begged them to stop. But each time they had beaten him with clubs until he shivered like a child, curled up in a ball in the corner of the cage in a puddle of his own piss. He had tried to fight them, but they were quick, strong and numerous. They had beaten him until he broke. Until he was compliant and sedated. A mindless automaton.

He forgot what clean air smelled like. The feeling of sunlight on his skin became a complete unknown. He knew no taste other than the porridge they threw at him through the bars. No smell beyond the damp, stale stench of the cellar and his soil pot. Day and night were irrelevant under the permanent yellow glow of the bare bulb hanging just out of reach of his grasping fingers. The point where he could take no more came and went with barely a whimper. He lay unflinching on the cold concrete floor as ice cold water was thrown over him. When the steel-capped boot smashed into his legs, he did nothing but blink, lost inside the universe of purgatory that had once been his mind.

He wasn't sure when they had clothed him. Nor when they'd placed him in a bed, a thick duvet covering his now frail form. He might have slept for a day, a week, a month – who knew? He wasn't sure if he remembered the injections themselves or just finding the plaster over the wounds. It was just vitamins and antibiotics though; he'd found that out later. When at last he had woken, they had come for him. He'd been dragged from his cell and up into the soft sun of a spring morning. They'd settled him into a wicker chair, a blanket over his legs, beside a table filled with fresh fruit, pastries and – of all the blessings – fresh coffee. Despite the clearly audible growl from his belly, he'd been too scared to eat. Unsure if he was allowed, or if this was even real or another phase of the torture. Then, emerging silent from the sun, Grantham had met God.

Grantham clearly remembered their conversation. The voice that had wormed its way into his mind and laid roots through his psyche. The kindness and love that soaked each syllable as they ate together, talked together. He understood Grantham like no one ever had. He knew his every thought and feeling, urge and pain. It had been so easy for Grantham to love him. It was as though it was always meant to be. When He had told Grantham a cure was possible, he had agreed to the treatment as willingly as a child about to receive an ice cream. The smile He had given him still warmed Grantham's heart to this day. He had led him into the warm, light house and introduced him to his carers and told him they would begin the treatment right away. Grantham had wanted nothing more than to please Him.

What followed was brutal. The scars that criss-crossed his back were a tribute to that. The ice baths were to cleanse the skin; the whippings were to cleanse his soul. There were prayers five times a day and a strict diet of fruit, vegetables and homemade bread. No contact with anyone outside of the house and no contact at all with the opposite sex. He had lived this way for three years and, for the first time in his life, had found a certain peace and tranquillity in the simple quiet life. His corner of the large, sprawling house was secluded, the pace of life regular and sedate. He would wake at six, shower and dress in a T-shirt, thin jumper and chinos. A breakfast of yesterday's bread and butter was preceded by prayers and followed by Bible study and self-actualisation lessons. Afternoons were spent painting, gardening or repairing the house. He learned what God had planned for him. His life's purpose. He understood why he had been made this way with the love of watching life disappear from someone's eyes. He had been made for the cause. For the mission. Until recently, that had been enough. He had lived to serve.

The painting had helped. Had given him an outlet for his thoughts. His life committed to the canvas. The temptations tempered and subdued.

But they had all come rushing back to him that night last week. He had become so aroused watching his mother's bemused expression as he lifted his balaclava and grinned at her before pulling the trigger and watching her whore brains splatter out over the room. God that felt good.

The one thing that had surprised him about that night was that it had been surprisingly hard to kill four-year-old Emily Price who lived in Bakers House. She'd been asleep when he'd entered her room and he'd noticed the bruising on her arms and legs. The clear signs of abuse spread over her thin, soft

I Vow to Thee – William E. H. Walker

limbs. A flood of memories of his own childhood washed over him and he had growled and nearly woken her. Were her parents not dead already, he may have exacted his anger on them for pushing memories of his youth into his mind. His bitch of a mother shoving him out of the way to embrace her latest lover. Shoving him into his room and locking the door so she could dance the night away with God knew who. Bringing men half her age into her bed and not caring what he saw her doing with them. Spreading her legs as easily as most women spread butter on bread.

He remembered the man who'd broken into his room and forced himself on his six-year-old body, pushing his head so violently into the bed frame he broke three teeth. His tongue subconsciously ran over them now, a shiver flashing down his spine.

Well, she was dead now, the bitch whore from hell. Lying in a fridge somewhere, a hole in her head as big as the one in her heart. He laughed at the memory of her last expression, a joyous mix of disbelief and confusion. Then she was nothing more than a bloody stain on the pillow. He felt himself stir and patted his crotch. Maybe a quick one before work?

And, of course, now he'd found Freemark again. The bitch who'd rejected him. She still looked good, and now he'd seen her naked he wanted her even more. She looked like she worked out, all sinew and muscle. He liked that. A bitch who felt capable would be fun when he dominated her, put her in her fucking place.

We will have her.

He sang along to Lily Allen's LDN and turned down the heat on the onions. She would pay for what she had done, embarrassing him like that. First, he would kill her husband, then he would make her watch while he sliced up her daughter, then he would take her. Hold her down, open her up and watch her bleed out. The plan could still happen, it wouldn't get in the way. He hadn't been involved in London and wasn't needed again until stage four, so he had plenty of time. Plenty of time to finish what he'd started all those years ago when she'd stopped him. How had he let her do that? A girl so weak prevented him from his prize. Well, Francesca had paid for that. She had been an experiment, he realised that now. His first attempt trying to work out what it took to make him happy. What it took to make him feel joy. He had perfected the art since then, the eight bodies buried across England were testament to that. He'd never even been considered as a suspect. How could he be? He had been so careful. And Freemark would make nine as her husband and daughter didn't really count, they were just collateral. His mum though, she was something else, something special. She stood alone, and then there was the fun to come. More opportunities for release in their plan.

We're going to love this, but let's have some fun before then. That's still days away.

I Vow to Thee – William E. H. Walker

He'd be able to play again soon, just as soon as they gave him the go ahead. He knew what he was to do next and, just to make it even better, they hadn't told him it needed to be neat and tidy. Unlike the village, which had strict discipline and a code of conduct, he was almost given a free licence with what he could do. Maybe he would take his time? Had they meant to let him play? They had been annoyed with him about the letter to Freemark, but he couldn't resist it. She was too much fun to play with. Maybe they had forgiven him for it and were willing to let him enjoy the next one? Maybe that's why the brief had been so simple. Effectively just "kill her." No further detail, no restriction, just the freedom to play. They must have forgiven him.

They know you're better than them.

There was a knock on the door and he frowned. 'Who the hell can that be?' he muttered. He left the stove with the pan on a low heat and walked through to the living room, the lamp on the bureau casting his exaggerated shadow over the room. Scratching his buttock through his jeans he leaned over and pressed his eye to the window in the door. There was a small noise, no more than a suppressed pop, but Grantham didn't hear it.

His left eye disappeared and the bullet blew out the back of his head, leaving a baseball-size hole in its wake. His lifeless body jerked backward as he hit the deck, his remaining lifeless eye staring up at the ceiling.

The Man clicked open the door and pushed until it met the resistance of Grantham's corpse. He put his weight against it and shoved his way inside. His cold dark eyes looked down at the bewildered expression on Grantham's face. 'You shouldn't have written those cards,' the Man said to the corpse.

Without wasting any more time, he crossed into the kitchen. The frying pan was still on the hob and he turned up the heat and added more oil to it. He poured more oil into the pan, took a small glass vial containing a tiny lump of metal from his pocket and placed it in the centre of it. Without a backward glance he turned, walked past the body by the door and out into the night.

Behind him the oil bubbled and sizzled around the glass. Under the pressure of the heat the vial split and the caesium inside exploded as it met oxygen, sending a shower of now flaming oil over the kitchen. The house stood no chance and the flames spread quickly throughout the room.

It reached the first stack of paintings and the dry canvas fed the flames, spreading the fire over the walls and floor. The paintings would never be world renowned; he would never be listed among the world's greatest artists. No one would ever see any of his art again, they were now just kindling for his funeral pyre.

I Vow to Thee – William E. H. Walker

The fire engulfed the kitchen, the radio melting halfway into Ben E. King's Stand by Me, made its way upstairs and spread hungrily through the rooms. Before long, the thatch ignited and sent a tower of flames into the dark sky and lit the land up for miles around. The people who owned the place across the valley saw the flames and dialled 999, but by then the fate of the house was sealed. The roof collapsed and created a furnace.

In the living room, the look of surprise melting with the skin from his face, Grantham burned.

I Vow to Thee – William E. H. Walker

23:46

Miller

She woke from a dream about speaking to the EU trade delegation about the importance of fridge magnets to the UK economy to the sound of the urgent knocking on her bedroom door. It took her befuddled brain a moment to work out what was going on, having spent the past few hours trying to persuade the French President that he needed to buy her relief magnets of the Tower of London at just 99 pence a magnet, or Sussex would be given over to the sea. She rolled over to see the clock and knocked the half-empty bottle of whisky onto the floor where its contents bubbled out and immediately started to soak its way into the 19th century rug. 'Shitting bollocks,' she swore under her breath. The knocking again. 'What, what, WHAT?'

Stewart's voice from behind the solid oak. 'I'm sorry Prime Minister, I have some urgent news.'

She felt the sudden need for a cigarette. She'd not smoked for over 20 years but for some reason at this moment she needed a cigarette. And a kebab. She ran her hand under her nose and wiped the crusted drool from the side of her mouth. 'Give me a second, I'm not…dec- decent.'

She rolled out the bed, her head foggy and her eyes watering, and fished for the bottle that had unhelpfully rolled under the bed. Collecting it she grabbed the cap from the side table, screwed it tight and hid it under the duvet. She switched on a bedside lamp. Why hadn't she done that first? The light stung her eyes as she swung her legs over the edge of the bed. She overbalanced, swung too far and swore again as her toe connected with the leg of the bedside table. The squeal that escaped her mouth resembled a pig running from a butcher. Her sight was refusing to focus properly as she limped over to where she had thrown her dressing gown at a chair.

'Prime Minister?' Stewart's voice, insistent.

'One second!' she screeched back, her voice ragged and petulant. The dressing gown forgotten, she checked herself in the mirror, screwing up her eyes to bring herself into focus and being only partially successful. Her hair was glued to one side of her face and she had mascara rings spreading from her eyes. She tried in vain to wipe some of it off but instead spread it further over her cheeks. She ran her hands through her hair and attempted to appear as though she was awake and alert. In her mind she saw a woman ready for action. In reality, she looked as though she'd been run over by a combine harvester.

'Prime Minister, this is urgent.' He was sounding anxious now, she thought.

She spun on the spot and immediately wished she hadn't. It took a second for the room to catch up with her. When finally it had, she stumbled over to the door, focused on the handle and opened it, letting it fly backward to crash into the wall before bouncing back, painfully, into her right leg. The bright hall lights caused her face to contort and resemble a Spitting Image puppet. When her eyes unscrewed themselves as the shock of the door and light subsided, she saw Stewart standing before her in a tux, looking flustered for once and carrying a sheaf of papers.

Before she could say anything, Stewart barked out his reason for coming to see her. 'Prime Minister, the UN has concluded the evidence for the war is faked.'

'What?' She didn't quite comprehend his words, not helped by the fact there were at least three of him right now.

'Also, we've lost a Tempest in Qatar – it was brought down and the pilot captured. The generals are asking if we should attempt a rescue.'

'What?' She tried to keep the various Stewarts in some sort of focus.

'Prime Minister, how much have you had to drink?' She heard judgment in his tone.

Miller bristled, letting out a loud snort. 'Not much. Hardly a thing in fact. A whisky. No, I mean a wine. No, a…' She waved vaguely in the direction of her room. 'I had a couple of drinks before bed, nothing really.' Her head wobbled like a nodding dog as she leant heavily on the doorframe. Could she go back to bed now? No. There were pilots to fight. Or to fake? No. Finding fake pilots, that's what she had to do.

'Prime Minister, I don't think you're in a fit state to make these decisions.' His voice was like ice. He seemed to have grown a couple of inches as he stood rigid before her.

She waved her hand dismissively. The gesture was over flamboyant and nearly hit him. 'I'm fine. Fine, Stewart. Fine. Now, we need to fake our rescued pilot… fighter…' She lurched up from the wall and made to move past him, but he didn't budge. She gave him a look she hoped was outrage. 'Come now, Stewart. To flight.' She stepped forward once more and bounced off the wall. He caught her and pushed her back against the wall. It wasn't a hard push, but she felt indignation rise like bile. 'Don't push me. I'm the Prime Minister of England.'

She saw his brow set, saw the decision made. 'Prime Minister, I believe you are not in a fit state to make decisions. As such I am going to have to call the Home Secretary and form an emergency meeting of COBRA to take action on these matters.'

'You what?' She couldn't believe what she'd heard. Her head was swimming, but his words were clear.

'May I suggest you go back to bed now, Natasha?' Stewart's voice was firm.

Natasha? Who the hell did he think he was? Miller tried once more to pass him but instead found herself leaning on his surprisingly strong arm. She threw her head back in disgust. 'You are in my way. I have a job to do. Prime Minister.' She jabbed her finger in his chest. The three Stewarts had amalgamated themselves into one, silent and furious Stewart who gripped her arm tightly in thin, firm fingers. Miller's mind cleared as the threat held in his clear blue eyes cut through the fog of whisky.

'Let me put it this way.' His voice had turned so cold it stung. The look he gave her caused a whimper to escape her lips. It was all malice and rage. No, worse – contempt. He was no longer the smooth and sophisticated Cabinet Secretary. He was dangerous, full of untapped threat. When he spoke, his voice was quiet but firm. It chilled her to the bone. 'You, madam, are a disgrace. You bring shame to this office. You bring shame to yourself. You are in no state to look after yourself let alone a country. You're so devoid of sense you have not even noticed that you're not wearing a dressing gown.' Miller looked down at her sheer nighty. Her breasts, clearly visible beneath the thin fabric. 'You, madam...' There was a definite sneer to the word "madam," '...have a choice. Either return to your bed and sleep this off while I make arrangements to cover the shit show you have made...' Was he really talking to her like this? '...or I shall personally drag you into the cabinet room in your current attire and invite your colleagues to come and see you. See how long you last as Prime Minister then?' Miller felt the bottom fall out of her stomach. Stewart may have been a pompous arse but he'd never so much as spoken a bad word to her before this. She couldn't believe her ears. He flicked his wrist, sending her lurching back against the doorframe once more. He took a step back from her as though she were diseased, his eyes alight with fury. 'Now, turn around, lock yourself in your room and sleep through till morning when you may find yourself with the need to write a letter to the cabinet.'

Miller had no fight left in her. She felt drained and as weak as a starving kitten. She shuffled meekly around, her head slumped forward and fell back into her room. She heard the door close behind her and Stewarts clipped footsteps marching away.

She stood near her bed, for a moment lost in her emotions. Fear bringing sobriety, followed by pain and ultimately regret. Tears rolled from her eyes and down her cheeks. She had considered several times over the past week that she had reached the end of her time in office, but she'd ridden those moments and was still here. This was different. Within minutes Stewart would be on the phone and informing the cabinet and generals that she was unable to carry out her duties. In the morning they would ask for her resignation and she would give it to them.

She didn't care anymore anyway. She didn't care that the UN knew the evidence was fake. She didn't care that the press would destroy her. She didn't care who took over from her. In that moment, as her world fell apart around her, she only cared about her husband. Fishing in Scotland and keeping well out of her way. He'd said that if she ever got bored of climbing the ladder she should come and find him. That had been two years ago and they'd spent approximately 30 days together since then. Would he still want her? This broken wreck of a woman? She leaned down, flung the duvet out of the way and fished out the bottle. She didn't bother with a glass but simply swigged the whisky from the bottle, gasping as it burned her throat and slumping down on the bed. This would be her last night in Number 10, her last night as Prime Minister. And what was her legacy? Death, destruction and war. Was that all she had to show for her time in office? For her time in the sun? Had she really been such an abject failure?

She shoved the bottle between her legs and leaned over for her phone, which clattered to the floor as she grasped for it. Reeling it in by its charging cable she sat the screen in her lap. Her head wobbled and her finger stabbed at the display, looking at his name. She pressed dial and he answered on the fifth ring. His face materialising on the screen like a most welcome of visitors to her home. She felt her heart squeeze as soon as she saw him.

'Hello darling.' She loved him for that. For calling her darling after all this time.

'Hey you.' She was crying. The tears welling up and rolling slowly down her cheeks.

'Has it all gone wrong?' He was being kind. She'd missed him, oh how she had missed him. How could she not realise how much she had missed him?

She nodded and sobbed, the whisky bottle once again leaving her grip and falling to the floor. 'I'm done, John. I'm done.'

He smiled warmly at her. His expression without pity, just love and understanding. 'Are you coming home?'

She laughed. The sound gurgled from her chest and shook her body, sending tears raining onto the bed. Home. Where was home? This wasn't home. This was the home of Peel, Churchill, Thatcher and

Blair. But it wasn't her home. Her home was with him in Scotland. She found herself nodding. 'Yes. If you'll have me?' She felt childlike, small and insignificant. Just wanting to be cared for and loved.

'Come home darling.' His smile was warm and inviting. The words touched her heart.

She cried and nodded. It was over. It was finally over. She was going home.

00:23

'You didn't tell me it would be like this. You never said I'd feel like this. I can't sleep. I can't eat. Every time I close my eyes, I see their faces. I was better off on the drugs than I am now, they don't even help anymore.' The tears ran freely down her face to mix with the snot from her nose. 'What have you done to me?' She'd felt surrounded by the dead. Clothed in them. They sat with her as she ate breakfast, they lay with her in bed. She was never alone. She was walking with the dead.

The voice in her ear was soothing, like balm on a fresh burn. But she had been burned too much. The wounds so deep the balm barely touched them. 'When? When will it get better? When exactly will it get easier, huh? I'm taking double the dose I used to and it's not helping.' She reached up and touched her wrist below the phone. Tracing the ragged scar from when her husband had stopped her. Bursting in and finding her in the bath.

She listened to the words. She had once believed this voice to be the only voice that mattered. She had gobbled them up like a child given free rein in a sweet shop. She had worshiped this voice. This voice that had cured her of her paranoia, her anxieties, her postnatal depression and drug addiction. This voice had saved her life.

But now, as she sat huddled in her pyjamas on the large living room chair, shaking and unable to stop crying or sleep, she hated that voice. 'You bastard. You utter, utter, utter bastard. I did it because you said it would help. I did it because you said it would change the world! And now I can't even…I can't…' She broke down, dropping the phone on the floor as she wailed.

It was a good five minutes before she had recovered enough to collect the phone.

The voice spoke again. She listened again, but the balm had turned to hot oil. 'No, I've sent them off. I can't be around her now. I keep seeing her lying there in place of them. They've gone to his parents for a few days.' The once honeyed, now poisonous voice seeped into her. 'But you never said it would be like this. You never said I'd remember them all. What have you made me into? What have you done to me? I was suicidal before, but now? How can I live with myself?'

I Vow to Thee – William E. H. Walker

The voice was entering her again, as it once had done so easily. It slipped inside her and made her feel. That feeling had once been heavenly, but now it ate at her like a parasite. 'No. I don't want to see you. You can't help now.' A pause. 'No, don't come round. I don't want to see you. You've ruined me.' She was sobbing again. Her words coming between heaving breaths. 'I just want to sleep... to not feel like this... I just...' Her voice cracked and she slumped to the floor, cradling her head in her hands.

There was a knock at the door. A soft knock, gentle and discreet. She froze. The voice was talking again. Encouraging. 'You... you there?' She raised herself to her knees. Every nerve quivering, eyes wide like a cat on the hunt. 'How did you get here so fast?'

Without realising it she was on her feet and moving toward her front door, the voice drifting like smoke through her mind. Persuading. 'But... but you can't help me now.' Her voice was small and fragile and barely more than a whisper. She shuffled and swayed into the hall, the phone to her ear, her eyes set on the shadow that loomed behind the frosted glass of the door. 'I can't see you. I don't know what...' Her whispered protests were cut off by the soothing voice. Comforting.

She reached the door and lifted her shaking hand to the lock. 'We can make it better?' she asked, her fingers wrapping themselves around the cold metal of the key. She didn't hear the man behind her. He'd used the back door and slipped into the hall, following her silently. She clicked the lock open.

The hand moved silently over her mouth and nose. Realisation hit her and she inhaled in shock. The chloroform washed through her body and she slumped into his arms.

The second man entered, a long piece of rope in his hands as he closed the door quietly behind him and lifting her still body.

I Vow to Thee – William E. H. Walker

Day 8

'Do your best to present yourself to God as one approved, a worker who has no need to be ashamed, rightly handing the word of truth.'

—Timothy 2:15

08:42

Loach

The small UHT chocolate mousse tasted like mouldy luncheon meat and he ate it sparingly while watching the tiny television that was costing him £10 a day to hire.

Lying in his hospital bed, having posted on Frog that he was mending slowly but stronger than ever thanks to the Glory of God, and skimming through the comments left by his supporters, he'd got bored and decided the ridiculous drivel of the telly was better than going crazy.

The sound coming through his headphones was tinny and annoying, as though a fly was translating what was on the screen. That could be due to the quality of the ludicrously expensive headphones he'd been forced to buy to hear what was on the hired television, or the fact that his hearing was still struggling as a result of the explosion, or a combination of the two. Either way it made every sound incredibly frustrating.

The news today was that Qatar had brought down two US fighter jets and were holding the pilot of one prisoner. They had paraded him on TV to show how well he was being treated. He looked bruised and battered and ashamed as he scowled at the camera.

The American aircraft carrier USS *Abraham Lincoln* had been joined by the UK carrier HMS *Queen Elizabeth the Second* and were launching raids on the Qatar military sites while the Qatari claimed thousands of civilians were being killed in the bombardment. The report was being rigorously denied by both governments orchestrating the attack.

'Qatari officials continue to assert no evidence links them to the attacks on Lesser Worburston and London. They claim the UK government, together with the US, fabricated the evidence to establish a motive to attack them,' the news anchor was saying. 'The UK and US presented their evidence to the United Nations amidst widespread condemnation of the actions taken against Qatar at this time.'

How quickly things escalate, Laoch thought, smug at being on the winning side.

I Vow to Thee – William E. H. Walker

'…Prime Minister Miller made a statement yesterday condemning what she called Qatari lies and propaganda and their refusal to give up Sa'ad Essa, leader of the Islamic Terrorist Group Islamic Jihad who the UK government claims is hiding in Qatar.' The news cut to Miller standing outside Number 10. 'We do not accept the Qatari government assurances that Sa'ad Essa is not hiding in Doha and we will do whatever is necessary to bring him to justice for the atrocities he has committed against this country.'

Laoch allowed himself a small smile. *They sure managed to fix the blame on him quick enough*, he thought.

The news anchor again. 'We have received reports that the Prime Minister called an emergency meeting of COBRA at around midnight last night for reasons yet unknown, although sources in Number 10 tell us a UK fighter was shot down late yesterday evening. It seems the whole of Whitehall is working overtime. We will bring you more news as it comes in.'

Laoch could guess what had happened. Miller was being forced out just as they had told him she would be. They had also told him how best he could benefit from it. He just needed to wait for her to speak today. She would have to; it was bound to happen.

He closed his eyes and relaxed in bed. Not long to go now. She would speak by lunchtime and then he would have her.

***

He awoke two hours later with a start. He'd not meant to sleep and was annoyed at himself for doing so. As his eyes cleared, he saw Miller standing behind a podium on the television. *Shit!* he thought, scrambling around as best he could for his headphones. They'd fallen off the bed and it took him a good minute to reel them back in. He composed himself as he put them back into his ears.

The Prime Minister was answering questions now. From off screen a reporter asked, 'Prime Minister, both the German and French governments have condemned the actions of the coalition and have publicly stated they doubt the legitimacy of the evidence you claim you have. How would you respond?'

Interesting… Laoch thought. *Our allies desert us so quickly. Though they were little more than scum.*

'I have faith…' Miller was saying, '…that once they have had time to study the evidence they will be right behind us.'

Another reporter, 'Prime Minister, do you have a drinking problem?'

He watched Miller's face flicker with anger. No – embarrassment. 'I do not, nor ever have, had a drinking problem and I will do nothing to further the anti-British lies being spread by our enemies.'

The reporter interrupted her. 'Had you been drinking last night? Were you unable to attend the COBRA meeting due to drink? And are you going to resign?'

Miller looked as though she was about to burst into tears. It took her a good few seconds to steady herself and respond and when she did, her voice caught in her throat. 'That's all for now. God bless you all and God bless the United Kingdom.' She turned and walked back inside Number 10.

Laoch sat up straight causing a sharp pain to run from his bruises. *She's going to resign*, he thought. *She knows the evidence is fake, it's probably been proven by the UN. Does that mean that the British government has falsified the evidence or the Americans?* Well, he knew it wasn't Islamic Jihad so clearly Miller did as well. He reached for his mobile and called his assistant.

The phone was answered within two rings; Laoch didn't wait for a hello. 'Peter. I want a statement put out. Right now.' His voice was still hoarse, his throat still burned with each syllable, but the fire in his belly was not caused by pain. He could smell the opportunity. 'First, mention how I am recovering valiantly from my grievous injuries, but that's not from me – that's your personal statement. Then say this: my thoughts and prayers go out to the victims of this savage attack against our great nation. All the more heinous for it taking place on a day of national mourning when we joined together as one in the sight of God to pray for peace in the spirit of love. These vile acts that continue to be inflicted on us by the beast that calls itself Islam are not a symptom of our country's failure, but of our success in bringing God back into our lives – did you get that? Once again, we are shown the dangers of accepting the perversion that is Islam into our country. Once again, the liberal elites will tell us we need to acquiesce to them, just like they do with homosexuals and paedophiles. Once again we are shown how right we are to follow God's chosen path to ensure we are truly worthy of being God's chosen people.' He paused waiting for the sound of typing to end and collected his thoughts. 'That being said, while I agree with the UK government that Islamic Jihad are behind these cowardly and vicious attacks, I do not believe that the UK government has evidence of this.'

'Sir,' Peter interrupted him. 'Why not try "positive proof"?'

'Fine, Fine,' Laoch spluttered. *How dare Peter interrupt me?* 'I saw her face, she's lying and she knows it, now write what I say. I. DO. NOT. BELIEVE the UK government has the proof it claims and therefore, while the attacks against our enemies are just in the eyes of our Lord, the claim that the UK government is making is a lie and must be exposed. Natasha Miller must resign today.' He knew it was good. 'Now, read that back to me in full.'

I Vow to Thee – William E. H. Walker

He listened as Peter recited what he had said, made a couple of small changes and then hung up with an instruction to send it out to all the networks, news sites and official social media channels within the next 10 minutes.

He lay back satisfied. What they intended for him was now clear. His path was laid out. The pain he had experienced was justified. Like Jesus on the cross, it was needed for him to suffer to cleanse the nation of a corrupt and evil regime. He would be the hero. He would be the voice of the revolution. He would be the leader of the new Great Britain – One Britain Under God. He would lead them out of darkness and into a glorious new era. He would be the next Prime Minister.

Within the hour his statement has been circulated, digested and repeated ad infinitum. An hour after that he had another 20,000 followers on Frog, another 14,000 on Bamboo and a crowdfunding page set up in his name to aid his recovery, which he naturally said he would put toward supporting the families of those who died.

His phone was ringing almost constantly with reporters vying to be the first to interview him with his reaction to other people's reactions to his statement. Such was news these days. Journalists no longer reported the news but the reaction to it.

By 11.00 am the hashtags #Millermustgo, #Justiceforthefallen and #Millerresign were trending across all social media. Number 10 had called his statement misguided. The Archbishop had wished him a speedy recovery but had refused to be drawn on political matters. No word had been heard from Miller. The initial whispers from the UN were that the Security Council wasn't buying the evidence, which threw more petrol on her already brightly burning pyre. She would roast in hell and he would be her successor.

Pundits were asking where he had got his information and how he knew. The behavioural psychologist on Sky was demonstrating how the Prime Minister's facial expressions gave credibility to the claim that she was lying, had lost control and was hitting the bottle hard. Commentators, those people who 20 years ago would have been called "busy-bodies," were relaying his message as though they were their own, drawing out other times Laoch had seemed to know what was going on long before anyone else had worked it out. His statement had made an impact the size of Canada, and he lay back content in his bed.

The next Prime Minister of Britain.

I Vow to Thee – William E. H. Walker

14:42

Miller

'Good afternoon. I would like to make a short statement; I will not be answering questions. Every premiership has a lifespan, and I believe that my premiership's lifespan has come to its end. I would like to thank you, the great British public, for the opportunity you have given me to serve you. I hope I have done you proud. I shall be stepping down with immediate effect for reasons of my health. In my absence, the Party has agreed that Denis Patterson, the Leader of the House, will act as interim Prime Minister until a new leader is elected in two weeks. Once again, I thank you for the opportunity to serve. God bless the United Kingdom.'

PART 2

'The two most powerful warriors are patience and time.'

—*Tolstoy*

I Vow to Thee – William E. H. Walker

Prologue

'I know I'm asking much of you; you are taking the biggest risks. You're going to be exposed and you may have to pay the ultimate price.' He lowered his head in a moment of silent reflection. They waited for him patiently. 'What is asked of you over the coming week will be hard and it will be dangerous, but we will succeed. You have been chosen not because of the training you've had, but because of who you are. You're the best of us. You're ready for this.' He paused once more, his eyes drifting over them. 'At the last minute you might be tempted to run. To turn and hide and escape your destiny. But be assured. In those moments do as you have been instructed and all will be well. Breathe in. Hold. Release. God is in breath. And God will be in you.'

Day 14

'The world breaks everyone, and afterward, some are strong at the broken places.'

—Hemmingway

08:56

Freemark

'The angle has yet to be properly explored, but I think there might be a bit of interest.' Frank was determined to persuade her, and she could see there was no arguing with him, despite how pointless she thought it would be.

'Farmers though?' She couldn't hide the resistance in her voice. 'I didn't even get to cover Miller's resignation and now you want me interviewing sodding farmers?'

He sighed a little too theatrically. 'Everyone covered Miller's resignation. All the nationals had that. Haven't we heard enough about her drinking, the lies and the misleading evidence? If it comes to trial you can cover that, okay? We're a local paper; we want local stories.' They still called them papers, despite not a single sheet being printed in years.

'But farmers?' She heard herself sound petulant.

His expression showed his annoyance. 'Aye, farmers! They've been kept off their land now for two weeks. How's it affected them? What's the impact on their business? Do they know who's going to compensate them for their losses? Are the crops dying in the fields, their kids going hungry, their lives falling apart? We want stories that reflect the area we live in, the people who live here.' He leaned back in his chair, his porky beer belly spreading the buttons of his shirt to reveal tufts of coarse brown hair, making her mouth twitch. 'Also, what've they seen, what's been said to 'em? What've they heard on the grapevine, so to speak? They might have insider knowledge.'

She narrowed her eyes. 'You realise they probably had friends in the village, right? That they may have even lost family?'

Frank scratched his chin and picked his nose. She'd always liked him but that particular habit of his was vile. 'We've got the full list of the deceased now. Check out the farmer's names before you go down there, any match and you don't talk to them. If they're not on the list, make that your first question.'

I Vow to Thee – William E. H. Walker

'"Excuse me, don't suppose any of your relatives were brutally murdered in the village, were they? No, great! Can I have an interview?"' Heavy on the sarcasm. Frank's smirk was humourless, a hint of the old-times investigative journalist in his bloodshot eyes. She looked sheepish. 'Sorry,' she said, 'but you must admit there's a high chance that some of them will have lost at least friends if not family. Maybe even in London at the memorial?'

He wiggled his finger in his left ear. 'Yep, but we need this. The nationals have spoken with one or two, but I want the local care angle. "Who's looking after them now" and all that. Here...' His fingers ran nimbly over the virtual keyboard. 'The Independent interviewed a... Fred Savage.' Freemark snorted and Frank looked at her confused.

'Fred Savage was in The Wonder Years and The Princess Bride,' Freemark explained.

He raised his eyebrows, not looking impressed. 'Somehow I doubt they're one and the same. But anyway, they didn't seem to get much more out of him than an overview of what was happening on his land and his sorrow and all that crap. You'll go in there with the caring "what's next?" Right?' His face was set. Argument over.

Freemark sighed and rubbed her eyes. 'Yes boss.' She rose from her chair. 'Apparently they've stopped blocking the wi-fi in the area so I'll get something over to you by four.'

She left his office, collected her bag and the remaining half of her beef-flavoured muffin and made her way to the exit. She tapped her thumb to the new security doors installed just the previous day and out into the mid-May sun.

Lighting a cigarette as she unplugged her car, her phone jingled in her pocket. It was Stephen. She dropped the cigarette, crushing it under her heel, and answered. 'Hey, hunny.' She smiled at him.

'Hey, you've not been smoking again have you?' She looked at him, pouting theatrically. He laughed at her, a genuine laugh full of love. 'You always have that look on your face when I catch you smoking a fag.'

She flushed red and grinned. 'What can I do for you?' she asked, getting into her car and pressing the start button.

Stephen's picture moved from her phone to the central console display. 'I wanted to ask your opinion. Ash's got these shutters installed on his house. Says they'll keep out even the most determined intruder. He's said we can get a good deal on them at the moment as they're selling like hot cakes.'

'Shutters? You mean like the Swiss have? The wooden things you see on ski chalets?' she teased as she pulled out into traffic.

I Vow to Thee – William E. H. Walker

'No hun, like they have in Russia. Metal ones that come down over your doors and windows at night or when you're out. No one can get in through them.'

Freemark was unconvinced. 'Well, how much are they?'

He hesitated before replying. 'Ash says he paid 25k for them.'

She spluttered. 'Did you just say 25 grand? Are you taking the piss?'

He tried to look put out, as though he'd invented them and she'd scoffed. 'Everyone's getting them, just in case of another attack. After what happened in London sales have gone through the roof. Apparently there's already a six-month waiting list.'

'So how did Ash get them so fast?' she asked, with an eyebrows raised and giving him a sideways glance.

'He said he got in straight after the village. Said his wife wouldn't go another night without some protection and it was either that or a gun!'

A pause while she negotiated a roundabout, annoyed at the person next to her who was in the wrong lane. 'You know I wanted to get a self-driving car, right?'

'I know, but I was thinking of you and Maddie and—'

Freemark interrupted him. 'Do you think they're likely to do it again?'

Stephen looked serious. She realised then he was genuinely worried. 'I don't know. Who thought they could actually pull that off in the first place?'

She had to agree with him there. She moved into the outside lane of the dual carriageway and passed the first in a line of trucks. 'But it's been over a week and nothing…'

'Nothing yet. Who knows what's next after we started this bloody stupid war?'

She felt herself beginning to relent when a lorry suddenly pulled across lane her causing the car's automatic braking system to kick in. Freemark swore loudly at the driver as she pulled in behind the truck. 'Listen hun, can we talk about this later? It just sounds like 25 grand to protect us against something that's less likely to happen than getting hit by lightning seems like a lot of money. Can I think about it?'

'Sure. We can chat later.' He sounded disappointed but was trying to hide it. 'Where are you off to?'

'Interviewing farmers near the village. See how they're feeling and how it's affecting them. Although what Frank is expecting I don't know. I could probably write this from home and still get as much value. You?'

'Usual crap; different day. They've just installed new retina scanners here. No access to the building without at least one working eye.' They smiled at each other. He was trying so hard to be strong for her.

'Yeah, we've just had new fingerprint and voice-linked security installed at the office. So you get a sore throat and you're fucked. It does seem a bit overkill really. I know it's been bad, but are they really going to attack us again? Here?'

He shrugged. 'Depends if they get what they want or not. And we don't even know what that is yet…'

'Islam for all, surely? And Sharia Law across the world,' she replied, laying on the sarcasm.

'Still not convinced it's Islamic Jihad then?' They had discussed this possibility often and neither were convinced.

'Are you?' She smiled at his face on the screen.

'Well… anyway. I best get back to work. Have fun interviewing them farmers.'

'Thanks hun. Have fun at work.'

She was leaving Oxford now and heading up the M34 to join the M40. She decided it was music time. 'Fiesta, play Ariana Grande.' The car's central console graphics flicked over to music mode and the sound of Don't Call Me Angel came through the speakers. Freemark started to sing along as she joined the M40.

Some 45 minutes later, she came again to the hamlet of Little Tipton, the hill ahead showing the first houses of Lesser Worburston peeking through the trees.

She thought back to her first visit to the village. Her efforts to gain access through the woods only to be suddenly confronted by soldiers with dogs. That was a stupid idea. What had she expected to happen? That they'd welcome her in and show her the carnage? Would she really have wanted to see it? Could she stomach it? She hoped she'd never have to find out.

She pulled up the map on the console and asked the Fiesta to pick out the Savage farm. It was four minutes away. She noted how all the roads leading into Lesser Worburston were shown as closed on her map. *How long would that remain the case?* she thought. *Who would want to live there now?* As she turned down a single-track road surrounded by high hedges smothered in the green beginnings of black berries and the stunning white flowers of bindweed, she pondered on the practicalities of what would have to happen.

Eventually, once all investigations had run their course, all stains cleaned away and every inch of every house searched, the village would be reopened. The families would be allowed in to collect their

I Vow to Thee – William E. H. Walker

relative's possessions. Most likely they'd try to sell the houses. *Bloody hell that would be a bargain.* She wondered if they should buy one when they came on the market. Could she? No. Too close to home.

The Fiesta was telling her to turn left. The drive had grass growing down the middle of it that brushed against the undercarriage of the car. Ahead of her was an old red-roofed barn and large grey stone farmhouse. To her right, a self-driving tractor was spraying the young crops, while just down the hill she could see the seven-foot-high blue cordon that separated the village from the rest of the world. Behind that, sitting in the bright sun and surrounded by all the joys of spring, the houses and church tower of Lesser Worburston.

Stopping the car, Freemark pulled out her phone and snapped a couple of photos through the open window. There was still activity there. Still a swarm of SOCO units and officers hunting, desperate for some clue.

As she turned back, she saw a figure standing by the entrance to the farm watching her. She moved the car slowly forward, the electric motor sounding abnormally loud with just the soft brushing of grass under her feet. The man stood tall against the gate post, intently observing her approach with a quizzical and reserved look in his eyes. *Not friendly*, she thought.

She pulled up in front of him and stepped out, giving him her most winning smile. 'Mr. Savage? I'm Julia Freemark. I'm from the Oxford Times.'

'Right?' An articulate, plummy voice.

She regarded him closely. The clothes were fine, tailored and expensive. The beard well maintained. He was a man of means. Was he swaying slightly? 'I'm wondering if I might ask you some questions?'

He took off his cap and picked at the seam. Mid-fifties she guessed, but well preserved. 'I've said all I want to say to the gentleman from The Independent.'

She smiled again, willing him to like her. 'I didn't want to talk about Lesser Worburston, I wanted to ask about you. How all this has affected you. Who you are, a real profile if you like?'

He looked intrigued at this, his face lightening somewhat. 'Oh, my dear, there's not really much to say about little old me.' He was already making his way back toward the house, gesturing for her to follow.

Sitting in the large soot-stained, musty living room adorned in ancient wallpaper depicting fading ivy and roses, the scent of lavender filling her nostrils from the bowl on the small coffee table between them and an old spaniel sniffing at her shoes, Freemark felt herself relax. Fred was explaining the government had advised him any money lost due to the cordon around the village would be compensated, but he was unsure as to if he would take it or if it would be in bad taste.

He was on his second whisky since Freemark had entered the house and was growing merrier by the minute. 'Sun's over the yardarm somewhere in the world,' he'd exclaimed when she'd turned down his offer to join him.

Freemark had been at her most charming. She'd started off asking him what he farmed, and he answered oilseed rape and GM barley. How long had he farmed here? It was coming up to 55 years, with his parents at first obviously. She'd learned all about his past, how he'd been born here and inherited the farm from his mother when she had passed on. She cooed as he spoke of his divorce and the horribly expensive settlement. She threw in a few sympathetic "oohs" and "awws" at appropriate moments, along with "Well, you're clearly a strong man" and "You do look like an intelligent man" accompanied by a light hand on the shoulder or knee. Within 20 minutes of her arrival he was laughing and joking, insisting she call him Freddy and willing to answer anything.

Keeping him on topic proved tricky. She sipped her tea as Freddy started telling her how, thanks to the inventions of soil regulators, nano analytics and self-drive farm equipment, 'Farming isn't the same mucky, grubby business it was in the old days.' He downed his whisky. 'Really now, I'm more of a computer technician than I am a labourer.' He snorted, reaching for the decanter. 'And you know they even repair themselves. I know! I don't really have to do a damn thing.' He guffawed in the way only a man born to wealth can do.

'That must make life simpler,' Freemark stated, and before Freddy, who was nodding briskly, could continue, she added, 'Freddy, you said you're getting compensation for your losses, but you don't know if you'll accept it or not. Is that because you lost friends?'

Freddy's face darkened slightly. Adam's apple bobbed as he swallowed and nodded slowly. 'Yes, I lost friends, many friends, many friends.'

Freemark sat still and silent. She let the silence drag out, watching his expressions move through the memories of days gone by. His head wobbled slightly on his neck, like it was just a little too heavy for it to bear. 'Mary's gone, you know?' he said, almost as though she was more a friend than a reporter.

'I'm sorry, I didn't.' She didn't want to ask who Mary was.

'Not on, not on.' He said, shaking his head and downing his drink before robotically refilling it for a fourth time. He pondered the glass for a moment, swirling the dark amber liquid around its base. 'I don't drink, you know. Not a drop. Not since... Well, after the divorce I did. Drank the whole of the Thames in whisky and gin. Too much, too much. It wasn't good for me, you know. But then I met Mary and I

I Vow to Thee – William E. H. Walker

changed. Not a drop since till, well...' He looked up at her, a world of sadness in his eyes. 'It's hard, you know? Being one that survived. Mary didn't. She was killed in bed, I believe, though they won't tell me details, we weren't married so...' His voice trailed off. 'Not on, not on,' he sighed.

Freemark's response was instinctive. She moved a little closer to him, as though her presence was a comfort. 'You were close?'

He nodded a little too enthusiastically, the drink making his movements jerky. 'Yes, she was... she was kind to me. Always kind. Would bring me jam and honey or those delicious cakes she used to make. You know the ones? Where the middle bits scooped out and replaced with cream and jam? Lovely cakes. Lovely. Full of jam and cream, real cream mind – real cream. And homemade jam. My goodness, such delicious cakes.' He smiled wistfully but all too quickly it faded and his brow furrowed. 'She was so gentle. So kind. Didn't even live in the village, you know. No. She lived in a cottage on the road to Morton. She didn't deserve it...' He lapsed into silence again, studying the glass. 'Didn't deserve it.'

Freemark realised this line of conversation would get her nowhere. She sympathised with him hugely, could see the pain etched into every fine line of his face, but she needed him talking. A thought struck her and she changed tack. 'Freddy, did you know Mrs. Grantham?'

Freddy made a sound in his throat like a gutter unblocking. 'Huh, that old dragon. Yes, everyone knew her. She used to be fun, always had parties and the like. We all knew her, the kids from the village. Fun parties.' He paused, remembering. 'Then, about 10 years or so ago something changed. She turned sullen and angry. Would just rattle on about how she used to be famous and now no one respected her. Offended and overly dramatic when she wasn't asked to open the village fetes or the school extension. Airs and graces that woman, airs and graces.' He burped and mumbled an apology before reaching for the decanter.

'She had a son, didn't she?' Freemark pressed.

He didn't seem to have heard her. 'Did you know she once told me she'd partied with Presidents Bush and Clinton? She told me she'd been so popular with them they'd asked her specifically to play at their birthday celebrations. Load of old tosh if you ask me. Who'd want a woman like that at their birthday?' He sipped yet more whisky.

'A woman like what?' Freemark sat forward slightly, trying to impress urgency on him.

'A whore.' He spluttered the word out, spilling his drink and staring at Freemark. Then it seemed to dawn on him that Freemark was also a woman. Propriety kicked in and he waved his arm as though trying to swat the words away. 'Sorry, I mean... sorry. I don't mean to...'

'It's fine.' Freemark smiled as though nothing had happened. *Keep him talking*, she thought.

'I don't drink,' he said, lifting the glass to his lips and throwing back the contents.

'I take it she was promiscuous?'

He looked at her like the answer was obvious. 'Everyone knew it. She'd have parties round her house and invite people over, take a different man up to her room each night and, well…' He tapped his nose and smiled indulgently at her. 'Delicate ears.' He snorted as he said this. 'Though I expect you know what I mean, don't you?' he said with a flourish of his glass, throwing another good glug of whisky onto the chair and floor.

Freemark nodded and smiled that polite smile that didn't reach her eyes. The one she reserved for men who would spout scarcely veiled innuendo or make unwanted advances. She again attempted to keep him on track. 'Did you know her son?'

'Jack? Oh yes, I know Jack. A nasty little boy that one. A terror. He's always causing trouble. Breaking windows or drinking in the bus shelter. Troubled, troubled. But with a mother like that, well…' He trailed off again. Freemark realised he was talking as though Jake was still a child.

'Did he cause you a lot of trouble?' Freddy nodded. 'What did he do?'

Freddy harrumphed. 'Oh, you know, all sorts of things. I'm pretty sure he stole little Tim's bike? He did, he did. Rode it out to Little Tipton Lake and just threw it in.' He looked incredulous. 'I know! Just because it was nicer than his. Nasty bit of work that one.' He seemed to remember where he was, his eyes focusing momentarily on the room with a slight surprise. He sipped his drink. 'Years ago, of course. Years ago now.' He refilled his glass.

'When did you last see him?' She noticed his eyelids were starting to grow heavy.

'Who dear?' His eyes were starting to cloud over, the alcohol winning the battle for his mind.

'Jake… Jack… when did you last see him?'

He screwed up his brow in thought. 'Oh, I don't know… all grown up now I suppose. Do you know I once caught him with that Barrows girl in the hay bales? Hands all over each other… I don't know. Must be 10 years ago…'

'You mean 10 years since you last saw him?' He was starting to pitch forward, his movements slowing. Freemark guessed he must be getting his dates mixed up. Around 10 years ago Jake Grantham wouldn't have been rolling in hay bales, he'd have been in his twenties. But a moment ago he had been talking as though he was still a boy himself. She realised he was probably close to passing out now.

'Ah, 10 years, yes.' He raised his glass to his lips and seemed surprised it was empty. But then his arm fell heavily to his side, the glass falling on the soft rug at his feet, his body slumping further back into the chair. 'He swore at me last year... when he came to see her...'

'Jack did? Last year?' Freemark was excited by this news.

'Yes. Or the year before? Found him standing in the field. Tried to say hello but...' His chin was nearly resting on his chest now. 'Bloody boy. Killed my dog...' A snort. He mumbled something but Freemark couldn't pick it up. Then his head lolled slightly, eyes closing, his breathing turning deep and regular.

Freemark watched him sleep for a moment before placing her practically full cup of now cold tea on the side table and standing.

She scanned his sleeping form. The gentle folds of skin over his restful brow. The lines of a life spent competing with the elements. Still, it was a soft face, one that might once have been considered handsome. She looked about the room, taking in the old world feel of the place, and noted an antique oak bureau on which stood several framed photographs. One was black and white, a couple getting married. The outfits looked to be 1950s or 60s. His parent's maybe? She walked over it and peered closer. The spaniel looked up at her from his place by his master's feet for a moment, before lowering its head to sleep.

Held in a thin silver frame was a woman in her mid-twenties. She was model thin with jet black hair to her Barbie waist, from which stretched long, tanned legs. Her eyes were full of life and joy, and a wicked smile showing just the hint of brilliant white teeth. She was standing on a beach in a bikini so small it may well have been two bottle caps on string. Everything essential barely concealed beneath the minute wisps of fabric. For a second, Freemark envied her large, tanned breasts and curvy body. Her clear skin and high cheekbones. She was stunning, this woman. Freemark touched her own stomach beneath which her six pack was fading. She'd not exercised properly in a while and not been to jujitsu for a month thanks to work and family commitments.

Beside the bombshell stood a handsome, muscular man with a square jaw, two-day stubble and an intricate tattoo of snaking black lines down his right arm. The arm that was fully extended and raised out of shot. A selfie. She flicked her eyes between the snoring Freddy and the young good-looking man in the photo and smiled. *How life catches up with us all*, she thought.

This must be the ex who had, according to Freddy, taken his best friend and his wealth from him in a messy and miserable divorce. She could see the appeal. This woman looked like she could control a room with a smile and light up the life of any man fortunate enough to be caught in her gaze. Might explain why he'd kept the picture so visible. He'd never quite got over her. She replaced the picture with a pang of sadness for Freddy and moved on to the next.

This photo was more recent and showed an easily recognisable Freddy standing behind a stall at a fete. Beside him was a woman in her mid to late forties. They were smiling at the camera and pointing to the pots and jars laid out neatly on the gingham-covered table. This must be the fabled Mary with her homemade jam and honey. The pang of sadness became a sudden wave of sorrow as she looked at the two pictures sat side by side on the bureau. The only three women, it seemed, Freddy had ever loved, all now gone.

Having lost the beautiful model, he'd found himself stuck in a solitary life but eventually met someone he thought he could end his days with, only to have it snatched away again in the cruellest of ways.

She looked at the now sleeping farmer and smiled sadly at him, feeling a tear leak from her eye. Would he cope now or would the drink keep hold of him? Would she read in the months or years to come of his lonely death locked away in this big empty house of loss? She hoped not, he deserved more.

She returned the picture to its rightful place and, still curious despite feeling so sorry for him, gently opened the bureau to reveal a green felt-covered writing station complete with tiny drawers and shelves. There were more photos here. Stacks of them, spread higgledy-piggledy over writing pads, loose rubber bands, paperclips and unopened junk mail. She picked up a small pile that was sitting on top of a newspaper from nine years ago and flicked through them. These seemed to be holiday snaps taken around the time of the one in the frame. The happy couple participating in beach and sea activities. She put them back and picked up another pile. Freddy as a kid, all 1980s clothing and big teeth. Playing in the garden, eating birthday cake or flying a kite. A happy childhood it seemed.

The first photo in the next pile was of a group of men standing in a kitchen. The table in the middle of the room was covered in wine bottles and crushed beer cans. Overflowing ashtrays and the detritus of smoking cannabis. The men themselves were all young, teenagers or early to mid-twenties at best. Judging from the hair styles and clothing she'd guess this was taken in the late 90s, maybe early 2000s. One was wearing ludicrously baggy jeans and a cap. Another had a skinhead and a T-shirt bearing the logo "Helter Skelter." He was grinning at the camera, beer in one hand and a fat joint in the other. His spotty face like a kid at Christmas. They were all smiling broadly or laughing at something. A happy party scene, she thought. Teenagers acting as they do, and indeed as she had done on more than one occasion. She remembered the party at Sam's house. The dubstep and trance blaring from the speakers as she snogged…what was his name? Dean? Darren? No idea. She'd been hammered, her first time doing both those things.

I Vow to Thee – William E. H. Walker

The next photo was of the same kitchen, although the focus of this picture was of the woman whose face had been plastered over TV and the papers as soon as it was announced she had been killed not two weeks earlier. She was tall, slim and still beautiful. Maybe in the mid-thirties, earlier forties at this point? In one hand she held a half-finished bottle of wine, the other was grabbing the crotch of the young man standing next to her. Her face was a mix of feigned surprise and joy while the man in question looked shocked, the other three in the photo pointing and laughing.

Clearly Myris Grantham liked to party. She was older than any of the boys in the photo by at least 10 years, but it appears that didn't bother her.

The next photo was of her next to a different boy on a sofa. Her arms around his neck and she was planting a kiss on his cheek. Eyes smouldering to the camera, an unmistakable look of temptation and lust. She liked to play games.

The next was of her again, this time with a young lad pretending to spank her while his friends egged him on. The next, she was sitting on a lap, the next she was kissing a boy in a hallway with her hands on his belt. In all the photos there were alcohol and drugs. Cannabis was smoked, cocaine chopped into lines, pills strewn across tables. Freemark struggled to keep her hands from shaking as she studied each picture to see if she recognised any of the faces. This was news. The rumours of Myris' affairs after falling from grace had, of course, been reported in the days and weeks since her death, but there had never been any evidence of it. Certainly nothing like this.

She flicked through the images, some of which were bordering on the explicit, when a face stopped her and she gasped. Freddy was lying in a bed, soft sunlight filtering in through white curtains. He'd turned the camera round and was giving a big thumbs up, a wide grin on his face. Beside him lay Myris Grantham asleep and seemingly naked. He looked to be about 18 or 19. Freemark started, mouth ajar, at the picture. Freddy with the woman he'd just called a whore. He'd not just known her, he'd partied with her and slept with her.

She flicked to the next photo: Myris sitting on Freddy's lap, legs either side of him, her hips pushed forward, his hands on her buttocks, hers around his neck and the pair of them locked in a deep kiss. Another boy stood behind them making a suggestive gesture. Another boy in the corner, laughing and pointing. Freemark's eyes flicked to the other side of the picture and gasped. A small boy stood there, holding a plastic Action Man toy close to his chest. His small face a mixture of fear and desperation. He stood in his Transformers pyjamas watching his mother kissing and groping Freddy. There were tears in his eyes as he watched his mum with what Freemark supposed to be yet another man. Jake, aged no more than 10, watching his mother getting wasted and screwing teenagers. *No wonder he's so fucked up,* she thought. Poor kid. But then that poor kid was capable of… she didn't want to think about it. She pondered her options a second longer, then pocketed the stack of photos.

Freddy was still snoring as she left. As she pulled back on to the road to Middleton, she called her editor. *Send me nasty notes, will you? Sod you Jake Grantham!* she thought as Frank's face appeared on the car's console. 'Frank, I hate to say this as it might make your head swell but you were right. Boy have I got a story for you!'

09:35

Suss

They had nothing in the file. No hints or tell-tale lies that she could see. She'd read each page a dozen times already and she couldn't see anything untoward. No clue that would prove Kinsella a liar. It had taken Nigel over a week to get Kinsella's employment file for her. He'd apologised, blaming some sort of funny added security that he couldn't explain. Apparently it hadn't been where it was meant to be either, but filed away somewhere he'd not expected. She knew he was being honest when he'd said there was nothing more he could have done.

She swore under her breath. Debs, pretending to watch TV, turned and studied her. Suss knew she was worried. Debs had gently tried to persuade her to leave this alone, to pass it on to her superiors and focus on herself. But she gave up after Suss had nearly growled at her to back off. Now Debs had a pained look in her eyes as Suss threw the tablet on the sofa and wrapped her arms tight around her body.

Was she losing it? Had the loss of her parents been too much? No, Kinsella had lied and she needed to know why.

It had been over a week, wasn't she meant to be feeling better by now? Wasn't the funeral meant to have closed down the pain and end that chapter? Why focus on a woman lying about her family? Who didn't tell themselves some lies about their family? Who doesn't forget that their father was absent most of the time when they're telling people how successful he was in business? Or that their mother was depressed when they're remembering how attentive she was as a child?

Maybe it was a simple answer: Kinsella's parents weren't nice people, so she'd pretended they were dead? Suss had known others who had done similar things. They'd run away from home claiming to be orphans, only for it to be discovered their actual biography was far worse than just experiencing a simple loss. A lifetime of abuse, neglect, suffering. History that could turn children into feral animals.

I Vow to Thee – William E. H. Walker

There were plenty of them on the estate. Kids whose lives had turned as hard yet as brittle as coal. A life where they were left to cope alone as though orphaned, but still have to go home and find mum passed out on the sofa with a needle in her arm.

Like Sabra's mum. She was only about six when Suss met her and already tougher than most. A look in her eyes like that of a cornered cat. Life had given her a mother who spent every penny they had on heroin, a father she'd never met and she'd spat back at the world that she wasn't done. She would survive. She died though, killed on the estate over some trivial argument. She was 13.

She'd known so many that died so needlessly. The old hippy, as they'd called her, in her sixties but still believing the world would find peace and love, bludgeoned to death for her glass jewellery. Teenagers had died every week on the estate from knives and guns to drugs and alcohol.

She'd been the lucky one, her parents had loved her and had done their best to protect her. Still wanted to know her and be a part of her life even after all her "friends" had drifted away when she'd said she wanted to be a copper. They had stood by her through it all and now someone had taken them away from her.

'Two from the top and four from the bottom, please.' The TV cut into her thoughts, both an annoyance and a welcome distraction from the ghosts that plagued her. '…75, 60, 3, 2, 6, 9. And your target is 387.'

Suss hardly needed to blink. '75 times three, times two, minus 69, plus six.'

Debs was shaking her head, a small smile on her face. 'I still don't know how you do that.' She returned the smile as best she could, noting the hope in Debs' expression that her Suss was coming back to her.

The contestants on the TV weren't finding it quite as easy. Suss flopped down onto the sofa, suddenly exhausted. Her head resting on the fluffy white cushion they'd bought at a market in Camden a month earlier.

'You wanna tea?' Debs asked.

'I'd love a beer,' she retorted.

'It's 9.30 my love, bit early.' She was keeping it light. She stood to make their drinks but Suss waved her back down. For the love of everything, no more tea.

Suss expelled all the air from her body. Breathing out through her mouth till her lungs felt ready to collapse. She held her muscles tight, enjoying the burning sensation that spread through her body as it starved of oxygen. She held it for as long as possible, then a little longer, before she sucked in deeply, noticing how quickly the body cooled. She was alive, she just wanted to confirm it. Why was she always the one who lived?

Back when she was 10 or so, she was involved in an accident. On her way to school she and a friend were hit by a car that threw her friend into a lamp post, but just clipped her. The driver hadn't stopped, just sped off to leave the small children to bleed on the road. She remembered none of this but woke to find herself in a hospital bed several hours later with her parents by her side.

Her friend had died on impact with the post, her spine broken. The driver was never found. Her aunt died in a fire caused by a faulty oven, her friend from bad cocaine, but always she lived.

She was staring at the TV, not really taking anything in. On the screen the woman had just picked her letters and the timer had started.

'T, N, O, E, R, E, P, I, A.'

'Peritonea,' she said quietly.

Debs looked incredulous. 'Are you even watching this?'

'Not really,' Suss mumbled, pulling the cushion out from under her head and hugging it close to her chest. Her thoughts moved back to Kinsella. Why had she claimed the message was from her Nan? Her file had confirmed she was an orphan. Parents lost at six years old, she had moved into the care system, so no grandparents. *Maybe it was possible she'd met them later*, she mused. No, that didn't sit right. She wouldn't still be saying she had no family, would she? She wasn't the type to fish for sympathy.

The most obvious answer, Suss thought, was that Kinsella was having an affair and had received a message from her lover she hoped to disguise. But Kinsella didn't strike her as the type for that either. She was too prim and proper. Too middle-class and predictable. She remembered Kinsella's reaction to her cursing. The looks of annoyance and once, when Suss had exclaimed 'Jesus!' she had even winced. A religious woman then. Pious even. But that still didn't explain Nan.

Suss thought back through her memories to find mention of Kinsella's husband, but there was nothing. She'd not mentioned him, ever. Not a peep. That was odd. Most people would talk about their partners. Make jokes, tell anecdotes and stories. Even just that their partner was cooking dinner or collecting them or being a pain in the arse. She often did with Debs who was, Suss truthfully thought, kinder, more thoughtful and funnier than anyone she knew.

Yet Kinsella kept silent and Suss realised she didn't even know his name. Problems at home? Was Nan someone who she confided in?

'Insulants,' she said to the TV.

I Vow to Thee – William E. H. Walker

'Piss off,' laughed Debs, visibly pleased to see her engaging a little.

It was the timing of the text right before the bombs that bothered her. As well as her body language, the sudden effort to hide her phone screen with her body. Angling herself away from Suss and Singh even before she'd opened the message. She'd been expecting it, there was no surprise when it came through, so why had she been so secretive?

Suss tried to connect some dots in her investigation. What she knew so far was that a man and woman had bought cars. Upon further investigation the guy who'd sold them suspected the woman wasn't as old as she looked. She was too flexible was the word he had used, leering at her. Suss had felt like punching him but had held her cool. She had established that it was possible the woman was much younger. Also, and most interestingly, he did have CCTV that actually recorded.

She had persuaded him that playing it back for her was far more beneficial to his future than waiting for a warrant, which would lead to the police thoroughly checking the status of every car on his lot. Twice.

They had squeezed into his tiny Portacabin office and peered at the blurred figures on the flickering monitor. The system was at least 20 years old and battered next to useless, but it was most definitely a black police-issue BMW that had pulled up in the street just in view of the camera but not close enough to make out the number plate.

The two visitors had been careful to keep their faces away from the camera that stood sentry over the lot. They had also waited for the owner to join them at one of the furthest points from his office, making them even harder to identify.

The woman was tall, the man shorter. His hair clearly white even in the grainy black and white footage of the CCTV. Was she taller than Kinsella? Maybe. It was hard to tell, but, using the angles, she had her height at about five 10. There was something else though, something about the way they moved that pricked her interest. It was joined up in some way, like two parts of a machine. Military training? If they were the perpetrators of the attacks, they would have had significant training. They even stood in similar ways. She had snatched off a copy of the recording and thanked him, sure she was on the right track now.

What had confirmed to her she was right was that he had been found dead two days later. Suicide apparently, an overdose of painkillers. It was too much of a coincidence for Suss. She'd looked up the High Wycombe dealer Kinsella had been to see and tried to make contact, but he'd apparently gone away for a while. Another coincidence or just bad luck?

She reminded herself she couldn't be sure it was Kinsella. She was pointing the finger without evidence and going on just a gut feeling. But it was a feeling she couldn't shake.

If Kinsella were involved in this then Suss would need to tread carefully. The woman was smart and had been careful to cover her tracks these past years. It would have to have been years as well. You don't plan all this in a week. You don't get promoted to DI as young as she was without being exceptional at your job. Suss, who was younger than Kinsella by several years, knew that. She would ask her little things, engage with her as a friend. Make her feel safe. And then she would have answers.

She'd used this method with people before. The expression "you catch more flies with honey than vinegar" had not been lost on her. She'd find out what was going on and if Kinsella was involved, then God had better help his devoted child because Suss would kill her.

Without warning the memory of her parents pushed to the forefront of her mind, but instead of crying Suss got angry.

I Vow to Thee – William E. H. Walker

10:56

Shanks

'Ladies and gentlemen, can we please bring this meeting to order?' The fat, balding twit Party Chairman stood before the assembled mass of sheep who gradually, reluctantly, ended their bleating. His cloudy eyes scanned the room, his hunched back making his upper body bob like a toy. 'As you are all aware, we are here to ascertain who among us...'

Just get to the sodding point old man! Shanks thought.

'...believes themselves both capable and willing of becoming the next leader of our Party, and subsequently the next Prime Minister of this great nation of ours.' He paused, surveying the room, his mouth chewing the air like an old dog. Shanks wanted to slap him and watch his cheeks wobble. 'In so much as it is both necessary and right for us to decide who among us should be allowed to be put forward for this high office, it is the responsibility of our members to make the final decision.'

Shanks imagined putting the fat old git over his knee and spanking him like a naughty puppy, although he'd probably like that, the dirty old bastard.

'Due to the nature of the crisis we find ourselves in, the decision has been made by the Executive Committee to expedite proceedings. Therefore, the vote will take place in six days' time. Now, this will be a Friday, as you know. We have invoked article 14 of our Party Charter to ensure a speedy and sensible transition of power. We cannot allow the country to continue on without a leader for much longer.' There was a murmur of agreement from across the room. 'I therefore open the floor to allow those among us who deem themselves worthy to step forward and be counted.' He shuffled back to his seat at the back of the dais and sagged into it, a balloon slowly losing air.

The room was hushed, expectant. All eyes searching for who would be first. Who would put themselves forward? Shanks placed a bet with himself and won it almost immediately. Marko Flint, the erstwhile Defence Secretary, was wobbling his way to the front of the room. A walrus on the march. As

I Vow to Thee – William E. H. Walker

people around him started to notice the movement, the white noise of whispering and lowered voices filled the room. Several hundred people all talking at once making it impossible to work out what anyone other than those stood directly beside you was saying. Martin, standing to his left, chuckled quietly and whispered some insult to someone and the laughing spread about him. Shanks himself remained silent.

As Marko huffed and puffed his way forward the murmurs turned to shouts. Some in support while others in derision. Bringing himself to a stop with what appeared to be some considerable effort, he held up his hands for quiet. Slowly the room stilled, and his beady eyes peered out at them from under their chubby eyelids. Shanks called him Pork Chop and smirked at the funny-looking fat lump. 'Esteemed colleagues. I thank you for the opportunity to talk to you today.' His belly hung low over the top of his trousers. Shanks wanted to try to scoop it up to see if it would all fit inside his belt. 'I have been Defence Secretary now for a little over a year—'

'And we've been attacked twice!' yelled a voice from the back of the room. It was met by laughter from various factions.

Marko ignored it. 'And yes, we've had our difficulties.' Shanks almost laughed out loud. *Difficulties? Is that what you called the past few weeks?* Others in the room failed to contain themselves quite as well. 'But we will go on and, I think…' he shuffled his feet, his belly wobbling in time, '…in the round, when all is said and done, that I have performed my duties to the best of my abilities.'

'Which is why we were attacked!' someone else yelled. This time Marko looked a little sheepish but struggled on nonetheless.

'And, as such, I would like to carry on doing my bit, working hard for the nation and serve as the next leader of this Party.' His supporters cheered while those against him shouted insults. Marko, unsure of what protocol dictated, stood and wobbled like a jelly at the front of the room. After a few moments the Party Chairman leaned forward and prodded him in his ample back and he stumbled off to the side of the stage.

A few seconds later he was replaced by Angela Rainsworth, MP for Hampshire East and Minister of State for Housing, Communities and Local Government. A very junior position and Angela had only held it since Miller's ascension to power. She was generally thought of as a bit of a waste of space.

This time the cheers were quieter and there were still a fair few who didn't like what they saw in the mid-forties former RAF pilot. Personally, she reminded Shanks of a stuffy librarian who regarded herself as superior to those around her. She marched onto the platform with military precision and stared down the baying crowd. Lips pursed and arms folded until the cheers and jeers quietened.

I Vow to Thee – William E. H. Walker

Her voice, when she spoke, was thick with Liverpudlian pride. 'I will stand for leader of this Party. We're at a crisis point and we need someone who can show strength of will and...' Here she glanced at Marko. '...body. I will not stand by and allow this great British Christian Party to fall from grace. You need someone who can command the respect of the public. That is me.' She nodded sternly out at the room as she said "me." Somewhere at the back of the room someone shouted 'Atten-shun!' and she shot him a look that reminded Shanks of a primary school teacher. 'I will bring our country together and forge a New Britain for all.'

'Save it for the punters,' someone called out and Shanks couldn't help but smile.

She scowled and moved off to stand beside Marko. She was followed up by Susan Fortescue, MP for East Sussex, who seemed to have most of the MP's support. She talked of uniting the country in its hour of need and bringing people together. She left the stage to moderately enthusiastic clapping from the crowd.

Harrold Chapman, Secretary of State for Transport, was next, followed by Roger Boldermore, MP for Darlington, who waffled on for so long the old dog Chairman practically barked at him to shut up. Shanks watched them all and smiled inwardly. They were nothing to him, just obstacles to be overcome or pushed aside.

The room was growing restless after Roger had left the stage to more than a few cheers and a few more jeers to stand beside his fellow leadership candidates. There was a lull while everyone waited to see if any others wanted to put their hat in the ring. Shanks bided his time. Martin nudged his shoulder, but Shanks waited.

The Party Chairman was bobbing his head over the room to see if the five were all he was getting, a slight look of disappointment in his eyes. Around the room people started to talk among themselves. Boredom setting in, the discussions grew louder, pocketed with bouts of laughter or good-natured teasing.

Shanks, who was standing with his closest allies Martin, Brian and Hugh, waited until the old man put his hands on the side of his ornate chair to rise before striding forward confidently and standing before the room. His eyes sparkled in the bright lights. He stood still and quiet. His stomach flat and his suit cut impeccably. He crossed his hands in front of him and waited. He waited as the realisation he was there drifted over the room. His eyes scanned the room, making contact with many of those who were gradually turning to face him. He waited until every set of eyes was on him. No one spoke.

He let the silence linger.

He could taste their need for him to speak. A rallying cry was what they wanted, what they desired and what they thought the Party needed now. So he would give them the opposite. When he finally spoke, his voice was soft and melodious. 'My fellow Members of Parliament, we are here today not because we have lost our leader, not because we need to find a replacement, but because we have lost all credibility.' He paused to let the more vocal of his colleagues shout their opinions, waiting again until the room was silent before he continued. 'The British public believe we are a bunch of self-serving narcissists who play politics for our own games.' Here the calls of righteous indignation were much louder and lasted far longer. Shanks let them go on for a while before smiling broadly and raising his arms for quiet. 'My friends, I know that for most of us this is totally inaccurate. We, like so many, are coloured by the few. This…' His arm shot up, finger rigid to emphasise his point, '…is our biggest challenge. Last week we…' arms spread to encompass the whole room, '…didn't just suffer an attack on Lesser Worburston and London, we…' he pointed to the crowd and then himself, '…suffered an attack on our Party.' They were all watching him closely now, and this is when he felt most alive. 'Our leader was attacked from within by a cross-dressing pervert.' Sniggers from some, but he shot them a look and they quelled beneath his gaze. 'He was unsuccessful, but how? Because our leader chose to publicly shame him. What does this say about our Party? What does this say about us?' He clenched his fists in front of him, his voice full of passion. 'I think it says we're not a real Party. That we have no unified direction and purpose. That we are nothing more than a bunch of squabbling children.' His voice had been rising slowly and the last word of his statement made a few jump. He paused and watched them. Even Marko was enthralled, his mouth open and his chins for once still. 'How can we hope to command the respect of the public when we cannot even give it to each other?' His voice rang out across the room. 'Those of you here over the past year who have leaked, who have given off-the-record interviews, who have taken money, liquor, meals or sex for a story, I say shame on you.' A pause, some of the Party were looking guilty. 'The reason we are here today, at this low point for both the British Christian Party and the country, is because we have put ourselves here. We have acted in our own self-interests and not in that of the Party.' He let the words sink in. His voice softened when he started again. 'But there is a way forward, my friends. If we can unite, if we can come together and speak with one voice, we can be the true and unequivocal power in this country.' His voice was rising again. 'We will be untouchable by Labour; we will be free of the Liberal Democrat Opposition. We will end the Greens. We will be the British government forever.' His supporters cheered, gradually others joined in and before long the majority in the room were clapping and hailing him. He stood accepting their applause. Smiling broadly at them.

This wouldn't be a contest. This would be a walkover.

I Vow to Thee – William E. H. Walker

13:12

Laoch

'Peter? Peter!' Where was that boy? Loach sat in his drawing room. His leg, the last part of his body still bandaged, elevated to "aid healing." He'd returned from hospital to his North Oxford residence the previous evening and had tried to sleep but the last of the bruising kept him awake, along with the thoughts of the glory to come. Having eventually fought his way to a fitful, dream-filled sleep, he had woken in a foul mood and it had taken a visit from her to turn his day around.

She had appeared in the drawing room, as though materialised through a wall. Standing tall and severe before him, he'd first wondered if he was in trouble for something, but she had surprised him by joining him on the sofa, her hand on his arm, asking him how he was and how she was so grateful that he was well. She had been falling over herself to express her sorrow for his injuries. She said they'd planned well but it seemed the support structure wasn't as good as it should have been, which had led to the walls collapse. She was very apologetic and pleased he was recovering. She was also sorry that it could not have been she who had visited him in hospital. That her sending of a subordinate was not meant as a slight, but as her desire to express her regret at his injuries as soon as she was able. And now she was free to come and see him and ensure herself of his returning health.

He'd been taken aback – she'd always been so cold, so distant. It warmed his heart when she prayed with him for his swift recovery. He dismissed her concerns as unwarranted, he was on the mend and ready for action. He was ready to be useful.

She beamed at him and exclaimed how pleased she was. How grateful He would be to hear Laoch was feeling better. Laoch asked her to send his respects and thank Him for His concern. She agreed willingly.

Then they spoke about the next phase and he listened intently as she'd outlined their plans. He started to grow concerned when she finished talking and still hadn't mentioned his rise into politics. He asked the question and for a second he thought he saw the cold distance returned to her sparkling green eyes.

But then she smiled and assured him the best was yet to come. He would rise higher than anyone. He was pleased with that and assured her he would do his part. She left him feeling buoyant and ready for action.

Four hours later he rehearsed his speech for that afternoon and was ready to deliver it. He just needed Peter, who was missing. 'Peter!?'

The door to the drawing room opened and Peter entered. 'I'm sorry, Your Excellency. I was in the kitchen with the chef.'

'Well stay at your bloody desk in future! I need you boy.'

Peter had turned away and was already pouring a glass of whisky for him. Laoch's eyes flicked up as Peter reached for the crystal glass. He was wearing tight trousers again this morning, his buttocks clearly defined under the thin cotton. He saw Peter was watching him in the mirror and looked quickly away, pretending to be deep in study of his speech but feeling his cheeks start to glow.

Peter placed the glass beside him. 'Is there anything else, Sir?'

Was there a twinkle in his eye? Was he hinting at something? 'Yes Peter.' His voice caught and he cleared his throat. 'I'm ready to record my speech. Do you have the camera?'

'I shall fetch it now, Sir.' He turned, walking toward the door. Was he wiggling his bottom more than usual? Laoch felt his breathing flutter and forced the thoughts away.

Peter returned a few minutes later with the camera, which he placed on the table before Laoch, adjusting the position via the small screen while Laoch sipped his whisky and turned the speech over in his mind.

When everything was ready Peter appraised Laoch. 'Sir, you need a tidy up.' Without warning, the man who had worked for him for the past two years suddenly started to run his hands through Laoch's hair, smoothing his eyebrows, brushing dust from his shoulders. Peter stood so close to him Laoch caught his scent. The slight musk of deodorant and the freshness of youth. As he straightened his hair Peter's belt was at Laoch's eye level. Loach struggled not to look directly at him but failed. As he brushed his shirt down and straightened the older man's jacket, their eyes met. Laoch held Peter's gaze, his heart thumping loudly in his ears. There was a small smile on the younger man's face. A teasing, tempting smile. Evidently satisfied, Peter straightened up. Laoch couldn't have if he tried. 'There. Now

I Vow to Thee – William E. H. Walker

you look presentable.' He grinned at Laoch before returning to the camera. He moved a chair to behind the screen and sat down, giving Laoch an expectant look.

Laoch was still working through the close and personal contact they had shared when he realised Peter was waiting for him. He sat up straighter, realised he couldn't, and fumbled with the top button on his shirt to show the bruising underneath. He was ready... ish. What had he done to him? He cleared his throat once more and nodded to Peter. 'Begin.'

13:35

Singh

Singh sat in his cramped magnolia office, the one window behind him affording a view of tarmac and spiky dark bush. The coffee he'd made to keep himself fresh had gone cold. The voices on the small radio on the standard-issue pine shelf making overly chirpy efforts to be interesting.

Singh wasn't listening and he wasn't drinking. He was reading a report, his eyes focused on the impersonal language describing the alleged suicide of the woman found in Blackbird Leys that morning.

She'd been dead for two days. Hanged from the banisters in her hallway, bruising on her neck...

Singh hadn't been sure what about this case had piqued his interest. Normally it would have stayed with Wentworth, maybe reaching his assistant. But something about it had touched him, so he'd asked to read the report.

"Body found by her husband Jeremy Simms, age 41, and daughter Caroline Simms, age five."

'Could it be connected?' Singh murmured the words. He was feeling useless, he needed to be involved. Last week all investigation into both the village attack and London bombing had been passed to a special task force made up of MI5, MI6, GCHQ and the Met Counter Terrorism Group, and both Singh and Thames Valley had been left out in the cold. He resented that decision, despite the fact they'd made next to no progress. Which is why he was looking into this file. One last desperate hope.

'Sir?' Wentworth sat opposite him, looking slightly awkward as his boss perused his work. 'Was there anything in particular you were looking for?'

'No.' Singh didn't usually offer one-word answers, but something in the report had caught his attention.

"Mr. Simms said that his wife had suffered from nightmares, insomnia and paranoia for the past week. It had started suddenly after she had stayed the night with a friend in Richmond, North Yorkshire, and was getting worse. She had sent her husband and daughter to his parents to try to pull herself

I Vow to Thee – William E. H. Walker

together. Mrs. Simms has a history of mental illness prior to her death and was being treated for anxiety and post-natal depression up until around two years ago. She was hospitalised after an attempted suicide attempt…"

'Is that accurate?' Singh was pointing at the paragraph. 'About the nightmares?'

'Yes Sir.' Wentworth was unsure where this was going, Singh could see it in his eyes.

'I'm not questioning your work, Phillip. It's as impeccable as always.' He saw Wentworth visibly relax. 'But there's something in this that's bothering me.'

Wentworth expanded on his report. 'According to her husband, it started on a Tuesday night two weeks ago. He said she came back from her friends looking exhausted, acting distant and distracted. He'd tried to find out what was wrong, but she wouldn't say. He said she woke up twice during that night screaming.'

'Did she say anything in her sleep?' Singh asked.

'Nothing he could remember, apparently it was a lot of screaming and blind panic. I've sent a message to North Yorkshire Police to visit the friend, see if we can find out what happened to her when she was there.'

Singh leaned back in his chair and rocked gently, the small squeaks of the motion bouncing round the room. 'The timing bothers me,' he said eventually. 'All started the day after the village shooting.'

'You're thinking she managed to escape somehow? She was there and saw what was going on and ran?' Wentworth's assumption she was a victim was the most logical.

'Maybe.' Singh wasn't convinced by that argument. He'd never really bought into the idea that Islamic Jihad were behind the attack. It was too cold and calculating for them. Too clinical and too well executed. Then, when the UN had rejected the evidence put forward by the UK and US, he'd started to think it was more likely that a group in the UK were behind the atrocity. 'Why wouldn't she come forward if she'd survived? I don't believe it was IJ but…' He didn't articulate his thoughts. 'But a mother from Blackbird Leys?' He closed the file. 'On its own I'd probably not think too much of this. But…' He pulled another file from the pile on his desk and passed it to Wentworth, who opened it and started to read. 'Colin Farrow, age 36. Died in a house fire a week last Wednesday. He was found in his living room burned so badly it took DNA reconstruction to identify him.'

'Poor bloke,' Wentworth said, a note of real sympathy in his voice.

'Thing is, it didn't make sense to me either. His house was one of those 1960s square build with the living room and dining room separated by an arch, kitchen taking up the other side of the house. Small hallway in the middle and front door opening into that.' He could see Wentworth was still unsure, but he didn't interrupt. 'He was found on what remained of a chair, the pathologist said he'd been sitting on it when he died.'

Wentworth had caught up. 'Was he drunk or asleep or something else?'

'According to his neighbours he lived alone, no pets or partner. He was pleasant and friendly, a churchgoer and not a drinker.'

'So asleep? Died of smoke inhalation before he woke up?'

'Normally I'd agree with you, but pathology found traces of coarse hemp burned into his body.' He waited to see if Wentworth got his meaning. He had.

Wentworth's eyebrows rose toward his hairline. 'Hemp like that isn't used for clothes.'

Singh nodded. 'No, but it could be used for rope.'

Wentworth looked excited. 'So he was murdered? Why?'

Singh shrugged. 'That's what I've yet to work out. Fire started in the kitchen and was hotter than one would expect for a pan fire. According to the report it spread through the house at incredible speed.'

'Arson then? Church going, non-drinker…' Wentworth was chewing through possibilities. His mouth moved silently as he did so. 'Any abuse or other issues?'

Singh shook his head. 'Again, according to his neighbours he'd moved to the village from Oxford about three years ago and had been quiet but friendly ever since. He didn't bother anyone or have many visitors. They said he generally kept to himself. DS Mulligan is investigating, and I've asked her to keep me in the loop.'

Wentworth tapped the file on his lap. 'What's this got to do with Mrs. Simms?'

Singh grimaced. 'Maybe nothing, but then this came through from our colleagues in Cornwall. Took a few days till someone realised the connection.'

He passed over a second file to Wentworth, whose expression turned to one of shock as he read the name. 'Grantham? You don't mean…'

Singh was nodding. 'The very same. Her son in fact. We interviewed him afterward, not the nicest of gentlemen by all accounts.'

Wentworth was reading the file. 'Says here he died in a fire as well?'

Singh nodded. 'Again, fire spread rapidly through the house, body burned beyond recognition, DNA tests required but there's more. Check page four.' Wentworth turned the pages.

'Jesus.' His voice had the tone of someone who really didn't believe what he was reading. 'He had a body buried in the garden?'

Singh's face was grave. 'Indeed. A recent addition as well. He'd planted vegetables over it, dogs were brought in to search for other bodies in the house and found her. She's yet to be identified but the body was less than a week old.'

'Why wasn't this on the news?'

'So far we've done a fairly good job of keeping it quiet. The neighbours who called it in have been obliging and the press don't seem to have picked up anything. Local force is also cooperating now they know the possible link. At the time, it was reported locally but the connection doesn't seem to have been made with Myris Grantham.'

'Grantham is looking likely for the village?' Wentworth shrugged. 'Seems a bit of a stretch still, even with the body. Though his mother was there.' He mulled it over. 'It's possible he did it, I suppose. If we're assuming he was killed to keep his part in it quiet. And this Mr. Farrow as well. But Mrs. Simms?'

Singh could understand his scepticism. 'Maybe. Either way, what we have is two deaths by fire and a supposed suicide of a woman who seems to have had a personality transplant from the day after the village attack, all in the space of a week.'

'The burnings I admit seem suspicious, particularly considering who Grantham was. But how do you connect the suicide?'

Singh shrugged. 'I don't, that's the problem. Other than the timing of her nightmares, I just can't seem to let it lie.' He turned it over in his head for a moment. Was he going down the wrong path with this? Could there be another reason that poor woman took her own life? The timing though. It all came down to the timing. 'Anyway Phillip. I want you down in Cornwall, see what you can find out about Grantham.' He saw the look of protest in his subordinate's face. 'I know, it's unlikely you'll find anything the locals haven't already, but I need your experience and expertise to be sure.' He smiled to soften the blow and saw Wentworth relent.

'Of course, Sir.' Wentworth sat up a little, the reluctance gone. He was onside.

'Right, now that's settled, how about some lunch? The chicken place down the road?'

Wentworth snorted. 'Is it still actual chicken?'

Singh laughed. 'I doubt it, isn't it all grown in a lab these days?'

He held the door open for Wentworth and walked with him for lunch, leaving the three files on his desk.

Day 15

'In the animal kingdom, the rule is, eat or be eaten; in the human kingdom, define or be defined.'

—*Stephen Szasz*

09:07

Kinsella

Listening to a news report of Laoch's speech, Kinsella laughed at his choice of words. The reporter had told the audience there was language that may offend, and he'd been right.

'We've been in the grip of fear for decades, first it was the IRA, the bloodthirsty murderers posing as Catholics. Then when we finally made peace, we let the Muslims into the country in their droves and we've been fighting them ever since.'

The news reporter's voice again. 'His Excellency Bishop Laoch of Oxford went on to say he expected the day to come soon when every, and I quote, "right-blooded Britons" would rise up and cast down those who have sought to keep them cowed and in fear of the true light of the Lord. His Excellency has generated quite a following over the past two years. He is now one of the most recognisable figures in the church and has utilised social media in a way only seen before in politics. He has over 33 million followers on Frog and Twitter, and even though he was caught in the explosions that devastated London, shows no signs of slowing down."

A different voice now.

'Mat Arnot there. In Wales tonight the people of Powys have marched on the town hall demanding the removal of all immigrants from their town saying they pose a threat to society. Placards, showing the face of Bishop Laoch calling for him to become the next Prime Minister, were brandished along with various anti-immigration slogans. Local officials have spoken out against the demonstrations that have followed in the wake of similar scenes in London, Nottingham, Manchester, Bradford and Birming—'

She switched the radio off, satisfied. She was waiting for Suss, they were meeting agents from MI5 to hand over the final pieces of their investigation and she was late. Kinsella didn't like lateness, although she suspected it was normal for Suss. She didn't dress like a copper, talk like a copper or even really act like a copper. She was all together a bit too... funky?

I Vow to Thee – William E. H. Walker

Even though she knew she shouldn't, she liked Suss. There was something about her that kept her interesting. Kinsella hadn't had any real friends in years, and she hadn't realised she missed them until working with Suss. Maybe she could make a friend of her? A real friend. Someone to confide in, not everything obviously, but the stuff that she'd not spoken about with anyone since... she really didn't know when. *"Where'd you get your hair done? I love it. Shall we go for a glass of wine? Girls' night, girls' night!"* She'd not had a girlfriend since she was married. They'd drifted away like mist, taking her laughter with them.

Once everything was done and finished, it might be nice to have a friend. To not feel so lonely.

The car caught her attention and she realised Suss had arrived. She climbed out of her BMW and affected a look of concern. Suss was moving slowly, taking her time exiting the car. She seemed different somehow, on her guard.

Kinsella moved round to the driver's door and opened it for her. 'Hey. How're you doing?'

'I'm all right.' She paused. 'Thanks.'

Kinsella realised her happy tone might not have been appropriate. 'I was so sorry to hear—'

'I know, I got your card. Thanks for that.' She smiled at her, looking strained.

Kinsella tried again. 'How've you been holding up?'

Suss shrugged. 'Good days, bad days. Well, you know.'

She seemed to eye Kinsella closely until she realised Suss meant her own loss. She felt her cheeks flush. 'Yeah, but I was very young. It's never easy I know but...' They were struggling through this, both feeling the raw pain of the void left by a loved one. Both unsure and unused to comfort and comforting from anyone other than their closest family. 'How's the hotel?'

Suss shrugged. 'It's ok. Was nice to spend some time at home though. I've missed it.' Her shoulders dropped as she spoke. Clearly she'd rather still be at home.

Kinsella brought the awkwardness to a close. 'Right, shall we get going? I'll drive.'

They left the station and drove in silence to meet the two MI5 agents.

09:34

Suss

Some 20 minutes into their journey and she could hold it in no longer, she'd have to tread carefully but she needed to know for sure, her questions fighting to be given breath.

They were speeding down the M40 on their way to London, handing over the last of their official reports to MI5 now Suss was back at work. Sitting in the outside lane thanks to a near constant stream of middle-lane drivers. They'd talked initially about their mutual loathing of this particular type of motorist. The type who stays at 65 miles an hour in the middle of a motorway. Pootling along seemingly oblivious to the left-hand lane, clogging up the network. The conversation would have helped bond any normal relationship but Suss was too unsure to allow that. After 10 minutes or so they were resigned to the fact that none of the drivers were going to change their behaviour due to Suss and Kinsella being grumpy about it, and so they had lapsed into silence.

Kinsella, despite police regulations telling her to use autopilot when motorway driving and not in a pursuit, was practically flying. Suss saw she was an excellent driver, even at over a ton.

'Mind if I ask you a question?' She looked over at Kinsella who was driving her BMW awfully close to the tail of the car in front.

'Sure,' she said, not taking her eyes from the road. Suss edited her earlier thoughts. She was a good driver but took risks.

'What happened? To your parents I mean?' There was a flicker of emotion in Kinsella's eyes. A tightening of her jaw. 'I'm sorry, you don't have to answer that.'

'It's okay,' she answered quickly, flashing the car ahead of her. 'It's natural, I suppose. What with everything you've been through.' The Astra ahead moved aside, and she accelerated into the space it left and quickly gaining on a van. Suss could tell she was building up to the confession. When she spoke, her voice came in spurts like she was forcing the words from her body. 'I was six. They went out to a party

I Vow to Thee – William E. H. Walker

at a friend's house. Lots of wine and beer and whatnot. They drove. Dad wasn't meant to be drinking.' She flashed the van ahead and it started to slow down. She saw her face set in anger. 'They drove home. Well, they meant to drive home.' She jabbed at the touch screen on the dash harder than was necessary and the car's blue lights flashed on. The van, which had been gradually slowing down from 90 to 60, quickly moved over. Kinsella prodded the screen again to turn off the siren and accelerated past the van as it finally got out of their way.

Suss remained quiet, waiting for Kinsella to continue. She was almost ready to prompt her when she started talking again. 'Dad had been drinking whisky, he'd always liked whisky. His friend had been plying him with it. Some friend.' She undertook a Mini, making sure to give the driver a cold, hard stare. 'Mum was on cocaine.' She shrugged as if this was totally normal. 'It was the nineties, and she was a successful woman. Dad was in finance and mum had her own business selling houses to rich folks. It's the only reason I'm still here, what they left me.' She pressed the horn as a Volvo pulled out in front of them causing her to slam on the brakes. She had been going nearly 120. Suss unconsciously gripped the side of the seat and held her breath until she was sure they'd managed to slow down enough to not hit it. 'Anyway, late night, both messed up, all it took was a tired van driver and that was that.' She had sounded so matter of fact summing up the fate of her parents. All the emotion of earlier had left her voice. It was clearly how she dealt with it: shutting out the pain. Suss almost envied her that. Her loss was still so raw. Like exposed flesh under boiling water, it had scolded her to the bone. 'They were young when they had me. Mum wasn't yet 20. The invincible ones, you know?'

'I'm really sorry.' Suss forced herself to sound sincere.

Kinsella flicked her head as though batting her sympathy away. 'It happens. But thanks.' She was chewing the inside of her lip, anxiety in physical form.

'What happened to you?' Suss wanted to know it all.

Kinsella made a clicking sound with her tongue. 'Same as happens to all orphans: the care system. I was lucky. Spent nearly 10 years with the same family. They were lovely and looked after me well. Educated at private school even..' She snorted at the luxury.

'You got lucky with them though.' Suss' mind conjured the pretty little Kinsella in pleated skirt and cardigan, skipping up to the gates of her posh school. Then her mother's face washed through her mind and she felt bile in her throat. She just wanted to scream at her, to beat her into a confession, but she restrained herself. She wasn't there yet. Her nerve endings prickled as though someone ran a current over her skin.

I Vow to Thee – William E. H. Walker

Kinsella seemed to ponder this for a moment. 'I did. I know. But then at 16 I inherited and I'm out on my own.'

'They didn't want you to stay on?' Suss was surprised.

'They offered, but no. I wanted to experience life.'

The atmosphere in the car was uncomfortable, thick with memories of lives lost.

Suss rested her head on the seat. 'It's hard, innit? I know I lost my parents more recently but, no family to count on. I ain't even got grandparents. No other family now. You?'

Kinsella gave her a watery half-smile. 'No, but it does get easier. You don't forget them but I suppose you just get used to it. The absence I mean.'

As they flew past three cars in the middle lane, Kinsella visibly shook. 'Middle lane drivers huh?' An attempt to return to a simpler, less emotional conversation.

'Yeah.' Suss' mind was elsewhere.

'I don't know, motorway driving has been taught for years now and still idiots think they're meant to sit in the middle lane.' She was trying to sound normal again, perhaps trying to block out the thoughts of death.

'How long have you had this now?' She patted the dashboard.

'The car? About six months. Goes well, don't like autopilot much though. Can't get used to letting a car drive me.'

Suss replied with a grunt, no longer in the mood for sharing, but she needed to keep Kinsella onside. Keep her thinking Suss was simply missing her parents. "Simply". When did the loss of her parents become simple? When did it become something she had to hide behind? She was lying. Suss was sure of it. Not a mention of grandparents or extended family. Why would she be so secretive about them when she was appearing so willing to share? She wanted to punch Kinsella square in the face and break her nose. Even now, traveling at just under 130 miles an hour. Jesus! Knowing what would happen if they crashed. Knowing it would end their lives as assuredly as if she drew a gun and shot her, she wanted to beat the truth from her. Was this grief driving her? Did she just need someone to blame? No, Kinsella had lied from the start and she needed to know why. She nursed the anger inside of her. Fanned the flames and kept it hot.

Her world consisted of one question. The question she couldn't ask and the only question she wanted an answer to: If you're an orphan, who is Nan?

12:00

Laoch

'We're being punished by God for our crimes! That's why He sent the Muslim here to destroy us!' He was holding them in his grasp, his to play with. To twist, turn, spin and manipulate. 'We allowed ourselves to become decadent. We allowed our government to lie to us, abuse us and destroy our souls for their own gain. That is why we are here now. In a country that's falling apart around us and overrun with vermin.' *Dance my pretty puppets, dance.* 'My brothers and sisters, you are being led to hell by the politicians who pay lip service to God while at the same time accepting bribes and corrupting themselves and our great nation. Look at the antics of our former Deputy Prime Minister!' On the huge screen behind him appeared the photo of Mathew Parsons that had gone viral. It had been taken through his bedroom window as he was standing before a mirror wearing nothing but a black teddy and knee-high boots. Someone near the front of the crowd laughed loudly. Laoch hissed at them, 'This is no laughing matter.' The man's head dropped and he stared at his shoes. More than 3000 people were watching Laoch speak and he had still known exactly who had laughed because he had been placed there to do exactly that.

'My brothers and sisters, this is the problem we face. We have been trained to view our politicians as comedians rather than hold them to account for their actions. For their lies! They play to our emotions by acting the fool, while inside their corrupt hearts and minds they dream of power over you. Subjugating you for their pleasure.' Some applause from the crowd and shouts of agreement. 'They seek nothing more than power and wealth and will crush you and your families to get it. They gave us the wars in Iraq and Afghanistan, sending our soldiers to die for oil. They gave us ISIS, born from that conflict and inflicted upon us, the common people of Great Britain.' More shouts of agreement, this time with curses toward politicians. 'They gave us Brexit, which they promised would return us to glory but instead they used it to strip away our rights and line their own pockets. They gave us the Syrian wars. The most pointless conflicts in our lifetimes with hundreds of soldiers killed for nothing.'

I Vow to Thee – William E. H. Walker

His voice was loud and confident, carrying easily to those at the back even without the help of the speakers. 'And what have they done for you here in Cardiff?' There were shouts of 'nothing' and 'fuck all' from the crowd. 'No, my brothers, it's not nothing. Quite the opposite in fact.' He waited for them to still, shaking his head sadly. 'They have stolen your livelihoods. They have reduced your chances of finding work and owning a house to a near impossibility. They've filled your town with immigrants, thieves and rapists. They have stripped you naked and flayed you all to increase their own wealth and power and I say enough is enough!' He slammed his fist down on the podium as the cheers rolled over him.

'No more must we accept the word of a government who forces us into poverty and servitude!' Another cheer. 'No more must we accept the laws that allow immigrant rapists to go free but punish you for parking on a double yellow line!' The cheers grew louder. 'No more must we bow down to an illegitimate government hellbent on destroying our country for personal gain!' Even louder still.

'My brothers and sisters, four days from now I march on Westminster. I shall demand entry to the Houses of Parliament and I shall tear down this falsehood of a democracy in the name of God. Will you join me?' The cheers and shouts almost overwhelmed him. He threw his hands in the air, shaking his fists and screaming over the noise. 'Join me, join us and together we will create a new world for us all!'

He left the stage to thunderous applause.

His assistant was waiting for him as he came down the rear stairs. 'How did you find that?' Laoch asked, grinning.

'Superb, Your Excellency.' His face lit up and he grinned at Laoch.

'Thank you Peter, thank you.' He nodded, reliving the speech in his head. 'Yes, I think that went rather well.' His stomach growled. 'Right, time for a bite to eat I think?'

Peter directed him toward the waiting car. 'I've booked James Sommerin for you, Excellency.'

Laoch's smile broadened. 'You do look after me, Peter. Thank you.'

Today, Peter wore a tailored navy-blue suit that hugged his slim form closely and brought out the blue in his eyes. Laoch admired him as he moved to open his car door. Realising Peter was watching him back, and feeling weak, Laoch dropped his gaze and got into the waiting Ford. Laoch had chosen the car as it made him look more approachable. More in touch with the people. Let the politicians drive around in Jaguars, he was with the common man.

Peter sat beside him. He smelt of cedar wood and fresh sweat. He smiled at Laoch and placed the iPad down between them, brushing his fingers against the older man's thigh as he did so. *Did he mean to do*

I Vow to Thee – William E. H. Walker

that? Laoch thought. What would this 20-something-year-old want with a sexagenarian like him? Though in truth, he had found some younger than this to warm his nights. Maybe it was true? He was famous and that could have a strange effect on people. Made them more open to suggestion and temptation. But it was one temptation he had to resist. He hadn't before, it's what landed him in that hole of a church in the arse-end of nowhere, rotting away. He had to be strong. Ignore the peach and blush lips, the eyes so blue they mirrored the sky. Skin so clear of wrinkle and blemish it looked ironed on to his slender jaw.

The car swung past the crowd leaving the hall. He received cheers and waves as they passed, and he returned the appreciation with a small smile and a gentle wave of his hand. 'They certainly were an appreciative bunch,' he said, watching a group of leather jacketed skinheads waving the flag of St George and singing loudly as they stopped outside the pub. 'Though probably not the most well educated.' Peter gave a small laugh. 'Still, we don't need them to be, do we?' Laoch continued. 'We just need them to act and act quickly. Where were you hiding that?' Peter was pouring Laoch a whisky into a crystal glass from a hip flask that seemed to have appeared from nowhere.

'Don't tell anyone, but I'm full of surprises.' His look was coquettish. Laoch felt a stirring inside him.

'You most certainly are my boy.' He patted Peter's knee, letting his hand linger there for a moment too long, noting that Peter didn't flinch. 'You most certainly are.'

I Vow to Thee – William E. H. Walker

15:52

Wentworth

Wentworth was as stiff as an iron rod. He enjoyed driving and the police-issue BMW was a comfy ride, quick as well, but the regulations meant he'd had to use autopilot on the motorway, making him nothing more than a piece of useless meat along for the ride.

Sitting for six hours straight while the car did all the work of keeping him in lane at a constant speed and distance from the cars in front made his joints ache like buggery. He pushed himself against the side of the car, stretching his limbs, trying to get his mind working again. He was reminded he wasn't 20 anymore as he walked over to meet the Fire Investigations Officer.

Introductions done, Wentworth stood in the wreckage that had once, apparently, been a tumbledown thatched cottage. 'You can't be sure it was an accident?'

''At's right.' The Fire Investigations Officer had a thick Cornish accent and Wentworth was struggling to understand him. 'Fire star'ed in the kitchen. Stove most like. But it's burned quick through the 'ouse. Quicker than I'd expect anyway. 'otter too'

He must have been close to 70. Short and slightly bent. The little of the hair he had left looked like it hadn't seen a comb in a year. Instead, it was left to float ethereally around his head in all directions at once. Wentworth's own hair was always carefully maintained. Died and gelled to hide the rapidly encroaching grey.

The older man picked his nose and scratched his arm as he spoke. Wentworth realised he was rubbing what came from the former onto the later and felt a little grossed out. Still, Wentworth had to admit he knew his stuff. The initial conversation had told him as much. 'What could have been used to start the fire?' he asked.

The man shrugged. 'No acciden' I can tell ya. Any number o' things. Oil, pe'rol an'alike. But see this 'ere is the oven. The me'al 'as mel'ed. Normal 'ouse fire wudna do that. Need summet more than tha.'

It took Wentworth a moment to work out he had said the metal had melted. Wentworth wondered if this man had ever been introduced to the letter "T" but kept quiet as he continued.

'Fire spread through 'ere. Seems there were a fair few pain'in's abou' which 'elped. Bi's of frames left all over, like.'

'Where was the body?' Wentworth asked.

'O'r 'ere' He pointed toward a spot near the front door. It was slightly less covered in ash and debris than the surrounding floor.

'How was he found?' Wentworth bent down and ran his fingers over the floor leaving dusty furrows in the ash as he did so.

'I dunno.' The man scratched his chin. He looked up, searching for someone. ''ere Joe!' He called to a constable standing nearby, who walked quickly over to join them. 'Joe 'ere was on the scene early on. Joe, tell DCI…'

'Wentworth,' he reminded the man for the fourth time.

'Aye. Wen'worth. Tell DCI Wen'worth 'ere bout the body.'

The man looked too young to be a copper, barely out of his teens. They made an odd couple, Wentworth thought, the young and eager-looking constable next to the aging Fire Investigations Officer. The fleeting flash of brilliance that was life. Wentworth brushed the uncomfortable thought aside.

The constable spoke quickly, pleased to be involved. His accent wasn't as thick as the older mans but still distinctly Cornish. Wentworth found himself liking it. 'Well, 'e was by the door 'ere, wasn't 'e. Must've been runnin' or sommet. 'e was black as pitch 'e was. No much of 'im left. All burned away.'

Wentworth studied the floor. 'Which way was he facing?'

The constable looked perplexed. 'Erm…'

'Was he facing the door? Was he face up or face down?' Wentworth was feeling annoyed at the delay. He was tired after his drive.

'I think 'e was facin' away.' He didn't sound sure.

Wentworth stood and moved to where Grantham's head would have been. 'As in head positioned here?'

'Aye. Thas right.' The young man was nodding, happy again.

'And face up or face down?' Wentworth pressed.

'Well, there weren' much face left if I'm honest with ya', he said, grinning.

'May I remind you, constable, that we're dealing with the murder of a young woman here?!' Wentworth's voice, although not raised, cut like a knife. His hazel eyes fixed on the laughing policeman. The young constable fell silent, his head dropping, ashamed. He mumbled an apology. 'Now, if we've finished the comedy hour, was he face up or face down?'

'Face up, Sir.' He was being careful now.

'Good.' Wentworth studied what remained of the room, working things through. No, it didn't make sense. If he were running toward the door and was overcome by the smoke, he'd have likely fallen forward. Lunging for safety, desperate to escape. 'So why was he facing away from the door?'

'Wha'ya say?' asked the FIO.

'I was just wondering why he'd be facing away from his point of exit, and facing up? If he was trying to escape…' he made a slow running motion toward where the door had once stood, '…and was overcome with fumes and smoke, he'd have most likely been found face down with his head nearest the door. Do you agree?'

The FIO fished some dead skin from his ear while he pondered the question. 'Soun's about righ' to me.'

Wentworth had moved to the small sprays of glass on the floor. 'Andrew, come and look at this.' The old man bent down beside him with a groan. *Me in a few years*, Wentworth thought sadly. 'See here.' He pointed at the shards. 'There's a large block of glass here, just outside the house, which would have melted when the door burned, yes?'

Andrew ran his tongue over his lips and sucked in some spittle. 'Aye, given the hea' it would 'ave.'

Then why are there pieces of melted glass over here?' He pointed behind him. 'And here.' He indicated the right and left sides.

'Glass broke when it got too hot?' Wentworth had noted the young Joe had crept forward for a look.

'Unlikely son,' replied Andrew, sniffing loudly. 'If the glass 'ad broke due to the heat, it would be ou'side. No spread ou' over the 'ouse.'

'Exactly.' Wentworth felt like he was onto something. He stood in silence for a while, his eyes unfocused as he thought the evidence through. Joe was shuffling, unsure what to do. 'You said there wasn't much of his head left.' When Wentworth spoke again it took Joe by surprise and he jumped.

'Wha'? Sorry I was… erm… yea'. The 'ead 'ad half melted like.'

'Melted?' Wentworth didn't seem convinced. 'Where?'

I Vow to Thee – William E. H. Walker

The youngster shrugged, swinging one leg as he answered. 'Well, I dunno exactly. Back of 'is 'ead I suppose.'

The back of his head? But he had been facing up when they'd found him so how was that possible? Wentworth turned from the door frame and bent slightly at the hips. Trying to line himself up with where he thought the window in the door must once have been.

He adjusted himself and stared directly ahead. Then walked slowly toward the chard wreck of the wall. There! *A small hole in the dirt.* 'Andrew, do you have any forensic equipment with you?'

The bullet came out easily and he placed it in a small plastic bag – one of the few exceptions for plastic use these days. 'I want this fingerprinted and DNA tested ASAP. Joe, you're to take it directly to the lab, understand?'

'Direct to the lab, Sir, aye,' he said and jogged off toward his car.

'Taking this with you if you please,' Wentworth called after him, holding the bag at arm's length. Joe turned and saw the bag, hurried back looking sheepish, mumbled an apology and hurried back to his car.

Wentworth watched him go.

''e's alrigh' 'e is.' Andrew was standing beside him. 'Jus' young is all.'

Wentworth wasn't listening. Singh had been right. Grantham had been murdered and his house torched to try to hide it. Was it retribution? Revenge? Or something far worse than that? Was it connected to the others? There was a part of him that thought Grantham was offed in a simple act of revenge for the poor girl he had murdered as that would make things simpler. But then a much bigger part of him wanted it to be a lead into the attacks. A route in. A beginning.

A commotion made him turn. A young woman was standing a little off from the house, arguing with an officer. She was holding a camera.

A reporter, fuck's sake! he thought.

He left Andrew pondering the newly discovered murder scene and hurried over to intervene. As he drew closer, he heard her Oxfordshire accent. It seemed surprisingly out of place down here. She was an attractive woman. Lean and fit. *Just my type as well*, he thought. 'May I help you madam?' He affected his most polite Oxford tone.

Her words were breathy, as though she'd run to get here. 'Julia Freemark. I'm here because you've found Jake Grantham dead, right?'

He was surprised by this and tried to hide it. No one was meant to know. 'What makes you say that? Do you know Mr. Grantham?' Present tense, see what she actually knows.

I Vow to Thee – William E. H. Walker

There was a change in her, something bubbling to the surface. Hatred barely contained. 'I knew him. I know a lot about him and his past. And I think you and I should talk.'

16:47

Freemark

They pulled up outside the Stag Inn in St Cleer, Freemark offering to get the drinks while Wentworth sat on the bench out front against the newly painted blue facade.

Approaching the bar, she noticed the three young lads sitting in a window seat, all on the wrong side of tipsy, stop their conversation and turn bleary eyes on her. She recognised the look. Like she was a piece of meat. She'd had to deal with men like that before and, if need be, she knew how to again.

The bar man greeted her and she asked for two pints of Tribute. While she waited for her drinks, she noticed the hushed tones and giggles between the lads. One, clearly the wannabe alpha, his T-shirt a little too tight to show off his time in the gym, sidled along the bar toward her. Freemark sighed. She didn't need this.

'Alrigh' love?' His voice was slimy and carried the undertones of someone used to getting what he wanted. 'You alone here?'

'No.' Freemark deliberately didn't make eye contact, instead taking her phone from her pocket to give her something to focus on.

He made a show of looking around. 'I don't see anyone with you. Why don't you spend the evening with me and my friends here?' He gestured at his giggling mates. 'We'll look after you right.'

Freemark chose to ignore him. He couldn't have been older than 19, hair spiked and dyed blue at the tips. Face still showed the signs of teenage acne and he looked like he was trying to grow sideburns.

She focused on her messages. Stephen had sent her a picture of Maddie holding up a drawing she had done, apparently it was a cat. Her daughter was beaming from ear to ear and Freemark's stomach tightened, she was everything to her. The increasingly close proximity of this annoying youth soured her moment and she was prepared to make him leave if needed.

He waited for a second to see if she would respond. His mates laughed that he'd been rejected. 'Hey baby...' he slurred, 'you're not deaf are ya?' He smiled at his mates who jeered, driving him onward.

Freemark was ready. She replaced the phone back in her pocket and put her hands flat on the bar.

He leered at her a moment longer before seemingly making his mind up and pushed up against her, crotch first. His hand slid over her bottom and squeezed. 'Hey baby, why don't you... AAAAAAH!'

Without even looking at him, Freemark had taken his arm by the wrist and twisted it hard, pulling it round and up, forcing his head into the bar. She simultaneously put the heel of her right foot hard onto the top of his knee cap. He squealed and collapsed on the floor, whimpering like a newborn kitten, clutching his damaged arm and drawing his legs up to his chest. Freemark took a second to look at his friends, her expression fierce, her eyes alight with anger and cold determination. She felt taller somehow.

The jeers and catcalls had ended abruptly as their friend had gone down. Their faces now ashen in shock at how quickly she had dispensed with their leader. She made sure it was over and turned back to the barman who was wearing an amused expression. Clearly he didn't mind seeing the youth brought down a peg or two.

He put the beers on the bar and accepted her wrist tap. 'Fair play to ya love,' he smiled. She returned it, feeling both exhilarated and embarrassed.

She picked up the pints and turned to see Wentworth standing in the open doorway, a look of curiosity and surprise on his face. He looked from Freemark to the now quietly sobbing man holding his arm and knee, and back to Freemark. 'Remind me not to piss you off,' he smiled at her. She couldn't help but laugh. Some of her pent-up emotions expelled with the moment. The floored man protested, and Wentworth flashed his badge at him. 'What did you want to say son?' he asked, smiling broadly. The youth saw the gleaming badge in its leather case through watering eyes that were a mix of pain and tears, and meekly shook his head.

Freemark sat down at the bench outside, putting Wentworth's pint down opposite her. She reached into her pocket and pulled out her cigarettes, lighting one and enjoying the sensation of the nicotine entering her bloodstream, calming her after the brief exchange. Her body tingled, excited and wanting more.

She'd been surprised to discover how much she enjoyed a fight. She'd taken up jujitsu after a night in the pub where one of her best friends had extolled the virtues of martial arts as a way of staying thin and fit. Eventually, after more than a few G&Ts Freemark had agreed to accompany her to a jiujitsu class.

The first few lessons she'd found quite dull and only continued to go out of a sense of obligation to her friend. That all changed after her first sparring session. She'd been paired up with a man who was a purple belt, while she still a white. He'd delivered a hard kick to her midriff that took the wind right out of her and forced her to the floor.

She remembered gasping for air, the pain spreading from her belly, the feeling of being alive. She was hurt and aching, but she was loving it. Now, a second-degree black belt, she was still loving the feeling it gave her every time she fought. Her life was amazing, her family was amazing, her daughter was amazing and she wouldn't change anything about her world. But there was something that changed in her when she fought. She seemed to be able to close off her mind to the pain and find a cold, hard joy in the fight. She became a warrior.

'I take it you've had training?' Wentworth asked, interrupting her thought. He refused a cigarette, taking out his own.

'A few years of jiujitsu.' She shrugged, not wanting to seem boastful and appraised Wentworth. A good-looking man, no doubt. A little polished maybe, but he seemed to look after himself. His eyes were something special though. The whites were clear, untouched by blood vessels or a yellow hue, and were surrounded by long eyelashes that gave him almost an innocent look, but seductive also. His skin was like polished oak, smooth and silky. Maybe soft to touch?

Right now, he was grinning at her, perhaps aware of her thoughts. 'I take it that...' he gestured over his shoulder, 'was self-defence?'

'He grabbed my arse.' She scowled into the bar window where the youths were all studiously making efforts not to catch the eye of the two strangers outside.

Wentworth held his hands out in front of him, palms out as though in surrender. 'I'm not arguing.' They grinned at each other and sipped their beers, Freemark taking a long drag from her cigarette. 'So,' he put his glass down and stubbed out his half-finished smoke. She saw the change in his demeanour: professional time. 'What do you know?'

She sat a little straighter. 'Jake Grantham, son of Myris Grantham, found dead in his house. Questioned the day after the village attack in Oxford Station.'

She could see Wentworth appraising her. She blushed slightly under his gaze. 'All right. Now tell me something you couldn't have found out online.'

Freemark composed herself. She sipped her beer and took another drag on her cigarette. She could see Wentworth was happy to wait for her. 'I met him when I was 16. He assaulted me in a pub in Banbury. He tried to get into my knickers and got aggressive when I said no.' Another drag on her cigarette before continuing. 'He also had a girlfriend called Francesca Moss, he raped her and sliced up her stomach with a knife while he did it.' She'd spoken quickly, wondering if her confidence would last long enough to get it all out.

Across the bench Wentworth had stilled. There was something in his expression that showed he was affected by her words, but that he was trying his hardest not to show it. 'Right.' He sipped his beer. Was his hand a little too tight on the glass? 'Did you report this?'

She shook her head and smoked. Under the table her right knee jiggled and she placed her hand down to still it.

'What about Francesca?' Again, she shook her head and sipped her beer. 'Okay.' He ran his hand through his hair. 'Do you know of anyone else he might have assaulted?'

'No.' She found her voice again; his reaction had been serious. No attempts at dismissal or sympathy. Just cool professionalism and the tell-tale signs of emotion bubbling under the surface. 'But he's also been sending me notes.'

'Notes? Like what?' She saw a hint of intrigue in the raising of his brow.

'Innocuous ones really, nothing sexual or violent but they were... creepy. You know? They were written on pink cards that showed a beach scene that I'm guessing is from round here somewhere. The first said "great to see you," which came when I bumped into him the day after the village attack.'

'Where did you bump into him?'

She looked embarrassed. 'Outside Oxford Police Station. I was cautioned for trying to get into the village.' He gave her a disapproving look. 'Reporter,' she said by way of explanation. That drew a smile. 'Anyway. I bumped into him then got a card saying, "great to see you." The second came after the bombs in London. I'd been in Banbury and got knocked down when the news came through. That note said, "Hope you're okay." It was also delivered by hand.'

'How did you know it was him?' Wentworth didn't look totally convinced.

'Other than him, the only people I met were either police or army. Plus the beach on the front looks Cornish.'

'Do you still have the cards?'

She shook her head. 'No. I reported them as they made me nervous. There was something off about him when I met him. I gave them to DI Kinsella of Thames Valley.'

Wentworth nodded his understanding. 'She's good, Kinsella, she'll look into it for you.'

Freemark shook her head. 'I don't know, she seemed to think there was no crime committed. No implicit threat or anything, just a card.'

Wentworth seemed to be considering this. 'She's right I suppose. There's no law against sending someone a card providing they're not threatening or there's no restraining order in place.'

He'd finished his pint. 'Another?'

Her eyebrows rose as her lips curled upward despite herself. 'I'm driving.'

'Back to Oxford?' The corners of his mouth twitched up as though he suspected he already knew the answer.

'No. Staying down here tonight at a b&b in Darite.' *I should be back with my daughter*, she thought.

'Where the hell is that?' he laughed.

She smiled back. 'About two miles that way.' She pointed up the road.

'I won't tell if you don't?' He didn't wait for her answer, turned and went into the pub.

She checked her phone, another photo from her husband. Their daughter on a swing, giggling away, loving the thrill. She suddenly felt a little guilty. She wasn't doing anything wrong; she was working. But still, there was something to feel remorseful about. The small feeling of lust she held within her. Wentworth was an attractive man. She replied with several hearts and a laughing face emoji. Then, after a moment's consideration, a separate message simply saying, "Miss you X."

Wentworth returned carrying two more pints and a bag of Walkers Salt and Vinegar. She grinned, her mouth salivating. 'I've not had Walkers in ages. I can't bring myself to pay the premium.'

'And I can't bring myself to eat those paper-wrapped chewy crisps.' He opened the packet up down the seam, like her father had done, so it formed a plate under the crisps. 'Remember when these used to be 50p for, what was it, 35 grams? Help yourself,' he said, picking out a large crisp and biting into it with a satisfying crunch.

'Yep. How time flies when you're eating crisps.' Freemark eyed the packet and picked out one and placed it on her tongue. She pushed it against the roof of her mouth and sucked the flavour from it. He was right, it was worth spending the extra. 'Okay,' she said, swallowing, 'I've told you my bit. Your turn.'

He gave her a shrewd look. 'Police investigation doesn't work like that.'

'It's not for the paper, it's for me.'

He seemed to be studying her again. She couldn't work out how it made her feel, but she didn't mind. 'Fine, but this stays between us. Our secret.' Was it her imagination or was he flirting? She glanced at his left hand. No ring.

'Deal,' she said, leaning in.

He leaned in also, his warm breath on her skin. 'I believe Grantham was murdered.'

Freemark had the sensation someone had run ice down her back. She knocked her pint, but her quick reactions caught it before it went over. 'Jesus, I'm sorry!' She mopped up the little that had spilled with her sleeve. He waved her away, taking a handkerchief from his pocket and dabbing it on his arm. *He carries a handkerchief?* 'He was murdered? Are you sure?'

Wentworth nodded. 'From what I can tell, he was shot and the house was set alight to try to cover it up.'

'By who? Why?' She was rushing again. Her brain wanted every detail. *Murdered?*

He bit into another crisp. 'Can't say and not sure. But there's something else.' She could tell he was weighing up if he should tell her, but she was impatient. He seemed to decide and leaned in close again. They were barely inches apart; she could smell his cologne and the scent of his skin beneath it. It was smoky, earthy. She liked it. 'There was a body in the garden. A woman.' He met her gaze, 'It looks like he killed her.'

Freemark didn't know how to react. She was torn from her position of inquisitive reporter with the undercurrent of relief that Grantham was dead to suddenly be confronted with the fact he was a murderer. Not only a murderer but that he had killed a woman and buried her in his garden. She felt... she really didn't know. Was it guilt? Pity? Fear?

'How did she die?' she heard how quiet her voice was.

'Strangled,' Wentworth said simply.

'When?'

'Looks like 10 to 11 days ago. Why?'

She did some quick maths in her head. 'That would have been the day after I received the second note from him.' The realisation that she had been stalked by a man capable of murder was making her head swim. Would he have done that to her had he had the chance? Would he have eventually tired of writing notes and decided to meet her somewhere quiet for a final rendezvous? Was that his plan all those years? She swayed in her seat. Wentworth saw her pale and moved round the table to sit beside her. He held her steady.

'Easy, easy. He's dead. He can't hurt you.' He seemed to have read her mind.

'I didn't… I mean…' She took a large gulp of beer. Wentworth released his grip from her arms but kept one hand on her elbow. 'I knew he was capable of rape. But not murder. I mean, not killing.' She nearly added "me."

'He's gone, he won't hurt anyone else.' Wentworth's voice was quiet, soothing. His thumb rubbing gently against her skin.

Was she shaking? Why was she shaking? Was she more scared of him now than she had been when he was alive? That made no sense to her. But then when he was alive, he hadn't been a murderer. 'Do you really not know why?' She failed to keep the shock from her voice. She didn't need to clarify; Wentworth knew what she meant.

'Not yet. But…' Again, he was deciding if she could take it.

'I need to know.' She tried to sound in control.

'It looks like he enjoyed it.' Wentworth had clearly decided not to pull his punches. 'Similar to what you described he did to Francesca.'

'Jesus.' The word slipped out between gritted teeth. She fought to bring herself back, hating her weakness. She was all right by herself; she was strong. 'There's more I have to tell you,' she said, sounding more herself now. She was resolved to being strong, capable. The beer helped. She pulled out her phone and flicked through the photos. 'Here.' She showed him the picture of Myris on top of Freddy with others standing around watching, clearly jubilant, Grantham in the corner watching his mother screw yet another man.

'What's this?' he asked, taking the phone from her.

'That is Myris Grantham circa 1997/98 on top of Freddy Savage. Don't laugh.' She'd seen the corners of Wentworth's mouth curl upward. 'But…' She leaned over him, and her proximity made him flush, but he didn't flinch as she zoomed in on the young child in the corner of the picture. 'That is Jake Grantham.'

Wentworth whistled 'Well, fuck me sideways.' Freemark smiled at the expression, beginning to feel herself again. 'Talk about good parenting. Are there more?'

'More than a few, we've got them at the office. My editor wants to publish them but we're waiting to see what I come up with here.' She realised she was still leaning in close to him and moved back, suddenly embarrassed.

His face took on a sudden look of surprise. 'Wait, you came down here to interview him, didn't you?' Incredulity filled his voice.

She blushed, her cheeks burning. 'No. Yes. I don't know exactly. I found those photos and I wanted to understand what happened. I just…'

He was shaking his head at her, his face a mix between disbelief and admiration. She was unsure if it was a compliment or not. 'Well, forgive the expression, but you've got some balls on you.'

She laughed a little shyly, curling a loose strand of hair behind her ear. 'No, I just needed to know. I mean, look at him.' She pointed to the small, pathetic boy hugging his toy to his tiny chest.

Wentworth tutted as he studied the photo. 'So, the rumours about Myris were true. And it seems Jakey-boy here was privy to more than a few of her encounters. Poor kid.' He'd relaxed a bit, more of a friendly tone although it was clear he felt sorry for the young Grantham. 'He looks to be about 10.'

'I said the same. Look what she turned him into.'

He was looking at the other men in the photo. 'None of these guys could be older than 20. You said 1997?'

'Roughly'

'Know who any of the others are?' She shook her head. He was pondering the photo. 'But that would make her…' She was amused to see him flick his fingers over as he worked it out. 'Late thirties, early forties?'

'She clearly liked them young. Freddy would've been about 17 when that was taken.'

Again, he whistled, handing the phone back to her. He seemed to have made his mind up about something. 'When are you publishing these?' He'd turned professional again, the friendly lilt to his voice gone.

'My editor wants to publish tomorrow once I've written up what I've found here.'

He shifted so he was facing her, his startling eyes focused on her own. She felt the pang of guilt again as she returned his gaze. 'I need you to do something for me,' he said.

'Maybe.' She wasn't sure where this was leading, but she wasn't sure she minded.

'Can you sit on this as well? Just give me some time and then you can publish the whole lot. How he died and everything.' There was an urgency to his voice.

Freemark had instantly realised why. 'You don't want to tip off his murderer that you've worked it out.'

He nodded but held eye contact. 'Whoever killed him went through a right royal pain in the arse to hide it. I want to know who and why before it's released to the public. Frankly, I'm amazed we've held it this long, but it does seem to be keeping shtum.'

'I get it.' He did intrigue her. She made a show of thinking about it. 'If I get to be the one who releases the details of the murder when it's time, sure.' She held out her hand and he took it in his. *Warm*, she thought.

'Deal.' He downed the last of his pint. 'And on that note, I'd best be getting back to work.' He stood and faced her, then bowed at the waist. She laughed. 'A pleasure to meet you, Miss Freemark.' He grinned at her.

'And you, Mr. Wentworth.' She smiled and watched him walk to his car. As he moved off, she felt that pang of guilt again. He had called her Miss and she'd not corrected him. She was clearly wearing a wedding ring, but he'd still called her Miss and she'd not said a word. She pulled out her phone and opened messages. There was one from Stephen. "Miss you too X."

She sighed and dropped the phone onto the table. It had been a long time since someone had shown interest in her rather than just trying it on or attempting to grope her like the twat in the pub. Wentworth had seemed interested in her. Not as a mother or even as a woman, but as an intelligent reporter and an equal. It was a refreshing change.

Even Stephen occasionally patronised her. Unwittingly she knew, but sometimes. 'It's all right, I'll change the tyre for you, dear'; 'I helped with the washing'; 'When you do the shopping this week.' He didn't mean it; he was just a product of his upbringing. There were boy jobs and girl jobs. Still, it was nice to not sense that at all in Wentworth.

She finished her drink and stood to go. Through the window the youths noticed her stand and quickly turned back to their drinks. 'Nice meeting you,' she called out and grinned all the way to her car. Grantham was dead. Whoever had killed him had done the world a favour in ridding it of that piece of filth. Still, there was something about this that bothered her. Why had he been killed? Was it the girl in the garden or was it connected to the cards sent to her? Or something else entirely?

18:02

From his vantage point up the road on Fore Street, the Man sat quietly in his Ford Caesar ES. He watched her cross to her car and get in. A little unsteady at first, he thought.

He noted her number plate and watched her drive past. He wasn't going to follow her. They had a fairly good idea who she might be. He was assigned to watch Grantham's house and see if anything interesting turned up. Like the body in the garden that, when he'd reported it, had clearly been a surprise to his superiors.

The discovery of the bullet was the only other thing worth reporting that day, and they'd not been too worried about that. That was until the journalist had turned up and distracted the Oxford detective away from the scene.

He'd followed them to the pub and watched them drinking and talking. Saw their close contact and the charged looks they gave each other. They must know each other to act like that. An affair maybe? These sorts of people often cheated on each other; they had no morals.

Then, when he'd driven off and left her sitting there, an affair seemed less likely. He had been unsure what to do next. Now he would await instruction and see if she would live till morning.

19:00

Shanks

'Welcome to Channel Four News, I'm Cathy Newman. Our headlines tonight: who will be our next Prime Minister? The candidates have come forward to be counted. Tonight, we interview the Defence Secretary Marko Flint about the process and his candidacy.

'Water rationing enters its third month in the South East as the UK braces itself for record temperatures. Could we see 40 degrees this weekend?

'Scientists have warned of the increasing risk caused by the melting of the Greenland ice shelf. Speaking at the UN, Professor Julian Hopper of Stanford University told reporters the melting of the ice shelf poses an extinction-level event for humanity.

'Engineers have completed the Amsterdam Water Defence Systems designed to prevent further flooding of the city. The barriers are motorised and can rise to a height tall enough to hold back sea level rises of up to 10 metres.

'And the President of Bangladesh pleads for international aid to prevent his country sinking beneath the ocean.'

Shanks snorted. 'It's funny, isn't it? The whole world's going to shit and we're wondering how to sell salvation.' He bit into the apple, savouring it before switching the car's TV to mute.

'People don't always know what they really need, or else there wouldn't be a need for government,' his aide replied.

'How right you are Brian.' Shanks shot him a grin. 'Now, what are we selling to Leicester?'

Brian, an eager and zealous man who was recruited straight out of Oxford University, flicked his fingers nimbly over the TV's screen and replaced the Channel 4 news with their itinerary.

I Vow to Thee – William E. H. Walker

'We start at 9.00 am in the Highcross shopping centre talking about the death of British business and expanding on the plan to increase taxes on online sales to 40 percent. Be sure to mention only on companies earning over £100k though. Don't want to piss off the little guy, do we?'

'I'm not going to say that,' Shanks said through a mouthful of apple. 'We're going to level the playing field. Scrap business rates for any business earning less than £200k a year and...' He thought for a moment. 'What about supporting the little employer over the big corporations? No. I'll say Britain used to be made up of real people owning their own businesses doing the things they loved, not working for a big corporation doing a job they hate.'

'The big money-grabbing corporations?' Brian suggested.

Shanks gave him another grin. 'Aye, the big money-grabbing corporations. I like it. What's next?'

He rolled down the window and threw the core out onto the M1.

Brian tapped his pad 'After that you're speaking to a group of party members who happen to all be former Next Fashion employees. When the company was sold, they all lost their jobs to Germany and are pretty pissed off about it.'

'That'll be the usual bollocks. Government treats them like sheep if we don't change then nothing will. The lies, the lies.' He made ghost noises and Brian laughed.

'You'll need to offer them something.'

Shanks thought for a moment. 'I'll talk about how we shouldn't be buying medication made by foreign companies when we could be making it ourselves for less. And the new National Police Service with an extra 100,000 officers. That ought to do it.'

Brian smiled. 'I should think so. Maybe launch the National Essentials Industry Division?'

Shanks nodded in agreement. 'Seems like the right time: start of the campaign, hit them with a biggie.'

The plan was simple, but Shanks was sure it was a vote winner. The National Essentials Industry Division was designed to provide jobs to the hundreds of thousands who had lost theirs over the course of the past few years as more and more companies closed to go online or relocated overseas.

The factories would make everything from TVs to toasters, fridges to sofas. Everything a modern family needed to live would be sold to the public at cost.

The factories would have a limited life span of 10 years. During that time, they would train up their employees to be able to open up businesses either making or repairing the products they'd helped produce in the initiative, but at a small profit.

I Vow to Thee – William E. H. Walker

Thus, they would solve the unemployment crisis and the skills crisis in one swoop, and garner much needed popularity with the populous. Shanks had been looking for an opportunity to present this. Maybe Leicester was the right time and place? He'd see how the speech went down and decide then.

Brian flicked the pad again. 'Now, at 12.00 pm—'

'No more for now.' Shanks waved his arm at the screen, which flicked off. 'How long till we're there?'

Brian checked the central console. 'Hour or so.'

'Right, well, I'm going to close my eyes for a bit.' Shanks pressed a button in the door and his seat lowered into the horizontal position. 'Wake me when we're 10 minutes out. Jaguar…' The car gave a soft bong in reply, '…dim lights.' The interior lights dipped as the Jaguar R7 Autodrive Limousine sped along the motorway.

Shanks relaxed against the headrest and closed his eyes. Tomorrow would be a long day and getting a little shut-eye before they arrived couldn't hurt. After all, there may be press waiting for him at their hotel. *Always pays to look your best*, he thought.

Growing up on a farm near Yarnton in Oxfordshire had prepared him surprisingly well for politics. The young Shanks had worked 12 to 15 hours a day with his parents, desperately trying to secure their farm against the banks calling in of their loans. It hadn't worked, but he'd learned to carry on working long after most people had fatigued and given up.

They'd lost the farm when he was 18, which had been the death of his father. He'd not lasted six months after they'd come to drag him, screaming, off his farm. After the death of Shanks' mother not two years earlier, it had all been too much for him. His father died of heart failure, which Shanks had always described as a broken heart.

Shanks had found himself penniless and alone. He'd slept rough for a while, stealing and begging or doing things to earn money that would haunt him forever. He had thought that was it for him. He would die on the streets alone. Then came that November night when he was 20. He'd intended to try to sleep on someone's porch, just to give him a break from the biting blizzard. Shivering and near starving, he'd tried the door with the thought that he could try to break it open if needed, but it had been unlocked. The interior was in darkness, save for a solitary candle at the far end of the wide, echoing space.

He'd paid it no heed, too cold, too tired, too desperate to worry about a random candle. He'd tried to quietly close the door, but the click of the latch echoed loudly in the silence. He'd shuffled inside, shivering with teeth chattering, creeping through the hushed void to find somewhere to sleep.

I Vow to Thee – William E. H. Walker

The man's voice had shocked him. Frightened him half to death. He'd made to run but a firm grip on his shoulder had held him in place. The man had been friendly, kind. He had fed Shanks and talked with him, listening as he described his unfortunate life to that point. Shanks had returned with him to his house, been showered, clothed and put up for the night. The following morning there had been a cooked breakfast and a shave. Clean clothes and a toothbrush.

Then came the offer. The offer to stay and work with him. To live with him and take lessons. Shanks had been unsure; he'd met men who wanted the boyfriend experience and was wondering if this man was just another pervert. But he was different, and everything about his life after that was different.

It was a clean and sober life. A life of relative luxury. It wasn't that the man didn't want anything from him, he wanted a great deal. He worked him hard and gave him lessons in everything from etiquette to Russian and Mandarin. He now had a working knowledge of subjects as diverse as the Treaty of Antarctica to the biology of measles. The history of Putin's Russia to traditional Romani weaving. His mind was filled with facts and figures he may never need but would never regret having.

Every day from five in the morning to 11 at night they would work. He'd grown strong with him, both physically and mentally. He had considered himself the luckiest man alive. For a while at least. Father, he squirmed at the word, had treated him well. And here was his reward after the childhood of failure, the loss of his parents and the subsequent homelessness. If only he had listened to his ideas more. That would be nice. But there was still time. Enjoy it for now. Today he was lying down in a brand-new Jag, the Premiership of the nation within his grasp and a smile on his face. *I'm a lucky fucker*, he thought as he drifted off to sleep. *And about to get luckier still.*

I Vow to Thee – William E. H. Walker

20:32

Kinsella

She opened her front door and entered the house, bones aching, the long days catching up with her. Her tired brain was gradually shutting down. Every muscle felt weighted with spiky, prickly creatures that threatened to break skin with every step.

It had been a strained drive home, Suss clearly still dealing with the loss of her parents had spent most of the journey lost in thought and sullen. Kinsella had left her to it. There was nothing she could do to help.

It had been a pointless trip to London. MI5 had kept them waiting for nearly three hours just to take what they had, barely thanking them for it before dismissing them. As they'd returned to their car, Suss had overacted and called them every name under the sun. She seemed on edge since her parent's death. As though she was fighting herself at every moment. Kinsella had to acknowledge one thing, MI5 hadn't a clue what was going on. Either way they had taken their files, listened impatiently to their brief and bid them adieu. Her mind was humming softly to itself. It was in "home now, bed next" mode and was quite content to ignore everything but the desire to curl up under her duvet and sleep.

It took her a moment to notice her husband's shoes and case next to the door. Had they been there before? Were they there this morning? No. Definitely not. She'd packed away most of his stuff weeks ago. It could mean only one thing. He was home.

She was suddenly awake, her mind shedding its weariness and firing up neurons. Why was he home? She stepped out of her shoes, her feet padding as gently as possible against the oak floorboards. From the kitchen came the sound of cooking. In her bag she had a very unappetising beef substitute lasagne and garlic bread for one, which she'd bought from the local garage on her way home. Right now, she felt she might prefer that to whatever was behind the kitchen door.

I Vow to Thee – William E. H. Walker

Working her way quietly through the hall toward the kitchen she heard a voice. She strained her ears, trying to work out if he was on his own or not. Could he have brought her here? Would he be willing to humiliate his wife like that? Did he not know how she would react if he did? Did he think her meek? She reached the door and pressed her ear to its cold wooden surface. Was that frying and muted singing? If there was someone else in there, they weren't speaking.

'I know you're there, Mari, you're not that quiet.' His musical voice came floating through the wood to her.

Shit! He'd heard her. She tried to hide her annoyance as she confidently pushed open the door, so it hit the wall on the far side.

Their kitchen was alive with the sounds and smells of cooking. He'd been busy. Three separate pans were steaming on the hob and there was an open bottle of wine on the island. Actual wine, not the synthetic American crap most people brought. He was putting on a show.

'When did you get in?' No "hey hun" or "hello lover." Down to brass tacks. 'And I've told you, I prefer you actually call me by my name.'

He had his back to her, focused on the hob. She watched him pour stock into a pan, releasing a cloud of steam and the scent of fowl into the room. 'Okay, sorry, I forgot: Maria. I got in this afternoon. I realised I've not been back in a month and thought I'd come and see you.' He turned and smiled at her. He was still so handsome. His smile was easy and genuine, his eyes alive and seductive. She still loved him, despite everything. She would always love him no matter how badly he treated her. That hurt her more than the affair itself, she just couldn't shake him from her. He had burrowed inside and had grown like a tumour in her brain that, for a while, granted the infected unbridled joy before it killed her.

'How are you?' He was still smiling at her as he crossed the room and hugged her. Kinsella found her arms glued to her sides as he wrapped himself around her and gave her a little squeeze. She had no idea how to respond to this. They hadn't been physical in any form since they'd found out they couldn't... well. He took a step back and examined her face. She felt exposed, a microbe under a microscope. 'You look tired.'

'I've had a lot to deal with.' Her voice was hoarse because she was angry with him. Angry at his sudden return and his easy manner with her, as if there was no problem. No fault to be found or blame placed here. Her anger was a small ball of flame in her belly, no bigger than a golf ball, but it scoured her as it grew, slowly, within her. She could feel it rising and fought to keep it down. 'Terrorism and all that.'

I Vow to Thee – William E. H. Walker

'Oh yeah.' He looked as though he'd suddenly made a connection. 'That was fairly near here, wasn't it?' He looked for confirmation and she simply nodded, unable to speak. Was he so wrapped up in his own life and his new lover that he'd failed to notice where the first attack had taken place? 'You didn't have to get involved, did you?' he asked.

'Well.' She took a step back and stepped round him to the cupboard, taking out a glass. 'It was one of the biggest attacks on our country ever so, yeah, I had a bit to do with it.' *More than I'm willing to tell you, anyway.*

'I brought real wine…' he said as she turned on the tap. It was almost like he hadn't heard a word she'd said. It didn't involve him, so he didn't care. Was he always so fucking selfish?

'I don't drink, remember?' She couldn't keep the bitterness out of her voice. He seemed surprised by her reaction. There was an uncomfortable pause. She needed to fill it to keep her anger in check. 'What are you cooking?'

He seemed pleased by the change in tack and moved back to the hob, waving his hand over the pots with pride. 'Wild duck in spiced honey with turnips in orange juice.' He beamed at her, pleased with himself.

'Since when could you cook?' She wondered if she had taught him.

'Didn't I tell you?' He looked at her from the corner of his eye. 'I did a course with Gordon Ramsey last year. A client bought it for me. Cost him an arm and a leg I can tell you, but it was worth it.' His pleasure was evident in his smile. A self-centred smile that spread over his smug face.

'A course with Gordon Ramsey? Are you actually kidding me? I'm here working my butt off and you're swanning about with Gordon Ramsey?'

Her anger was baseball-sized and growing.

She felt a huge wave of resentment toward this man who had ruined her life, had taken her dreams of a happy home and family and dashed them against the wall like an unwanted puppy. *How dare he swan in here like he's the light of my life and try to cook me dinner? He's been gone a month with that whore and now he expects to be able to act like he's God's gift?*

She had been left alone, stranded and abandoned. A kitten in a box on the motorway hard shoulder. She'd had to move on, find a new life without his presence, without his influence, his love and she'd done it. In his shadow she'd been a moderately happy DS. Now she had purpose, she had a mission, she had a life. Who the hell was he to poke his nose back into it now?

She placed the glass onto the counter and picked the lasagne out of her bag. She tore the paper cover off and threw it into the microwave.

'What are you doing?' He seemed genuinely confused.

'I don't eat meat,' she replied without looking at him, focusing instead on the slowly rotating plate of the microwave.

'Since when?'

'Since 18 months ago.' Of course he'd forgotten, because it didn't involve him.

'But I've made you dinner?' He was gesturing weakly at the duck in the pan.

'I've brought my own.' Kinsella wasn't going to look at him. Her anger was the size of a football now. She needed it, it was a part of her and she wanted it. She wanted to feed it.

She could see his reflection in the microwave glass, he stood stock still for a minute, seemingly unsure how to react. *Go on then, what are you going to do?* Even her thoughts sounded venomous to her.

He turned back to the hob, assessing his work. The care and labour he had put into its creation. He picked up the pans and threw them, food and all, into the sink. Kinsella didn't move, trying not to flinch as the pans smashed into the enamel sending pieces of duck, carrot and sauce splattering over the floor and wall. When he was done, he rested his elbows on the central island with fists clenched on the counter, his head bowed. He seemed to be trying to control his breathing. After a minute, he picked up his wine and downed the glass before pouring himself another and drinking half of that in one. The reflection was staring at her back. She could feel the look and it helped her anger grow.

A ping told her the meal was ready and she took the grey-brown slop over to the island and spooned it onto a plate. She reached round and opened the drawer on the side, taking out a fork. She cut a small square from the quivering mass and put it in her mouth. It tasted like feet, but she was determined to show no emotion while she chewed the rubbery muck. She took a sip of water, his eyes still burning into her. She enjoyed the feeling.

'You never told me you didn't eat meat.' A cold voice. There was no love there.

'You never told me you had cooking lessons.' Her anger was close to snapping. The ball misshapen, trying to force its way up through her throat, through her chest, out of her fingers, anyway it could find to be given breath.

Kinsella watched him move round to stand on the opposite side of the reclaimed oak and Victorian marble island in their huge empty kitchen of their huge empty house. She glanced up and saw him watching her eat. 'You want some?' she asked, lifting her plate slightly to show him the mush.

He smiled a mirthless smile. 'Surprisingly, no.'

She met his gaze; their look was that of strangers who take an instant dislike to each other. There was something in his manner. Despite his earlier easy charm that had quickly dissolved into the naked hate he gave her now. There was something else. A tick in his face, a fidget in his leg. He was hiding something. Or was about to reveal something.

The realisation hit her like a fist. She felt the physical damage it caused as it landed. The tearing of her flesh, the bloody rivulets left in its wake. She knew why he was here. Then the second punch landed, and this one hurt more than the first. It left her with a bloody gash that would never heal. A wound that would last until her death. She couldn't give him what he wanted.

As though he'd read her thoughts, he raised his head to meet her eye. 'I've come home for a reason.' He was speaking calmly now, trying to sound reasonable. The businessman in control of his world. His domain. His destiny.

Kinsella hardly heard him. She was caught between her logical and emotional minds. Her logical mind told her he had a purpose and that must not be forgotten. Justice was not yet hers to administer. Her emotional mind wanted to leap over the table and tear his eyes out with her fork. The fork that was gripped so tightly in her hand it was starting to bend. This had not been lost on her husband, who took a step back in trepidation.

Not now, not this way, control yourself. She forced her hand to release the buckled fork and stabbed it forcefully into the globules of fungus on her plate. *Control your emotions. You're better than him*, she told herself. It took everything she had, every shred of her body and soul to do it, but she wrestled herself under control. Pushing and driving her anger back down her gullet. She would address him as though he were a dog or child. As though he lacked understanding. She set herself to her task. Her anger was punching at her from the inside, desperate to be released, to live, but she would be civil. She would be better than him.

After a moment, when he'd seem to realise she wasn't about to leap out of her seat and gouge him, he gathered himself to go on with his speech. 'I've… I've met someone.'

'Silvia Hutton.' She spoke the name without emotion through a mouthful of foot-flavoured pretend beef fungus. Her husband looked stunned and she couldn't help but laugh at his expression. A short, hollow laugh, devoid of joy.

'You know?' His voice was quiet. She nodded, the laughter dead in her throat. 'For how long?'

Kinsella chewed on a particularly nasty piece of her meal, a small part of her wondering why she was still eating it. 'About three years.'

I Vow to Thee – William E. H. Walker

She watched the air escape from him. He wilted onto a stool like cut flowers left out in the sun.

'Jesus,' he whispered.

Kinsella slammed her fork down onto the table. 'No!' She stared at him, her anger had been begging to be let loose and now she gave it short relief. 'He doesn't have anything to do with this.'

He looked confused 'Okay. I'm... I'm sorry?' She held his stare for a moment longer before retrieving the fork and taking another small mouthful of what was now little but a grey paste.

He waited to see if she would talk. Clearly this hadn't gone the way he had planned. 'Anyway... like I said, I've come home for a reason.'

'You want to go live with your whore?' Her tone matter of fact.

'Don't call her that!' His voice rose, the reaction genuine. There was the love that had been missing when he spoke to her.

She held the fork rigid in her hand, the two sides of her brain still deciding her best course. A battle she was worried logic might lose. 'What would you like me to call her? Your lover? Your beau? Your hussy?' Her voice had taken on a sardonic high-pitch tone.

'How about the mother of my child?' He spat the words like venom.

Kinsella was blindsided. The words smashed into her like a freight train. She felt faint. The mother of his child? *His* child? She was carrying his child? How was this possible? He couldn't have children.

He was talking but she couldn't hear him. Something about a procedure in Switzerland, insemination and a boy. But it was as though he spoke to her through a stormy ocean. Her mind drowned and lost in the deep.

It was all over now; she had truly lost her husband. She had lost their life together. She had lost his children. She had lost.

She was having his child. His son.

Something inside her broke. She would never find the name for what it was, she would never find a way to express the feeling, but it was shattered by the revelation. Blown to dust. scattered into a million pieces, never to be whole again.

She swayed on her feet. When had she stood up? She gripped the edge of the island for balance. Her head disconnected, her legs on autopilot. Escape must be found.

His child. My child?

She had a vague awareness of him saying her name as she drifted across the room and into the hall. She had no idea where she was going.

Her child was being born to someone else.

Outside the house, she stumbled down the steps and onto the driveway.

Her son. Lost. Stolen.

She felt a tug on her arm. He was pulling her sleeve. She turned to face him, her expression a canvas of agony. The pain had stripped her bare. Taken her ability to process and express how she felt. She simply gaped.

Her son.

He was speaking, his tone aggressive. His arms flailing as he tried to cajole, push and pull her back toward the door.

She hadn't meant to bring the fork with her. She'd forgotten it was in her hand. There was no thought process. She plunged it into his arm with all her strength and he screamed, collapsing to the floor and clutching the wound.

She didn't stay to watch. She was in her car and on the road before she realised she was crying. The tears streaming down her face, her cries of anguish filling the vehicle. Her mind so torn she didn't hear the blaring horn or screeching brakes behind her.

Her internal autopilot took her where she needed to be. Stumbling from the car, she lurched into the porch and hammered on the door. She was screaming and wailing. Her strength gave way and she fell to the floor.

The door opened, the light from inside flooded over her. The strong, kind arms wrapped around her and held her close, letting her cry. Safe. She was safe. But she had lost her son.

I Vow to Thee – William E. H. Walker

21:45

Suss

Sitting in her car in the shadow of a large hawthorn, Suss watched Kinsella exit her house. She hadn't known she would, but she'd suspected it. Had felt it. Kinsella had a secret and Suss needed to know what it was.

It was her expression that surprised Suss. Haunted. Like someone had stripped her of her personality and left her shell to wander the Earth. What's going on? What had happened to her? The front door was opening again. The tall, toned man on the stairs calling her name. Was that her husband?

She watched him striding after Kinsella who was half-walking, half-stumbling toward her car. She let her window down an inch or so to try to catch his words. 'Come inside. Where are you going? Will you get inside? Mari? Mari, are you pissing well listening to me? Fuck!'

Suss jumped, hand to her mouth to stop herself crying out as she watched Kinsella stab her husband in his arm. She couldn't see the weapon but, whatever it was, it remained sticking out of his bicep. Something was seriously wrong here; this was way more than just an argument. A final argument maybe?

Her husband was lying on the driveway, hand clutching his wounded arm. Shouting and screaming at her. 'Bitch… you fucking bitch! You've fucking stabbed me… You… Come back here you fucking bitch!'

Suss ducked down as Kinsella's BMW backed out of the drive at speed and pulled up practically next to her before screeching off up the road to the junction and left toward the Wolvercote Roundabout.

Suss had no time to waste. Kinsella didn't look in the mood to observe speed limits and the police BMWs were not fitted with speed limiters. She pressed the engine start and accelerated off after her. Whatever had caused this was far worse than any normal marital disagreement, surely?

I Vow to Thee – William E. H. Walker

Although how much did she know about Kinsella's private life? Could this be normal for them? She'd known that to be true for other couples. During her time as a constable, she'd been called to a fair few domestics. It had surprised her how often the wife or girlfriend could be the abuser. Sure, most of the time it was men, but still there had been times when the woman was the controller, the alcoholic, the sadist. She remembered she'd been based in Lewisham, being called to reports of violence in a house on… where was it? Chalsey Road. Not a bad area. Just row upon row of three up, two down houses with tiny gardens.

She'd arrived to find a man sitting on the front step, blood pouring from a deep gash in his head. Through the open door in the thin, decorative hallway stood his 56-year-old wife brandishing a fire poker, screeching like a banshee.

She'd found out later, after succeeding finally to wrestle the mad cow to the ground, that she'd hit him because he'd forgotten cat food for the second day in a row. When he'd been examined in hospital his body had been a crisscross of scars and bruising. He'd gone home to her as well. Some people just didn't learn.

Maybe Kinsella and her husband had a relationship like that? But that didn't fit with the woman Suss knew. She was together. The type of person who thought before they spoke and ensured every word was worth speaking. Suss just liked to talk. She part envied and part mistrusted people who didn't.

Kinsella was turning right onto Squitchey Lane. Suss hung back until she'd completed the turning and followed her. In her haste, she narrowly missed a Vauxhall coming the other way. She cursed herself as the driver swore at her and blasted their horn into the warm evening air. Would Kinsella have heard it? She hadn't looked overly focused leaving her house, but she knew Suss's car. If she looked behind her, she could easily recognise her. What would she say if she had? 'Following you? Nah, just out for a drive in the evenin'.'

She felt a chill run through her, her palms a little sticky. She'd tailed suspects plenty of times. She'd followed the would-be Oxford Circus Bomber for three miles on foot and he'd not noticed her till it was too late. But this was different. Kinsella was one of the team. She was a copper. But she might also be a liar, and maybe worse.

Left again on to Banbury Road. Suss arrived at the junction in time to see the rear of her car disappear into a small drive. She drove slowly and pulled up opposite the entrance to the Sunnymead Church of St John. Choosing a spot where she could just see the church door.

Kinsella was out of her car and walking, no, staggering, her head in her hands, wiping tears from her eyes. Through her open window the gentle breeze brought her the faint sounds of despair. Despite everything Suss couldn't help but feel sorry for her. Having cried so hard, so recently, the rawness was something Suss could relate to.

The door to the church was opened, a figure cast in shadow in the doorway. Was that a vicar? She saw Kinsella fall into their arms and they embraced. They held her in their arms for a moment longer, before moving to one side and letting her pass into the church. The door was closed.

Suss had guessed Kinsella was religious. The fish on her necklace, her ticks of annoyance when Suss had sworn. Clearly, she had a good relationship with her vicar. A very close relationship? Could that be the cause of the argument she'd witnessed? But then why would Kinsella be crying so hard? Would it not be her husband who would do the storming out? No, it wasn't that.

Could it simply be she was reaching out to someone she trusted completely in her darkest hour? Maybe her husband was cheating, and she'd just found out and she'd come to her vicar for guidance and moral support. A more likely scenario.

The car's central console lit up. Debs was calling. Shit. It was nearly 10.00 pm and she had a good hours drive ahead of her. 'Hey sweets.' She tried to sound cheery.

'Hey love. You ok?' Her voice carried concern. The almost parental worry of a partner for their recently bereaved lover out late at night so soon after the trauma.

'Yeah, look, sorry, I've been working. I didn't see the time. You okay?' She rubbed her eyes, suddenly feeling tired.

'Yeah, it's okay. I'm not doing much. What are you up to?' She was nervous. Debs could never hide her emotions in her voice. Not with Suss.

'I'm jus' following up on a lead. I'm done anyway and just comin' home.'

'Okay.' Deb's relief was evident. 'When you getting here?'

Suss checked the time. 'Not till gone 11. You want anything?'

'Just you.' Suss smiled. Debs was such an old romantic.

'I promise ya that. I'll see you in a bit, yeah?'

'Okay, I'll make you tea when you get here. I got you some custard creams as well. Love ya!'

'Love ya.' Suss was smiling despite herself. Deb's had a way of making her feel better. It was the little things. Her voice gave her a sense of peace that spread over her body, a blanket for her life. Debs loved her. She said it often, but that was habitual. Suss knew Debs loved her because her every action reinforced that knowledge. She would never knowingly hurt her. She was her safety net.

Suss tapped the screen and pulled up directions for home. One hour 19 minutes. She selected autopilot and pulled away from the curb for home. Debs was waiting for her. Tonight, they would snuggle up and try to forget the world. Try to forget the hole in her left by the loss of her parents. Try to forget Kinsella and her lies. Debs was all she needed tonight.

22:02

She'd sat in the same place for six hours now. Waiting. Watching. For what, no one had told her. It was simply her job to watch. This was day six of her current rotation and she had been thoroughly bored and disinterested by the first five days, five hours and 49 minutes.

Now though, things had changed. Now things had got interesting. Now there was the black woman in her car, watching the white woman go into the church. Who either of them was she didn't know, but this was her moment. She finally had something to do.

She dropped her sandwich and reached for the camera and started snapping away. The white woman first, crying, desperation writ large in her features. Then the black woman, her face hidden at first as she watched the white woman. When the white woman disappeared the other turned to stare out the front of her car. She looked confused and angry.

She watched the black woman start talking, a phone call maybe? Her face lit from below as she strained a smile. She would love to know the conversation. Maybe she was a spy talking with her boss getting ready to go in guns blazing and take them down? That would be fun. And she needed some entertainment after her days of boring monotony. Maybe she should get out of the car, make her way across the street and…

Without warning, the black woman drove hurriedly off into the night.

She swung the camera around bringing the church back into view. No sign of the other. She sighed and let the camera fall into her lap. Her moment of excitement over, she adjusted herself in her seat and settled back in for a long night. Her mind drifting off to a world of villains and spies. It would be a great story for mum in the morning.

Day 16

'Give me six hours to chop down a tree, and I'll spend the first four sharpening the ax.'

—Abraham Lincoln

10:23

Shanks

'…It is not fair that we have suffered because of the incompetence of past and current governments. It was their job to protect us, to help us in our hour of need. Not to just let the companies we worked for be sold out from under our feet and moved to foreign lands.' A murmur of appreciation and agreement from the crowd. 'We deserve better than this.' They were nodding along like machines. He was pacing the boards of the small temporary stage, throwing his passion out to them in both words and gestures. 'We do! We deserve better! And I say it's time we take it.' A small cheer this time. 'WE must be strong and resolute. No more will we vote for those who act in the interests of the greedy money-grabbing corporations.' *Thank you Brian*, he thought. 'WE will vote for people who swear by God to work for us! For the Great British public and not the billionaires.' Applause with more cheering this time, he waited for it to die down. When he spoke again, his voice was soft, inviting. 'Who really needs a billion pounds anyway? I mean, what are you going to do with it that can justify keeping it when others have nothing?' Shouts of agreement.

The crowd was a mix between those who had once been middle class, those who still were and those who wanted to be. Most had lost their careers when the high streets finally failed and the big retailers had shut up shop or been sold off for parts. All were bitter, all were angry, all could vote him into Number 10 in just three days. And he would unleash a furnace of anger that would burn the country down. 'You know what I will do?' he asked in conversational tones. 'I will bring that money back into public ownership and redistribute it to you. No one needs £1 billion, so why do we let them keep it?'

Cries of 'Take it back!' and 'Tax them to hell!' were shouted from the crowd.

'We all deserve a life that's worth living, yet we allow ourselves to be subjugated into slavery by the billionaires who work us to death for their own profit. Well, I say no more!' Spittle flew from his lips as he screamed the last words. 'Enough is enough! You deserve to work to live, not live to work! You are not less worthy than them, you are better than them because you do not steal from your countrymen and

I Vow to Thee – William E. H. Walker

leave them with nothing!' They were enraptured now. The crowd was still and silent, drinking in his words.

'Today I stand before you, a candidate for the leadership of the BCP. If I am successful in that race, I make these promises to you. No!' He shook his head, a wry smile on his face. 'No, not a promise – politicians lie like weeds grow in excrement and promises from them are not to be trusted.' There was some laughter, smiles and nods of agreement from the crowd.

He paused as though lost in thought. Then slowly he raised his head to the sky. 'I swear this to you before God. If I am privileged and fortunate enough to be chosen to lead this Great Nation out of the darkness, I swear that I shall work every day, from dusk till dawn…' his voice was rising again, his body shaking as he brought them with him into his vision, '…for the benefit, not of those who would steal your life and future from you, but for you and you alone. I shall work every day to ensure this country is the greatest country in the world and I shall be judged, not by the lying press or the fake social media stories, but by you!' He opened his arms to the crowd, his voice a war cry. 'The wonderful British people! Everything I do, I do for you! Thank you.'

The crowd erupted in a cacophony of cheers, whoops and applause. He waved at them and shook hands with the man who had introduced him before stepping off stage. He was warm now, beads of sweat on his brow, but it had gone well. Very well indeed. It would get people's attention.

As the car took him onward to Nottingham, Shanks checked his phone for news. He fully expected to be the lead story, but his eyebrows rose sharply as his jaw tightened. The headline of the Independent Online wasn't about him.

Bishop Blames Bumbling Bureaucrats

He skimmed the article. It seemed Laoch had been speaking in Bristol the previous evening, blaming the Civil Service for Britain's woes. Not hiding his irritation, Shanks said, 'Laoch thinks the Civil Service is responsible for the terrorist attacks. He's quoted as saying, "Civil Servants tap all our phones and internet data, they must have known the attacks would happen and chose not to act because of their pro-Muslim and atheist agenda."' He couldn't keep the envy out of his voice.

'Is that possible?' Brian asked, his look earnest.

Shanks laughed, a joyous belly laugh. 'Of course it's not. But it helps our argument that the government is to blame for all our woes. Bastard nicked my headline though.'

'You realise you didn't mention any of what we discussed again, just like in Leicester. The NEID plan.' Brian sounded amused.

Shanks grinned ruefully. 'Yeah, might have got a bit carried away. I'll bring it up in Nottingham as long as you prompt me.' He smiled at Brian before returning his attention to his phone. His opponents had barely made the headlines.

"Marko Flint meets factory workers in Rotherham." *Boring*, he thought. "Harrold Chapman visits Weymouth Virgin Hospital." *Predictable*. "Roger Boldermore pleases crowd in Durham." *Interesting...* He read the details and was pleased to find nothing new in Boldermore's speech. 'What's Rainsworth and Fortescue been up to today?'

Brian tapped his pad. Did that thing ever leave his hand? 'Fortescue was in Committee and Rainsworth...' He tapped a few more times. His brow furrowed in confusion. 'No idea?' She's not showing up anywhere.'

Shanks smiled inwardly. 'Really? How strange.' He sat up, noting where they were on the motorway. 'Hungry?'

Brian looked up from his pad and shrugged. 'I could eat something.'

'Good, I fancy a cheeseburger.' Shanks leaned forward, 'Jaguar. Alter course. Visit McDonald's.'

10:45

Wentworth

'Sir, I wanted to let you know something.'

'Yes, Phillip?' Singh's voice was calm, but Wentworth knew he would be anxious for news. His expression on the phone's screen was tense.

'It's been confirmed that Grantham was shot, the bullet we found in the wall was a .45. The same calibre used in the village attack.'

'Any leads?' Curt but interested. No, excited by this news.

'Not here in Cornwall sir, no. The girl found buried in the garden was a local, identified this morning. Seems he may have picked her up from the street and brought her home. A chance meeting, I suspect.'

'No motive?'

'Not in isolation Sir, no – looks like a kill for fun. But a reporter showed up here yesterday afternoon by the name of Julia Freemark.' Her beautiful face appeared before him, but he forced it away to focus. 'Seems she knew Grantham. He assaulted her in a pub in Banbury some 20 years ago when she was 16. She had a lot to say about him.' There was a pause. Wentworth knew Singh would be digesting the news, but he interrupted the process. 'There's more, Sir. Miss Freemark told me about another woman, one Francesca Moss who she believes was assaulted and raped by Mr. Grantham at around the same time. Seems he may have sliced her stomach in a similar way to the girl we've found here.'

He watched Singh expel air through puffed out cheeks. 'Where's Miss Moss now? Can we corroborate this story?'

'According to Miss Freemark…' *The lovely Miss Freemark*, he thought, 'she's in Banbury working as an accountant. I've got the address; I was going to go there on my way back to the station.'

I Vow to Thee – William E. H. Walker

There was another pause. 'I think I'll get a couple of constables round to collect her, bring her back here. I'd like this recorded properly.'

'Very good, Sir.' Wentworth couldn't hide his disappointment.

'So, Mr. Grantham has form, which automatically gives motive to his murder. Someone finds out what he's done and decides to end him. But it doesn't link him to the other murders, apart from the timing.'

'No, not currently. What are the chances of the others being involved with him in some way?'

'A grooming or rape gang you mean? I suppose it's possible Colin Farrow might have been involved with something like that, but Mrs. Alice Simms?' His voice rose in speculation.

'I suppose not,' Wentworth agreed. 'But we shouldn't rule it out. She might have been supplying the women?'

'Must admit I doubt it, but you might be right. I'll sequester their bank accounts. We should keep it as a working theory at present, don't get the husband or the press involved. Which reminds me, Miss Freemark isn't going to publish, is she?'

'No.' He thought of her bright smile in the Cornish sun, the way she had dispatched that lad in the pub. He'd always been attracted to strong women. 'She's going to sit on most of it, but she's got photos of Grantham as a kid, his mum sitting on top of a fellow of about 17. In flagrante, if you know what I mean.'

'I see, and they're going to publish those?'

'Seems her editor is dead set, Sir.'

Singh was tapping his fingers on the desk. 'Right, well, that's annoying as it'll refocus minds on Grantham and the news will probably leak. Which paper does she work for?'

Wentworth noted it was still a "paper" to Singh rather than an online news platform. 'Oxford Times, Sir.'

'I'll get on to them, see if we can put him off. In the meantime you come back here, unless you think you can get anything more useful out of Cornwall? Or fancy a holiday?' The last remark was clearly a joke.

Wentworth wondered if Freemark might still be in her hotel and if she'd be free for a coffee or lunch. He'd seen the wedding ring of course, but that didn't bother him. He'd been with married women before. Often they were the most grateful. Sex starved and hungry for attention.

He'd seen the glint in her eye, the slight hesitancy as she had drawn close to him. He knew women found him attractive and, as he grew older, made efforts to remain so. The plastic surgery he'd had not six months ago was tribute to that. Plus, he made sure to run at least five miles every other day and exercise each morning to keep his body looking as close to his once 22-year-old self as possible.

He reminded himself that he was single by choice. He wasn't ready to settle down, not until he'd had his fill and lived first. Kids and stuff could wait until he was older, although he was now 43 and not getting any younger. Maybe he should start to consider it? Leave a legacy and all that? 'No holiday for me Sir, I'll come straight back. Should be in the office before five.'

Singh nodded, already distracted. 'Fine, see you then. Have a safe journey.'

'Thanks, Sir.' The phone went dead and Wentworth sat back in his car, his head resting on the faux leather headrest. Would she still be there? Could he find some excuse to pop by and see her? He'd forgotten to ask her a question and, "Oh sorry, I didn't know you weren't dressed yet... No, I don't mind waiting..." He grinned and shook his head. *Stop fantasizing about a woman you've met once you idiot.*

He pressed the car's start button and pulled into traffic to go home, images of a semi-naked Freemark roaming around his head. He barely registered the blue Ford following him. It wasn't until he'd gone through five junctions before he realised it was there. Was it following him? There must only be a few ways to get back to main roads from here. Maybe it was just going in the same direction? He didn't know why he felt uneasy, but he trusted his instincts.

His sat nav was telling him to turn right ahead, so he turned left instead. A couple of seconds after he pulled round the junction the blue Ford followed him round. He sped up to 40, quite fast for the single-track Cornish roads, and the blue Ford matched his speed.

To his left was a road leading to a junction. He took it and slowed, almost to a stop, just out of sight from the road he'd turned off of. After a moment, the Ford swung round behind him. It slammed on its brakes as it nearly rear-ended him. He was out of the car in seconds, but the driver had already slammed the car into reverse and was backing out into the road they'd just left.

'OI!' Wentworth yelled, breaking into a jog. 'Police! Wait up!' But the driver ignored him as the car's tyres screeched and the Ford sped off, disappearing round a corner.

Wentworth stood in the middle of the road as the car vanished from view. *Partial number plate only, damn it.*

12:45

Shanks

'I'd like to end today by encouraging all of you to vote on Friday for the next leader of our great Party. Even, and I hope this isn't the case,' he shot them a winning smile, 'even if it's not for me.' A warm laugh from the audience. Shanks joined them. 'Seriously though, our democracy has been decimated over the past 10 years to the point where it is now no longer fit for purpose. If you will allow me, I shall work tirelessly to fix the problems created through the greed and ineptitude of both your Labour town council and my predecessors. And through programs like the National Essential Industry Directorate and Integrated Emergency Services, we can restore this great nation to its rightful place. Thank you.' He left the stage to thunderous applause, smiling and waving at them warmly as he departed.

Once out of view of the stage he allowed himself a moment of self-congratulation. Just the right tone for the Nottingham Small Business Association's BCP membership. He was winning the leadership race by miles, all the polls had him out in front. His lead was such that already Harrold Chapman had withdrawn his candidacy and phoned to congratulate him. Voting hadn't even happened yet.

He saw Brian waiting for him looking grim. Beside him stood a tall and angry-looking gentleman who Shanks didn't recognise. 'Brian, please see that the car is brought round, I would like to be on the road by one.' Brian nodded and pulled his phone from his pocket. He caught Shank's looking at him and rolled his eyes at the man beside him. Shanks appraised the man. Standing at nearly six and a half feet, he was taller than Shanks by almost eight inches. His face looks as though it lived in a permanent state of disapproval with the world. His hands wedged in his jacket pocket and his fox-like eyes fixed Shank's with a look that could cut glass.

'Mr. Shanks.' A gruff, unfriendly voice.

'Yes.' Shanks held out his hand and smiled. Neither were returned.

'Darren Forelock, Daily Mail. I wanted to ask you why you've gone all communist on us?'

I Vow to Thee – William E. H. Walker

A fucking reporter, Shanks thought, although his smile never wavered. *No, worse, a fucking Daily Fail reporter*. He straightened a little, although it made little difference to the height gap between them. 'A communist? I'm sure I don't know what you mean?' He kept his voice light, as though amused by the idea.

'Your proposal for the NEID. That's nationalising production, the four-day working week, maximum earnings for CEOs, maximum profit limits for companies and removing all competition to nationalised products? Sounds like communism to me.' His voice was accusatory. Shanks noted he wasn't writing anything down. Recording the conversation, maybe?

Shanks shook his head as though it was all so obvious. 'It's not communism my dear fellow, its pragmatism. We're in a situation where we have over 10 million people out of work and nowhere for them to turn to. They can't afford the products sold from the companies of which you speak, so what are they to do? I am not proposing we make products that are already made in this country, but that we make products that we currently import. Products made by companies who don't pay taxes here, who don't employ people here, who don't support us and just expect us to buy from them. You want to write a story? Write about the companies who abandoned us after Brexit. Write about tax avoidance. Write about the rubbish produced in Europe and Asia leaving our hard-working citizens on the breadline.

'You should write about those companies who have never supported us. Those who pay no corporation tax thanks to the loopholes created by previous governments who were in bed with them. Look at how many former civil servants and politicians are now directors and advisors to these companies. The gravy train has gone on long enough and we will end it. WE…' he spat the word, '…will tear down this paper democracy and give it back to the people. We will ensure we look after our own through education, employment and healthcare. I don't work for the big corporations; I have never worked for the big corporations. I work for the British people and I will let them be my judge, not you. Not the Lord who owns you or the money-grabbing politicians or corporations.' His neck was hurting slightly with the effort to maintain eye contact, but he pressed on. 'I will work night and day to give a fair chance to everyone who calls this great country home.' His voice was raised, strong and powerful. 'So, if you're looking for an interview with me you can't have one. I want nothing to do with an organisation owned by a Peer, and which will print any lie it feels like just to boost sales.' He breathed deeply, holding eye contact with the man who was smirking slightly.

'Interview?' He lifted his phone from his pocket, the screen showing their conversation being recorded. 'I don't need one thanks.' He clicked the record button off, smiled and walked happily away.

Brian moved back to Shank's side. 'What did you tell him?'

'Exactly what I wanted him to hear. He thought I didn't know he was recording it.'

Brian tapped the iPad. 'Car's outside.'

Shanks was feeling better than ever as they left the Nottingham hall. The warm sun seemed to reflect his mood. Shining down on to the Earth like a benevolent king distributing his wealth to the poor and needy. A good meeting. No. A great meeting and some great newspaper coverage to come. He was whistling to himself as he got into the Jag. Diane by Therapy? He'd not listened to it in years. Today was a good day. Tomorrow, that would be a hard one. But one he must endure to succeed.

23:45

Freemark

It had been another hot day and the lack of breeze had left the night stuffy and overbearing. Just one of Stephen's T-shirts tonight and the Egyptian cotton sheet to cover her. She retrieved her bag from the boot and trudged up to her front door. Her drive home had been uneventful from a physical perspective, but her mind had been whirling with the news she had learned over the previous two days.

Grantham had been a murderer, capable of atrocities to women. He had plenty of reasons to hate his mother, a hatred he seemed to have projected onto all women. Her lack of love, care and guidance driving him to pursue women and see them as objects to be used. No, worse – things to be abused and despised. Did that make him capable of not only her murder, but of taking part in the atrocity that had happened in Lesser Worburston? Potentially, yes. With the right motivation. The question really was, what was the motivation? What was it that had driven him to do it? Assuming he had.

Even her conversation with Kinsella hadn't helped, it had felt like the detective hadn't wanted to discuss it with her. She'd listened as Freemark had told her about her trip to Cornwall and her meeting with Wentworth, but then Freemark had got the distinct impression Kinsella was trying to blow her off and shut her down. It bugged her. She'd experienced it before from the police. They didn't like it when they thought someone was trampling on their investigation. Maybe it was just that? Anyway, it was too late in the night to worry about that now.

She tapped her phone against her door and it unlocked. It was a compromise she'd made with Stephen. She'd refused to have the steel blinds over both windows and doors, instead opting for the far cheaper and, as assured by the online sales consultant, equally secure mobile phone or fingerprint recognition locks. Combine that with the offsite monitored CCTV ("monitored by a dedicated handler 24 hours a day, 365 days a year with a direct line to the police," as the advert had put it), she had managed to persuade him that it was enough.

I Vow to Thee – William E. H. Walker

She reflected on two points as she entered the house. The first was that everyone had a direct line to the police, it was called 999. She felt a slight annoyance at the program that had sold the security system to them. Although why she should be annoyed at a digital reproduction of a smartly dressed saleswoman, programmed to respond to people's enquiries, she didn't know. It seemed totally pointless. Plus, it transpired after they'd signed the contract, the 24 hour a day dedicated CCTV monitor team were based in China. Stephen had pointed out that it didn't matter where the team was located. 'Besides,' he'd said, 'the camera's presence will be enough.'

The second point was on how the village attack, followed in such quick succession by the far more devastating London bombings, had succeeded – more so than any previous terrorist assault – to put the fear of God into the populous. The country was changed, perhaps irrevocably, through the knowledge that it was now both theoretically and actually possible for a terrorist group to hit anywhere in the country and commit horrendous acts seemingly without fear of reprisal. Suddenly no one was safe. Not the farm isolated on a mountainside in the Highlands or the tiny hamlet in the arse-end of beyond. Everyone was vulnerable.

The mass slaughter of 15,539 people in London. That was a real show of strength. Enough to bring down a Prime Minister and start a war. One that still raged while party politics took precedent and Britain was left without a real leader – Miller hadn't even hung around for the handover. The rumours she'd been drunk during a crisis had circulated quickly and had never been officially denied. Freemark almost couldn't blame her. Who'd want to have to deal with the aftermath of these two attacks?

Was that it? Was it all over now? She moved through the silent hallway and into the kitchen, placing her bag down next to the sink. She opened the fridge and looked inside for something to fill the gap left by many hours driving. A half bottle of white, was it genuine wine, the real deal? No. Synthetic. Some American-style cheese, which was neither American or cheese, and eight textured vegetable protein ready-to-eat sausages. Well, that would have to do. She grabbed a plate from the cupboard, sat down and cut some of the cheese and sausages onto a plate, poured a little wine into a glass and ate greedily.

What would she do next? Wentworth had asked her to sit on the Grantham story, but he hadn't said not to investigate him. Where would she start? She could go back to Freddy, apologise for borrowing the photos (if he'd even noticed) and ask him some more questions? She could go back to Kinsella, but Wentworth would most likely do that. She saw his face before her, an extremely attractive man, and felt guilty.

'Hey.' His voice came out of nowhere.

'Jesus!' She exclaimed, spilling her wine. 'You scared the shit out of me.'

Stephen moved forward, collected a tea towel and cleaned up the wine. 'I'm sorry, I heard you get in. I didn't mean to scare you.'

Freemark was smiling at him. 'Well, you did.' She hit his arm playfully. A soft, welcome kiss on his warm lips. 'I didn't mean to wake you.'

'I wasn't asleep.' He patted dry the last of her wine and took the bottle from the fridge, refilling her glass. 'How was the journey?'

Freemark shrugged. 'Same old, same old really. Interesting trip though, I found out loads.'

She filled him in on everything she had learned, only leaving out that Wentworth happened to be a good-looking copper with a rather flirty manner. She loved Stephen and would never do anything to hurt him, so the fact she'd found Wentworth attractive was inconsequential. She belonged to Stephen and he to her. Till death do they part.

When she'd finished, Stephen looked slightly shell-shocked and ran his hands through his hair. 'So, he was a proper nasty piece of work then?' Freemark nodded through a mouth full of plastic cheese.

'Well, I'm glad you met him outside a cop shop. Can't imagine what would happen if you bumped into him somewhere quiet.' He looked as though he wasn't sure if he should be relieved Grantham was dead or still fearful he might be a threat to his wife.

'I'd kick his sorry little arse!' Freemark wanted it light. Don't worry him.

Stephen laughed softly. 'Of course you would. Still, I'm glad he's dead. I know that's not the nicest reaction to have to someone's death but, well, he murdered that poor girl and…' He paused looking for a word. 'Fuck it… he sounds like a cunt to me.' It was Freemark's turn to laugh. Her husband never swore.

Her food wasn't good. She held up a small block of yellow. 'Why do you insist on buying this crap?'

Stephen smiled at her. 'Your daughter likes it. She tears it into strips and plays with it. Besides, real cheese is so expensive and they add all the vitamins, protein and calcium to that…' He took the small block off her and popped it into his mouth, chewing it down and trying to maintain a smile. Freemark watched the display, amused by her husband's attempts to appear as though what he was eating was appetising.

'Like the taste of sweat then, do ya?' She smirked at him as he swallowed.

'Mmmmmm. Nom nom.' He said, rubbing his belly in mock appreciation.

'Aha, of course! Can we not afford the real stuff?' She laughed at him.

Stephen's manner turned more serious. 'Not really. Our gas bill came through. It's £550.'

I Vow to Thee – William E. H. Walker

Freemark swore. 'Why so high?'

'It's for last winter. We didn't have the biofuel attachment then. Anyway, with that, the cost of the new locks, CCTV and the council taxes, we're pretty much broke till payday' He noted her expression of concern. 'I've budgeted, but you should check. We've enough for food et cetera, just maybe not real cheese.'

Freemark scratched her head. 'I've not really been involved, sorry. I'll do my expenses tomorrow, that'll help.'

'How much are they?' He sounded hopeful.

She thought for a second. 'Maybe 50 quid or so?'

He picked up her glass and took a sip of her wine. 'Well, every little helps. You coming to bed soon?'

She nodded. 'Yeah, just let me…' she gestured at her remaining food.

'No worries.' He leaned in and they kissed. He smelt of mint shower gel and comfort. She felt her tired limbs relax as he drew away, turning to leave the room.

As he reached the door he turned back. 'Incidentally, Monkey thinks she saw a man watching the house earlier. I've tried telling her it's nothing, but she got quite scared. I said we'd keep an eye out.'

'A man watching the house?' Freemark was confused. Her daughter wasn't the anxious type.

'Yeah, I think it was probably just the van that was parked opposite today. She's maybe seen the news and got worried. Anyway, I've told her she's safe with us as her mummy kicks arse!'

Freemark laughed 'Please tell me you didn't say—'

'I said bottom.' He read her mind. 'She thought it was very funny and agreed that mummy could kick anyone's bottom.'

Freemark felt the squeeze of love for her daughter. 'I'll take that. Good night,' she called to her husband's retreating back.

She chewed the last of the sausage and she washed it down with the dregs of wine. The plate and glass went into the dishwasher and she switched off the kitchen light. As she passed the window to the garden a slight movement caught her eye. She crossed to the back door and switched on the garden light. Lawn and flowerbeds were suddenly illuminated, standing out against the pitch black behind. Nothing stirred. *She's got me at it now*, Freemark thought. She switched off the light and made her way to bed. She was too tired to think about Grantham now. Too tired to think about connections through. Too tired to worry about spectres in the garden.

I Vow to Thee – William E. H. Walker

Day 17

'Holding on to anger is like grasping a hot coal with the intent of throwing it at someone else; You are the one who gets burned.'

—Buddha

06:23

Suss

The office was still nice and quiet at this time of day, she always preferred it like that. The secluded stillness of early morning before 100 officers arrived to attempt to solve 1000 crimes.

On her screen was the website of the Church of St John. She tapped the table as she read the guide.

"Originally built in 1467, the church is home to an array of beautiful 17th-century stained glass windows featuring scenes from the New Testament."

She skipped forward to more current times: "In 2007, the Right Reverend Jowan Cross joined the church and has been instrumental in bringing it into the 21st century through a program of local initiatives, support groups and children's play groups. For more information click here."

Suss clicked the link. A picture of a vicar surrounded by beaming children filled the top half of her screen. She studied the man. Mid to late sixties, pure white hair flowing loose to his shoulders. No more than five foot nine and stick thin. His skin had taken on the look of melting plastic, sagging over his jaw as though attempting to escape his face. Across his brow a long, thick scar tore into the hairline. Harsh and jagged. Torn apart, that's what had happened there. His skull had been torn apart. His eyes had an almost dog-like quality. Puffy, giving him the look of the perpetually tired. The eyes themselves though were sharp and clear. Despite his looks, Reverend Cross stood straight and strong, a man who took care of himself.

She clicked open a new tab, typing in Reverend Jowan Cross, Oxford. The search came back with the same website she currently had open and several articles from local papers reporting on his good works. "Vicar Starts Alcoholics Support Group"; ``Vicar's Mental Health Charity"; "Reverend Offers Rooms to Orphans"; "Vicar Runs Drug Rehab Course".

A proper nice bloke, Suss thought. She scrolled down the list, clicking open pages and skimming articles before moving on. After about 20 minutes or so she leaned back in her chair, mouth pouting in

I Vow to Thee – William E. H. Walker

thought. There was nothing about the man prior to 2007. Not a whisper. She minimised the pages and tried the police database. Nada.

Returning to the web, she tried looking for social media. No profile on Frog, Bamboo or Twitter. She tried searching for Jowan Cross 2001. Nothing; 2002, still nothing; 2003, 2004 and 2005. Empty handed.

How could there be no reference before he started in Oxford? Not a single mention of the man anywhere? Had he not been a vicar then? She returned to the church website, but there was nothing about the man's ordination or personal history. Where had he been? Was it possible there was nothing?

'Hey, what are you up to?' The voice had appeared behind her. It was Kinsella and she was early.

Suss closed the internet pages and spun quickly in her seat. Kinsella was standing a couple of feet away, but Suss couldn't read her expression. She looked almost like she was trying not to run, keeping her face neutral.

Suss smiled, looking innocent but feeling like she'd been caught stealing. 'Not much, just thought I'd get in early.' She was conscious of the now blank desktop betraying her lack of work. 'How's you?'

Kinsella passed her a cup of coffee, her face still a mask. Suss smiled her thanks. 'I'm okay, not sure what to do now we're not investigating the village.' An uncomfortable pause. Suss wondering what Kinsella had been up to the previous day. She'd been out of the office, Suss thought she knew why after what she'd witnessed outside Kinsella's house. 'What are you working on?' Kinsella was eyeing her screen.

'Oh, you know, nothing really.' Her mind raced for a response. 'Just still wondering about the cars. Felt like we were onto something.'

'Yeah, still, it's with the bigwigs now.' Kinsella sipped her coffee. 'I suspect you'll be back off to London soon?' Was there a note of hope in her voice?

'Yeah, I guess so.' In truth, a part of Suss would've loved to be back home right now. Back where she could forget about all this crap and just snuggle up with Debs. But another part of her, the bigger part, wanted to know what was going on with this woman who stood so innocently before sipping her coffee.

The silence stretched into awkwardness. Finally Kinsella said, 'Well, I'm going to get on with some work.' She smiled at Suss and left quickly. Suss watched her go, thinking again how she might be so wrong, but there was something.

She opened her browser again. Reverend Jowan Cross, Maria Kinsella. Nothing. She tapped the desk, thinking. Glancing up she saw Kinsella at the far side of the office, typing quickly into her phone, her face held a look of furtive panic. *Interesting*. Suss absentmindedly clicked the images link. The screen

I Vow to Thee – William E. H. Walker

was filled with pictures, mostly of the smiling Reverend Cross at various charitable events. She scrolled down the page, her eyes drifting from image to image. After about a minute or so when she was almost ready to give up, she landed on a picture. Her eyes widened as she stared at a man with his arm resting around the shoulders of Jowan Cross. He was much younger, with short, neat brown hair and an infusive smile, but still very much Cross. Both men were wearing running gear, paper numbers fixed to their shirts, mud splattered over them and broad grins on their faces. She knew that man. She enlarged the picture. It was from an old Myspace profile and carried the caption: "Me and Joe after the cross country run." The picture was dated September 21st, 2001. The profile belonged to a Gerald Piper. She knew that name.

The profile was inactive and most of the personal information was gone, but she was sure she knew that face. He wasn't that young. He'd had grey hair when she'd seen him. Where had that been? Her mind suddenly flashed a picture before her. A family photo, grandparents holding a baby. They had been killed. Killed in Lesser Worburston. Gerald Piper was the paedophile in Lesser Worburston. Now she realised the photo was taken in the village. The green in the background with the curious stone once used to mount horses. The manor house a blur behind that.

Her hands shaking slightly, Suss typed, "Reverend Jowan Cross, Lesser Worburston" into the search engine. At first there was nothing. Hundreds of articles on the village massacre but nothing linking the vicar to the village. But then, on page nine, one result. A comment from a blog written by someone calling themselves "BeansSpilled16." Suss glanced up from her screen and noted Kinsella had left the office. She looked around but there was no sign of her. She opened the blog:

December 14th, 2005

I've got to get this off my chest. It's hurting too much to hold on to it. I think I've killed a man. At least I've hurt him more than he ever deserved. For reasons that will become clear, I will stay anonymous and change any names in this blog.

It all started about a year ago. When I was 15 I was going through a bit of a rebellious phase, smoking weed, drinking and stuff. We had this vicar in the village. He was about 30-odd. But a young 30, I mean he looked after himself. Always saw him running through the village and that.

Anyway, my parents kept us involved in the church. We'd always be doing things like book sales and fetes and stuff. We became friends. I thought so anyway. He was always so nice to me. He'd make me laugh and that. He tried to persuade me to not drink and smoke. Told me how pretty I was and how I looked nicer sober. Helped me stop. He was always looking out for me.

Over the next six months I realised I had started to fancy him. He'd rest his hand on my shoulder or place it against my back and I'd get this feeling like excitement but different. I thought he felt the same way. I would find reasons to be alone with him and we'd always be laughing and joking about. I was sure he fancied me too.

I'd not been with anyone and I wasn't sure how to tell him how I felt, so I decided to seduce him like I've seen in films online. I'd been watching porn for a few years so I knew how to do it.

I started to make sure I was always wearing tight clothes or short skirts and no tights. I'm thin and fit and wanted him to look. Once I "accidentally" fell over and scraped my knee. He washed it clean and was so gentle. I was wearing a skirt and I was sure he was looking. I was so excited. Anyway, this went on for a few weeks and I started getting desperate. I even went so far as to "accidentally forget" to put on underwear and bent over in front of him but nothing happened. I couldn't get him alone long enough for us to act on our feelings. I knew he had feelings though.

Then came the day. We were alone in the church. I was helping him sort out books for the book club. We'd recently had a donation that needed sorting. I was wearing a crop top and this skirt that barely came over my arse. I knew I was having an effect on him, he kept dropping books and was stuttering. I was desperate and realised now was our chance.

I decided to make my move. I found a book that needed to go on the shelves behind him. I walked over and leaned into him, pushing myself against him. He looked surprised but I was sure he wanted me too. I kissed him and he pushed me away. He told me I was too young and that I'd misinterpreted his feelings. I was gutted. Like, I knew he wanted me. I tried again telling him how I knew he liked me and that I wanted him but he refused. He told me to get out. He actually shouted at me. I was devastated. I cried all the way home and hid in my room. I'd never been so humiliated.

Dad come up and asked me what was going on. I'm not proud of this, but I told him Reverend Cross had tried to force himself on me.

His face scared the shit out of me. He left me with my mum and went out. Next thing I know we don't have a vicar. I asked dad what happened and he wouldn't answer me. His knuckles were swollen and cut though. I'm worried he had done something stupid and killed him. I didn't know what to do? I lied as I was scared and now I think I'm responsible for the vicar's death. I needed someone to help me?!

Suss exhaled slowly. *That's quite a link*, she thought. She scrolled down to the comments.

"Hey Stace, Cross was his real name. You forgot to change it! This is so obviously about our village."

I Vow to Thee – William E. H. Walker

The sub comment:

"Shit. How do I change it?"

The reply: "Haha, man you best hope no one in Worburston reads this, you'll be in the shit for real."

The other comments were a mix of people laughing at her mistake, offering condolence, condemnation and unhelpful advice. The occasional troll comment thrown in by someone without the intelligence to add anything worthwhile.

Suss ran her hands over her hair. He'd been the vicar in Lesser Worburston, he'd been run out of the village for something he hadn't done. Her mind was racing, making connections.

The probability that the former vicar was linked to the attack was, superficially, tiny. What was his motive? Revenge. Sure. If what Stace, AKA "Beansspilled16," was hinting at with her father's actions had happened, he'd certainly have motive to hate the village. This had happened in 2004, in 2007 he'd joined a church in Oxford and, from the look of him, he was a changed man from the fit and healthy "young" 30-year-old mentioned in the blog. What happened between 2004 and 2007? A lengthy stay in hospital followed by recuperation? Maybe. Not much of a stretch if he'd been seriously hurt. But then why wait till now to get revenge? And why bomb London? What was the connection between that and the beating he must have taken because a young girl lied?

She pictured the girl, Stace, 15 and flirtatious, dressing in skimpy clothes to attract him. All health and hormones the way only teenagers can be. What was it she'd said? *"I decided to seduce him. I'd been watching porn for some years so knew how to do it."* Suss had learned the same way, although she suspected from different movies to Stace. All wrong, of course. You don't learn anything from porn.

He'd objected to her advances, or at least had done so at the last minute. His reaction had suggested he was angry at himself as well. Might she have been right and he had been tempted? You don't shout at someone to get out like that unless you're feeling shame. Could this be about his faith? He was tempted and he didn't give in, only to be beaten half to death for his troubles. She sipped her rapidly cooling coffee. Or could this be about her? About what she stood for? Her clothing, her lifestyle? Could this be a revolution against modern life? That would tie in Laoch as well, he's out there spreading the Christian mess—

She sat bolt upright in her chair, realisation flooding through her. Here you have a simple village vicar, happily living life in a quiet environment in Oxfordshire. Then into this world comes everything the church is supposed to teach against manifested as a teenage girl. He'd tried hard to help her and she'd repaid him by lying and getting him beaten up. He'd been angry, embarrassed, humiliated. Not by her, but by society. He'd moved to Oxford, used the groups he set up to recruit other desperate, lonely people to commit murder for him. But to what end? Change of government? Yes. Laoch. He wanted Laoch. He was running Laoch. He orchestrated the village massacre and London bombing to get Laoch into power. He'd killed more than 15,000 people to do it, he'd killed her parents to do it. Killed her parents. The pictures forming in her mind were instantly replaced by one of her own parents as she always remembered them, hugging and kissing her goodnight.

'You fucking scum-sucking motherfucker.' The words machine gunned out of her mouth. The chair flew out behind her as she turned to stalk out of the room. She would find him, she would expose him, she would beat him. And yes, she would bring him in. Or kill him.

10:03

Castle Way didn't look like the type of road you'd build a castle on, but then she supposed it would've been built long before the dual carriageway. The little she could see from her vantage point in the back of the van gave her the impression of a town that had never quite recovered its former, castle-dominated glories. The van took the slip road and headed into the town proper, her first visit to Carlisle.

'West Tower Street, two minutes out,' the driver called back to her.

She adjusted herself in her seat, fidgeting with the balaclava that covered her face. Why were they always so itchy? She wrapped her gloved hand on the cold handles and breathed in deeply.

Focus on your breathing, control it, feel it within you. You are alive, the voice inside her said.

Her second attack in two weeks. Did she pity them? Yes, it was sad that they had to die. But was it necessary? Most definitely. For the sake of all their souls, it most definitely was.

The van swung a right onto Market Street, then a left onto Fisher Street and round to St Mary's Gate.

'ETA 15 seconds! Get ready,' called the driver as they approached the crossroads with Castle Street.

This isn't murder. This is the creation of a new world for all of us. The words revolved around her head as the van pulled into the centre of the crossroads, blocking both lanes to the consternation of other drivers, and stopped. The side door opened automatically, and she aimed the M134 minigun mounted on its tripod at the fat man on the dais erected in front of the cathedral. The crowd, roughly 200 people, were all listening to him speak, their backs to her.

She opened fire.

The fat man's belly exploded like a balloon popping. She kept the barrel aimed squarely at him until his body was little more than red mist. The crowd seemed frozen in place, stunned into silence by what they had just witnessed. She smiled to herself and lowered the smoking barrel, pointing it directly at the rear of the mass.

She opened fire again and unleashed 4000 7.62×51mm rounds per minute into the crowd.

I Vow to Thee – William E. H. Walker

10:06

'Mr. Boldermore, Mr. Boldermore! What's your stance on education?'

'Mr. Boldermore, do you believe homosexuality is a sin?'

'Mr. Boldermore, do you support Mrs. Fortescue's policy on immigration?'

He ignored the rats climbing over each other to get to their meat. The prize rump steak of a politician trying to force his way to his car, his bodyguards attempting to hold back the plague.

Go straight for him. Don't stop, don't blink. Just head right to him and then do it.

He knew he must fight his way past them, push himself through the melee. But his size would help that. He'd always been small, even with the 20 extra pounds he was currently carrying he was slim and could slip easily between the gaps in the rabid crowd.

You are joining God. You are becoming a part of God.

The cacophony increased as he neared, the prop camera dangling uselessly from his neck. Then he was among them. They squeezed in tightly, but he angled his body like a boat navigating a river, and slid between their pressing desperation. He was worried for a moment that the explosives fastened around his waist and torso might be loosened by their pressing, sweaty bodies and he squeezed tighter, the dead-man switch in his hand.

Suddenly he was beside him. Their eyes met. He read the confusion and surprise there. The recognition that this wasn't a chance meeting. The realisation this was something more.

He released the trigger and the world vanished.

I Vow to Thee – William E. H. Walker

10:06

Shanks

Shanks stood to the left of the makeshift podium set up outside the Royal Wootton Bassett Town Hall Museum, listening to the introductory address by the local Party Chairman. He was gushing in his praise of Shanks' bravery after the attack on London. Shanks couldn't say he minded.

As the praise ended, he stepped forward and shook the man's hand. He fixed the political smile on his face and stepped behind the microphone. Waving to the crowd he waited for the applause to finish.

'Thank you, thank you.' A deep breath. He sneezed, his body doubled over with its force.

The podium in front of him splintered as the bullets smashed into it, ricocheting off the ground beside him. Shanks dived to his right, his suit tearing on the rough stone. The second shot hit next to his head and suddenly there was a body on top of him. He was lifted roughly and thrown forward under the cover of the building.

His breathing was ragged, sweat poured from his brow. The crowd were screaming and running as he was pushed hard against a wall by one of his minders.

The bullet had been inches away, they'd almost taken his head off. But he had survived.

10:42

Freemark

Freemark was feeling nervous now. The feeling tingled through her chest and arms like ants on her skin. The sustained ability of this unknown group to attack the country seemingly at will and without trace was proving hard to fathom. Three more attacks that morning. All aimed at the BCP party leader candidates. Two fatal and one near miss.

She sat in the cramped office at the back of the supermarket, alone now as the manager she'd been interviewing on the recruitment issues had been called out front after the news of the attacks came through. It seemed these atrocities might be a tipping point for much of the populous into near total panic.

Freemark had sat, slightly bored, listening to the grumpy young man, his moustache pointing in every direction but down, blaming everyone but himself for his store's inability to recruit and retain good staff, wondering if maybe he'd shut up and listen to his team who might tell him he was the problem, when one of his team leaders had rushed in.

The radio was switched on and the reports started coming in.

'Defence Secretary Marko Flint was gunned down in Carlisle this morning while giving a speech on northern industrial growth. Reports are that the shots were fired from a van that had pulled up at the junction of Saint Marys Gate and Castle Street. The Minister was killed instantly before the gun was turned on the crowd. At least 50 are known to have died before the van took off at speed and has yet to be found.

'Roger Boldermore, leadership challenger and MP for Darlington, was killed in what appears to be a suicide bombing in Hastings. Mr. Boldermore had just finished giving a speech to local Party members and was returning to his car when the attack occurred. At least 15 members of the press were caught in the explosion. The exact number of casualties is as yet unknown but is expected to be significant.

'Mark Shanks, the MP for North Oxfordshire, was also the target of an attack today in Royal Wootton Bassett in Wiltshire. A gunman fired twice at Mr. Shanks, narrowly missing him. Mr. Shanks is reportedly shaken but otherwise unharmed.'

Within 30 minutes the supermarket had filled with panic shoppers. Bread, milk and water were bundled into trolleys as worried families tried to secure themselves against further attacks.

Five attacks in two weeks, no wonder people were frightened. This was unprecedented. The IRA had come close to this level of violence, but they had at least called in the bomb locations before detonating them. These attacks were different. Each unique in its execution and target. Each planned, precise and merciless. Each designed to invoke the maximum amount of fear in people, and it was working. It truly seemed no one was safe. From babies asleep in their beds to potential Prime Ministers, everyone was vulnerable. Anyone and everyone a potential target.

Freemark was feeling at a loss of what to do. Part of her wanted to join the shoppers as they raced from aisle to aisle buying up tinned goods and toilet roll. Part of her wanted to be with her daughter and husband. To hold them and feel the security they provided. Part of her needed to listen to the unfolding news.

The van had been found ablaze just outside Carlisle. Police were on the lookout for a man and woman driving a blue car seen leaving the area. The shooter in Royal Wootton Bassett had not been found.

Freemark took out her mobile and saw a message waiting for her. It was from Stephen.

"Hey, tried to call but went straight to voicemail. Work has closed early for the day. I'm going to collect Maddie and take her home. Have spoken with the school, they're fine with it, lots of parents doing the same. Call when you can. Love you. X"

A moment of intense relief washed over her. Choice made. She tapped, "Coming soon, love you. X" into her phone and rose to leave. The news reader's voice had changed. A note of excitement in his tone.

'We've just received a report that police dispatched to the home of Susan Fortescue, MP for East Sussex, have found three bodies. Reports are sketchy at present, but it seems that they might be of Mrs. Fortescue, her husband and their nine-year-old son. No word yet on how they died, but we are told that police had arrived at the scene to secure Mrs. Fortescue against an attempt on her life and found that they were too late. We can tell you that Angela Rainsworth, MP for Hampshire East and Secretary of State for Transport, who is also running as candidates for leadership of the British Christian Party, has been taken to a secure location for her own protection. We shall keep you updated as this story develops.'

I Vow to Thee – William E. H. Walker

Freemark was out the door and running for her car before the end of the statement. It was clear the attacks were targeted and deliberate, but with such capability no one knew where they would strike next. She needed to be home with her husband and daughter. Safe.

16:04

Wentworth

Standing at the mirror of the station toilets, Wentworth picked yet another tiny white hair from his head, wincing slightly as it came free. Blinking, he studied his features in the soap-splattered glass. The skin was starting to sag a little. He pinched his cheek between his fingers and released it. Losing its elasticity, maybe? The creases at his eyes were becoming more pronounced. And what was with the random fine hairs that grew seemingly overnight to an inch long from his ear lobes? When did that become a thing? Was his body rebelling against him for his mistreatment of it as a teenager? Was he really so old? He'd been 21 just last week, now suddenly he was less than seven years away from 50. Middle aged and in danger of developing a beer gut. That was an exaggeration, his stomach was actually more toned than it had been when he was 21. He exercised every day without fail. He flexed his arms under his suit. Could you tell? Maybe.

He told himself he just wanted to be healthy, to be fit and to feel good. Not haunted by the thought of dying. Forgotten, lost in the earth with no one to remember him. He had realised a couple of years ago that it was very possible he was over half way through his life. He was now on the downward slope and heading for the finishing line, so to speak. The thought had struck him so violently he had lain awake for most of the night staring at the TV, unable and unwilling to let himself sleep lest he miss even more. Where had this fear come from? What was driving it? He'd always been so confident and capable. He knew he was fairly smart and logical, yet the thought he had probably already lived for longer than he would do was a mind fuck he was struggling to deal with. But then his body was telling him so. The eyebrow hairs that grew to three feet long before standing directly out from his face. The grey hairs he shaved or cut or plucked or dyed. The sudden twinges in his back and knees. The nostril hairs that were an inch wide and as black as night. He was fitter than he had ever been but still scared that it wouldn't be enough. Sometimes he just wanted to cry.

But not today. Today he had to continue being the DCI. His officers were scared and unsure what to do, he had to help them, give them that reassurance, be their rock. He straightened and picked fluff from his suit. 'Look good, feel good,' he said to himself, and left the toilet.

Outside the office was quiet, most personnel had been deployed with the military to quieten down the brewing panic that was threatening to spread into all-out riots. Bishop Laoch had given a speech via Frog calling for the expulsion of all non-Christians and called on the people of the country to revolt against our attackers. Oxford Mosque had been attacked that afternoon, an Indian man was beaten half to death in Headington and similar kneejerk brutality was being repeated right across the country.

Wentworth crossed to the operations control room and walked inside. The difference between the deserted communal office and the control room was equal to the difference between living alone and flat-sharing with a wild Tasmanian devil. The room was alive with noise. The vibrations of pent-up anxiety, anger and fear spread throughout the room, infecting everyone as they went about their work. Officers and admin staff screaming out incidents and directing officers to support, running between terminals or making phone calls. Panic threatening to overwhelm.

Wentworth stood in the middle of it, the large 3D map of Oxford projected onto the desk before him. Small red dots highlighting the sites of 999 calls while blue dots denoted where the officers currently were deployed. Every now and then one of the blue dots sent out a long green line that connected with a red dot. A clock appeared above it, showing the time it would take for the dispatched officers to arrive at the scene. Wentworth took it all in and wondered what to do. So many red dots.

Curfew, he thought to himself. *It needs to be a curfew.* He picked up his phone and dialled the Superintendent. 'Sir, we need to install a curfew.'

'I agree, I'm in the town centre right now with the CC. I'll get it done.' He hung up. No time for pleasantries, just get the job done.

'Hi, what can I do?' Kinsella stood beside him, seeming to appear as if from nowhere.

He jumped slightly before recovering himself. 'Hey, you can give us a hand in Iffley if you don't mind. We've got students using this shit as an excuse to fuck around.'

'Sure, no problem. Can I take anyone?'

'You've got a couple of officers already there, if needed I'll see if I can spare anyone else. Singh is in town as well. He had a meeting with the Super and they're taking control of the centre of town.'

'Great, I'll get over to Iffley.'

She was about to go when a thought struck Wentworth. 'Hey,' he called her back. 'You know Julia Freemark, right?'

Her face twitched slightly. 'Name rings a bell, why do you ask?'

'I saw her in Cornwall. Jake Grantham, the son of the singer who was killed in the village. He was murdered in his home.' He'd walked round the table to face her. He'd always found her pleasant enough, but she'd often come across as quite cold and aloof, like she was holding something back.

Her eyebrows crept up her forehead and she tutted and shook her head. 'Murdered? Well, he didn't come across as the nicest bloke when I interviewed him, but I didn't expect that. Do you know why?'

'Not 100 percent, no, but he had a body buried in the back garden.'

Her face definitely twitched that time, but she recovered quickly. 'A body? Oh wow. I really didn't see that coming.' She ran her hand through her hair, chewing her lip.

'Well anyway, I understand you spoke with Mrs. Freemark about some cards or letters he'd written to her?'

Kinsella looked distracted, 'What? Yeah. I did. They didn't seem that serious at the time, nothing malicious in them anyway. I told her I'd investigate it but also that it wasn't a crime to write to someone. Not if it's inoffensive anyway.' She shook her head. 'Had I known he was a murderer...'

'I very much doubt you'd let him go swanning off out of here to write more if you did,' Wentworth assured her. 'Anyway, I'll need those letters for my file on him. Drop them off on my desk, thanks.'

'Sure... no problem.' She stood for a moment, looking like she wanted to say something, then left without another word.

He watched her go and pondered her reaction. She'd seemed unduly concerned over his interest in those letters. Maybe it was simply because she'd told Freemark not to worry and then found out Grantham was a murderer? She might think she'll get into shite for it. He should remember to reassure her that she couldn't have known.

He picked up his phone again but spotted Suss stalking past the door. He'd not really had much chance to talk to her. He knew she lost her parents in London and that he should check in. He poked his head out the door. 'Suss?' he called.

She turned and gave him a look of inquisition. 'Boss?' she replied, walking back to him.

'How are you doing?' he smiled; she didn't return it.

'Fine, boss. Thanks.' She seemed anxious to be away.

'What are you up to at the moment?' He held his smile in place.

'I'm, erm… I'm looking into a lead.' Why so hesitant? What's going on with his officers today?

'Tell me more then.' He leaned on the wall, ready to listen.

'Well, it's a bit loose right now. I'd like more time.' She gave a quick glance back in the direction she'd been travelling. She was definitely anxious to be away.

'What've you got so far?' *You're not getting rid of me that easily*, he thought.

She seemed to resign herself to his line of questioning but didn't spill the beans straight away. She seemed to be weighing up what to say.

'How did they get into the Lesser Worburston houses so easily?' The question took Wentworth by surprise.

'Laser pick locks, that's been established.'

She shook her head. 'That's not what I mean. Not one alarm triggered, not one dog missed. And as far as I can see, they didn't even knock over a pot plant. How is that possible?'

Wentworth felt like he was being schooled. Her expression was that of someone expecting the question to be obvious. After a moment's silence, she answered it herself.

'They knew the village. Not just the village, but the houses inside and out. Which ones had dogs, which ones were alarmed. They even went through the back door on a few rather than the front. Why is that? Because the front door was noisy and the back door was the better option? How come they were so quick as well? What, 15 minutes or so based on autopsies? They couldn't do that without knowing everything about their targets.'

'I see your point.' He itched his neck. 'But the task force must have worked that out by now. What are you seeing that you don't think they are?'

'I want to know who told them.' Her eyes were glistening with passion. Had she got too close to this since London?

'And who do you think told them?' Wentworth felt he should tread carefully. She held the air of someone teetering on the edge.

'That's what I want to know. I think it's the people we'd never think of. The cleaners, the odd job guys, window cleaners, rubbish collectors.' She paused again, 'Police.'

The word hung between them like a spectre. Wentworth had to admit it was an interesting theory. A thought occurred to him. 'You think a local cop was involved?' Wentworth thought the idea had legs. Suss didn't react, she just stood silent, vibrating with energy.

Wentworth was starting to like her way of thinking and decided to trust her. Even though she dressed like a teenager – was that Mighty Mouse on her T-shirt? – and looked ready to snap, her mind was evidently still working at full capacity. 'You know, before all this kicked off,' he signalled toward the control room, 'Singh asked me to look into the murder of Jake Grantham and two apparently unrelated deaths in the past week.' He filled her in on the details of the two suspicious deaths and an overview of what he'd found in Cornwall.

Behind Suss' eyes he could see her mind working. 'It's a clean-up,' she whispered after a good minute's silence.

'A what?' Wentworth hadn't heard her properly.

'Boss, I think you're going to have a fair few more suspicious deaths before the week is out.'

'How can you know?' But Suss was already walking away from him, her fingers tapping out a tattoo in the air, her mind working overtime. 'Suss, Suss,' he called after her.

She turned just short of the door that led to the carpark. Her face was set and severe. 'Boss, I need to look into this. Can you get me those files? Also…' She hadn't waited for him to respond, 'I think I might know why this happened.' Without another word she left.

Wentworth watched the door swing closed; her words worried him. He knew she was meant to be super intelligent and a highflyer, but he'd only seen a young woman in jeans and a scruffy T-shirt who looked almost ready to crack. Could she really be so far ahead of them with her chain of thought? He should probably call her back and get her to explain more concisely what she was thinking.

Just when he had made up his mind to go after her, he was tapped on the shoulder by a young admin assistant. 'Sir, we've got a Co-Op on the Abingdon Road being broken into. It's on fire.' Wentworth sighed and turned his attention back to the issues at hand, Suss, Kinsella, letters and murder pushed to the back of his mind. Only Suss' last words stayed with him a little longer: 'I think I might know why this happened.'

19:26

Laoch

'You're a racist, it's as simple as that.' The presenter was angry. Laoch could tell he'd railed him, and that was exactly the point.

Laoch kept his voice quiet and reasonable. 'I'm not a racist John. I'm fine with people from all over the world. I just don't see why we need them here. We are God's children and look at what they do to us. Today is yet another example of what they are capable of.'

'But how can you say that isn't racist? We are a multicultural society, we promote tolerance and—'

'Yet you seem unable to tolerate my view John.' Trap sprung.

'I find it hard to tolerate a view that is so inherently racist,' Caught.

'Oh, I see.' Laoch nodded in an exaggerated way for the camera. 'We should only tolerate some views and some perspectives, providing they align with what we want people to believe.'

'That's not what I said.' He was on the ropes.

'It's exactly what you said. It's what our society has been told for years. We must accept people. Have to. We must welcome people. Have to. *We* must do what *we* are told because *we* are the people and not those in change. The people who tear us apart, *we* must tolerate then and allow them to murder *us*.'

'You're twisting my words—'

'I'm twisting nothing.' His accent grew thicker as his voice rose. His eyes burned into the presenter, who shrank back slightly. Such a young man, such limited experience. 'You claim that my views are abhorrent yet all I do is work for the good of this nation. This one nation under God. All I do is fight with my brothers and sisters against the oncoming storm that is waging war against us. Today we lost more soldiers in the fight and while they may have only paid lip service to our Lord, and while some may have been politicians, we cannot afford to lie down and let our enemies stamp all over us as if we're nothing. As if we'll just take it. *We* cannot. *We* will not.' John Hampton, the new ITV political journalist, didn't even try to interrupt now. Laoch was standing, towering over him, a beacon of righteousness. 'We must show them we are not afraid. We must show them who we are and what we are capable of. This is why I will be holding a rally in London's Parliament Square in two days' time. This Friday we will come together in our nation's capital to stand up against those who would destroy us. We will pray together for our fallen brethren. We will remember those we have lost to the virus that calls itself Islam. We will stand tall and show our government that we will not be cowed into submission. That we will rise and show the world that we will not be defeated.' He sank back into his chair. There was a moment's silence as the young reporter stared at him. Then, his wits returning, he ended the show.

Laoch left the studio and got into his waiting car. Peter was talking quietly into a phone and shot him a look. Laoch didn't know what to make of it until Peter, without a word of warning, pushed the phone into his hands. Laoch was confused but put the handset to his ear. It was her. And she was pissed. There wasn't a question, there was a statement of fact. It stung him like a hornet.

'I don't see why I needed to—'

'No, I didn't mean to not mention him…'

'No, I don't want to—'

'Yes, I understand…'

'Yes—'

'Yes…'

'Yes… I will. But you said I would be the lead… okay… later… okay… but— yes.' He handed the phone back over to Peter who listened intently for a minute. 'I understand,' he said and hung up. He rolled down the window, removed the sim card from the phone, snapped it in half and threw one half out onto the road.

Laoch was feeling perturbed. Whichever way you looked at it, he'd just been thoroughly bollocked. This wasn't how it was meant to be. He wasn't the one who was meant to be bollocked. He was meant to be the one who did the bollocking. Was he not their leader? How dare she raise her voice to him? He was the Bishop of Oxford. The Leader of the Revolution, the Voice of Freedom. Oh, he liked that one. The Voice of Freedom. He'd have to remember that.

He became aware that Peter was asking him a question. 'Huh? What?' he snapped at him.

'I was asking if you'd like to go out or home for dinner, Your Excellency.' Peter's voice was honeyed.

'Oh, right. Erm… home I suppose.'

'As you wish, Sir.' He leaned forward and placed his hand on Laoch's thigh. 'And don't let it bother you, Sir. She doesn't understand.' He left his hand there a moment longer, his young fingers moving imperceptibly over Laoch's trousers. The Bishop merely stared at him, unable to speak. The boy had an effect on him, that was for sure.

The car pulled into the courtyard of his 17th century manor and Laoch extricated himself from the vehicle as quickly as possible. His mind conflicted between his hurt at the scolding and the flurry in his stomach at Peter's touch. As he marched quickly toward his front door, he heard Peter call after him, 'I'll bring your dinner to your rooms, Your Excellency.'

Laoch waved a hand in acknowledgment and went inside. He changed out of his robes and into a pair of loose-fitting chinos and a shirt. Feeling more relaxed, he poured himself a whisky and switched on the TV. It seemed Mark Shanks, who was being interviewed by Channel 4, was calling on everyone to back his new ideas for Britain.

'Our country has been without a leader for too long. We cannot go on like this.'

Too right, Laoch thought, *and in two days I'll take my place as that leader. You and your cronies can go hang.*

'We deserve to live our lives, not be worked to death for the benefit of the super-rich.'

That's what you think, Laoch smiled to himself and sipped his whisky.

The interviewer asked a question that immediately caught Laoch's attention.

'What do you think of Bishop Laoch's call to arms? His desire to take on parliament while the Leadership vote is being counted?'

Laoch watched Shanks' slimy smile spread over his face. 'Now, I may not agree with his rhetoric but I must admit Bishop Laoch has a point.' Laoch sat up in his chair. This shit was going to pay him a compliment. 'Politicians have paid lip service to God for too long. They have stolen our livelihoods for too long and praised God for the privilege. Bishop Laoch is a unique individual. He is blessed with the ability to draw a crowd and speak most eloquently.' *Why was this toad paying him compliments?* 'I believe that he works tirelessly for our country and, as I have already said, while I do not agree with some of his rhetoric, he is a man of principles. A man of honour, and I believe he will continue to work hard for this country.'

The interviewer stepped in. 'But with regards to his protest outside parliament, has he spoken of taking over?'

Shanks shook his head. 'I don't think Laoch means to do it literally. He's too sensible for that. I think, fundamentally, he and I are on the same side. We both want change in this country. We both want God back at the heart of everything. We're on the same page, just reading different verses.'

The interviewer again. 'So, you back the Bishop?'

Shanks gave a small chuckle 'Funnily enough, I believe Laoch has tweeted just this afternoon that he's backing me.'

'Like fuck I am!' Laoch screamed at the television. Dropping the whisky noisily on the glass table, he scrambled for his phone and opened twitter. His app didn't show his account, so he entered his username and password. Both were unrecognised. He tried again, same result. He clicked the "reset password" link and opened his email, but nothing came through. He tapped his foot rapidly on the carpet as he waited but still nothing. He opened a browser window and searched for his own twitter feed. Sure enough there was a tweet there from his account endorsing Shanks as, "The type of righteous man this country needs." Laoch was beyond furious, crazed by the very idea. Like he would tweet that? Like he would rally behind scum like that? Did they not know who he was? He opened his messages and typed a quick one-line message to "Nan."

"Twitter account hacked. Not my tweet. Trying to fix it. "

A reply came through within seconds. "Okay, no problem, let me know when fixed."

No problem? This would seriously dent his chances. If all his supporters went out and voted for Shanks, then how could he hope to seize parliament? Fucking hell, it was just one thing after another. He tried several different variants of his email address and password, but his account remained stubbornly closed to him. He searched how to report his account being hacked and completed the report form. When he'd clicked send, he felt a strange mix of fear and anger. Would he be punished for this tweet? How could this happen to him? He suddenly felt very tired and downed his drink. He flung himself into a chair, flicked off the television and brewed over his predicament.

If we withdrew his support now, he would be a laughingstock. He would be mocked for allowing his Twitter account to be hacked, and he couldn't have that. On the other hand, if he did nothing Shanks would most likely get elected Prime Minister. Did that matter though? He could be thrown aside with the rest of them, maybe even easier as he was so young and inexperienced. Plus, he didn't have the backing Laoch did. Maybe this would work out for the best? Laoch didn't really care who stood in his way, he'd have his revolution anyway. This would still work out fine. He could get Mark-sodding-Shanks out of the way easily enough.

I Vow to Thee – William E. H. Walker

Feeling more relaxed he turned the TV back on and settled down with another drink. A hiccup, that's what this was, a hiccup. He could deal with hiccups.

There was a knock at the door. Peter entered carrying a tray with a silver plate on it and what looked like beef steaming from on top.

Laoch returned the proffered smile, the memory of his hand on his thigh flashed before his eyes and looked hurriedly away. *God do not tempt me now, not when we are so close.* He opened his eyes to see Peter bending over the table in front of him, his tight trousers leaving nothing to the imagination. Laoch felt himself stir and gulped down his remaining whisky.

Peter turned and saw the empty glass. 'Let me fill that for you, Sir.' He smiled and took the glass, young fingers brushing lightly against his hand. *Please don't tempt me*, Shanks thought. He filled it from the decanter and turned back toward Laoch.

Just before he reached Laoch he seemed to trip on something, sending the whisky over the Bishop's lap. Laoch jumped up in surprise, the front of his trousers now thoroughly wet. 'Oh my word, Sir, I'm so sorry.' Peter put the glass down and reached for the napkin.

'Now, now, don't worry I…' Laoch's words faded to dust in his throat. Peter had dropped to his knees and was dabbing the napkin firmly against Laoch's trousers. Laoch's mouth opened and closed but no words came out. He tried his hardest to focus on the banalities of the television as the young man pressed his hand firmly against his crotch. *Don't think about it, don't think about it. Damn, damn, damn.*

Peter had stopped. He was kneeling in front of Laoch, who was staring as hard as he could at anything but the man before him. Trying for the love of God to stop himself from reacting, but knowing it was already far, far too late. Peter's grip told him that.

'I can help with that too if you like?' Peter whispered. A soft, honeyed tone. A voice of youthful interest and curiosity.

Laoch hated himself for a moment. This was a mortal sin and one to which he had succumbed too often in the past. One that had got him transferred from parish to parish and had left him bereft and alone. But this boy was older, an adult who knew what he wanted, and his hand was moving so slowly over him. Still, it was a sin. He was so close to achieving more than he ever thought possible, and this was a sin. A sin against God. He preached against it daily, told others they would burn in hell for it, but he wanted it almost as much as he wanted to be the Voice of Freedom.

Without a word, Laoch nodded once, his eyes now closed, his heart pounding in his chest as he felt his belt loosen.

I Vow to Thee – William E. H. Walker

I Vow to Thee – William E. H. Walker

20:48

Singh

'I'm too old for this, you know.' Singh spoke to the two disembodied heads that floated over the small projection units on his desk. 'I'm planning to retire next year.'

Commissioner Slender, her face a slightly blue tinge from the projection light, smiled at him. 'I feel you there, Alex, but you're clearly still as sharp as a tack. It's an interesting line of inquiry.'

Christine Gout looked less impressed. 'A mother in Oxford hangs herself and you think it's connected? I'll admit the timing is intriguing, but I think we'll need more to go on before I give it serious credence. She's got zero background in anything even remotely linked to terrorism. She's average in the extreme. Husband too – hell, even his porn habits are bland.'

Slender looked disapproving. 'I think it's worth looking into further than his porn habits. If we can prove both Grantham and... what was the other guy's name?'

'Colin Farrow,' Singh informed her.

'Yeah, Colin Farrow. If, as you believe, he was murdered as well, I see a possible connection.'

Singh was grateful for her support. He'd been concerned about telling them with so little to go on, but after the attacks today he felt he had no choice. He felt it was important to give them everything and anything possible to investigate.

Christine was still not convinced. 'I don't know. I still can't picture what would turn a middle class, middle England mum into a terrorist. That Grantham guy, fine. He was clearly a psycho and, as much as I'd like to have talked with him about his possible involvement, in a way we're better off without him. But this woman was about as normal as it gets. She earned 22k a year working part time in a local office as an admin assistant, always took her kids to school. Regular churchgoer, no outlandish debts or gambling problems. Fine, she suffered for a long time with anxiety and post-natal depression, but I don't think that's enough. She's just not the type.'

I Vow to Thee – William E. H. Walker

Slender was looking torn so Singh sought to cement her opinion. 'It's the less obvious of the two, I'll grant you, but I would suggest that you look into all unexplained or sudden deaths in the week after the village attack. Might find there's more?'

Slender nodded at this. 'I agree, can't hurt?'

Christine's hands came into the picture as she held them up in surrender. 'Fine. Slender, can I leave this with you? We've our hands full guarding every politician out there right now. Civil servants as well. Which reminds me, I'm borrowing some of your officers.' She gave Slender a smile to suggest it was a request not an instruction.

'Okay, we can talk about that after. Singh, I'm going to need Suss back here, plus I may have need for more. This rally the Bishop Laoch has planned is set to be a nightmare.'

'Anything you need.' Singh was grateful for her support.

'What do you both think of Laoch?' Christine asked.

'I think he's the worst sort of hypocrite.' Slender spoke without emotion.

'You think a racist bigot like him could be wrapped up in all this?' Christine asked.

'If we're throwing out the IJ angle, then it's a possibility.' Singh was thoughtful.

'Right now, I don't think he's the top of our list,' Slender put in. 'He's all piss and wind. I just need to deal with his army of idiot supporters who want to smash up my city this weekend.' She grimaced.

'Like I said, anything you need,' Singh smiled at her.

'Thanks Alex, Keep in touch.' She hung up.

'Good luck to you.' Christine's blue-shaded head vanished from the tabletop.

Singh leaned back in his chair. The Bishop of Oxford, now there's a thought. A knock on his door. 'Come in.'

Abboud opened the door and stood rigid. 'Sir.' His black eyes stared at a spot about an inch above Singh's turban.

'PC Abboud, come in.' He waved him inside. 'How are you?' He tried to not be disconcerted by those eyes.

'Sir, I wish to request a transfer. My Sargent's out of the office and the Super told me to come back later, so I came straight to you.' Abboud's voice was without emotion.

Singh was taken aback by the request. 'A transfer? I'm sorry to hear that Abboud, may I ask why?'

'To put it simply, Sir, I am not being allowed to work. I am being side-lined and given admin duties. I wish to go somewhere I can be useful.'

Singh took his time replying. He'd never trusted Abboud, not because of anything the man had done. It was his eyes. Singh suddenly realised he may well have been totally unfair about him. It had been Singh who had side-lined Abboud in the village and it seemed possible others had taken their lead from him. He may have inadvertently wronged him for no reason other than prejudice. He sighed and scratched his forehead. 'Abboud, I am terribly sorry you feel this way and, should you wish it, I shall back your request for a transfer. However, if you decide to stay here I shall ensure you are fully supported and active.' That sounded like he was some sort of charity case. Singh was annoyed at himself.

Abboud seemed to consider this, although his eyes never left the spot just above Singh's head. 'Thank you, Sir, but I think I'd like to try something new.'

'Did you have anything in mind?' Singh asked.

'I wanted to go to the Met, Sir. It's more diverse, Sir.'

Singh knew what he meant. Ethnic minorities in Thames Valley accounted for less than five percent of the total and that was pretty much the norm for most of England. Only the Metropolitan police had a higher percentage at close to 20. Singh felt bad, he had wronged this man and had failed to both spot his mistake and put it right. He must do so now. 'Very well, I shall put in a word and get you moved across.' He stood and held out his hand.

Abboud hesitated for a moment, then took it and shook it once. 'Thank you, Sir.'

He stayed stock still. It took a moment for Singh to realise why. 'Dismissed Abboud.' Abboud turned and marched smartly from the room.

A misjudgement, and it had cost him an officer. He had not treated Abboud fairly, and he would regret that. He checked his watch, time to go home. Time for a late dinner and some TV with his wife. He switched off his light as he left the office. Terrorism could wait till morning.

21:46

Three motorbikes sat quietly on the side of Victoria Street, just off Parliament Square. Their electric engines on standby, their riders still and ready. At 21:47 three cars pulled out from the rear of the Supreme Court, their occupants three of the highest judges in the land. As the cars passed them the riders followed, keeping back until it was time to move.

They reached the junction with Vauxhall Bridge Road and Grosvenor Road where one of the cars took the right-hand turn and moved off along the river. One of the bikes followed. They had expected this.

All three riders felt a vibration on their wrist and knew it was time. Two of the cars were in traffic on the bridge, the third moving slowly taking its occupant home to Chiswick.

As though operating through telepathy, all three riders moved closer to their target. As each drew level with the rear of the car, they drew their weapons. Each fired five times through the window breaking the glass and skulls of those inside. Even before their victims' bodies had hit the cushioned seats the riders had hit the accelerators and disappeared into the night.

Day 18

'No matter how much suffering you went through, you never wanted to let go of those memories.'

—Haruki Murakami

I Vow to Thee – William E. H. Walker

05:30

Kinsella

For the first time in years, Kinsella woke in bed next to her husband. Turning off the vibrating alarm on her wrist she rolled to face him, studying his features, listening to his gentle snore.

He had always looked content when sleeping. There was an innocence that belayed the truth of him. Ever an attractive man, she felt a sudden remnant of the love that had once consumed her. The man who had, at one time, occupied nearly every thought she had. She felt weak for it.

Watching his nostrils flare as he inhaled, she could almost fool herself into believing this wasn't the end. That he didn't have to die.

She pulled herself back to reality and crept from the room. Closing the door so slowly it was practically silent. She slipped into the bathroom and undressed for a shower. She needed to be out of the house in no more than 15 minutes, so she kept her hair out of the water.

She thought back to the previous day when she'd seen Suss on her computer, Jowan's face on the screen, the moment of pure fear. How much did she know? She had, of course, immediately contacted Him and explained what had happened. His reply had surprised her, which maybe it shouldn't have. He'd been calm, as always, and simply told her everything would proceed as directed. She wasn't sure what that meant, but as always his voice had been so reassuring and loving, the love of her mother and father rolled into one, that she had complied without further question.

She knew her part for the day, it was simple enough: get out of the house and to the station. Be there by 6.30 am and stay there. Talk to people. Be out of the way, then know how to react. How to react? How was she meant to react? When they'd talked it through, they'd said her reaction was meant to suggest a deep loss. A heartfelt loss. Crying wasn't needed, she knew not everyone cried when they first learned of the death of a loved one. Some people clammed up and sat like stone, others broke down in a flood of tears. Some denied the truth, while others beat their fists against the closest wall, door or desk.

I Vow to Thee – William E. H. Walker

How would she react? Laughing and jumping for joy? 'Everyone acts differently with bereavement. There's no right way.' She'd said that line so often to bereaving family members it was almost meaningless. And now she was saying it to herself. How would she react?

She dressed quickly and snuck downstairs, desperate not to wake him. How would she react? After all, they'd practically been strangers for the past few years. Even with the sex last night – a necessary evil – she had not felt the connection she'd expected. It was like having sex with a machine. Was he like this with her? Grinding away till climax without even the thought of foreplay or her enjoyment? Thinking back, he'd always been like that with her. Humping on top of her like an over enthusiastic piston. Head buried in the pillow and that weird grunting sound emanating from him. Shaking as he pumped his seed into her and leaving her feeling a little let down before having to stroke his ego. 'Oh joy, it's magical. You're a god amongst men. Horary for sexy times.'

She'd made the first move as well. She was the one who had seduced him, however alien that felt to her.

It hadn't been difficult. She'd made one suggestion of opportunity and he'd climbed on top of her faster than a rattlesnake taking down its prey. Two days after he told her he was leaving her and she'd stabbed him with a fork, he still couldn't resist an "easy lay." She hated that expression, but she remembered it was one he'd used. Years ago, with friends in the pub, talking about an ex of John. Or was it James? Or Derrick? Who cares?

She slipped into her shoes and collected her bag, taking care to close the door slowly, turning the key to prevent the lock from clicking as it shut.

She couldn't remember the last time she'd had really good sex. She couldn't remember the last time she'd had an orgasm. Jowan had forbidden them masturbation and so she'd not had an orgasm in over three years. Had it really been that long? When was the last time? On the sofa, that guy online. What was his name? Humpstar69? A little overweight and very hairy, he'd at least spent about 10 minutes with his face buried between her virtual legs. She shook her head, remembering. She needed some good sex. After today, maybe she could remarry? Find someone who loved her, worshiped her. How would that feel? To be the centre of someone's attention again after all this time? Wonderful, she supposed.

Lost in thought, she got into her car. The possible futures causing a warm, inviting feeling to flow through her. She could find a man who loved her. A husband who wanted to come home early from work just to be with her. They could go for long walks over hills or snuggle up cosy under a blanket. Drink tea and talk about books or drink real wine and eat real cheese on homemade biscuits. With

I Vow to Thee – William E. H. Walker

grapes. Oh, grapes! She'd not had a grape in years. But he would buy them for her, he would seek them out and bring them to her just to see her smile. Because he loved her.

And they'd have kids. The realisation struck her, and she laughed. She could have kids. Three, no – four. Two girls and two boys, two years between each. She was still young enough. Four kids of her own. She could play with them and teach them. They would learn to ride bikes on the country road in the village where they lived. In the thatched cottage with the rose garden. Her kids running around, playing games and getting into mischief. Her kids, whose father wouldn't be spending his days in a flat in London with a moribund slag, would be at home with them. Would want to be home with them, playing with them, tending to their needs.

She could bake. She could teach her little daughter to make biscuits and bread. She could teach her son the piano, although she'd have to learn first, but she could do that. She could learn to play the piano.

And she could see her friends again. Go out with them for nights on the town, meet guys in bars and have drinks. Maybe bring them home for coffee? Why not? Who was going to tell her not to? She would live. She would have a life, a lover, a family. After today she would be free.

All it took to get there was one more person to die. Her reward for her part in all that had happened. Her reward for her night stood guarding the road into the village. For the hours spent nervously watching for movement in the dark. For being their eyes and ears in the investigation. She was finally about to get her reward and all it took was for an adulterer to die.

Reversing the car out the drive, she deliberately ignored the van parked four doors down and turned toward the Headington Roundabout.

She didn't realise she was grinning like an idiot, picturing her children playing in the sandpit her new husband had made them. She was feeling genuinely happy for the first time in years, and it felt simply awesome. She turned on the radio and cranked up the music. Joss Stone's Fortune Favours the Bold. It sure did. She belted out the chorus as though she was on stage at Wembley as she made her way to work, leaving her old life behind her. Today was necessary, not just for her but for the others who would lose today.

Tomorrow both she and the rest of the country would start anew, and she would be rewarded with a new life of her own.

I Vow to Thee – William E. H. Walker

05:43

Suss

Suss watched Kinsella drive away. She watched her turn out of her road and toward the Headington Roundabout. She watched the van move silently down the street and pull up in Kinsella's driveway.

She hadn't returned to London when the instruction had come through from Slender, she'd needed to see this through. She had spent the previous night in a local hotel piecing everything together, and she thought she now had a coherent picture of what had happened and why. The deaths of the candidates had been the final piece of the puzzle.

She had been unable to sleep so had gone for a drive. Just to clear her mind. She hadn't meant to drive past Kinsella's house, but was unable to move on once she'd seen Kinsella's car there. She'd come home. Was this reconciliation or further aggression? She'd expected to watch Kinsella or her husband storm out at some point. The public ending to another private argument. But she had to admit, she hadn't expected this. To watch Kinsella sneak out of her own house, creep to the car and slink away. It had only taken a second after she left for the van to pull into the driveway. Suss knew what was about to happen.

She wasn't armed. Hadn't thought she'd need a gun this morning. She knew there was nothing she could do; the police would be too late. Had she been in a police car, she'd have put the siren on and tried to scare them away, but she had hired one so she would not be recognised by Kinsella. There was nothing she could do.

She watched the two men get out and open the front door to the house, pulling their balaclavas down over their faces as they went in. She didn't try to stop them.

She needed to be patient, to bide her time. To get them all when they were at their most vulnerable. The only problem was Suss was in no mood to be patient. She wanted revenge. Knowing what was going on in that house, that yet another person would lose their life for this man's vision, she made up her mind. Fuck procedure, fuck process, fuck it all. She'd go meet the man who had killed her parents.

I Vow to Thee – William E. H. Walker

08:54

Wentworth

'Sir, I need a word?' Wentworth had found himself jogging after Singh and he was feeling foolish. He wasn't sure how to run unless he was really running. Jogging in a suit made him feel foolish, especially when carrying a bunch of papers. He felt like he was wobbling along with his hands tied.

'Phillip, how are you?' Singh smiled at him. Singh was a good five inches taller than Wentworth and it sometimes made him feel slightly insecure, particularly when he wanted Singh's approval for something. Years of working together with Singh's unwavering backing of him throughout his career, and he still felt like he needed his approval.

Wentworth thought of the older man as a friend and enjoyed his company, but he'd never truly accepted Singh felt the same way, which always made his conversation stunted and a little off balance. After the panic brought on by the three attacks had died down, Wentworth had found himself returning to the word's Suss had told him: 'You're going to find more.'

He'd pondered her meaning while sitting in the Subway near the station, the Mushroom 'n' Facon Sub going cold on the table before him. He'd noted her lack of surprise upon hearing that Grantham had been murdered. Also, that he had himself been a murderer. It was after he'd finished filling her in on his demise that she had spoken.

'You're going to find more.'

The photos of the woman found in the garden popped into his head. She had been strangled, her windpipe crushed. But before she had died, Grantham had sliced her stomach apart with a knife. It was so brutal that even Wentworth, who had seen more than his fair share of violent death, had felt a little queasy. He thought back to what Freemark had told him. He had experimented, started with a fumbled attempt in a pub and moved quickly on to cutting and raping Miss Moss and then... His mistake hit him like a steel bar to the face. This wasn't his first murder. He'd killed before because he liked it. He'd enjoyed what he had done to her. He was out of the fast food restaurant in a second, running back through the rain to the station.

Five hours later he had enough to go to Singh. He had gone home only to find sleep eluded him. Spending the rest of the short night tossing and turning and unable to relax. Now here he was, chasing down his boss to put forward his theory for his approval. *Confidence Phillip, confidence.* 'Sir, it's about the Grantham murder. I have a theory.'

'Well, let's hear it.' Singh sipped his morning coffee, looking down over the rim at Wentworth as though he were a child covered in chocolate.

'As you know, Grantham was sending notes to the reporter I met in Cornwall. Nothing sinister by all accounts, more creepy than anything.' He was speaking quickly, wanting to get this off his chest. 'He also attacked and raped a former girlfriend, I met her yesterday. He did a real number on her, slashed her across her stomach…' Singh raised his arm to quieten him.

'Why don't we continue this in my office?' Wentworth was led into the room and directed to a seat. He waited for Singh to sit before he continued.

'Anyway, he cut this girl up bad but didn't kill her, I think that came later.' He pulled the first page out and handed it over to Singh.

'Have you actually slept?' Singh asked, giving him a friendly smile as he took the printout.

'A little, Sir,' he lied. 'Came in early, wanted to find out if I was on to something. I wasn't the only one either. Kinsella's looking into who smashed up the supermarket in town, thinks she's got a lead.'

'Yes, I saw her. Dedicated as always.' Singh hadn't raised his eyes from the page. 'You think this was Grantham?'

'Fits his M.O. if you imagine he started young and worked his way up to murder.'

'He would've been what? Around 22 years old at this point?'

Wentworth nodded. 'Yes Sir.'

Singh was still reading. 'This was in Bristol? Do we know if Grantham was ever in Bristol?'

Wentworth shook his head. 'No, but the cuts across her stomach like that, it's remarkably similar. Particularly…' he pulled a second sheet out from his pile, '…when combined with this.' He handed it over to Singh. 'He would've been 25 at this point. The marks here were done post-mortem.'

'Over eager?' Singh replied. Wentworth could tell it wasn't meant as a joke.

'I don't know. She was killed after a night out on the town and found three days later in a layby on the A5 in Denbigh County.'

'Do we know if he was in Wales?' Singh was still reading as he spoke.

'Again, not yet.' Wentworth was wondering if Singh could see his chain of thought. As though Singh had heard him thinking, he said, 'I can see a pattern emerging here.'

Wentworth felt relieved. 'Indeed Sir, and I have identified three more. Two that fit the pattern and one that I suspect was him.'

'Two more?' Singh looked up and studied him. 'What made him stop? There's a pattern of behaviour here that suggests he would have carried on.' He gestured at the pages. 'Did he serve time for an unrelated offence?'

'No Sir, that's where I'm a little stuck.'

'What's the one you suspect?' Singh sat forward to receive a third page.

'She was found just off the old A34, I actually assisted DCI Fox in the investigation. She'd been strangled the previous night about 10.00 pm and thrown from a moving car sometime later that night. The bruising and cuts all occurred post-mortem.'

'What makes you think this was him?' Singh asked.

'The finger marks around her neck. It's the same grip. Grantham liked to squeeze his victim's windpipe till he crushed it. This girl had that done to her.'

'How old would he have been then?' Singh was intrigued. He sat forward, spreading the pages out in front of him.

'He'd have been 29, and then he just stopped. I can't find any records after this that fit. I suspect he was interrupted, but by who…' he spread his arms, '…I haven't a clue.'

Singh was nodding enthusiastically. 'I think you're onto something though. What's the connection with the notes to the reporter?'

'I think he was choosing his next victim and they had history. He tried to sexually assault her when they were teenagers and I think he was trying to finish what he started.' Wentworth hadn't shared this theory with anyone yet.

Singh breathed out deeply. 'Do we know if any of the other girls received notes, cards, letters?'

Wentworth again shook his head 'No, not as far as we know, but then she'd be different, wouldn't she? The one that got away.'

Singh was silent for a long time. Wentworth knew him well enough to respect these silences. 'Right, talk to the Oxford girl's family again, see if your findings brings anything new to bear. Contact the other forces where the girls were found and see if there's anything they've not included in their official reports. Tell them we suspect he was a serial killer. Also, contact the reporter who received the notes and see if she can remember anything else. Anything he might have said or she heard about him. And most of all...' He leaned further forward; his eyes focused on Wentworth. He felt again like a child before a teacher rather than an old friend and colleague. 'Find out where he went for 10 years.'

15:07

Laoch

'You're determined to go ahead with this?' Peter stood in front of his desk, his manner more formal since the previous evening. Did he regret what they'd done?

'Of course I am.' Laoch didn't look up from his draft speech.

'You know they'll be upset.'

Laoch slammed his pen down on the desk and eyed Peter, his rage born of a lack of restraint, a moment's joy and subsequent rejection. 'They had best not be bloody upset, they told me to do this. Besides…' He sat back and puffed up his chest. 'I am their leader; they do as I determine. They will follow me.' He stared at the seemingly unaffected man before him a moment longer, a more than small part of him wanting to take back his anger and return to the previous evening's bliss, but Peter simply nodded curtly and left the room. Laoch stared at the closed doors like a puppy awaiting the return of his owner before going back to his notes, resolute. This speech had to be perfect.

Nearly 50,000 people were expected to turn up to hear him tell them to tear down parliament and join the revolution. And He would rise to be their monarch, appointed by God Himself.

He smiled and sipped his whisky. Tomorrow he would fulfil his destiny and become the new leader of Britain.

16:17

Freemark

'What are you up to now?' Stephen crossed the room to lean over her shoulder. 'Why are you looking at his profile?'

She had been staring at the Frog page of Jake Grantham for half an hour or more, convinced there must a clue to his involvement in… murder? Rape? Terrorism? She wasn't yet sure, but it had to be something.

'What?' She blinked to clear her mind and looked up at her husband. 'Oh, hey! I'm just…' she wondered what to say, '…finishing off.' Her inflection on the last word rose like a question.

'Aha.' He nodded, but his expression showed he wasn't the slightest bit convinced. He walked over to the sink and poured himself a glass of water, watching her over it as he drank. She squirmed under his gaze. She didn't like this feeling. 'Is he really that important?' he asked.

It was a fair question, Freemark knew, but she didn't want to answer. 'I don't think he's…'

''cause you've been staring at pictures of him for days now. Were he not dead, I'd be worried you were having an affair.' He'd tried to make it sound like a joke, but there was real concern there. The words spoken just a little too harshly. He must have seen the shiver that engulfed her body because his whole manner changed. Gone was the half-joking, slightly annoyed at his wife for taking an afternoon off work and spending it sitting on her laptop looking at pictures of dead murderers. Instead, his eyes filled with fear and concern for her. He crossed the room quickly, pulling out the chair and sitting beside her, taking her hands in his. 'What is it?' His voice was a whisper.

Freemark hadn't intended to react as she had; she'd thought she was stronger. Though Grantham could no longer affect her now he was dead. The reaction surprised her as much as it had him, just the thought of that filth climbing on top of her, it was too much.

She looked into the pained, worried eyes of the man she loved more than anyone, save the daughter they had made, and came to a decision. 'Stephen…' She rubbed the back of his hands with her thumbs, his skin creasing under her touch. He met her eye with nothing but love. She laughed despite herself and stroked his cheek. 'Stephen, I need to tell you something. And I'm sorry I didn't tell you this before.'

She talked for the next 20 minutes. She told him about that night in the pub, what Grantham had done to her, what she thought he would do, what he had done since and how it made her feel. She told him of Francesca Moss, of the cards, the visits to the police, the way it all made her feel and her fear he was involved in the terrorist attacks.

Throughout it all Stephen sat and listened patiently, only asking questions to clarify a point here and there. He was still and focused, his expression unreadable at first but gradually evolving into a look of pain and regret.

When she was done, he exhaled loudly and looked like he'd been through the mill. Freemark felt her chest tighten, worried she had ruined something beautiful.

Then a change came over him, he rose quickly but calmly from his seat and knelt before her. Freemark was confused, her face scrunched up like a quizzical cat. He reached out and pulled her to him. She went willingly and they held each other tight. Tears were leaking from her eyes and she tried to bite them back, but he kept her close to him and she failed to prevent herself crying. 'You know, you're the strongest person I know?' His voice was loud in her ear, although he whispered the words.

'Shut up,' she said through her sobs.

'It's true. You're hardcore!' The word made her laugh. A wet and noisy laugh that burst through the tears. She wiped her sleeve over her nose as he released her. 'You've been carrying that around all these years and I've never known?' he shook his head. 'Frankly, that stuns me. You're proper hardcore.' She laughed again and kissed him. A hard kiss that clashed teeth and hurt their lips but filled her heart with joy.

He stayed there, holding her for some time, his thumb stroking her cheek as she regained her composure. 'Wine?' he asked, and she smiled and nodded her head. He stood and walked over to the rack. 'You know, I think this calls for some of the proper stuff,' he said, trying to sound jovial. He picked up a bottle from the bottom of the rack and it came away with a puff of dust. He blew the remainder off the label.

'Châteauneuf-du-Pape,' he read. 'Sounds delicious!'

She laughed again. 'We can't waste real wine! You know how much that cost?'

He made a show of thinking. 'If I remember rightly it was about 15 quid in Sainsburys in 2018.' He made her laugh yet again. He opened a drawer and searched for a bottle opener. 'Besides, what are we saving it for anyhow?' He shot her a wide grin and pulled the cork. 'Glasses are your job!' He nodded toward the cupboard where they kept their few precious crystal. Freemark retrieved two, setting them carefully on the table. His grin broadened further when he recognised them. They were the pair they'd purchased on their honeymoon, engraved with "Wife" and "Servant." He'd bought them from a small Mexican man who'd sat, bent almost double, over his tiny hand-operated engraver and etched the beautiful cursive in the crystal. She'd loved them from the first, they were perfect.

They sat in silence for a while, enjoying the wine and the company. An easy silence that comes with years of trust and love.

Stephen stirred first. Freemark suspected what was coming, almost welcoming it. 'I think you should stop this.' He'd spoken quietly, watching her for a reaction.

Freemark sighed and put her glass on the table. 'I know.' She nodded and reached for him. They held hands over the table. 'I was thinking the same thing.'

He smiled at that. 'Leave it to the police? Go back to supermarkets and fetes and farmers?'

She chuckled warmly. It was an old joke about local papers and their preoccupations. 'Yeah. Go and interview locals about dog mess and roundabout markings.'

He squeezed her hand. 'You're damn good at it. Best there is.'

'Maybe.' She sipped her wine; it was nice to be drinking the real thing for a change. She suddenly realised she was tired, bone tired. Her body seemed to become several stone heavier in the same few seconds. She'd not understood how tense she had been, how much this had been affecting her.

'He's dead, Julia.' His voice had become serious, solemn.

She knew that. She mostly knew that. 'I know. I just wanted to know if...' She struggled with the words, 'I got lucky.'

His look showed understanding. 'I get that, but it's time to let it go.'

He was right, sleeping dogs and all that. Not even DI Kinsella had thought she was bringing anything new to the investigation. Time to move on, and thanks to the love of this wonderful man she could.

'Okay, it's a deal. I'll leave it be.' Stephen looked relieved. He leaned forward and kissed her gently, all tenderness, on her forehead.

The weight was gone, Grantham would rot in his grave. She would enjoy her life with her wonderful husband and beautiful daughter.

I Vow to Thee – William E. H. Walker

17:32

Shanks

'Welcome to tonight's ITV British Christian Party Leadership debate sponsored by Richmond Sausages, I'm Jeremy Vine. Tonight, our debate comes in the shadow of the war in Qatar and the attacks that have continued to be directed against our nation, reportedly by Islamic Jihad. So far, these attacks have claimed the lives of nearly 400 villagers in Lesser Worburston, over 10,000 in London, three Supreme Court Judges and three of the candidates vying for Party leadership. Tonight, you the viewers will have the opportunity to put your questions to Mark Shanks, the MP for North Oxfordshire, and Angela Rainsworth, MP for East Hampshire.' He gestured to each candidate who nodded respectfully. 'In response to the ongoing situation, tonight's debate comes from an undisclosed location without a live audience. Each candidate will have one minute to give their response to the question, and we ask that you each allow the other to speak without interruption.'

That'll last for about 30 seconds, Shanks thought.

'Without further ado, let's get right to it. Our first question comes from Mrs. Kylie Bellamy from Egremont in Cumbria. A squat, middle aged woman with the features of a kindly nanny appeared as a hologram in front of the two podiums, her head bobbing around as though looking for someone. Shanks thought if there was anyone in history who looked less like a Kylie he'd eat his shoe.

''ello? Can you 'ear me?' she asked in a thick Cumbrian accent. Shanks wanted to laugh but managed to contain himself as Jeremy prompted the woman to ask her question. 'Right. What would you do to combat the terrorist attacks? Would you continue the bombing of Qatar?' She pronounced it Qu-a-tar, but no one corrected her.

'Mrs. Rainsworth?' Jeremy prompted.

Shanks watched Angela stand a little straighter and adjust her traditional black power suit. Angela was old school, and although only in her fifties she held true to what were now called old Conservative values. 'Thank you, Kylie.' Shanks saw her set her face to what was clearly meant to be an expression of sincerity and remorse, but in reality made her look like she had trapped wind. 'Before I answer your question, I would again like to extend my condolences to all the families and friends of those we've lost over the past two weeks. What our country has gone through has been unprecedented and we must meet this aggression with action. Firm action that will ensure we provide the peace and security our country and our people deserve. I shall ensure that you are secure against all attacks. I will ensure your safety is our top priority. I will work every day to ensure you don't suffer attacks like this again.'

Shanks thought she looked pleased with herself as she ended her answer. *Well, we'll wipe that smugness off your face*. He felt the excitement stir within him. He loved this. Turning to face the hologram, he leaned forward on the podium. 'Kylie, may I call you Kylie?' His eyes twinkled at her.

'Oh yes, sir,' she preened at him.

'Kylie, what you've just heard from my colleague here,' he gestured at Angela, 'is a masterclass in how to speak without actually saying anything.' From the corner of his eye, he saw Angela's face twitch. *Strike one.*

'She talks about how she would meet aggression with action, but not what that action would be.' He stood straight 'Now, I would stop the attacks on Qatar as I don't see how us bombing civilians helps prevent us getting attacked. All we do is create more enemies.' A slight pause. 'Angela, you'll have noted, performed what's known as the rule of three at the end there. What that means is she ends her speech with three statements that resonate with people but don't actually mean anything. They're taught it at the posh school she attended. The likes of you and I don't get that.' Angela looked ready to interrupt but Jeremy held his hand up to stop her. *Strike two*, Shanks thought. The Kylie hologram giggled. 'Now I shall do the same but with actual actions. I promise you I shall stop the war with Qatar. I shall launch an investigation into the truth of the evidence we were given for the war, which I believe was falsified.' He paused again and looked directly at the holographic Kylie. 'And I promise you, by adding an extra 100,000 police officers we shall never suffer like this again.'

The hologram woman's head was bobbing away in agreement.

Shanks placed his hands on the sides of the podium. *Strike three.*

'Mrs. Rainsworth, your response?' Jeremy prompted her.

She looked a little lost for a second but recovered quickly. 'I disagree with Mr. Shanks. The war in Qatar is necessary to protect us from Islamic Jihad. There is no proof the evidence presented for the war was or is false. The United Nations has yet to give us their official response, but I believe they will agree with us.' She pointed at herself. 'He promises an extra 100,000 officers. From where will these officers

I Vow to Thee – William E. H. Walker

be recruited? Where will he get the budget to recruit them? He gives these sweeping statements but no detail behind them. I will work with the security services to do everything we can to prevent further attacks against us. I shall work hard every day to ensure we don't suffer like this. I…' She stopped herself. He'd gotten to her. She adjusted her stance as though she had meant to finish there. Jeremey looked mildly amused, then offered the floor to Shanks.

'She claimed I'm light on detail so let me rectify that.' He moved from behind the podium, ignoring Jeremy's muffled protests. 'Despite the turmoil we've suffered over the past few years – the recession, the coalition increasing the national debt to its highest level ever,' he turned to face Angela, 'and our current government's ineptitude…' he saw her bristle before turning back to Kylie, '…we're still one of the richest countries in the world, part of the G8, and yet millions of us don't share in that wealth. We don't benefit from it. Our economy is worth £2.6 trillion pounds, but our police force only gets three percent of that. Our education system gets four percent. Our health service, nine.' He held his hands open in confusion.

'Mr. Shanks, time,' Jeremy interrupted him, but Shanks ignored him.

'What are they doing with the other 84 percent?' He turned back to Angela, a questioning look on his face.

'Thank you, Mr. Shanks. And thank you Mrs. Bellamy for your question.' Shanks returned to stand behind his podium. He was going to walk this. 'Our next question comes from Mr. Hartness of Swaffham in Norfolk. Mr. Hartness?'

The man who appeared before them was so large his arms failed to appear within the confines of the hologram. He looked as though he had two short stumps that ended in hollow black circles. Shanks thought it was hilarious. 'My question is this. Why can't we afford the NHS anymore? Why's it being privatised?' He pushed his chin up as though he was challenging them to a fight.

'Mr. Shanks?' Jeremy invited him to speak.

'Thank you, Mr. Hartness, for your question. I would suggest that it comes down to choices. The choices we make and the choices they make.' He pointed at Angela again. 'We chose to elect people who have ties to corporations. Who use those ties to enrich themselves and their friends by selling them hospitals and paying them with our money. I happen to know Angela here is a very close friend of the CEO of Samsung Medical who were issued contracts for six hospitals last year.'

'I had nothing to do with that!' Angela exclaimed loudly.

'Oh, I don't doubt it.' Shanks smiled reassuringly at her, ladling the insinuation on so thick it might suffocate her. 'No one would suggest you did, but still, the ties exist. And you're not alone in those coincidental relationships.' He turned back to the questioner. 'I have no ties with corporations, I work for you and for you alone. My choice is that we have an NHS that does the same.' He returned to his podium, satisfied.

Angela's answer was predictable. The NHS works best when private and public expertise work together for the betterment of society. She commented on the drop in infant mortality and new medical breakthroughs. And then she stopped herself once again. She then said the one thing Shanks was waiting for her to say. 'Mr. Shanks has again promised the moon but has refused to tell us how he expects to pay for all this.' He was so pleased with her he wanted to thank her. This was his masterstroke.

'Refuse? You've not asked me. But I shall answer nonetheless.' He met the gaze of the hologram. 'Mr. Hartness, how many different types of tax do you pay?'

Mr. Hartness looked lost for a second. 'What?'

'How many different types of tax? Income tax, VAT, capital gains, stamp duty, National Insurance contributions, excise duties?'

'Erm…' The stumps seemed to windmill on the sides of the projection. 'I dunno really, maybe six?'

Shanks gave him a broad smile. 'Six? As many as that?' He again walked round from behind his podium, again ignoring Jeremy's attempts to wave him back. 'What if I were to tell you it was highly likely that you're paying upward of 20 different stealth taxes over the course of a year? How would you feel then?'

'Bit shit really.' The response prompted Jeremy to remind Mr. Hartness where he was.

Shanks smiled, indulgently. 'I happen to agree with you, but it's sadly true. It's how they hide money from you. A little here, a little there, and pretty soon you've no idea where your money is or what it's doing.' He was bouncing inside; this was so much fun. 'I would simplify the tax system. I would remove almost all taxes from goods and put them onto income. You'll pay your tax from your pay packet but that will be pretty much it. Everything else would be cheaper and it will give you visibility as to where your money is going and, therefore, they can no longer hide money from you. That will mean we can afford to remove privatisation from the NHS and fund it properly.' He stood back, watching Mr. Hartness' expression as he mulled this over. He looked like he might be convinced, and Shanks suspected the majority would.

Jeremy Vines flicked his fingers over his pad. 'Our next question of the evening comes from Ms. Agatha Jacobs from Exeter.'

The hologram of a tall, slim lady with hair tied in a tight bun and thin rimmed glasses perched on her nose materialised before them. Her hard, monotone voice punched through the room as she asked her question without preamble. 'How will you each deal with the rampant corruption that exists in government today?'

Jeremy nodded toward Shanks. 'Mr. Shanks?'

He took a moment to lower his head. Closing his eyes and slowly shaking his head, he said, 'You know, there is almost no greater threat to our country than corruption.' He raised his face to the holographic woman, his eyebrows dropping with the sides of his mouth. 'What makes it worse is, as you said, it is rampant.' He paused as though thinking. 'From the minute you join the government you're bombarded with people trying to bribe you. And it's not just the central government, no.' An exaggerated slow shake of the head. 'No, from the parish councillor being taken to dinner by a building contractor to the government minister receiving campaign donations from foreign governments in exchange for fishing rights or a construction contract, corruption is rife.' Shanks turned to face Angela, his expression severe. 'You'll even find it in leadership races. Someone could accept a £20,000 donation from a pharmaceutical company hoping to get their potentially dangerous drug fast-tracked for the NHS.' He savoured the expression on her face as she squirmed under his gaze. He held her eye for a moment longer before turning back to the hologram. 'I have taken no bribes. No lavish dinners at the Savoy, no exotic holidays or generous campaign donations, and I never will. Under my leadership all forms of what is laughably called lobbying but is in reality thinly veiled bribery, will be banned. No more will we allow ministers to work for the interests of the corporations of America, Japan and China. No more will we allow our government to be soiled by allegations of corruption. No more will we allow our ministers to receive donations from defence contractors or Russian billionaires. I have received no money from any of them and I challenge Ms Rainsworth to say the same.' The feeling of elation swept through him as he watched the beads of sweat prick her brow. She was done for – "fucked" to use the common parlance.

'Congratulations, Sir. Early indications are you're over 60 points clear in the polls.' Brian was beaming at him as he left the stage.

'Thanks.' Shanks couldn't help but return his smile. By the end of the show Angela Rainsworth had been shouting and ranting at him while he remained calm and collected. A very Prime Ministerial quality. 'What are the news reports saying?' Shanks leaned forward to look at the tablet Brian held when a hand landed heavily on his back.

He turned to see Angela Rainsworth, her face still furious and her body shaking. 'You lying little shit! You accuse me of pushing through better benefit rights for disabled people because my husband had MS? How fucking low are you willing to stoop?' She looked ready to punch him.

Shanks smiled and put his hand to his chest. 'I said no such thing, I simply pointed out it was a curious set of affairs that you would push for an increase in benefits for the disabled but not out of work benefits.'

Her voice was a shriek. 'My husband doesn't even claim benefits! He works for a living!'

'Really?' Shanks attempted to look mildly surprised but ruined it by smiling. 'I had no idea.'

'Fuck off!' Rainsworth spat. 'You're a charlatan and if you get into Number 10 you can expect my resignation within your first five minutes in office.' She stormed off before he could reply.

Shanks grinned at her back. 'Oh, and how you will be missed,' he said quietly. Brian laughed. 'So, what's next?' Shanks was feeling eager now, today had been a most excellent and productive day. He'd participated in a country-wide discussion through hologram with all bar three of the local party committees, conducted an online interview with party members and the public through Frog, Bamboo and Twitter, and then he'd slaughtered Angela in the TV debate. Where others might be feeling tired, Shanks felt like he was just getting started.

'We've got to get you ready for dinner. Tonight should be the final straw.' Brian was tapping the screen as he spoke.

Shanks nodded his agreement. 'Have the press accidentally been tipped off?'

The corner of Brian's mouth rose slightly 'Sun, Daily Fail, Independent and Times.' He ran the list off quickly. 'All by a "delighted volunteer".'

Shanks patted Brian's back. 'You're a bit of a legend.' He leaned in closer. 'Principal Private Secretary.' Brian's face beamed. 'Right then,' Shanks started to walk toward the exit. 'Let's dress for dinner. I'm thinking jeans and a T-shirt. Don't want to seem over dressed for the soup kitchen, do we?'

23:08

Suss

She clicked the magazine into the Lodestar 9mm Smart Pistol and threw onto her hotel bed. Tomorrow, she will catch the man who murdered her parents. She would either take him in or kill him. As of this moment, she wasn't sure which one it would be.

I Vow to Thee – William E. H. Walker

23:45

'Tomorrow is ready?'

'Yes'

'Your people are in their places?'

'They are. Are you ready?'

'I believe so.'

'You know what's going to happen?'

'I do, which is why I've asked for the precaution. Will you come?'

'I shall do what's needed, everything else is taken care of.'

'We've reached the start now. We're nearly there.'

'I know. And it's all thanks to you.'

'To us, my dear. To us'

I Vow to Thee – William E. H. Walker

Day 19

'The ides of March are come.'

—William Shakespeare: Julius Caesar

06:38

Freemark

'Mummy, mummy, wake up!' Maddie jumped up and down on Freemark's stomach, forcing her awake. Spears of morning light pierced the gaps in the curtains, creating a sparkling dance of dust from window to bed. She grinned at her daughter before wrapping her in her arms and spinning her onto the mattress. Maddie cried out in laughter and pretended to fight her mother away as Freemark blew a raspberry on her belly.

Stephen rolled over and groggily protested. Freemark kissed him and Maddie, her daughter's pudgy little arms wriggling about, trying to grab hold of her father.

'Right, little monster.' She tweaked Maddie's nose causing another outburst of laughter. 'Breakfast time. I'm thinking…' She made a show of pondering prospective recipes. 'Eggy bread and beans!'

'Yay!' Maddie wriggled in delight and poked her father on the nose. 'Daddy! Eggy bread! Eggy bread!'

Stephen opened one eye and smiled at her. 'Best get some eggs from the chickens then, hadn't we?'

Maddie vigorously nodded her agreement. 'I'll go!'

She clambered over Stephen, arms and legs in every direction, ignoring his protests, dropped nimbly from the bed and ran excitedly from the room. Freemark smiled after her, enjoying the sounds her tiny feet made as she hastily descended the stairs. Her heart squeezed inside of her, so much love for such a tiny person. Stephen reached out and stroked her cheek with his fingers. She turned and smiled at him, her heart content. 'How did we make something so beautiful?' she asked, leaning in to kiss him. He wrapped his arms around her and held her close. She breathed in his scent, fresh and clean. Security and happiness bottled.

'She takes after her mother,' he said as he released her.

'Mummy! Come ooooon!' Maddie's voice echoed up the stairs.

It was Stephen's turn to grin. 'Well, you heard her – eggs mummy!' He playfully made a whipping motion in the air that made her laugh. She slapped him lightly on the arm, stretched and started to rise. 'Fine, but you're cooking.'

'Mummy!' Maddie called.

'I'm coming monster!' Freemark slipped her feet into her trainers and rose from the bed. She'd slept well, her mind clearer than it had been in weeks. She felt truly rested, refreshed, alive. Happy and content in her little world.

The choice to let the Grantham crap go had been a good one. Telling her husband what had happened to her, no, his reaction to her telling him, had lifted the weight of the Earth from her shoulders. She loved him even more for it. He was her life now. He and Maddie were all she wanted. She would be happy covering the supermarket openings and village fetes so long as she had Stephen and Maddie to come home to.

Maddie was calling her again. 'Mummy! Mummy! Come o—' Her voice was cut short.

Freemark and Stephen shared a look. 'Maddie?' she called.

No reply.

Stephen got off the bed and reached for a T-shirt, quickly pulling it over his head. 'Maddie?' he called.

There was the sound of movement from downstairs. Slight and so quiet they almost missed it.

'Hiding from us?' Freemark asked.

'Maybe.' Stephen didn't look convinced. He walked past her, opening the bedroom door. The landing was small and in the shape of the letter T. In front of them was Maddie's room, it wasn't that big and, with the door open as it was, they could see most of the empty room from their doorway.

'Maddie?' Freemark's heart was starting to beat loudly in her ears, her breathing quickened.

Stephen stepped out of the room and walked quickly down the stairs, bare feet making soft patting sounds on the carpet. 'Maddie, this isn't… the fuck? Julia, ru—'

Freemark had followed him and, from her position at the top of the stairs, she heard a soft pop, saw his body hit the floor in the hallway, the bullet hole clearly visible in the centre of his forehead. Freemark's scream forced itself from her lips before she could stop it. A billion ants and spiders scurried over her skin and she sank into a crouch, her hands instinctively over her mouth.

The black-clad figure appeared below her a heartbeat later, their vision moving from her husband's corpse to Freemark's frozen form. She didn't register the gun as it swung toward her but something from

I Vow to Thee – William E. H. Walker

her training made her move. Something from her years of jiujitsu forced her body to dodge to her right as the bullet slapped into the wall where her head had been just a second before.

Without thought she was running. She slammed her bedroom door closed behind her and twisted the lock, animal instinct picking up the sounds of pursuit on the stairs. She didn't think as she ran to the window. She was out of it and dropping into the front garden as the sound of the door lock being shot hit her ears. She landed hard but her body didn't let her stop. Ignoring the new twisted pain in her leg and wrist she dragged herself free from the flowerbed and was running again.

Maddie, she had to get Maddie.

She ran round the side of her house, legs moving as though weighed down by concrete, focused only on getting to her daughter. She saw her as she rounded the corner to the back door. Legs and arms spread in the kitchen doorway. Blood on her top and neck. Freemark made the noise of a mortally wounded animal.

Sprinting to her, she collapsed at her daughter's side and collected her in her arms. Maddie's eyes stared blankly at her mother, Freemark's pleas for life lost on her. No more breath in her tiny lungs.

Freemark heard the Man before she saw him. He had sprinted back down the stairs and into the kitchen. He was scanning the room as Freemark rose. Her eyes darkened as she set her daughter gently down on the tiled floor. She invited the Devil in. She let him fill her soul. She was beyond grief now. She was a primeval ball of rage. Fury incarnate. The Reaper. The Apocalypse.

She took the six steps between them at a sprint. Her hand snaking out, snatching the knife from the wash rack without conscious thought. The Man seemed surprised by her speed; his eyes widened as he lifted the gun and fired.

Freemark dodged the bullet but she was too close. It hit her in her left shoulder, scraping down the bone and tearing muscle. But Freemark didn't stop moving, avenging angels do not stop.

She brought her right knee up squarely between the Man's legs, not hearing the audible crack as it connected. The air left his body and he toppled backward as Freemark spun her right leg out and connected her heel with his nose, which exploded beneath his balaclava. He tried to cry out, but the blood gurgled in his mouth. The gun hung uselessly in his hand as she stepped into the space created as he fell and landed a third kick to his jaw, feeling it break. He hit the wall hard and bounced back off.

The knife took him in the neck, severing the jugular vein. She barely registered the surprise in his eyes as the gun dropped to the floor and his hands reached for his throat, frantically trying to stop the blood that flowed in a river down his chest.

Freemark's body was shaking, her face a mask of rage and hate. She tore the knife from his body, spraying blood over the wall, and took a step back before thrusting it forward again. Screaming as she drove it into him. Screaming as the knife broke through his ribcage. Screaming as it entered his heart. Her spittle flew in his lifeless face as she held him against the wall. As the scream died, she released her grip. The man fell heavily to the floor, dead at her feet.

For what felt like a lifetime, Freemark stood over him, her mind lost in her own rage, face splattered with his blood, left arm soaked with her own. A tear rolled out from her eye and she blinked as though waking. 'Maddie.' She spun and ran back to her daughter. Her emotions overran her and she collapsed on the floor beside the child, cradling her tiny head in her lap, every piece of her desperate for her daughter. *Live. Please, for the love of God, live.*

There was a shout from somewhere nearby. Mrs. Pembleton, her neighbour, was screaming at her from their garden. Mr. Pembleton had hopped the fence and was running toward her. Freemark didn't register their presence until he was right beside her. The pain in her arm was nothing to her. Her heart was broken. Her world was destroyed. She simply wanted to die.

17:06

Laoch

Laoch peeked out at the crowd from the side of the stage, letting their admiration wash over him like a warm bath after a long day. More than 60,000 people had made the trip up to London to see him. Him. And now they cheered him, they loved him. He saw the slogans and the flags. "Get the immigrants out!"; "Britain is white!"; "Laoch for PM!"; "Loach and Shanks!" That one was a little annoying. "Britain Without Muslims", although the last one actually said, "Britain Without muslems", but he got the point. God, it was good to be loved. Yes, Peter had been cold and distant toward him since that night, but he could either get on board or get gone. Laoch had no time for him if he was going to act like a petulant child, he had been gentle on him.

The crowd were loud in their anticipation. They cheered and chanted his name, they were buoyant and excited, they wanted change and he was their man. All around them were police and soldiers, a sign that his message was being taken seriously, but there were too few for the numbers he had. Too few for the 60,000 souls who had turned out to cheer him, to make him their next leader. The next leader of Britain.

He would let them cheer him for a minute longer before going on. *Today my rule begins*, he thought. He wanted to jump with joy, his belly churned with excitement. The speech was perfect, it would enthral them. They would cheer, weep and scream with rage, and by the end they would worship him. The roller coaster of emotions he held in his hand would drive them to fever pitch and they would do whatever he wanted. Whatever he required to bring him to power.

How could they be unhappy with him? He was doing what they asked. He had toured the country for two years, presenting the message they'd asked him to give. Had they not promised him this? She, the woman with the sparkling green eyes, had told him his part would be huge. That he would rise higher than anyone. This was his time, his future. The future of the country he would shape as a tribute to God. They would love him for it.

He was the leader of the revolution, they couldn't let Shanks get it – he wasn't one of them. Not one of the chosen. Laoch would rule the country. His followers would elect him by sheer force of will, Shanks was a nobody compared to him. It was Laoch's turn now. It was his time.

He looked down at the notes for the speech he knew off by heart. He swallowed; he was ready. His eyes rose from the pages and surveyed the baying crowd. Time to go. A hand tight on his shoulder, strong and slightly painful. He twisted to see Peter stood so close to him he could have kissed him had he wanted to. Did he want to? Was this reconciliation? Had he come to his senses? But there was no happiness in Peter's face. No admiration in his demeanour. 'Peter?' he stammered. 'What? What are you doing?'

The voice that came from the young man was unrecognisable. So cold it froze him in place. 'You will not be delivering that speech today.' It wasn't a request, it was an order.

What was happening here? 'What? No, Peter. What the hell?'

Peter pushed a pad into Laoch's hand and he blinked at suddenly finding himself holding it. The noise of the crowd fading as he saw what it was. Saw his naked body on the screen, saw the whip in his hands, the acts he had Peter perform, the whole scene laid out before him in glorious 8K resolution.

Peter's icy tones cut through his confusion. 'If you insist on giving your speech, this video will be put up on every platform known to man.' Laoch's stomach lurched, bile rising quickly in his throat. 'Also…' Peter twisted Laoch's head slowly around so they were looking out over the crowd, and he pointed toward the Cabinet Office. 'On top of that building is a police marksman who works for us. Unless I can assure him, you're on board…' He left the threat hanging between them.

Laoch was struggling to keep up. It was too much. The betrayal. 'Why?' he asked, his voice weedy like a small child.

Peter smirked at him. 'You really think someone like you would be the leader of Britain? You're a degenerate, a wastrel, a pervert.' He leaned in closer, his breath in Laoch's ear. 'You like fucking teenage boys.' He snorted. 'We're creating a Christian nation here, what makes you think we would let you run it?'

Each word bit into Laoch as though Peter was physically eating him. His flesh carved from his body piece by piece. 'It was all a lie?'

The question wasn't directed at Peter, but he answered it nonetheless. 'Not all of it if you read this speech.' He thrust the pages into Laoch's hand. 'You'll be Archbishop of Canterbury by the end of the month. Do as we say when we say and you'll be rewarded.' He smirked like an assassin. 'After all, you're a useful pervert.'

Laoch still couldn't take it all in. He gazed down at the pages in his hand, unsure what to do with them. He was meant to be taking over today, she had promised him he would rule. Hadn't she? She said he would rise higher than anyone, but what did that mean?

'You need to get out there.' Peter lifted Laoch's chin, forcing eye contact. 'You have a choice, it really is quite simple. Either say what we tell you to or don't live to see your reputation destroyed. Either way you need to decide now.' And he twisted Laoch around and gave him a firm shove in the back.

Laoch suddenly found himself on stage in full view of the tens of thousands who had come to see him. Feeling like a naked child in a school play. Their mouths were all open, they were jumping and waving at him. Banners and flags flapping and bobbing in all directions. Arms flung up in reverence toward him. Were they shouting? He felt sick again and made to turn back. Peter stood there, somehow looming over him despite his slight statue. The pad held firmly in his hand, the threat clear in his face. Laoch's eye lurched over to the roof of the Cabinet Office, scanning the sky for the gun that would end him. There was nothing to be seen. Was it a lie?

He glanced back at Peter who was now waving at him and pointing to the crowd. His arm raised by itself and fluttered like a lost bird in the air. The noise of the crowd hit him like a sandstorm, and he realised he was waving. Peter was motioning for him to speak. Despite everything, Laoch felt a longing for the boy – he was so beautiful. He had been so willing and capable, he had made Laoch feel young again. But it was all a lie, a betrayal, he didn't love him. He had used him for this. For delivering the words scrunched tight in his hand. What was he going to say? He was at the podium now, the noise of the crowd condensed to a regular chanting of his name. It buffered against him, stinging him. He was a joke, a fall guy, a laughingstock. What should he do now? If he told them to storm parliament, as he had intended, would they shoot him here? Was it worth the risk?

As though controlled by remote, he lifted the speech to the podium and spread the pages out in front of him. His eyes swam down to the first paragraph. If he read this, he would live. He would be the Archbishop, but he would still be a joke. He would still be in their power. To be used as and when needed, no freedom of his own. Or he could give his own speech and risk dying a martyr. Again, he scanned the roofs about him and saw no one. He could read his own speech, maybe die. But maybe, just maybe, get everything he ever wanted. He just needed to be brave.

He breathed in deeply, the crowd quieting and growing still. He glanced over their expectant faces and then back down to the pages. He made up his mind.

He picked up the first page and began to read.

I Vow to Thee – William E. H. Walker

20:39

Suss

Suss stood outside the church and breathed in deeply. She felt tight, like a stretched rubber band. Quivering, ready to snap. Her hands were shaking as she approached the large, ornate oak doors.

She'd been watching the church for the past hour. No one had followed the vicar inside; he must be alone. The pistol under her jacket felt heavy against her stomach. Almost warm against the cold fury she nurtured for the man who murdered her parents. She drew the pistol, thumbed the safety off and placed her free hand on the door handle and turned it slowly, trying to be as quiet as possible. There was a loud click as the latch reached its zenith. She cursed herself and pushed the door open, moving with it, bringing the interior of the church into view as she did.

It was a small building by church standards. A central nave but no aisles down either side. The nave ran from the raised chancel and altar down to the bell tower and ceremonial entrance, lined with a faded once-rich red carpet. Bell ropes hung limp and still in front of a screened off section in the back corner. Heavy cloth curtains on a bright brass rail, which caught the little remaining light and glinted softly. The pews were old and tattered, the wood chipped at the back but worn smooth on the seats by 100 years of prayer. The stained glass windows depicting the life of Jesus spread blotches of evening colour over the cold stone floor. The whitewashed walls adorned with monuments to the long dead.

The church was cooler than the world outside. She shivered slightly, unsure if due to the change of temperature or anticipation of the task to come. Her gun raised, she swept the space ahead of her. The building was so silent she could hear the blood pump in her veins. She crept slowly into the centre of the church, turning her head to peer into the shadows that seemed to move with her, covering the space behind her as she went.

Ahead of her, the altar was raised three steps from the chancel, which itself was raised by three steps from the nave. The elevation to God. As she crept forward, she focused her aim on the small squat figure

I Vow to Thee – William E. H. Walker

who knelt before the altar under the stained-glass vision of Christ on his Cross. The Lord's benevolent gaze turned down toward the huddled masses beneath him. The vicar had his back to her, seemingly deep in prayer.

Suss moved as quietly as possible, her breathing shallow, her heart racing. Her parent's murderer was here, alone and defenceless. She reached the chancel, a mere 20 paces from where he knelt in the apse. Kill him or take him in? She still wasn't sure. Fear, revenge, rage, hatred, grief flew through her like swarming wasps. Each one surging forward before retreating as a different emotion took hold.

As she reached the top of the steps, her feet almost silent on the old red carpet, he spoke. 'My dear child.' His voice was silk, almost mystical. It brought her up short. 'I was so sorry for your loss.' He had yet to turn around.

His words threw her. She had expected resistance, confrontation, argument. Not sympathy. 'You wha'?' she heard herself reply, her voice shaking like her outstretched arm.

He turned his eyes upon her. Blue like the Caribbean Sea and just as rich with life. His aged features were creased into a look of pure sadness and concern. 'I truly am,' he spoke slowly, deliberately. As thought to instil each word upon her soul. 'So incredibly sorry for your loss.' He rose easily from his knees, clearly fitter than his appearance would suggest, and stood facing her. His hand held together before him, his left holding the right. His robe settled about him.

Suss didn't know how to react. She had wanted him to resist her. She'd wanted anger and a chase. The chance to follow him and the right to shoot him for what he had done.

Lost in her thoughts she missed his movement. He had approached quickly down the steps and was walking toward her. His hands still held in front of him, his face still set with sadness. She snapped herself back into focus and pointed the gun firmly back at his centre mass. Gripping it with both hands to stop it shaking.

He stopped. His eyes sparkled in the light that seeped through the windows. She saw genuine pity there and didn't know how to deal with it. 'My sweet lost child, I would wish to hug you.' His voice did something to her she couldn't quite place. It was gentle, the embodiment of kindness, of love. But she knew what he was, knew what he was capable of and she felt herself sickened by her weakness.

He was moving again. His arms rising, palms spread to show he held no weapon. He was talking as he moved. 'I feel your loss, my child, and I share it. I wish only to comfort you.'

Her hand shook violently while her usual quick brain tried in vain to make sense of what was happening. Then suddenly he was in front of her, past her gun and within her arms. He smiled, the skin around his mouth creasing like old paper.

I Vow to Thee – William E. H. Walker

She held his eye; she couldn't help herself. She felt his arms around her, drawing her in close. His hand moved up her back to cradle her head, all the while talking to her in that voice, the voice of an angel. The words were irrelevant, the voice filled her, breaking her down. She felt tears sting her eyes. Felt her body loosen as though he was physically drawing her pain and anger from her. She felt she would burst.

'NO!' Her rage bit back hard, a lion's sudden roar of resistance. She pushed him hard away. He fell to the floor before her, crumpling as though made of matches, and she raised her gun again.

'STOP!' His voice held such authority she obeyed without question. The gun quivered in her hand, not quite fully raised. From behind her, somewhere in the shadows in the back, she thought she heard a soft click but ignored it, her world entirely focused on the man sprawled out before her. He was rubbing his elbow and studying her. 'You're strong.' He smiled easily. 'You should have some training.'

'I know what you are!' She needed to retain control. *Don't let this man get to you*, she thought as she built a defence in her mind. Walls against that voice.

He held his hands out and raised himself up to stand. Meeting her rabid gaze with calm acceptance. 'What am I, my child?'

'Don't call me that!' She fortified her defence. 'I am not your fucking child. You killed my parents.'

His expression didn't change, he retained his look of care and concern. He was moving again.

'My child, I am an old man, I cannot hurt you. Do you really need to keep that pointed at me?' He gestured at her weapon and, when she did not move, pointed to the choir seats. 'Come, sit.' Suss kept the barrel pointing at his head as he sat down in the choir and crossed his legs, silently waiting for her to comply. Unsure how to proceed she lowered the pistol but remained standing. 'As you wish.' He smiled at her.

Suss felt a fresh wave of anger. 'Don't you smile at me you bastard.' The words came through gritted teeth.

He watched her for a moment before responding. 'Why have you come here this evening, my child?'

'I said don't call me that!' She heard her voice raise. *Stay in control!*

He held up a consolatory hand. 'Forgive me, but why did you come here?'

'I wanted to bring you in.' She was still unsure if that was her reason for being there.

He seemed to read her mind and looked down at the gun. 'So not to shoot me?'

'I... I don't know.' Why was she talking to this man?

'Did you expect me to resist?' He gestured at his supposedly frail body. 'This tired old man against a fit young woman with a gun?' He shook his head and tutted. 'No, you were thinking of revenge.'

He was right, she wanted revenge. She wanted him to suffer as her parents must have. 'Yes,' she replied simply, the waves of anger ebbing.

'And how do you think that would make you feel?' He wasn't looking at her but looking into her. His eyes, so soft, seemed to be studying her from the inside out.

'I don't know.' She felt foolish, her control faltering. *Attack. Don't allow him to control the conversation.* 'How did your revenge on Lesser Worburston feel?'

If the question phased him, he didn't let it show. 'It nearly broke me. I shall carry that with me for the remainder of my life. It was the ultimate sorrow.'

'Sorrow?' She couldn't keep the disbelief from her voice 'You felt sorrow? You murdered children in their beds.' Her voice rose, the words echoed off the high walls.

He didn't react at first, again letting the silence rest between them. Allowing the natural stillness of the church to return. Then his head bowed and he slumped forward. 'Yes.' The word was spoken softly, with real pain held within it. Suss was again taken aback by the seemingly genuine emotion he displayed. He raised his head and met her eyes again. Was there a tear in his eye?

'You admit it?' She was unsure how to feel at his admission.

'Of course I do. And I regret each and every death.'

'And the 15,000 people in London?' Her voice cracked.

He was nodding but holding her gaze. 'Yes. Every one of them. They shall eat away at me until the day I go to be with God.'

Suss couldn't help but let out a bark of joyless laughter. 'God? You think God would take you? After all you've done?'

He seemed to consider this for a moment. 'Maybe not, but I have done all I can to bring about the restoration of this nation.' He turned to the effigy of Christ on the cross, preserved forever in the stained glass above the altar. 'If my fate is to spend eternity in hell then I shall do so willingly.' He turned back to her. 'How did you know?'

Suss hadn't planned to have a conversation with this man, let alone explain how she'd worked it all out. But he held such power she struggled to resist. 'It was Kinsella. She gave it away.'

'Kinsella?' It was the first time he'd seemed genuinely surprised. 'How did she manage to do that?'

'She said she's an orphan, then she got a text from her Nan.' Suss was struggling. She wanted to run and hide or raise her gun and shoot, but something held her to him.

He was nodding slowly, seeming to understand. 'I see. Yes, that makes sense. And that led to you following her here after she'd argued with her husband?'

It was Suss' turn to show surprise. 'How did you...?' she began.

'The family across the road are parishioners, they keep a watch out for me.' He smiled at her as though this was perfectly normal. 'Their daughter saw you in your car. But that alone wasn't enough, so how did you join the dots?'

She resisted at first, but he held her eye and she felt her resistance collapse. 'I realised the attack must have religious connotations. You don't persuade people to do what they did in the village unless there's a promise of redemption at the end of it.'

'Very good, yes, very good. Do go on.' He was nodding as she spoke, encouraging her.

'I didn't believe it was Islamic Jihad. They couldn't pull that off. It had to be a domestic attack. Someone who could train in this country without anyone knowing. You do retreats, don't you?' He didn't reply. 'You took your parishioners up to the arse-end of nowhere and taught them how to pull this off. Taught them to shoot and break into houses, kill without hesitation.' She saw his eyes betray him and she knew she was right. 'You got them to work in the village. Cleaners, repairs, decorators, plumbers, sparks and note down everything they saw. How long did that take?'

He might have told her she was wrong, but she could see she wasn't. 'Two and a half years,' he replied quietly.

Suss felt her first moment of success. 'Then London, you can't pull that off without someone in the police helping you. Kinsella got her text right before the bombs went off and—'

He interrupted her. 'Ah yes, a mistake of mine, I feel. Vanity.' He waved his hand. 'Every ass likes to hear himself bray.' He gestured for her to sit and she found herself complying. She took a pew just out of arm's reach from him. 'Sorry I interrupted you. Continue please.' He smiled kindly at her.

'I followed her here and looked into you. Your sudden move from Lesser Worburston because of tha' Stace.'

He shook his head sadly 'Ah Stacy. A lovely girl, but misguided, very misguided. Such a shame.'

He was lost in reflection for a moment. 'She moved to the US, by the way. I know you were looking for her.' Suss was surprised again. She had indeed been trying to identify the woman she had known only as Stace. But that had been from her police laptop in her hotel, how had he known? 'Go on, how did you realise I was involved in this?' he asked gently.

Again, she felt compelled to answer. She wanted him to know all was lost, that it was over. 'Your connection with Kinsella was the start. Then I investigated Jake Grantham and realised he must have been involved. The timing of his death and his general character both told me there was more to him, then there were the notes to the journalist, his mother living in the village and then I found he'd lived near here.'

That seemed to surprise him. 'You did? How?'

'It was a post he put on Facebook. Down at the Hangman pub. The Hangman Arms is just down the road. After I found out there was a murder of a woman here 10 years ago and then suddenly he went quiet, I suspected...' She held out her hands in front of her, the gun resting in her right. She bobbed her right hand up and down. 'One suspect murderer in need of a hiding place.' Now her left hand. 'One sadistic vicar with a score to settle and no qualms about murder. Made sense to me that you'd found him. You'd need vile bastards like that to do what you wanted done.'

Jowan was reflective. He was silent for some time before he replied. 'Jake was...' he seemed to look for the word, '...a monster.' He smiled grimly at his description. 'He was never going to make it in the new world. You know...' He stood, and Suss' arm flicked the gun up but he waved it back down, seemingly completely unconcerned. He spoke as he stepped silently toward a small cupboard on the wall beside the altar. 'When I met him nearly 10 years ago we had caught him after he had killed that poor woman in the church yard.' He pointed to a spot on the wall. 'Just out there. He was an animal. All lust and no judgment.'

He opened the cupboard and withdrew a bottle of wine from within. 'Would you care for a glass?' he asked over his shoulder. Suss shook her head, feeling slightly dizzy. Why hadn't she arrested him yet? He was talking again as he closed the cupboard and carried the bottle and a crystal glass over to where Suss sat. 'We tried to cure him,' he said as he sat back down and poured himself a glass, placing the bottle on the floor beside him. 'For a while we thought we had succeeded, but the demon inside him was too strong. Too much for any human to bear.' He appeared to contemplate this as he sipped his wine.

'Didn't stop you using him to murder though, did it?' Suss asked bitterly.

He bowed his head slightly in acknowledgement. 'No. He had his uses. But he wasn't for the long term.' He took a second sip of wine. 'Was that all you found out?'

'You're cleanin' up after yourself.' She saw the surprise in his eyes and it gave her strength. 'You've already killed at least six of those involved in the attacks, made them look like accidents or suicide or whatever.' Her emotions were running high, she was all over the place. She was angry at his acceptance at what he had done, strong in her ability to confront him and despairing at her inability to shoot him. Every emotion was welling up inside her. One would burst through soon enough.

'You are very clever, aren't you? I had heard you were. Yes, we are cleaning up, as you put it. Much like Grantham, some of those who participated in our cause were not the type of people you'd want living in your street.'

'So, you're jus' going to carry on killing then?' The question came out as almost a shout. *Do not lose it in front of this bastard!* Her mind was scrambling around, trying to rebuild her defences from the rubble.

He paused, his glass close to his lips, before placing it on the floor beside him and reached toward her. She recoiled instinctively, as though he had approached with a knife rather than wrinkled hands. He withdrew. 'I'm sorry. I didn't mean to frighten you.'

***

The Man moved silently to the front door.

***

Another hollow bark of laughter escaped her lips. 'Frighten me? You scare the shit out of me. You've murdered more than 15,000 people including my parents.' Their faces flashed before her eyes and she nearly broke, it was starting to be too much, a tornado ravaged her body and mind. Harder to keep focus. Harder to think. Harder to speak. Harder to breathe. She paced, the gun held to the side of her face as she ran her fingers through hair, her breathing fast and ragged. She saw her parents holding her, waving to her and felt their love and loss.

He sat in silence, watching her.

Stop it, not now, not now. She squeezed her eyes shut and held herself rigid. Forcing the images of her parents from her mind. Trying desperately to breathe normally.

'Breathe in through your mouth and hold it for four seconds.' He spoke quietly seated behind her. 'It will help.'

She did as instructed without conscious thought. It did help. She repeated the exercise three times before she felt strong enough to speak. 'I just need to know why.' She panted the words out, the first tear working its way down her cheek. 'Why?'

'Keep breathing and I'll tell you.' He sipped his wine and waited while she regained control. As her tears stopped flowing, her breathing near normal, she turned her eyes upon him. He gestured for her to sit and she sagged into the pew, her body feeling drained.

He refilled the glass and held it to her. She took it as though this was a natural gesture and drained it in one. He watched as the colour returned to her face. Feeling stronger as the wine hit her blood stream, she turned to him again. 'Why?' A whisper.

***

The Man picked the lock and silently turned the handle.

***

'You know why,' he replied, so gentle his voice was like a salve to her heart.

She shook it off. 'No. Not the Christian nation bit. Not the "bettering society" bollocks. Why for you? Why are you doing this?'

He nodded his understanding and considered his response before replying. 'Do you know what happened to me after that poor child Stacey told her father I had tried to rape her?' Suss shook her head, unable to speak. He took the empty glass from her limp fingers and refilled it. 'Her father and six of his friends came to the church.' He sipped his drink and studied the glass as he spoke. 'They dragged me out into the churchyard. They stripped me naked, beat me until I could no longer stand, then they kicked me until I could no longer see.' He pointed to the scar running into his hairline. 'This was a golf club, I believe. They would have killed me had it not been for an old lady coming to visit her husband's grave. She was the one who found me. They ran, of course, and the police told me they all had alibis for the evening. They refused to believe I hadn't tried to rape the poor girl.' He waved this away as though it was to be expected. 'But there was also no evidence, so I was in no position to be questioned.'

I Vow to Thee – William E. H. Walker

***

The Man crept into the flat's interior.

***

'It was about the same time as all the allegations against Catholic priests assaulting children came out, so they put me down as just another of those and decided I'd got what I deserved.' His tone had an edge of steel to it now. Suss found herself enthralled. 'You'd think I would be angry at the men, or the girl, wouldn't you?' He turned his bright eyes back upon her as though seeking agreement. Suss neither replied nor moved. He turned back to the glass, seemingly unconcerned. 'But they were just products of our time. You see…' he twisted round his body to face her, hooking one leg over the other. 'She dressed as she thought she was meant to dress, acted in a way she thought she was meant to act.'

Suss thought back to the blog post: "I'd been watching porn for a few years so I knew how to do it." He wasn't wrong.

***

The TV was on, volume low, the screen sending flickering lights over the room. The Man slipped into the short hallway.

***

'Likewise, the men who sought revenge were doing what they thought was the right thing to do. They've been conditioned by society to believe that this is how you react when someone threatens your daughter. Lord knows I couldn't say I might not have acted the same way once.' He closed his eyes for a moment before continuing, his tone now one of resignation. 'I do not blame those who beat me, I do not blame the girl, I blame all of us. We have all contributed to our current situation. We have all allowed ourselves to become lost in this world. Allowed our lives to slip by as we work ourselves to death for the benefit of a society that doesn't care about us.'

***

The Man stopped at the bathroom door. The sound of running water.

***

Suss considered his words. Could she really say she disagreed with them? 'That doesn't justify what you've done.' Her resolve hardened.

'No,' he replied simply, his honesty again disarming her. 'But if what we have done gives the people of this country a better world, then my eternal soul is worth the trade.'

Suss found this hard to swallow. The wine had emboldened her. 'Bollocks.' The word was spoken more loudly than intended. 'I don't believe you're so noble.' She stood and walked toward the altar. 'You've corrupted some of the neediest people you could lay your hands on. Those groups you've been running. Alcoholic's support, homeless people, all they were to you was a recruitment ground. You don't care about the people, only what they can do for you, just so you could get them to murder children and...' *Don't let your voice crack*, '...my parents.'

She heard him sigh behind her, but she didn't turn to look at him. 'I truly am sorry...' Suss swung round.

***

The Man placed his hand on the doorknob and turned it slowly.

***

'Don't say it!' The tears were welling in her eyes again. 'I am sick of hearing how fucking sorry you are about my parents! You made the choice to plant those bombs, you killed them!' She heard herself, shrill and desperate. *Keep control! KEEP CONTROL!* She turned from him again. He wouldn't see her cry.

Silence.

***

The Man aimed the silenced pistol at the shadow cast on shower curtain while moving slowly forward. She was singing softly to herself.

***

'I never wanted to kill anyone.' His voice was reflective, as gentle as a meandering stream. 'But there was no other way. We must change our ways, you surely see that? We cannot go on like this. Working ourselves to death for the sake of the few. Destroying ourselves and our planet for economic growth, for numbers on a computer. Nothing real, nothing tangible, nothing meaningful. Surely you must see that this isn't the world we were intended to inherit? This wasn't the future we were promised?' His voice was pleading, and she found herself swaying for a moment but resisted, focusing on the stain glass. Focus on the imagery.

She had to keep her distance. Something radiated from him, a force she struggled against. 'Is that what Laoch is for? To be your puppet leader?' She was staring up at the depiction of Christ, the crown of thorns upon his head. The small trickle of blood from the wound in his chest glistened in the evening light.

Jowan must have followed her gaze. 'You know Longinus, the Centurion who stabbed Christ, was blind?' Suss shook her head but didn't reply. 'It is said that the blood of Christ fell into his eyes and cured his sight.'

Suss found that hard to believe. She was struggling with the knowledge that, despite everything he had done, she agreed with his statements on the state of the country and tried to reconcile that with the knowledge he had murdered her parents.

***

I Vow to Thee – William E. H. Walker

Two steps to go.

***

'That's what I'm trying to do,' he said. Suss leapt back in surprise. He had moved silently to stand beside her, his face turned up to look at the window. 'A small drop of blood to heal the world. Surely that's worth the sacrifice?'

'Not to those who lose.' A renewed steadiness to her voice, although her limbs trembled.

'No, not to those who lose.' Why did he have to agree with her?

It took her a moment to realise he no longer stood beside her. She wheeled round and raised her hand. She was no longer holding the gun. 'Fuck!' she swore and searched around her, when had she put it down? She saw it sitting on the pew. He stood on the other side of the chancel, seemingly studying an ornate gravestone. She ran to the gun, snatched it up and pointed it at his back. 'If I wanted it, I would have taken it,' he said without turning round. 'You put it down when I gave you the wine glass.' He turned to face her again. 'I don't want to kill you. I want to help you.'

She felt incredulous, the loss of the gun had stunned her. He had managed to literally talk it out of her hand, something she had prided herself on being an expert in. She felt ashamed of her own weakness. She would end this now.

'I have to take you in,' she said through gritted teeth.

***

The Man whipped the shower curtain back and the occupant gasped in shock.

***

He turned back to the gravestone. 'This family rebuilt this church after a fire in the 19th century. They put in over £50,000 to keep it going. At the time it was a fortune.'

I Vow to Thee – William E. H. Walker

'I don't care about the fucking church.'

'Do not swear about the church.' His voice was so hard it was like being hit by a train, and she felt herself falter. As though nothing had happened, he continued, 'At the time, that money would have been enough to keep the church running for hundreds of years, but…' He turned round to face her again, finger raised to make his point. 'You know what has happened to that money?'

***

The gun fired and the woman died, her blood mixing with the warm water.

***

He continued without waiting for her reply. 'That money, sitting in the bank, and yes, with money added and spent over the years, has run out.' His tone implied this was somehow amusing. 'I know what you're thinking, £50,000 is nothing. Well, you'd be right. In today's money, it is nothing. But back then it was the equivalent of over £10 million.' He let the words hang in the air for a moment. 'But it's not worth £10 million is it!' It wasn't a question.

There was a soft ping, and he raised his eyebrow. 'Do you mind if I get that?' He raised his hand to his robe.

'Keep your hands where I can see them,' Suss barked at him.

He shook his head and sighed. 'I am going to get my phone. I have no interest in hurting you, nor will I attempt to contact anyone.' His hand had sneaked inside his robe to produce his phone while he was talking. Suss stared dumbly at him. He pressed a button on the side and glanced at the screen. 'All done now,' he said, returning the phone to the hidden pocket.

This had gone on long enough. Suss made up her mind. 'Jowan Cross, I am arresting you for acts of terrorism under the Terrorism Act 2000.' Suss wanted this over. She wanted him dead, but she knew this was the right thing. What her parents would have wanted.

He acted as though he hadn't heard. 'I think you and I share a great number of opinions about the world we inhabit.'

'You do not have to say anything…'

'All I ask is that you listen to me.'

'...but it may harm your defence if you do not mention when questioned something which you later rely on in court...'

'Suss. I'm trying to save you.' He held his arms wide in exasperation.

The words stung her ears. The nerve of the man. 'Save me? Save me? Who the hell are you to save me? I don't want you to save me.' She felt her anger renewed. Starting low in her stomach and building. 'I don't want you! I don't believe in your God. You don't get to decide how I live my life. I do! Yes, this country is fucked but you don't fix it by killing people. That's the only reason you're still alive. I want your trial to be for the world to see. That's what my parents would want.'

'And what would Debs want?'

**

Her lifeless body slumped against the wall of the shower.

**

The question threw her off balance. He'd called her Debs. Not Deborah or Debbie – Debs. Her pet name for her. How had he known?

'No, Kinsella didn't tell me that.' He had read her correctly.

'How did you...?' Her voice faltered.

'It was written on a card in your flat. A birthday card you gave to her. "Dear Debs, happy birthday".'

'Shut the fuck up.' She was shaking again. He had been in her flat?

'"You are my world..."' His voice had taken on that edge of steel again.

'Shut up.' her voice was rising. The anger rising inside her like a volcano.

'"You are my life…"'

'Shut UP!' she screamed at him.

'"Forever."' he said, his voice returning to its quiet, gentle tone. His expression was sad, defeated.

'You leave Debs out of this.' The gun thrust forward to emphasise her point.

He waited for her to take a breath before he spoke. 'I'm afraid I couldn't do that.'

It took her a moment to realise what he'd said. Past tense. Then she knew the truth. 'No?' Her voice quivered.

He had walked back up to the altar, standing before the large gold crucifix at its centre and making the sign of the cross on his body as he approached. 'I couldn't be sure what you had told her. I'm afraid I couldn't have that.' He looked back at her. 'I'm so very sorry.'

Suss felt numb. Her head shaking slowly from side to side as though she could will it to not be true. The pain spread through her like lava. Her muscles failed her, her soul shattered and she collapsed to the stone slabs. Her cries of anguish filled the church, her tears fell to form dark spots on the floor. Debs. Her life, her love, her heart. Gone. The pain fed on her body and turned to bile. She retched, spittle flying from her mouth as she coughed and spluttered, incoherent in her grief.

He wasn't looking at her. His face again turned to the image of Christ in the window. 'You must understand, it gave me no pleasure to order her death but she would not have made it in our new world. Unlike you she had never been with a man. She was sadly beyond curing.' He fell to his knees, adopting the position of a man at prayer.

Suss felt as though a colossal weight had been piled upon her. She couldn't think straight, she was broken afresh. And this fucker had been responsible once again for her sorrow. Then she saw the gun in her hand.

He was still talking. 'I genuinely wanted to help you, Anya. I wanted you to join us, but it wasn't to be. I'm sorry for that.'

Fuck arresting this piece of shit. Fuck process. Fuck the trial. He needed to die. For her parents. For Debs. For her. She channelled all her pain, all her anger, all her grief into her arm. She screamed as she raised the weapon, screamed as she pointed the barrel at him, screamed as she pulled the trigger, screamed as the gun fired.

Blood, bone and lung tissue splattered over the floor, forever staining the faded red carpet.

Suss had stopped screaming, she had drained herself dry, she was pure pain. She turned slowly, every nerve of her body faltering and protesting. Blood bubbling up from the hole in her chest, she turned to look into the face of her killer.

What? No. She had missed it all. She had missed the most important element. The CCTV in the car showroom had shown her this, but she would never have believed it. This was impossible.

His hand was on her shoulder, her breath was leaving her body, she had no strength left. Not you. Not you. It couldn't be you. But then, even as she coughed blood in her last moments of life, she knew it made sense. Somehow, she had missed it. But then, she could never have known. They had been too clever.

'Anya, you know my sister.'

Commissioner Slender nodded to her. The pistol by her side, her expression solemn.

Suss' mind reeled, there was nothing left. The last of her strength seeped from her and she folded onto the floor.

21:46

Shanks

'Ladies and gentlemen.' The thin balding man stepped forward to the microphone, the small piece of paper held tight in his hand. 'The votes for the election of leader of the British Christian Party have been counted and verified and the results are as follows.' Shanks stood stock still, his expression solemn as one would expect of a leader. 'The total number of votes is 143,204. There were 68 rejected votes and 117 spoilt ballot papers.' The thin man licked his lips before continuing. Shanks wanted to tear the paper from his hand but restrained himself. Across the room Angela Rainsworth was equally composed, although Shanks could tell she was on edge. The past few days had been bad for her, not least the debate.

'In alphabetical order...' He adjusted his glasses and looked down his nose at the page.

Fucking get on with it! Shanks thought. His hands tightening slightly.

'Mrs. Angela Rainsworth MP for East Hampshire...' a slight pause, '...32,312.' The cheers started immediately around Shanks. So loud the Teller was forced to wait before he could continue. Shanks found himself slapped on the back, his hand shaken and a myriad of smiling faces appearing before him. 'Excuse me,' said the Teller, clearly annoyed. Gradually the cheers and applause subsided. Shanks was trying hard not to grin. He noted Angela had already left.

The Teller turned his beady eyes on his audience. He coughed slightly before continuing. 'Mark Shanks, MP for North Oxfordshire, 110,707 votes. Mr. Shanks is duly elected leader of the British Christian Party.'

The cheers started again, even louder this time. Shanks was bustled and nudged forward to the steps that lead to the stage. Waving gratefully, aware he was on every channel in the country right now, he endeavoured to keep his expression respectful and calm, although inside he was buoyant. Alive with what he had achieved.

I Vow to Thee – William E. H. Walker

He shook the Teller's hand and approached the microphone, waving his audience to silence. 'Thank you, thank you. This is indeed an honour.' He had no notes, he knew what he needed to say. 'I'd like to start by congratulating my opponent on a well-fought contest. Angela is an excellent MP and I hope we can work together closely over the coming months and years.'

Someone called out, 'She's scarpered!' which caused some laughter in the room. Shanks didn't join in.

He thanked the Teller and the counters for their hard work. He thanked the Party for their support and the public for the honour they had bestowed upon him. As he neared the end of his speech, he lowered his head solemnly. 'We have suffered so much in recent weeks.' He let the silence eek out. 'Too much.' He raised his head, his eyes fixed firmly forward. 'We will suffer no more. I swear it. I shall do everything in my power to prevent further attacks, starting with ending our conflict with Qatar.' A solid round of applause from the room. 'I shall contact the Qatari Ambassador this very evening and present an offer to end hostilities. Furthermore, I shall start an investigation into the so-called evidence that led us to war and we shall prosecute anyone who is found to have misled us.' Another round of applause. 'Lastly, I will put to parliament a bill designed to overhaul our currently failing system and bring it into the 21st century.' The applause continued. 'We will have a new system of democracy! One that works for all of us, not just the few wealthy! This I promise you.' Cheers and shouts joined the applause. 'In order to achieve this I make my first order of business a vote in the house for an early election to be held six weeks from now. This is to allow the great British public a chance to vote on my proposals. To make them their own and to join us in our journey!' He was having to shout to make himself heard over the noise. 'I swear to you, no matter what obstacles stand in my way we will have a new, fairer and more equal Britain. This is my vow!' Having called out his war cry he stood back and let the applause wash over him. He had made it.

He was led off the back of the stage by the Teller. Brian was stood waiting for him. The two men hugged each other. 'Mate! We did it!' Shanks was jubilant.

Brian likewise. '*You* did it,' he said, his face all smiles.

'We did it! I couldn't have done it without you.' They hugged again, lost in the moment of victory. 'Right.' Shanks pulled away. 'To work, then to party.'

Brian tapped the laptop. 'The Prime Minister's Jag is waiting for you out back.' He shot Shanks an enthusiastic grin. 'The Qatari Ambassador is waiting. Apparently he's pleased to be meeting you.'

'Good, good.' Shanks slapped Brian's back. 'Let's getta groove on then!' They laughed and headed for the exit.

Shank's phone beeped in his pocket. He picked it out and looked at the notifications. One email. One message. The email was a letter from Angela Rainsworth, her resignation. Shanks smiled. She was a good MP, but it would never have worked.

The message was just three words long and made his whole body swell with pride. He had fulfilled his destiny. He had made Him proud. The message said simply: "Well done. Nan."

Epilogue

'I believe in a benevolent dictatorship provided I am the dictator.'

—Richard Branson.

Kinsella

As the coffin slowly disappeared into the cold ground, Kinsella wiped an imaginary tear from her eye. The crowds began to disperse, returning to their cars to make the short drive to North Oxford Golf Club for the wake.

She accepted muted words of condolence and regret from people she either didn't know or didn't remember. Returned Wentworth's awkward hug, thanked Singh for his words of encouragement and took the withered arm of her mother-in-law for the walk back to the limousine. Murmuring insincere agreement and pleasantries as she waffled on about how wonderful her son had been.

She knew she was meant to feel the loss. Knew they would expect her to be monosyllabic, withdrawn and defensive. A delivery driver had alerted police he'd found a front door open and that no one was responding to his shouts. Her husband's body was found beside the bed and identified. Official cause of death was a heart attack brought on by stress. It's amazing what could be achieved through an injection of air into a vein in a toe. Why would anyone look for that? It had given her old boss a stroke, though they'd injected him under his arm. Poor man hadn't really deserved that, he was just in the wrong job. It hadn't taken long for Singh to call her into his office to give her the news. When he'd uttered the words 'He was pronounced dead at the scene, I'm so sorry,' she had been surprised to find tears had sprung from her eyes. To this day, she couldn't tell you what they were for.

The car drove sedately around the corner to the golf club. Her mother-in-law still wittering on beside her like an incessant chaffinch for the length of the short journey. The last time she'd been here was a wedding some five years ago. What was the bride's name? Lucy something. She'd been his friend, not hers. Probably an ex. They were all exes though, weren't they? Seems the only women her husband knew were exes.

In the days since his passing with unfettered access to his phone and accounts, it had become increasingly clear that the woman he wanted to leave her for wasn't his only extramarital affair, she couldn't bring herself to use the term "lover." There was the French student he had put up in a flat in Marylebone, and, predictably, his assistant. All of whom she had invited here today. All of whom had turned up. All of whom she hoped would realise the truth this afternoon. She wasn't usually a vindictive woman, but she might find a little pleasure in that.

I Vow to Thee – William E. H. Walker

She entered the hall to the white noise of hushed conversations. Made efforts to look strong, together and thank people for coming. Her husband's brother would make a speech, she was too fragile to do so, and then it would be over and she could go back to the hotel she'd been staying in since his execution.

For now, though, she would quaff the cheap fizz and make polite small talk with people who seemed surprised to find out her husband had a wife.

Across the room, the Valkyrie warrior Silvia Hutton wept uncontrollably into a silk hanky. *Have some self-respect woman,* Kinsella thought. Her eyes drifted down to the swollen belly and felt her own twist itself into knots. How far gone was she? Five, six months? How long had he waited to tell her he was leaving? Had he resisted? Had he wondered if he could juggle them both once the kid was born? Had he torn himself to shreds over the prospect of losing his wife? Or had he just not thought of her? Amid their joy at becoming parents, had he simply forgotten the need to dismiss the wife from his life? Had they discussed marriage, was that his motivation to come home to her? What had he told the others? She focused on the skinny blonde in the short black dress and six-inch heels stood awkwardly in the corner of the room, desperately trying to look comfortable and failing in every way. She was 19 for God's sake – 19. She had one of those faces that older women look at and think, *I remember when I looked like that,* but knowing deep down they were never that attractive. Never did my hair tumble in glorious sparkling waves like that. Never were my legs so long and graceful. Never were my breasts so perky.

Kinsella had found a moment of amusement as she watched confusion spread over this teenager's face when they'd first arrived at the church. She'd clearly wanted to approach her, to offer some words of sorrow, regret or hope. But she had been caught between the quiet Kinsella, seated in what was clearly the most prominent position in the front row, and the howling mess of Silvia Hutton most vocally expressing the loss of the man she loved. Kinsella could tell she still didn't know which of them was his wife. Not the brightest spark then, but she had at least known he was married.

Then there was the assistant. Daisy. Daisy, what a name. Though in truth it suited her. She was petite with shining bobbed blonde hair and a dazzling smile. She looked as though she spent her life in a perpetual state of excitement. Kinsella had disliked her from the start. Never trust anyone who isn't unhappy about something.

It was then Kinsella noticed the correlation between the three, and subconsciously pushed her own copper-red hair away from her face. *He had a type, it just wasn't me.*

As the afternoon dragged on and people started to make their excuses to leave, Kinsella wandered over to the decimated buffet, wondering if she could stomach anything. There was nothing that appealed to her, but she picked up a tiny cheese and pickle sandwich and bit into it. Not good. Someone coughed

I Vow to Thee – William E. H. Walker

behind her and she turned to see, oh joy, the Norse Goddess Silvia. It seemed she had decided snivelling and sniffing were a suitable show of emotion for now.

'I wanted to talk to you earlier, but I didn't know how.' Her voice was hoarse from the hours of wailing. Kinsella didn't reply and, after a moment of looking through her long lashes, Silvia continued. 'I understand why you hate me.'

Kinsella felt the temptation to slap her, but just couldn't bring her arm up to do it. Her left leg jiggled and she clenched her fists, but she remained silent.

'I just wanted to say sorry,' Silvia whispered, her expression one of hope.

But hope for what? Kinsella couldn't hate her, no matter how hard she tried. Equally though, she couldn't forgive her. She couldn't give the woman who had stolen her life from her a sense of hope. When she finally spoke, her voice was brittle. 'When are you due?'

Silvia saw this as an entry to bonding and perked up a little. 'Three months. He's big though, don't you think?'

It took everything Kinsella had to not scream at her. To give vent to her bitterness and rage. To pour molten bile over this woman in a tirade so searing it would have scarred the Earth. It should have been her. Her husband. Her baby. Her life.

Silvia cocked her head to one side. 'You want to feel him kick?'

Do I want to feel my husband's baby kicking inside another woman's womb? No. I'd rather have needles inserted into my eyeballs. But Silvia had hold of her arm, moving her hand inexorably forward. Kinsella felt as though she were watching herself from across the room as Silvia's delicate fingers guided her hand until it rested on her belly.

Kinsella's eyes were glued to her fingers, why couldn't she move it? Then it happened. The pressure against her skin, the sudden wonderful movement that confirmed life. Silvia gave a little giggle as Kinsella's spirit crumbled to dust. There was no denying it, no way to convince herself it wasn't true. That a mistake had been made and she wasn't carrying her husband's child. No going back now.

The baby kicked once more and Kinsella jerked her hand away, not sure she could cope. It was only then she realised tears stained her cheeks. She wiped them away with the heel of her hand and fought back control. Silvia was looking at her, expectantly but uncertain. Kinsella knew she had to say something, she couldn't just walk away. She needed Silvia to know she wasn't the only one. She needed her to know why the French model was acting shifty and why Daisy had wept so quietly throughout the service. She needed to know how she'd made Kinsella feel. The pain, anguish and anger. The sleepless nights, sick with worry that she wasn't good enough. That she wasn't enough to be loved. That there was something wrong with her. She needed to know it all. Her hand twitched as though kicked, and she wiped her palm over her sleeve.

She swallowed and raised her chin to meet the taller woman's eye. 'I don't hate you.' She wasn't sure where these words were coming from. 'I wish you all the best.' She swallowed once more, unsure why she'd not said what she needed to say.

Silvia seemed equally unsure how to process these words. She blinked at Kinsella three times before spluttering a reply of thanks.

Feeling her head reel, Kinsella turned away from Silvia to find a toilet to be sick into.

Silvia's next words, although spoken in her light, gentle voice, slammed into Kinsella like a wave. 'I would like to name my little boy after him.'

Kinsella buckled a little, recovered, then swayed on the spot for a long moment before turning back to face her husband's mistress. 'I think he'd like that,' she replied honestly, in a voice barely above a whisper.

Just as she was turning back round, Silvia's second wave hit her. 'Would you like to meet him? When he's born, I mean?'

Kinsella didn't have the strength to turn back round. She didn't have the words. She allowed her head to fall forward and her feet to stumble forward and into the toilet.

As she wiped the vomit from her mouth, she felt her phone buzz in her pocket. She washed her hands and face, dried herself off and studied herself in the mirror. She looked as though someone had run her over before sewing her back together with rope stitches. This day needed to be over, now.

Her phone buzzed once more, reminding her of a message. She fished it from her pocket and, recognising the number, felt her first moment of hope in that long day. Opening the screen, she read the message.

I'm outside.

She breathed out deeply, feeling her shoulders drop and her back untense. As always, his timing was perfect. The effect he had on her was profound. Even as a child, she had noticed how easily He held a room. How captivating so many found His voice. How it seemed to flow through you like warm spring water, refreshing your essence and renewing your soul. Small wonder he was so popular as a vicar.

Ever since He'd had taken her in, the timid, broken child who'd just lost her parents to a car crash, He'd been so kind, so caring. Had taught her the truth of life. Taught her how broken the world was, how damaged its people. How they could make a difference. For God. He had loved her from the first, and she knew He would love her till the end. Whenever she needed Him, He was there.

And now once again he was here when she needed Him most. Here to spirit her away from her old life and into a joyful future. Freedom. The word tasted sweet. Before she could stop herself, she was moving. She was out of the toilet and through the hall with the stragglers looking on after her. She didn't realise she was smiling. Outside the world was still, calm. And there he was, standing beside the car, his

I Vow to Thee – William E. H. Walker

long white hair drifting down over his shoulders like a halo. She couldn't help herself. She ran to him and he scooped her into his arms. 'Dad,' she whispered.

'My child.'

Shanks

He stood, smiling and shaking his head in amusement as the jeering and catcalling continued. This was perfect, they were playing right into his hands. Leaning on the dispatch box he picked at some imaginary dirt under his manicured fingernails before raising an eyebrow at his new Home Secretary who grinned in reply. Shanks knew the cameras were on him. He knew the commentators would be speculating as to the reason for him remaining silent. Was it trepidation? Consideration? Anxiety? Or confidence? He needed to project the latter, which is why he leaned on the dispatch box, his free hand resting on his hip and a smile on his lips.

When he had stood, the jeering had started as a low rumble and so he had waited. His silence had spurred them on, and so he had waited. Before long almost the whole opposition were laughing and jeering him, and so he had waited.

And he waited now. Waited as they cried themselves hoarse. Waited until their enthusiasm drained. Until the cries of 'Order, Order' from the Speaker were finally listened to and obeyed. Waited until the room was hushed and still, waited until they almost ached to hear him speak. Then he waited some more.

When at last he spoke he kept his voice low and controlled, an almost conversational tone. 'You know, when I was a boy I asked my father what the point of this room was.' He waved his arm to encompass the chambers. 'You know what he said to me? It's to debate the important issues of the day, exchange ideas and views and to come to a collective decision as to the best way forward for the country.' From the benches behind him came the low growl of agreement. Shanks slowly waved his arm to quieten them.

'But that's not what I see. I don't see you…' he pointed at the leader of the Labour Party, '…agreeing with a single word I say.' Shouts of ridicule and laughter came from the opposition benches. Again, Shanks waited for them to still. 'And therein lies the problem. Say I were to propose an increase in funding to the NHS of £30 billion, you would immediately accuse me of penny pinching, whereas my side," he turned to look at his own MPs, "if we were in opposition, would accuse you of throwing money at the problem rather than fixing it.' There was a strange silence in the room, neither side sure which way this was going. Shanks smiled inwardly. 'We don't converse anymore. We don't compromise. We don't

I Vow to Thee – William E. H. Walker

work together.' He could see the calculating expression of his opposite number trying to find an argument to counter this, but he would be too late. 'Now I've only been Prime Minister for a few days, but already I can see the issues are systemic. This form of government might once have worked. Now, however, as far as I can see it's dead in the water.'

The shouts started again from the opposition benches and again he waited for them to finish before continuing. 'You see?' He pointed at the opposition benches. 'How does that help? I can't hear what you're saying as you all shout over each other. You're not offering anything constructive, you're just making noise.' He paused as more calls came. 'And you're still not listening to a word I'm saying.' He shook his head sadly. 'We used to be a great country, and we, in this chamber, have managed to reduce it to the disaster it is today with our partisan ways. Well, I say enough is enough.' For the first time his voice raised. The room was as silent as a tomb. 'I'm done with it. We're not achieving anything, all we're doing is reversing each other's policies each time we swap power. This chamber no longer works for the people of this country.' He saw the mouths open ready to cry shame. 'And if you try to shout me down all you do is prove my point.' The silence was re-established. 'You're too interested in stopping views being heard, you don't want debate, you want noise. The pretence of activity. Well, I am done with it.' He paused, glowering at his opposition. 'This country deserves a system of government that works for our people. We deserve a government free from corruption and party interests. We deserve a government who works for one goal, and one goal only: to fix. Great. Britain.' He hammered his fist down to illustrate each word. 'We need change. And we don't need you.' He waved his hand over the opposition who erupted into a frenzy of shouts and Shanks threw up his hands as though frustrated. He was loving this. It was as though he controlled them, had scripted their responses to him. The cameras would be soaking this up. The commentators would be pouring over his words and the opposition's response while Shanks himself stood tall and stared them down in the chamber. His own benches, still, silent and calm. He had warned them that anyone who cried out would find themselves replaced.

As the cries died Shanks shuffled his papers. 'I have no time for shouting. I have no time to waste with people who don't want to help fix Great Britain. I have no time for this shambles of a chamber, and that is why today I call a general election to be held in six weeks' time. Whereupon the British public will be given a clear choice between this antiquated redundancy that calls itself parliament or our new British democracy that will work for the people with one goal. To fix Great Britain.'

As the cries of shame and jeers of hate washed over him, he kept his expression set. His manner was firm and resolute while inside he laughed and danced.

Wentworth

It had been another long day. He felt like he hadn't stopped and was feeling himself near collapse.

Suss' funeral had been tough. He'd not really known her that well but he had liked her, and it had been hard to bury her. She was so young. It was almost a comfort she had been buried with her partner. Eternity together, even if their deaths had been pointless. A hate crime apparently. Another homophobic attack in London. He'd asked to see the file but had been shut out. It hadn't made sense to him at the time. He thought she'd been in Oxford that day. She was even booked into the hotel for that night. Seems something had taken her home. The Met Detective had said her suitcase was in the flat. Maybe she just missed her wife? Found it too hard to be alone after the loss of her parents? Who knew? Whatever the reason, had she stayed in Oxford that night, the two of them might have lived.

This came so fast after Kinsella's husband's funeral. A heart attack at just 44, stress was a bitch. It seemed everyone was dying right now, his department falling apart around him. Two more murders, three more deaths. He was feeling a failure. His investigations into Grantham's victims had hit a dead end. Yes, they suspected him and practically knew it, but they could prove nothing and there was even less to link him to the attacks.

He had nothing.

He flung himself onto the sofa and flicked through Bamboo on the TV. The upcoming election seemed to be all anyone was talking about and he was frankly bored with politics. He switched it back off and picked up his phone. At the bottom of the screen sat an envelope with a large number next to it. His personal email, untouched for weeks. Setting his expectations low, and feeling he should probably unsubscribe to some mailing lists, he opened his inbox. Sure enough, the usual crap. The running club he'd joined six months ago when he was feeling low and thought maybe jogging with company might help, but hadn't, was still emailing him weekly updates trying to cajole him back to their ranks. A discount website was offering him 15 percent off maternity clothing. *So useful*. His local MP had emailed him asking for his support. *Fat chance*. Another offer – 25 percent off purchases at the Siberian Supermarket. *No thanks*.

I Vow to Thee – William E. H. Walker

He closed his inbox, resenting the lack of interesting activities in his life, and noticed the number 432 sat beside the folder marked Spam. Maybe something slightly amusing at least? He clicked it open.

"My esteemed friend, I have come into the possetion" – he noted the incorrect spelling – "of $46 billion." *Of course you have mate*, he thought. Delete.

"You could live longer through cell cloning." *If only.* Delete.

Delete.

Delete.

Delete.

Jesus, life was dull for some people. He dropped the phone back down and flicked on the TV. It took a moment for the face on screen to connect with his tired brain. When it did, he sat up straight and turned up the volume.

'…her daughter Madeline, four years old, and her husband Stephen Freemark before going on the run. If you have any news on the whereabouts of Julia Freemark please call the Action line on 0800 245 6546. Do not approach her, she is considered extremely dangerous.'

It was Freemark. A murderer? Wentworth scrambled for his coat; he couldn't believe it. The woman he met wasn't capable of this, was she?

Freemark

She picked her way between the puddles on the dirt track that ran up the side of the steep hill, the rain beating down on her like a hammer. She had already run 12 miles that morning, but she had no intention of stopping anytime soon. It had been six weeks and she was still feeling raw, as though every emotion except rage had been scoured from her soul.

She would be running for some time to come. Her shoulder burned, jarred and throbbed thanks to the bodge job she had done on it. Helen had done her best to fix the damage, but even with her years of training she could only do so much from her bathroom. Still she ran.

Helen was an old school friend, a doctor and wife of a farmer of sphagnum on the Yorkshire Moors. Despite the arrest warrant issued for her five weeks ago for the murder of her husband and daughter Helen had not believed a word and told Freemark she could stay for as long as she needed.

Her. The murderer. She had killed the man who had murdered her family and now she was being harried and chased for the crime. How fucking dare they! Who could do that? Who could reinvent what happened so smoothly as to pin her as the culprit?

She crested the hill where the wind hit her hard and she screwed up her eyes to prevent them watering. She began her descent, running fast as though trying to outrun demons, her feet throwing great globules of mud up the back of her legs. She had to find out who did this to her, had to know why, but where to begin? How do you take down people like this?

She hit the bottom and slammed into the gate, almost enjoying the rush of pain as her body smashed into the wood. It was a feeling at least. She blinked into the rain and pushed her hair from her face. The world about her was awash with grey. The rain skimming across the earth in great sheets, driven by the even present gale.

She was alone now, alone in a world that had rejected her; her life was worthless.

Her daughter's face swam in the rain before her. Her precious toothy smile sparkled in the desolate landscape. Freemark's voice broke from within her like a trapped animal. Why? Why her daughter? Why her husband? Why her? Her screams were lost in the howling wind.

I Vow to Thee – William E. H. Walker

After several minutes, she stilled. She needed to know. She would find out. She would have her revenge.

I Vow to Thee – William E. H. Walker

Printed in Great Britain
by Amazon